THE HEALING TOUCH

The Healing Touch

ZOFIA VON HUCK

Cover art by Diana Krawczyk-Bernotas

Haus of Huck

Contents

Contents

The Healing Touch
ISBN 9781763517011
© 2024 Zofia von Huck
Published by Haus of Huck

The following story is fictional. Any similarities to people, places, or events are coincidental.

Possible triggers: medical procedures, medical abuse, domestic violence, eating disorders, depression, talk of suicide, bullying.

Maps

N
Desert of Rem
Morrock
Pelleas
Sirianna Mountain
Borla
Palinora
Palinas
SIRBANNA REGION
Sirrock City
Sirrock
Talinda
The Riveralands
Gidean
Dragon Island
Isle of Grynn
100 k
CONTINENT OF JAANIS

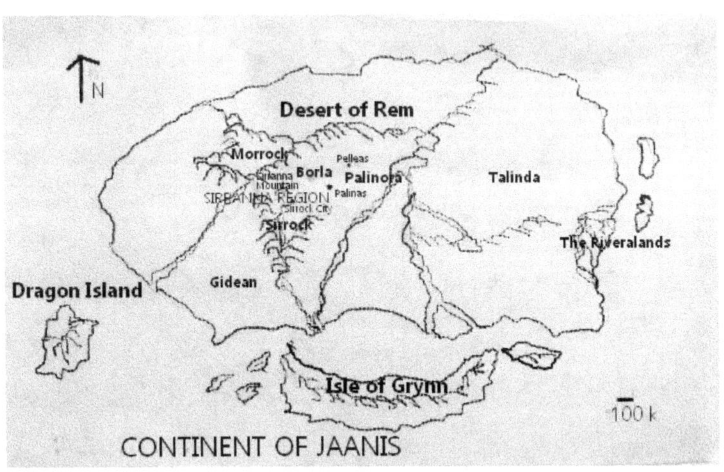

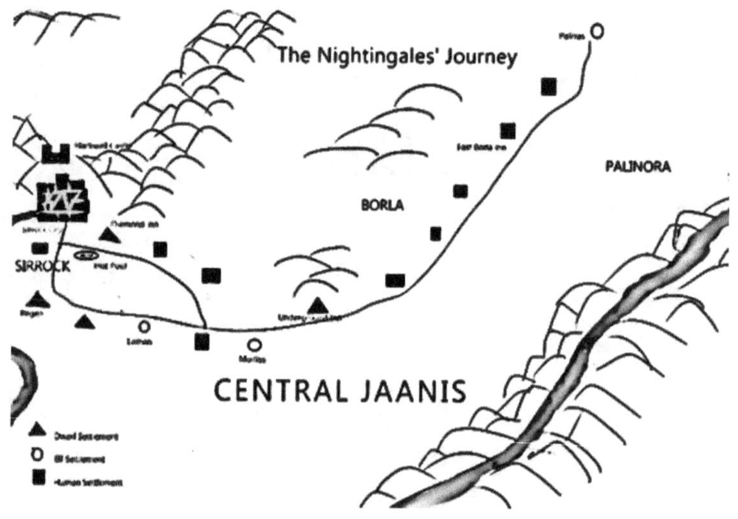
The Nightingales' Journey
Palinas
PALINORA
BORLA
SIRROCK
CENTRAL JAANIS
Dwarf Settlement
Elf Settlement
Human Settlement

Chapter 1

Lim Nightingale

One of Lim's most prominent childhood memories was waking in the night with a sense of desperate urgency. Something was wrong. As usual, when he was anxious, his breath caught in his throat and he started to cough, waking his twin brother, who slept next to him.

Lim reached to his bedside table and fumbled for his potion, which helped him to breathe, but couldn't get the lid open. Vaarem finally helped him, then after making sure that his brother was okay, he went back to sleep. Lim however, remained awake, staring into the dark with his sharp elf eyes, wondering what it was that was making him so uneasy.

Soon enough, he heard a noise, so he got out of bed to investigate. He tiptoed down the circular staircase, which wound around the centre of their house, that like all elf houses, was built within a large tree.

He reached the landing just in time to see his human half-sister Vada, dressed in her travel coat and boots, with her dark hair tied back, walking to the front door, a large bag slung over her shoulder.

"Vada!" he called. "What are you doing?"

"Shh." She put her finger to her lips irritably. She'd recently turned eighteen and was very vocal about the fact that she was now grown-up, even as her half-elf mother and her elf stepfather argued otherwise. Although humans technically came of age at eighteen, the legal age of adulthood across the continent of Jaanis was twenty-five. This was because the other races matured slower, and an eighteen-year-old elf, dwarf, or pixie was still considered a child. However, as the only human living in the elf city of Palinas, Vada had always insisted that she didn't belong, and was determined to leave at the first opportunity.

"I'm leaving," she said in a pointed whisper.

"Why?" asked Lim, distressed. Lim had been frail and sickly all his life, which set him apart from the other elves, who were known for being strong and robust, despite their delicate appearance. It was Vada who'd stayed home and played with him when he'd been too sick to go outside. She'd taught him magic, not just the everyday kind that all elves used to heat their food or light others' way in the dark, but also about the high magic, the complicated spells that could stop intruders in their tracks, or even move the very mountains (in theory, at least). Most of all, she was the only person who didn't treat him like he would break if they got too close. Why was she leaving him?

"Limmy." She put her bag down and walked up the stairs to meet him on the landing. She crouched down to be on his level, put her hands on his shoulders, and said, "I don't belong here. You know that."

"Yes you do," he said. "We belong together." He flung his arms around her waist, starting to cry. "Please don't leave," he sobbed into her coat. "I'll be good. I'll take my potions." At barely eight, Lim was still learning to manage his condition. A few weeks ago, he'd forgotten to take his morning medication and had fainted that evening at the dinner table. His parents had, quite unfairly he thought, told Vada off for not reminding him. Was she still angry at him for that? "I promise," he added earnestly. He couldn't imagine living without her. Who would read to him? Who would he talk to about his hopes and dreams? Who would understand him?

"Limmy," she said impatiently, taking his arms off her and looking down at him. "This is not about you, sweetie," she said more gently. "I'm sorry, but this is the way it's got to be."

"Why didn't you tell me?" He looked up at her, his heart dropping into his stomach and his breath catching, as he realised that she'd meant to leave without even saying good-bye. How could she do this? What had he done wrong?

"Because I was hoping to avoid this very conversation. You're too young to understand."

He looked up at her as fresh tears formed in his eyes. Why was she suddenly treating him like a little kid? "Please don't go," he said softly and tried to put his arms around her again, but she stepped away. "What will Mother and Father say?" he asked. Surely his parents would never let her leave.

She frowned down at him and even in the dark, he saw the flash of anger that crossed her pale, thin face. "*My* father is dead," she said coldly. "I don't give a shit what Garrett thinks. Mother doesn't care about me. She only loves you, and Vaarem. So, I am going back to Sirrock City, where I was born. Good-bye, Limmy. I'm sorry it's come to this, but one day you will understand." She kissed his forehead, then turned around and without looking back walked down the stairs, picked up her bag, and walked out of the house. And out of his life.

Lim stared after her for a long time, too shocked to move.

He didn't remember going back to bed, although he must have because he woke up the next day, sick and feverish, and unable to breathe. By the time he recovered, everyone had adjusted to Vada being gone, and she was rarely talked about again.

Ever since she left, Lim would scry Vada on her birthday. He would get his crystals, or a bowl of water, and try to contact her across the lands of Palinora and

Borla, all the way to Sirrock City. At least, he would try. Sometimes she didn't answer, which left him depressed for days afterwards, but there was never anything he could do about it, so he suffered in silence and kept his thoughts to himself. He still didn't understand why she'd left the way she had.

On Vada's thirty-fifth birthday, seventeen turns after she left, Lim woke up in the morning and tried to scry her, like he did every turn. Despite getting on well with his brother and having friends at school, he still missed her greatly. He still felt that out of everyone in his life, she was the one who understood him best.

It was winter, and the weather was exceptionally cold. Lim was feeling more ill than he had in a long time, so he wanted to speak to his sister, hoping that she would cheer him up. He'd recently turned twenty-five, the elven coming of age, which meant that he was now legally an adult among the elves, and thus able to make his own decisions. Now that he was finally old enough to travel alone, he wished to visit his sister.

Unfortunately for him, Vada didn't answer on this day. He tried to reach her all morning, exhausting himself until he nearly passed out and giving himself a headache, but all to no avail. Vada was not there. As a result, he didn't come down to breakfast with the rest of his family. He had no desire to talk to them, and he wasn't hungry anyway.

He looked at the carving of a spiral above his door, the symbol of The Faith, the main religion on the continent of Jaanis, and sighed. *In order to know joy, one must know pain,* he recalled one of the first lines in the Book of the Fates.

I sure hope I recognise joy when I finally see it, thought Lim, putting his arm over his face as his head throbbed.

His mother Zareanna half-elven came up to see him later that morning.

"Lim?" She knocked on the door softly, then opened it when he didn't reply.

The curtains were drawn, and the room was dark. Lim pretended to be asleep.

But no sooner had he curled up on his side, than a fit of coughing wracked through him, indicating that he was, indeed, awake.

"Aww, darling," said Zareanna kindly. "What's wrong?"

Lim turned around so that he could look at her, then sat up, so that he could breathe easier.

Zareanna rubbed his back as he coughed and waited until he could speak.

"Nothing's wrong," he said, when he could finally draw a breath. "Nothing more than the usual anyway," he added, laying his head back down on the pillow. Zareanna frowned at that, so he sighed, and said, "I tried to talk to Vada, but she wasn't there."

"Oh."

Lim knew that, like him, his mother was hurt by her only daughter's apparent disinterest in having anything to do with them. Contrary to Vada's assessment, her mother did care, but she was unable to express this in a way that Vada understood.

Zareanna looked at Lim for a few moments, as if trying to think of something comforting to say.

"I'm sorry, darling," she said finally. "But you know what she's like. She'll call when she can."

Lim didn't reply. In all the time she'd been gone, Vada had only initiated contact once, when Lim had been so sick that everyone, including himself, had thought that he was going to die. Other than that, she never called of her own accord. Lim wrote her hundreds of letters, and only occasionally did she reply. She never tried to scry him though (apart from that one time), which hurt, because she was a much more powerful magic user than he was, and scrying came easier to her.

Zareanna leaned over and stroked Lim's long blonde hair away from his forehead.

"Are you hungry?" she asked him. "Would you like me to bring something up for you?"

He shook his head. "No thanks. I have a headache. I'll just stay in bed and rest for a while."

She looked down at him with an anxious frown. Despite being as frail as he was, Lim didn't often rest. He would usually spend his days and nights reading books and scrolls and studying magic.

Lim had always loved magic. Now that he was a legal adult, he could officially apply to the Academy of Magic, the only institution on Jaanis that took in students from all four races and taught all of their different types of magic to them.

Each of the four races on Jaanis had their own magic traditions, which all drew their power from the same source, known as the Fates of the Universe, therefore a suitably gifted individual could learn all of these skills. It was individuals such as these, that the Academy allowed into its ranks and taught.

Despite wishing to apply, Lim doubted that he would get in. Magic required a great strength of body as well as of mind, and he was fairly sure that he wouldn't cut it.

Yet it was not this that prevented him from applying.

Ten turns ago, when she'd been twenty-five, Vada had written and told Lim that she'd applied to the Academy but had been knocked back.

If they hadn't accepted her, Lim didn't think that they would accept him either. Also, some fierce loyalty to his sister made him think that he shouldn't apply anyway, as a matter of principle.

When they'd been children, Vada and Lim had sometimes fantasised about studying at the Academy together. The training took ten turns, so theoretically, they could have both been students at the same time. Now, Lim thought that if Vada couldn't go, then he shouldn't either.

He sometimes wondered why he was still so fiercely loyal to Vada. It wasn't like she was loyal to him.

At midday, Zareanna came back into Lim's room.

He was still lying on the bed, staring up at the canopy, occasionally coughing, but otherwise being as still as he could. The interior of the house was heated by magic, so his room was warm and smelt of lavender and pine. But despite all this, his breath kept catching in his throat and his head and muscles ached.

Zareanna opened the curtains, and Lim put his hands over his eyes.

"Come on, darling," she told him. "I know you're upset, but lying here brooding is not doing you any good."

"It's not doing me any harm either," said Lim sullenly, then sat up again as another fit of coughing wracked through him.

"Come on down and have some lunch," said Zareanna.

"I'm not hungry," said Lim, lying back down.

"You never are." Zareanna frowned with concern. She sat down on the side of the bed, and took his hand in both of hers. "But you need to eat. You're so frightfully thin as it is, and I fear that you've lost weight recently, which concerns me greatly. I've called for a healer to see you this afternoon."

"Fucking dragon dung, Mother," said Lim, sitting up, then putting his hand to his temple as the sudden movement made his head spin. "Why? It's not like they can do anything."

Lim had been seen by more healers than he cared to remember, but none of them had ever really helped.

The elf healers that he saw most frequently would give him potions that made him feel momentarily better, but tasted so horrible that it was barely worth it. When he was really sick, they gave him energy healings, but their effects had only ever lasted for a few hours at most. He'd been treated by dwarf shamans who used crystals, but these too had only helped temporarily, and he'd once met a travelling pixie medic, who had given him some magically-infused water, which had only made Lim need to use the bathroom all the time; considering that their bathroom was three levels down from his bedroom, the whole experience had been excruciatingly uncomfortable.

None of them had ever been able to heal him, or to even work out what was wrong with him. He had trouble breathing, was prone to infections, and was generally weak. He would catch every bug that was going around and be more severely affected than anybody else, but nobody knew why. The healers theorised that it was due to him having human blood, but his twin brother had human blood too and wasn't affected, so Lim doubted that was the reason. In any case, even if it was, no one knew what to do about it. These days, he tried to avoid healers except for when he needed a new prescription for whichever potions he was currently using.

"There is no need for that type of language," scolded Zareanna.

"Aw, but it's so descriptive and poetic," said Lim, which made his mother sigh and shake her head in disapproval. He swung his legs over the side of the bed. It seemed that he would have to get up after all.

Zareanna smiled at him tenderly as he got out of the bed slowly and walked over to the dressing table, where he sank down into the chair, took a moment to catch his breath and looked at himself in the mirror.

He had the typical delicate elf bone-structure, with sharp cheekbones, a straight nose, pointed ears, and large slanted eyes. Despite this, he looked like he always did; pale, thin, and tired. His blue eyes, unusual amongst the normally green-eyed elves, were sunken and shadowed.

He picked up his brush and ran it through his long, pale-blonde hair.

Zareanna walked up behind him, took the brush, and brushed the rest of his hair out for him, before tying it back with a black ribbon. She then walked over to his wardrobe and opened it.

"Do you have anything that isn't black?" she asked.

"No," said Lim simply. "What for?"

She shook her head and smiled with wry amusement, then took out a black shirt and a pair of black trousers and laid them out on his bed. "It might make you feel better to wear a happier colour occasionally," she said.

"It didn't when you used to dress me," he said. "You used to dress me and Vaarem the same, but we were always different."

She looked annoyed for a moment, then she looked sad. She walked back over, and hugged him from behind, kissing his cheek. "I'm sorry, darling," she said. "I wish I could do something to make you feel better."

"It's okay," said Lim, letting her hold him. He didn't like it when he made her feel bad.

He didn't like making anyone feel bad.

Pity that he seemed to do it so often.

"I'm fine, really," he said, trying to smile at his mother in the mirror. "Now, let me get dressed, and then I'll come downstairs. I can do that on my own," he turned and smiled at her, to show her that he really bore no ill feeling towards her.

She kissed him on the cheek again, then left the room.

Lim stood up with a sigh.

He walked over to the bed and picked up the clothes that his mother had chosen for him, before taking off his black nightgown and putting them on. The linen shirt felt cold against his skin, and he shivered.

He'd always been skinny, but in the past couple of weeks his appetite, which had never been overly hearty, had become all but non-existent, and now all his clothes looked and felt a bit wrong.

After doing up his trousers and shirt, he went to his wardrobe and found a waistcoat, which he put on over the top, partly because it was cold and he needed an extra layer, but mostly because it completed the outfit. Just because he wasn't feeling his best didn't mean he wasn't going to make an effort.

Before leaving the room, he went to his bedside table and took a swig of his potion, which usually eased his cough and helped him to breathe but wasn't helping much today. Still, it was better than nothing, he supposed, so eventually he squared his shoulders and left his room.

It was the mid-winter holiday period in Palinas, so his father was home from his job at the Palinas City Council, and his mother, as well as his brother and himself, were home from school. Zareanna taught the younger children at the local junior school, so was currently on holiday, too. Today, the whole family was home.

Well, the whole family who lives here, thought Lim cynically. Everyone except for him seemed to forget that Vada existed.

Lim held on to the living-wood bannister as he made his slow way down the stairs that wound around the centre of the tree that contained their house, down the two levels that led to the dining room. It seemed that all physical activity, even something as mild as walking, was leaving him out of breath today. Usually, only strenuous exercise left him wheezing and unable to breathe, and he could otherwise, if he was careful and took things slow, function normally. Today, he found that he couldn't. He really was feeling awful.

He was the last to arrive for lunch, and his family were already sitting around the table when he walked into the dining room. Like the bedrooms upstairs, the dining room was built within the tree. The table was part of the design and grew out of the floor. It was covered in a pale green tablecloth with gold embroidery around the edges, a gift from their great-grandmother. There were a few shelves on the walls that were built out of the living-wood too, but the rest of the wooden furniture was free-standing. Like the bedrooms upstairs, this room was warm and cozy.

"Nice of you to grace us with your presence, Lim-nos," said his father coldly, as Lim sat down.

"Sorry," said Lim instinctively. He'd learned long ago that he would get no sympathy from his father.

Garrett Nightingale treated his youngest son's health problems like an embarrassment and a nuisance. He seemed convinced that Lim was either exaggerating or bringing everything upon himself on purpose, that if he only made an effort, he would get better.

Garrett pushed his golden-blonde hair behind his pointed ears and frowned at Lim, then closed his eyes and said, "We thank the Fates for providing us with this meal. May their blessings be upon us."

"May their blessings be upon us," repeated Lim, along with his mother and brother.

Typical, thought Lim. His family were not particularly religious or spiritual and his father only seemed to insist on a blessing before meals after Lim had missed one.

Lim picked up his fork and looked at the offerings on the table. As always, there were several platters of different foods in the centre, and everyone was expected to serve themselves.

"Try the fish," said his twin brother Vaarem beside him. His long blonde hair was up in a top-knot and he wore a red shirt and a blue waistcoat with purple and green embroidery. Whilst Lim dressed exclusively in black, to blend into the background, Vaarem always wanted to stand out as much as possible. He smiled at Lim and said, "Go on, I made it myself. I mean, I cooked it this morning." He grinned, then continued to eat his meal.

Lim gave his brother a small smile, then picked up the fish platter and put some on his plate. Then he got himself some vegetables too, because he knew that it was expected, and arranged them on his plate so that they didn't touch, then began to eat. Elf cuisine was traditionally vegetarian, however as more and more elves interacted with humans and dwarves, some of their customs, such as eating meat, were now common amongst elves too. Zareanna, who had lived amongst humans for over ten turns, was used to cooking meat, so the family would eat meat or fish most days.

Vaarem looked at Lim expectantly, obviously wanting to know what he thought of the fish.

"It's good," said Lim, smiling at his brother. He was only being polite though, because it seemed that as well as having faulty lungs and no stamina, he also had faulty taste buds; he'd never really, truly enjoyed the taste of anything that he ate.

But his performance was clearly convincing,

because Vaarem smiled proudly, then looked at his parents and said, "See? What did I tell you? I told you that I could do it."

Lim wondered why his parents had doubted his brother's ability. Vaarem was good at everything that he turned his hand to. He was a natural athlete, an accurate archer, a graceful dancer, and now it looked like he was a good cook, too. He was also a complete show-off and if he hadn't been so genuinely kind and personable, Lim would have no doubt found him annoying. But as it was, he and his brother got on very well and were as close as any set of twins, especially since Vada had left. On days like today, Vaarem was the only person whom Lim could tolerate for any extended period of time.

As he ate his meal in silence and his family made small talk around him, Lim thought that it wasn't Vaarem's cooking ability that his parents had doubted, but his own ability to like anything. That made a lot more sense.

"Why are you so glum, Lim?" asked Vaarem, taking him by surprise.

"I'm not," Lim started to say. Vaarem had never been as close to Vada, so he didn't miss her as much, and his father was already angry, so Lim didn't want to mention Vada and make him even angrier. He tried to think of something suitable to say when he was overcome by a bout of coughing.

"Could you not do that at the table, please?" asked Garrett irritably, as Lim struggled to draw a breath. His vision dimmed and for a moment he panicked that he might pass out, until Vaarem leaned over and patted him on the back.

"Sorry," gasped Lim, when he could finally talk. He could feel sweat running down his brow, and he wiped it away with his hand.

Garrett glared at him, then rolled his green eyes, and Lim looked down at his plate.

I'm not doing it on purpose for Fates' sake, thought Lim, but he didn't say anything. If he'd tried, he would have probably started coughing again, or worse, crying. He desperately wanted to go back to his room and back into bed. But he couldn't do that yet. His father would never let him hear the end of it.

Vaarem smiled at him kindly, then turned to his mother and asked about her work. Zareanna told the family about the children she was currently teaching, and they finished the meal without further incident, although Lim only pushed his food around on his plate, not trusting himself to swallow anything solid.

When they'd all finished eating, Vaarem got up and started to gather the plates to take into the kitchen. Lim stood up to help him, then had to put one hand to his forehead, and use the other to hold onto the table, as his head swam.

"You don't have to, Lim," said his mother, but his father interrupted her.

"He's not a complete invalid, Zara," he snapped. "He can help. Can't you, Lim?"

"Yes." Nodded Lim, managing to suppress a cough,

grateful that for once his father was on his side (even though he knew that Garrett's motivations were not so kind).

He picked up the rest of the plates, and followed his brother into the kitchen, where Vaarem pumped some water into the sink, that like the dining room table was built out of the tree, and they washed and dried the dishes in companionable silence.

Lim wondered whether Vaarem remembered that today was Vada's birthday, but he didn't know how to bring it up. Vaarem had always had a lot of friends at school, as well as partaking in many extra-curricular activities that kept him out of the house, so had never had much time to spend with his half-sister.

Just as they were finishing up, Lim doubled over in another coughing fit, gasping and wheezing as he tried to draw a breath.

"Shit, Lim," said Vaarem, rubbing his back when Lim had managed to get upright again. "Are you all right? I don't mean to sound nasty, but you seem really sick today."

Lim shrugged. "I feel like shit," he admitted.

"Do you think you should see a healer?" asked Vaarem with a worried frown. Unlike Lim, Vaarem still believed that healers knew something that Lim didn't and would therefore help him.

"Mother has arranged for one to come later today."

"Good," said Vaarem, looking at his brother with concern. "I hope they help you to feel better. I don't like it when you're sick."

"That makes two of us." Smiled Lim, starting to feel better for the first time since giving up trying to reach Vada that morning.

"Let me help you up the stairs," said Vaarem, as they left the kitchen. "You look really pale."

"Thanks," Lim put his arm around his brother's shoulders, and allowed Vaarem to put his arm around his waist. He usually hated to be touched, apart from having his hair brushed and stroked, which he enjoyed, but had learned to tolerate it from his family because the alternative was to sometimes be unable to get to where he wanted to go.

They walked up the two levels to where their bedrooms were, slowly. Lim, though annoyed with himself for having to stop and rest on each landing, was grateful for his brother's comforting presence. As he caught his breath, he looked at the pictures that adorned the walls. Before becoming a teacher, their mother had been an artist, and she'd drawn and painted many portraits of Vaarem and Lim as babies, as well as pictures of Garrett. There had been pictures of Vada too, and of Vada and her father Malkim, but those had been taken down after Vada had left. Lim wondered whether anyone else still noticed their absence. No one had ever mentioned it. No one had been in Vada's room, which was situated on the lowest level of the house, since she'd left.

"It's Vada's birthday today," said Lim, as he leaned against his brother on the last landing.

"Oh," said Vaarem, "that's nice. We should send her a letter or something."

"I did," said Lim. "Two weeks ago. I signed your name too. She hasn't replied."

"Oh well." Vaarem shrugged dismissively. "She was never the birthday celebration type. Did I tell you what happened at archery yesterday?" he asked, changing the topic. Vaarem's favourite topic of conversation was himself.

"So, then," Vaarem was standing in the middle of Lim's room, mimicking the story subject's clumsy movements, while Lim lay on his bed, "he was like this," Vaarem gestured, turning his feet outwards and spreading his legs, "and remember, it had been raining, right? So, the field was muddy. So, then I came over and said, I bet you can't hit that acorn from over here. So, he turns to me, but his foot slips in the mud, and remember he's got the bow drawn, so he falls on his arse and releases the arrow, and the arrow flies straight upwards and hits, get this, a goose, which then promptly lands on his head, arrow and all, but not before it has shit itself as its last, dying act." He laughed.

Lim laughed too, trying to imagine the elf that his brother was talking about. He thought that he knew whom Vaarem was referring to, and he laughed again. Vaarem repeated the movement of the elf falling, then having a goose shit on his head, before landing on him.

"So, what happened to the goose?" asked Lim, between chuckles.

Vaarem shrugged. "I don't know. I suppose he took it home to eat it."

"After cleaning it up, I hope," said Lim, with another laugh.

They were still laughing when the healer came, Lim having forgotten all about the morning.

Lim felt that all the healers in Palinas secretly resented him. Nevertheless, the healer that came, an ancient elf named Dr Fantail, was perfectly courteous and professional. Lim sometimes wondered how old Dr Fantail was. Elves lived to about five hundred turns, but only began to age visibly in their last century.

"Good afternoon, Lim," said the healer, inclining his head politely and extending his hand. He was dressed in the pale-green robe that all elven healers wore, and his brown hair, which was greying at the temples (the only sign of his advanced age) was tied back in a braid. He carried his bag of tools in his other hand. "Nice to see you again."

"Hello." Lim shook Dr Fantail's hand and smiled thinly.

"I'll leave you to it," said Vaarem, standing up, but Lim grabbed his sleeve.

"Stay," he said, then mouthed, "*please.*" He didn't like to be alone with healers. They never had anything good to say.

Vaarem nodded and went to sit on the chair by Lim's dresser.

Dr Fantail asked Lim to undress, which he did, then he lay down on the bed.

Vaarem looked at him, then when their eyes met, scrunched up his face, and stuck out his tongue, which made Lim laugh, while Dr Fantail ran his hands over Lim's head and body to measure his energy levels. He then got Lim to sit up and checked his breathing by getting him to blow into a crystal tube that registered different colours according to the strength of one's breath. The stronger that one could blow, the deeper the colour the crystal would turn. Vaarem had once made it look a deep purple like the night sky. Lim's best was a very pale blue. Today, Lim barely managed to make the crystal take on a frosted white tinge. He couldn't even get a colour. Finally, Dr Fantail checked his pulse and heartbeat by placing his fingers on Lim's neck, and then his wrist.

After the examination was over, Lim got dressed again, while Dr Fantail made some notes at the desk.

"Shit," said Vaarem, as he helped his brother tie up his shirt. "I didn't realise you'd gotten so skinny."

"What would you have done if you had?" asked Lim, with an amused grin.

"I don't know." Shrugged Vaarem. "Made you eat more. Or at all," he added with a raised eyebrow.

Lim chuckled at that, then sat back on the bed to wait for what Dr Fantail had to say. Vaarem sat beside him and put his arm around his brother's shoulders, the way he'd done since they'd been children. Lim looked at him, and Vaarem scrunched up his face, this time crossing his eyes, which made them both laugh.

Dr Fantail sat in the chair and looked at them with a serious expression.

"Uh oh," said Lim. "This doesn't look good," which made him and Vaarem laugh once more.

"It's good to see that you are in good spirits," said Dr Fantail, looking like he was picking his words carefully, "because I'm afraid that I don't have any good news."

"Oh," said Lim, sobering.

"As you are no doubt aware, your condition has deteriorated quite dramatically since the last time I saw you. Your breathing capacity has diminished again, and your overall energy levels are lower than I have ever encountered."

Vaarem hugged his arm tighter around Lim's shoulders.

Lim didn't respond. There was nothing to say.

"I will give you some more of your usual potion," said Dr Fantail. "It seems to still be holding you. But you need to be aware that there comes a certain point where the dosage becomes toxic."

Lim nodded. "Let me guess. I am at that point." It wasn't even a question. When he'd first started taking the potion, several turns ago, he'd only used it in the morning. Now it was only allowing him to breathe for a few hours before he'd start to choke and need another dose.

Dr Fantail's grim expression told him everything

that he needed to know. "You are nearing the point where increasing the dosage would do more harm than good. How often are you using it?"

Lim shrugged. "As often as I need to," he said. "Four, five times a day, maybe."

Dr Fantail considered this. "You can stay on that amount safely, as long as you don't increase it," he said. "However, you need to be aware that even five daily doses will only hold off the symptoms for so long."

"Right." Nodded Lim, then looked down at his hands in his lap.

This is why I don't like healers, he thought. *They never tell me anything good. This morning I felt like shit. Now I still feel like shit, only now I know that it's not going to get better.*

"So, what's he supposed to do then?" asked Vaarem, his arm still tight around his brother's thin shoulders. Lim hugged him back. He tried to live day by day, not focusing on the future because he was never sure if he would have one.

Is this the beginning of the end? he wondered, suddenly feeling scared.

Dr Fantail was thoughtful for a moment. "There is something that may help," he said.

"Yes?" Both Vaarem and Lim looked up at him, interested and hopeful.

"It's a new treatment, so still in the experimental stages, but so far, the results have been promising."

"Yes?" asked Lim, getting his hopes up, despite

telling himself that he never would again; he was always disappointed. And yet, he kept hoping. Because what else could he do?

"It's a human treatment," said Dr Fantail. "Designed for humans. But as you have human blood from your mother's side, I think you are human enough. As I said, it is still an experimental treatment, in its early stages, but you seem like a good candidate for it. It works by strengthening human magical energy with electricity and using this combination to jolt the patient's own energies into working more effectively. As I said, the results, so far, have been promising."

"Okay." Lim nodded thoughtfully.

Electricity sounded scary. It was a very human thing, as elves had little use for it. Still, if it was supposedly his human blood that was causing him to be sick, and if that part of him could somehow be healed... Did he dare hope?

"How does it work exactly?" he asked.

"For a long time, human mages have been looking at ways to augment their magic," explained Dr Fantail. "I am not sure if you are aware, but in humans, anytime they are sick or injured, their magic suffers while they recover."

"Yes." Nodded Lim. It was the main reason why he didn't think he'd ever be able to do high magic.

"It was discovered," continued the healer, "that magical energy, particularly in humans, is similar to electricity, so for a while now, human mages have been using electric jolts to boost their magic."

"Okay," Lim raised his eyebrows, interested. Vaarem frowned beside him.

"What one of the doctors at Sirrock City Hospital recently discovered was that he could isolate the magical energy in a subject, and target this specifically for the electric treatment. The idea was to make it less uncomfortable for the subject. What he found was that by targeting the magic and boosting it with electricity helped to not only strengthen the mage's magic, but it improved their whole wellbeing," he said excitedly. "He is marketing it as a miracle cure for all ailments, but of course, he needs to do more research, hence is looking for subjects. I think that you would be a good one."

"And he works out of Sirrock City?" asked Lim, finding this to be the most exciting thing about what the healer was saying. Vada lived in Sirrock City. If he were to travel there, surely she would come down to see him. At the very least, he would get to see her one more time.

"Yes," said Dr Fantail. "For the moment. He is looking to expand the treatment to hospitals in Borla, and Morrock, but at the moment, the treatment is only being done in Sirrock."

"Then I want to do it," said Lim.

Vaarem frowned at him, his arm still around Lim's shoulders.

Dr Fantail looked at Lim for a moment, as if wanting to make sure, then, when it was clear that Lim was onboard, he said, "Very well, I will talk to my human colleagues in Sirrock today. Provided that your parents agree, of course."

"I'm twenty-five now," said Lim. "So, you don't need their permission. But you can tell them if you want."

Dr Fantail looked at him with a wistful expression. "I remember I first saw you when you were less than a week old," he said. "It's hard to believe that you are now an adult."

"I am." Lim smiled thinly.

Is he surprised that I am still alive to reach adult-hood? he wondered. It seemed that some people had been planning his funeral for the past twenty-five turns.

Well, they can all wait a little longer. He smiled bitterly. *And who knows, this new thing may work out, and I may get better once and for all.*

He tried not to get his hopes up too high, but as usual, he couldn't help getting excited.

Chapter 2

The Journey Begins

"I don't trust those humans." Garrett shook his head. Dr Fantail had told the family about the experimental procedure and after the healer had gone, Lim had expressed his desire to do it. However, his father was not keen.

"You're an elf," said Garrett, as the family sat in the living room, "human medicine won't work."

"How do you know?" demanded Lim, coughing discreetly into his elbow. "Dr Fantail says it might. And I'm one-quarter human." *And what else do you suggest?*

"Yes yes," said Garrett dismissively, "Everyone has some mixed blood somewhere. But you are an *elf*. Stick to what you know."

"What I know doesn't work," Lim pointed out. "I'm an adult now, and you can't stop me. I want to do it." Despite his words, Lim was afraid that his father *would* try and stop him. After all, Lim was just barely a legal adult. He'd never travelled anywhere by himself, and he didn't really think that he could do it. Garrett, however, didn't like travelling outside of Palinas, and he didn't like the idea of anyone in his family doing it either, claiming it dangerous.

"Perhaps he should try it," said Zareanna. She was sitting on the armchair across from him, and she leaned forward towards him. "There have been a lot of advances in medicine over the past twenty-five turns," she said. "I think we ought to all go with him."

"But Sirrock City Hospital?" asked Garrett with a sceptical frown. "Don't you remember?"

Remember what? wondered Lim. *Had something bad happened?* Surely his healer wouldn't recommend that he go somewhere less than scrupulous.

"That was different," said Zareanna firmly, gripping the sides of her chair. "We're not asking them to come to us."

Garrett shook his head. "I swore I'd never go back," he said quietly.

"You did, did you?" said Zareanna sarcastically. "You can't avoid one of the biggest cities on the continent forever because-"

"It's Malkim's city," said Garrett tightly, interrupting her. "It always will be."

"He hardly ever left the castle," said Zareanna, just

as tightly, "and neither did his fanatical followers. We won't be going *there*. They can't do anything to us. Sirrock City is just a city like any other. And the hospital is doing good research. It's worth a shot."

Garrett sighed, "Fine," he said. "We can go to Sirrock City. But what about the boys' studies?"

"They're on winter break," said Zareanna

"Vaarem was going to be doing some work at the Council with me."

"What?" Vaarem, who was sitting on the couch next to Lim, sat up. "When? Nobody told me."

His father sighed, "Fates, Vaaremill, what is your problem? I would have jumped at such a chance at your age."

"Well I'm not you," said Vaarem, crossing his arms and leaning back in his seat.

"No, you're not," scoffed his father, "I wish better for you than I had myself, but fine, you can do the internship in the summer, I guess."

"I don't want to do an internship," said Vaarem.

Lim began to cough again. The negative energy when his family fought or argued always made his breath catch.

Zareanna came over and rubbed his back, "There, there," she said kindly, sitting herself on the arm rest. "This is Lim's choice." She looked up at Garrett. "I say that we should go. We are due for a family holiday. Fates know, we haven't had one since..."

Lim knew what she was going to say, "*since Vada left,*" but his father's frown stopped her.

"Not for a long time," she said finally.

Lim swallowed and closed his eyes.

Would his father stand up now and leave the room in a huff, the way he did when the subject of Vada was brought up?

Garrett was silent for a moment. He crossed his arms over his chest, then said, "Fine, we'll go. I guess it can't hurt. You're right, we are due for a family holiday."

Lim opened his eyes and breathed a sigh of relief. He coughed once, but managed to catch his breath.

"Great," said Zareanna. She smiled, then turned to Lim and stroked his hair, pushing a strand that had come loose behind his ear. "We'll be there for you, darling. It will all be wonderful, you'll see."

Lim hoped she was right.

After hearing of the family's decision, Dr Fantail contacted the Sirrock Hospital, and received an answer within two days, saying that Lim was booked in to begin the treatment at the start of the next moon. The treatment would take one to two weeks, depending on how things went. There was also a doctor at the hospital who was working on developing treatments for people of mixed blood and would be assisting with Lim's care. Because it was all experimental, the costs would be covered by the hospital, which made Lim feel even better about the whole thing. Although finances were never discussed, Lim was always aware of how much his mere existence was costing his family.

Lim immediately wrote a letter to Vada, telling her when he was going to be in Sirrock. He finished with *"Please come and visit me"*, which he hoped didn't sound too desperate.

His health had not improved since her birthday, and he still struggled to do the most basic things.

The day before they were due to leave, Lim packed his clothes, potions, and toiletries in a large bag. He felt equally nervous and excited, which made his breath catch, so he had to keep sipping on his potion. He hoped that he wasn't overdoing it.

After packing his things, he lay down on his bed, feeling dizzy. But he couldn't rest, so as soon as he felt able, he got up carefully, and continued to pack.

He packed some books and scrolls. He was planning to do some study in the carriage as they journeyed across the continent.

Finally, he looked in the bottom of the wardrobe for shoes. He would be wearing his usual black boots while travelling, but he wondered what other shoes to take; slippers, certainly, but anything else? He was looking at his three pairs of dress boots, wondering if he would need them, when his eyes fell on a box behind them.

He reached over and fingered the silver clasps on the side of the box. He hadn't played the violin for many turns now. He'd got it from his grandparents for his eighteenth birthday, and he'd been thrilled. His school friend Fen was a very talented musician, and he and Lim would often play together. Lim had been happy to have such a beautiful instrument of his own.

But then, as always, he'd gotten sick, and then his father had threatened to sell the violin to pay for Lim's treatment, so Lim had put it away.

Out of sight out of mind. Besides, he'd been too weak to play it anyway.

He put his hand down with a sigh.

Perhaps I should just sell it, he thought, *Or give it to Fen. It deserves better than to sit in the back of a wardrobe unplayed.* Because it wasn't like Lim would ever play again. Would he?

Maybe if this treatment works, he thought hopefully, taking a pair of light ankle boots with a pointed toe and a small heel out and shutting the wardrobe door. He'd decide what to do with the violin on his return.

Vaarem knocked on his door and came in without waiting for Lim's response. His face was flushed, and his sleeves were rolled up.

"Do you have any room in your bags?" he asked Lim. "I can't fit all my stuff in."

Lim stood up slowly, waited to catch his breath, then walked over to sit on the bed. "Yeah," he said, then coughed discreetly into his elbow, "I have some space. What do you want to pack?"

"I'll bring it over," said Vaarem, then returned a moment later with his arms full of clothes, which he dropped onto Lim's bed.

Lim looked at the pile and shook his head with a chuckle. "Do you not have your own bag?" he asked.

"I do," said Vaarem. "It's full."

"How much stuff are you taking?" asked Lim. "We're going to be gone for one moon, not a whole turn."

Vaarem rolled his eyes. "I know," he said, "but I want to be prepared."

Prepared for what? wondered Lim, then sighed, "Okay," he said, "but I don't have enough space for all that. Maybe take the blue shirt and the green one, and those dark red trousers."

Vaarem picked up the items and put them in a separate pile. "What about this one?" He held up a pink shirt with frills and lace on the cuffs and delicate embroidery around the collar.

"I don't think we'll be attending any weddings or other formal occasions," said Lim drily.

"Okay." Vaarem put the shirt down with a sigh. "What about these?" he held up a pair of trousers.

"They're very similar to those," said Lim impatiently, pointing to the other pile.

Vaarem frowned. "You don't have to get so snippy."

"It's nice that you're planning for parties, and have conveniently forgotten that I will most likely not be having any fun when we get there. Or before." He coughed into his elbow and felt his brow sweat.

"I'm sorry." Vaarem's face fell. He reached over and patted Lim's back, then passed him a glass of water. "I will not be doing any partying while you're sick," he assured him. "But I'm thinking about afterwards.

Because when you're up to it, I want us to go out somewhere."

Lim smiled thinly. "Thanks," he said. He couldn't think that far ahead.

The trip to Sirrock City would take two weeks with their two horses Sera and Clea, pulling their carriage. Although they were by no means poor, the costs of Lim's treatments, as well as Vaarem's extra-curricular activities, such as archery, dancing, and hand to hand combat, meant that they couldn't afford winged horses, which were faster and more resilient than their more common non-winged cousins, so they made do with what they had. The family would all go together. Vaarem and Lim, as well as Zareanna were on break from school, and Garrett would take time off from his job.

Lim felt good that his family were coming with him, but also anxious, in case the whole thing ended up being a complete waste of time. They didn't always get on, so he worried that they would fight. However, the thing he was looking forward to the most, was hopefully seeing Vada, as he'd not seen her since the night she'd left. She hadn't replied to his letter, but she rarely did, so he tried not to let this bother him.

They set out on a cold, frosty morning, after break-fast. Lim had felt too nervous to eat but had neverthe-less forced himself to swallow a couple of mouthfuls of porridge. Dr Fantail had warned him that if he lost any more weight, he might become ineligible for the treatment, as it would be too dangerous, so he did his best to try and eat regularly, even if he could only manage a few bites each time.

The cold air made Lim's lungs hurt when he stepped outside. He'd found though, that if he dipped a cloth in some herbal water, and warmed it up, then held it to his mouth and nose, he could breathe a little easier, so he tried to do this whenever he had to go outside. His father frowned at him but didn't say anything. Lim lowered his eyes, trying his best not to anger or annoy Garrett. He didn't want to deal with the added stress of family arguments.

They crossed the border from the elf country of Palinora to the mostly-human inhabited Borla in the late afternoon and reached a roadside inn in the evening. Apparently, the border crossing hadn't always been so easy. Lim had learned at school that, for centuries, the land of Sirranna, which was now known as the Three Countries: Borla, Sirrock, and Morrock was ruled by the dragontamers, a dynasty of powerful human magic users, who'd had the innate power to control dragons, and had used it to rule the land with terror and intimidation. Elves had avoided them, as the dragontamers would use them in their magical rituals, draining them of their blood, and their essence. After the dragontamers were overthrown and Sirranna became the Three Countries, their descendants and supporters had tried to get their throne and their power back. It took Zareanna's parents, the human Nellian

Goldsword, and the elf Gemill Bluebell, to unite the elves and the humans against the then-current dragontamer Bilrund Blackwell and his supporters. Bilrund was defeated and the Human-Elf Alliance was formed. Shortly after, dwarves and pixies had joined, and the Human-Elf Alliance became known as The Alliance. All four races living on the continent of Jaanis were given the same rights, and now followed the same laws. Lim and Vaarem had been minor celebrities at their school for a few weeks when the kids had learned that it was their grandparents, who had founded the Alliance, and for a while, everyone had wanted to talk to them. Vaarem had been particularly happy and had spent many lunchtimes regaling everyone with tales that his grandparents had told him of their adventures (never mind that their grandparents seldom visited so were highly unlikely to have told Vaarem that many stories).

After Bilrund Blackwell's defeat, Lim had learned that the remaining Blackwell supporters had tried to use Bilrund's young nephew, Malkim to pick up the dragontamer cause, but Malkim seemingly had had no interest in ruling. He'd married Zareanna Bluebell, the daughter of Nellian and Gemill, to seal his support of the Alliance, and the existing peace, which still remained after Malkim had died and Zareanna had moved back to Palinas and married her childhood sweetheart Garrett Nightingale.

Lim looked around curiously, thinking of his ancestors who had travelled this way before him. The country of Borla looked the same as Palinora, with the same trees, the same gentle hills, the same leafy, earthy smell. But the buildings were very different.

Unlike elf buildings, which were built within the trunks of the trees, human buildings were free-standing, so the inn was surrounded by trees, but not actually in one. Lim had traveled a little for some of his treatments, so he'd seen human buildings before, but he still found them curious. Vaarem was curious too, looking at the long, square inn with wide eyes. They would stay in these types of places each night. Garrett was used to a certain level of comfort, working for the Palinas City Council as he did, and everyone knew that Lim was not well enough to camp out. So, they'd planned their journey to make sure they reached a settlement by each nightfall. Garrett seemed confident about which roads to take, so they were sure to make good time.

The family checked into the inn and were led to a suite on the first floor. The building contained an elevator, which Lim was immensely grateful for, as he was struggling to walk up even one flight of stairs. The innkeeper opened the elevator door and ushered the family inside, then closed the door, pulled a lever, and the cage rose up with a rattle and a shake that reminded Lim of being in his room on a windy day.

"How does it work?" asked Vaarem with wide eyes, and even Garrett looked impressed. None of them had ever seen such a contraption before.

"It's powered by electricity," explained the woman,

which made Lim look around curiously. They had learned about electricity at school, but only as an abstract concept. Elves had no use for it, as everything that humans did with electricity, elves, and dwarves too, did with magic. Dr Fantail had said that Lim's treatment would fuse electricity with magic. It sounded scary, but if electricity could lift their entire family up one whole level so easily, then surely it was a force for good.

There were two beds in the single room suite, so Garrett and Zareanna would take one, and Vaarem and Lim the other. Garrett looked at Zareanna apprehensively, and she nodded. Although they never talked about it, Lim was aware that his parents slept in separate rooms. He'd never known them to share a bed.

Apart from the beds, the room had a water closet with a water pump, and a small dresser in the corner. A door beyond the beds led to a balcony. There was a vase of fresh flowers on the dresser, which filled the room with a subtle scent of lavender.

Zareanna smiled, "See?" she told Garrett. "It's all perfectly civilised."

Garrett merely grunted, then told Vaarem and Lim to go to bed.

Lim tossed and turned. He struggled to sleep at the best of times, and being stuck in a strange place made him that much more anxious. So, he lay in bed, listening to his family's breathing, and tried to breathe himself, only to be overcome by a fit of coughing, which he seemed unable to stop. He put his arm over his mouth to stop the sound, but this did nothing to help. Eventually he was forced to sit up.

His wheezing and hacking woke his family, which started the first argument of the trip.

"Could you try not to be so loud?" asked Garrett, annoyed. "In case you've forgotten, I've been driving all day and will be doing the same tomorrow. The least you can do is let me sleep."

"I'm trying," gasped Lim, when he could speak.

"Well, it looks like you're not trying very hard," said Garrett.

"Garrett, stop that," scolded Zareanna, then came over to comfort Lim. Because she couldn't see in the dark as well as the average elf, she summoned a small mage light, which hung above her head and illuminated her pale, worried face. It made Lim feel even worse, and he coughed again.

She sat on the bed and put her arms around him.

"I'm fine," insisted Lim, trying to push her away, without making it obvious that that was what he was doing. He didn't like it when she fussed. He coughed once more.

"Drink your potion for Fates' sake and let us sleep," said Garrett.

"I did," said Lim miserably, "I'm sorry. I'm not doing it on purpose."

"Well, have some more," said Garrett.

"I can't," said Lim between coughs. "It's toxic if I have too much."

"What?" demanded Garrett. "If it's toxic, why are you even taking it? What are you doing to yourself?"

"Garrett," said Zareanna, looking at him with stern eyes. "Don't. This is different."

Garrett looked at her for a moment, then shook his head and turned away, before lying back down.

"It's okay, darling," Zareanna drew Lim to her again. This time he let her and rested his head against her shoulder. "Are you okay?" she asked him softly.

He nodded, still struggling to breathe, but managing not to cough again. Zareanna kissed his head and went back to bed, her light blinking out as she did so.

Vaarem, who had watched the whole scene wordlessly, gave him a wan smile and lay back down. The one complaint that Lim had against his brother was that Vaarem didn't seem to think that Garrett's treatment of him was ever out of line.

"He doesn't baby you, the way that Mother does," Vaarem would say, "He treats me the same, and at least he doesn't expect *you* to follow in his footsteps." Their father was always insisting on Vaarem following him into a career in the Palinas Ruling Council. Fortunately for Lim, his father hadn't expressed much interest in his career aspirations thus far and had never said anything negative about Lim pursuing magic. Then again, he probably knew that Lim couldn't do it, so it was moot.

Lim looked at his brother with annoyance, then, when Vaarem didn't move, lay down too.

When everyone's breathing had slowed, indicating

they were asleep again, Lim got out of bed. He couldn't sleep and he didn't want to risk waking anyone up again. He put on his robe, and walked towards the balcony door. The balcony reminded him of the balconies in the elven tree-houses and he thought of going out there, but when he touched the window, he realised that it was freezing outside. His father was unlikely to be sympathetic if Lim made himself even sicker, so he wrapped his robe around himself and walked out of the room. The elevator was off, so he made his slow way down the stairs, holding on to the bannister and stopping every few steps to catch his breath.

By the time he got down to the lobby, he was feeling dizzy, so he sank into one of the chairs in front of the fireplace. Because elf houses were made in living trees, they didn't have fireplaces like human houses, and were heated using magic. However, elves still had bonfires, and used fire for cooking outdoors, so Lim knew that fire equaled warmth, therefore sat close to it now, stifling a cough as some of the smoke drifted toward him. He shifted the chair a little, to be out of the smoke's range.

The innkeeper, who was looking after the lobby, walked up to him.

"That cough doesn't sound good," she told him. "Would you like some tea or something?"

"Yes, please," said Lim, then took the cup gratefully when she brought it over several minutes later.

He sat in front of the fire and sipped on the tea,

as the innkeeper sat on the chair beside him. The warmth of the tea, as well as the air near the fireplace eased his throat, and he found that he could breathe easier.

"You should get that cough seen to," said the innkeeper.

"I know," said Lim. "I am. I'm going to the hospital in Sirrock City. That's where my family and I are travelling to."

"Sirrock City?" She frowned. "I didn't know that they treated elves."

"They do," said Lim. "Or they're making an exception for me, I'm not sure. It's supposed to be an experimental procedure."

She raised her eyebrows. "That sounds serious."

Lim sighed and coughed again. "Yes," he said. "It is, but I've tried every treatment that I've heard of, and I'm still sick. Experimental procedures are my last hope. And I'm one quarter human, so I guess I qualify. Elf medicine doesn't work on me anyway."

She smiled at him awkwardly, then she patted his hand, and stood up.

"Well, I hope it works out for you," she said.

"Thanks," said Lim. "I hope so too." He smiled cynically. He finished his tea, then stood up to go back upstairs, but then remembered that the elevator was switched off for the night, so he came back into the lobby and sat down again.

"Can I stay here?" he asked the innkeeper. "I can't breathe if I try to climb the stairs."

"Yes, of course," she said kindly, then she stoked the fire up, so that it burned warmer.

Lim sat and stared at the flames. After a while, their dance and the rhythmic sound of their crackling became hypnotic, and he closed his eyes.

He was woken up in the early hours of the morning by Vaarem shaking his shoulders.

"Lim?" His brother's voice was saying. "Are you okay?"

"Yeah,' said Lim, blinking. It was still dark, but he could see the sun rising through the window in the lobby.

"Shit, man," said Vaarem. "Mother is frantic. She freaked out when she woke up and you weren't in the room. Here, I brought you your potion." He handed Lim a small bottle.

"Thank you." Lim had a long sip, then closed the bottle and put it in his robe pocket. "I'm sorry. I didn't mean to scare anyone. But the elevator wasn't working, and you know I can't climb stairs at the moment."

"Yeah," said Vaarem. "It's fine. But come back up now."

"Is the elevator working?" asked Lim. Just the thought of climbing the stairs was making his breath catch in his throat.

"No," said Vaarem. "Not yet. Here." He leaned down and put one arm behind Lim's shoulders, and the other under his knees. "Hold on to me."

Lim put his arm around Vaarem's neck and allowed

his brother to pick him up and carry him up the stairs and into their room.

"Oh, thank the Fates," said Zareanna, when Vaarem put Lim down, and steadied him where he stood. "Where were you?" She ran towards him and cupped his face in her hands. "Are you all right?"

"Yes, I'm all right," said Lim. "Sorry, I didn't mean to scare anyone. I fell asleep downstairs."

"That's okay," said Zareanna, hugging him. "But don't do it again. Promise?"

"Yeah." Lim nodded, then sighed. It seemed that he couldn't win. If he tried to sleep in the same room as his family, he would keep them all up, yet apparently, he wasn't allowed to leave now.

He washed and dressed as quickly as he could, which under the circumstances was very slow, as he kept having to sit down and catch his breath. His father, fortunately, ignored him completely, as he and Vaarem packed their bags. Zareanna made them all a quick breakfast of fruit and porridge, after which they finished packing and left the room.

The elevator was still not on, so it took Lim a long time to get down the stairs. Vaarem carried his bags, which Lim was eternally grateful for but also made him feel guilty and useless.

He shouldn't have to do everything for me, he thought, as he leaned on the bannister to catch his breath.

The innkeeper was at the desk, and when he said

good-bye to her, she walked around, and put something in his hand. It was a paper bag, filled with something light.

"It's tea," she explained. "In case you can't sleep again. Good luck, and don't forget to say hi on your way back through."

"Thank you," said Lim, taking the tea, then, taking his herb-soaked cloth out of his pocket and warming it with his magic, before putting it over his nose and mouth in readiness to go outside. "But it will likely be several moons before we come back."

"Take as long as you need." She smiled, "and good luck."

"Thank you."

"May the Fates be with you," she told him.

"And with you also," he replied, then he walked outside, and into the waiting carriage.

Although he'd managed a couple of hours' sleep, he felt stiff and sore. He longed to lie down, but every time he tried, he couldn't breathe. Eventually, he managed to get semi-comfortable by sitting between his mother and brother and leaning his head on their shoulders, switching from one to the other as his neck got stiff, while his father drove the carriage again. Zareanna stroked his hair when he rested his head on her shoulder. He felt too sick to look at the books and scrolls he'd brought to read on the journey, his head starting to hurt whenever he tried.

In the early afternoon, they stopped for a brief

lunch and to rest the horses. Although Sera and Clea were used to pulling the carriage around Palinas, the forest paths were harder on their hooves, so the family were careful to not overtax them. Lim stayed in the carriage and nibbled on some fruit and bread, while Vaarem and Zareanna rubbed the horses down and gave them some oats. Garrett glanced in, to look at Lim, but thankfully didn't say anything. Lim normally liked to help with the horses. He liked animals in general and was the best at calming Sera and Clea if they ever got spooked, but today he was too tired. He hoped the mares would understand.

After half an hour, they set off again, this time with Lim leaning against Vaarem, who tried to tell him jokes, but Lim was too sick to listen.

"Did you hear the one about the tree that went to a party?" asked Vaarem. "It was asked to leave. Get it?"

Lim chuckled thinly. "Yeah, good one, Var," he said. "Sorry, I'm just not in the mood," he closed his eyes and crossed his arms, concentrating on keeping his lunch down.

"It's okay," said Vaarem, then put his arm around his brother and held him tightly to shield him from the bumps in the road.

Eventually, Lim managed to doze off.

Chapter 3

The East
Borla Inn

They arrived at the next inn, another human building in the middle of an orchard, in time to eat dinner.

After some consideration, the family decided to rent two rooms, one for Garrett and Zareanna, and one for Vaarem and Lim. Zareanna was apprehensive about this.

"Will you be okay?" she asked Lim anxiously.

He rolled his eyes at that. "Fates, Mother, I've been sleeping in my own room for many turns now. You'll be just down the hall, so closer than at home." At home, their parents' bedrooms were on the level below his and Vaarem's. "And Vaarem will be with me."

Vaarem stood behind him and laughed, which didn't do much to ease Zareanna, but finally she relented.

Lim went into his and Vaarem's room, and lay down

on the bed, while Vaarem dropped his things off, then went back out to have a look around.

A short while later, Vaarem returned, looking annoyingly cheerful.

"Get dressed," he said to Lim. "There's a restaurant in this place. We're going to dinner."

"I am dressed," said Lim. "And I'm not hungry."

Vaarem rolled his eyes, as he looked through his bag for something to get changed into. "Yes, yes," he said. "You're never hungry. But you still eat every day. Well, most days," he conceded.

"I had breakfast, and lunch," said Lim sullenly. He was still feeling decidedly ill and had even less of an appetite than usual.

"The waitresses are pretty," said Vaarem, sitting down beside him.

"So? What's that got to do with me?" Lim looked up at him.

Vaarem rolled his eyes again. "So, they want to meet you."

"Why?"

"Because I got talking to them, and they seem very nice, and then they asked me if I had a brother, so naturally I said yes, and then they asked me if he was cute, and I said, 'We're identical twins, so, yes, he is very cute', and then they got all excited and asked to meet you." Vaarem got up again, then crouched down and looked into Lim's bag. "Do you have any clothes that are not black?" he asked, looking up at Lim again.

"You know that I don't," said Lim dully.

"Do you want to borrow something of mine?" asked Vaarem, sitting back down on the bed again.

"Why would I want to do that?"

"Because I have stylish clothes that I'm willing to share with you," suggested Vaarem with a raised eyebrow.

Lim chuckled. "No thanks," he said. "But thank you for offering."

"So, does that mean that you're coming?" asked Vaarem.

Lim sighed. He knew that he had to eat something, despite his body trying to convince him otherwise. "Do I have a choice?" he asked grimly.

"Not really," admitted Vaarem, "but it is better if you come willingly."

"Ugh," Lim groaned, then sat up and coughed. He drank some of his potion, until the coughing stopped. His throat still felt raw.

"Can you get me a shirt?" he asked Vaarem. The mere idea of finding something suitable was too tiring.

Vaarem went over to Lim's bag obligingly, looked through it, then selected a cotton shirt with gathered sleeves and lace at the collar. He brought it over to Lim, who put it on, then waited to catch his breath, before tying it up in the front. Vaarem got Lim's brush out of his bag, then came back over and brushed his hair for him, running the brush through its silky length, before putting it up in a top-knot, matching his own hairstyle.

Lim frowned. He never wore his hair up in this way.

"Really?" he asked, getting up off the bed and walking over to the dressing table to look at himself in the mirror.

"Why?" asked Vaarem. "You look good."

Lim turned his head this way and that, looking at his reflection critically. The top-knot accentuated his sharp cheekbones and somehow made his face look less gaunt, his eyes less sunken. He looked reasonably good, which made him smile. Then, seeing his reflection smiling made him feel better inside.

Perhaps this dinner would be fun after all.

Before leaving the room, Lim put his waistcoat over his shirt, then he had another swig of his potion, putting the bottle in his shirt pocket.

"Are you monitoring your usage of that?" asked Vaarem.

"Yes." Nodded Lim. "I'm being careful not to have too much, but it's hard, as my breathing is getting worse. The lady at the other inn gave me some tea, which I may try tonight."

"Good man," said Vaarem, patting Lim on the shoulder, before taking a final glance in the mirror and adjusting his outfit. He wore the same black slim-fitting trousers and boots as Lim, with a sky-blue shirt, and a silver vest. His hair was up in a top-knot, in the same style as Lim's.

Vaarem smiled at himself in the mirror, and Lim smiled too. His brother's smile was infectious. "Well, if I say so myself, we make a handsome pair, don't we?" said Vaarem.

"I guess," said Lim, uncertainly, although he had to admit that he agreed with his brother. Vaarem was handsome, even by elf standards, which meant that Lim was handsome too. At least in theory... He had another sip of his potion and followed his brother out of the room and down the hallway.

The twins walked into the dining room and sat down at the table that had been set for them. Their parents hadn't arrived yet.

Two young human women came over and served them a bowl of vegetable soup each.

"Hello, Vaarem," they both said shyly.

"Hello, ladies," said Vaarem. "This is my brother Lim."

"Hello," said Lim, smiling, and doing his best to not appear as shy and awkward as he felt. Fortunately, the potion was coursing through his system, which was at least allowing him to breathe.

"Lim, this is Marla," Vaarem indicated the older girl, "and Jessa."

"Hello, Lim," said Marla, curtsying gracefully, and Jessa followed suit.

Marla was taller than her sister, with dark brown hair pinned up in a loose bun, and a few strands falling out and framing her face, a style that Lim had seen on several elf girls in Palinas. She was dressed in a blue and white checkered dress, and a white apron. Jessa was shorter and curvier, with bright red hair, tied back in a braid, and a friendly face, liberally sprinkled with freckles. She was dressed in a similar style to her sister, only her dress had green and white checkers, and her apron was trimmed with lace, whereas Marla's was plain. Lim wondered how they got the checkered materials for their dresses. Were they dyed, or woven that way? Elf clothes were all made of plain fabrics, with decorations made of beads or embroidery.

"Nice to meet you," said Lim to the girls. "I like your dresses."

"Thank you," said Marla with a curtsey. Behind her, Jessa smiled.

Vaarem raised his eyebrow suggestively and Lim shook his head a little. He hadn't meant anything. He looked down and began to eat his soup. The smell of it was delicious, and soon enough he found his appetite returning. He tasted some herbs that he wasn't familiar with, and decided that he quite liked them. He was halfway through the bowl (Vaarem had already finished), when their parents arrived and sat down at the table.

"You look nice, darling," said Zareanna to Lim, kissing him on the cheek before sitting down.

"Oh, and I look nice too, you say?" asked Vaarem sarcastically. "Why, thank you."

"I'm sorry, dear," said Zareanna. "I didn't mean to exclude you. I..." She trailed off.

"It's fine," said Vaarem, "I'm used to it," he added under his breath, but she'd turned to the waitresses, who had brought over some soup for her and Garrett.

After they all finished their soup (even Lim managed

to eat the whole bowl), Marla and Jessa brought over the main course, which consisted of roasted pork with pumpkin and potatoes. To Lim's relief, all the foods were served separately, so he put them on his plate carefully. Again, the smell was so delicious, with the same herbs and spices as before, that Lim found himself eating it with a small degree of pleasure. The family made the occasional small talk as they ate, but mostly they sat in companionable silence.

When they'd finished eating, they all stood up to go back to their rooms.

"Don't stay up too late," Zareanna told her sons.

"We won't," Vaarem assured her.

"Don't forget to take your potion," Garrett told Lim.

"I've already had it," he said.

"If you need anything," said Zareanna anxiously, "I am just down the hall. Come and get me, no matter the time," she said, looking at Garrett with a frown that clearly showed that her decision on this was final and he had no say. He nodded, but rolled his eyes a little.

"Yes, I know. Thank you," said Lim, trying not to sound as impatient as he felt. "I am no longer a child. I can look after myself."

"I know," said Zareanna, hugging first him, then Vaarem. "But I am still your mother, and I will always worry. So, are you sure you're both fine?" she asked.

"Yes, Mother," they both assured her, then they both went to their room, while Zareanna and Garrett went to theirs next door.

Chapter 4

Marla and Jessa

Lim had just settled down with a book, when there was a knock on their door.

"Our guests have arrived," said Vaarem, standing up to open it.

"What?" Lim looked up, momentarily confused, then, "Oh," he said, realising what had happened.

"I invited the girls over." Vaarem confirmed Lim's suspicions.

"Why?"

"Why not? They're nice, and much as I love you, I enjoy different company every once in a while. Come on, get up, it'll be fun."

Lim put his book down reluctantly.

"We don't have to have sex with them, sheesh," said Vaarem to Lim's unhappy expression. "We're just going to talk. It's not a double date or anything." He rolled his eyes.

"Oh good," said Lim, feeling a little more at ease. He was very uncomfortable with the idea of being set up to go on a date. Vaarem had dated several girls in Palinas and confided to him that he'd had sex on a couple of occasions, revealing that it had been fun and hinting that Lim should try it. Lim was glad that his brother was not planning on bedding any girls this evening. He did not want to have those conversations again. He himself had never had sex and had no desire to do it. Apart from the fact that he doubted that he had the stamina for it, he just wasn't interested in getting that close to anyone. He figured that this was simply another part of him that didn't work as it was supposed to, but unlike his breathing and lack of energy, he was fine with this. He found the whole idea a little gross.

Vaarem opened the door and Marla walked in, followed by Jessa. Both girls were still wearing the dresses they'd worn earlier, but they'd taken off their aprons, and tidied their hair.

Lim took a small sip of his potion, to try and prevent having a coughing fit while in their company, and arranged his face into a smile.

"Is it true that all elves can do magic?" asked Jessa. She was sitting on the bed beside Lim, while Marla and Vaarem sat on the couch across the room. The innkeepers' daughters had confided that although the inn had elf guests from time to time, they rarely got a chance to talk to them on a personal level.

"Yeah," said Lim, taking a discrete sip of his potion. "We use it for heat and light and stuff, so kind of instead of electricity in some ways. But also for art and entertainment. Some elves are better at it than others and can do more. My grandfather, for example, has very weak magic and struggles to do basic things, but his sister, our great aunt, is very talented, and studied magic at The Academy. I'd love to study there, but I don't think I can. They only accept two elves each turn. My grandfather now lives among humans, so doesn't need to use magic. Although some humans can use magic too." He trailed off, thinking of Vada. He hoped that there would be a message from her when he arrived in Sirrock.

"But can *you* do magic?" asked Jessa eagerly.

"Yes," said Lim. He lifted his hand and concentrated on the fire that was burning in the fireplace, adding his own energy to it. The flames started to burn higher. It was a simple enough trick that he could do without exhausting himself too much.

"Oh wow," said Jessa, impressed, and both she and Marla clapped.

"You think that's cool?' said Vaarem. "Watch this." He lifted his hands, palms up, and conjured three balls of white light, like the mage-light that their mother had summoned the previous night, and began to juggle them. Or rather, he made it look like he was juggling them. In reality, he was manipulating the lights with his mind and moving his hands to make it look like they were pushing the orbs. It was an impressive illusion and Lim smiled seeing it. He was capable of similar feats himself, but they took a lot of concentration and energy, which was usually beyond him.

Although perhaps tonight I could try?

Marla and Jessa clapped and laughed excitedly.

Lim lifted his hand and conjured a ball of red light, which he sent over to Vaarem, making it look like he'd used his hand to push it. Once the red sphere was in his vicinity, Vaarem took over controlling it, so that he was now supposedly juggling four balls. Lim then pointed, for effect, and the balls began to change colour from white to yellow to green to blue. It was usually difficult to control another mage's conjured light, however Vaarem and Lim had been playing with magic since they'd been young and were attuned to each other's energies. Another difficulty was that the mage-lights were moving, but as their movement was rhythmic, Lim could predict where each orb would be at each moment, so could send the thought-command to change its colour to its exact location at the right time.

"Hey," said Vaarem, as Lim made the balls change colour again. "Stop messing with my balls," which made everybody laugh.

The elves did several more magic tricks, such as turning the water in the jug to ice, then melting it and making it boil, after which they all talked again for a while.

It was well after midnight, when the girls finally left.

As they were getting ready for bed, Lim turned to

his brother. "Thanks for that," he said. "You were right. It was a lot of fun."

Vaarem smiled as he took his hair out of its top-knot and shook it out. "You're most welcome. As you can see, I'm not just a pretty face. I sometimes have good ideas too."

Lim took another sip of his potion as he lay down. He'd been swigging it all evening, and had successfully avoided having another coughing fit, as well as breathing relatively normally all night. He knew that he'd had more than he should have, having finished two full bottles, but it was now after midnight, a new day, and he resolved that he would watch his dosage from now on.

Lim woke up several hours after falling asleep with a stomach-ache, of all things.

"Ow," he groaned, curling his legs up to his chest, and hugging his arms around himself. He knew instantly that it was from overusing his potion, and he cursed himself for having been so careless.

He tried to take deep breaths and to breathe through the pain as his gut cramped but this only made him cough, which in turn made the pain so intense that he wanted to cry. So, he lay on his side, curled up and gasping, praying to the Fates for some sort of release.

"Lim?" Vaarem sat up in the bed, clearly woken by Lim's moaning and wriggling.

"Mmmm," replied Lim, unable to form any coherent words.

"Are you okay?" asked Vaarem, sitting up.

Lim winced, then when the cramp eased, he turned to his brother and said, "I've got a stomach-ache," then curled his legs into his chest as another cramp came on, "It's really bad."

"Do you want me to get someone?"

"No." Lim shook his head, then groaned, as the next cramp ran through him. "I think I had too much potion. Remember Dr Fantail warned me that it was toxic in high doses? Well, he was right. Ow," he gasped.

"Oh shit," said Vaarem. "Lim, you should know better than that." His voice was gentle though, not admonishing.

"I know," said Lim weakly. "But we were having so much fun, and I didn't want to spoil it." He winced.

"You wouldn't have spoiled anything," said Vaarem. "You need to look after yourself." He patted Lim's shoulder.

"I'm sorry," said Lim again. "I honestly thought it would be okay, and like I said, we were all having such a good time, and." He paused and grimaced as his stomach cramped, "I didn't want to ruin it. I always end up spoiling things for everyone."

"No, you don't," said Vaarem, still stroking his shoulder. Despite Vaarem's words, they were both aware that there had been many incidents where Lim's illness had disrupted an otherwise pleasant social occasion.

Lim looked up at his twin helplessly, then said, "Ow," again as his stomach pained him.

Vaarem looked at him for another moment. "Here, let me help. Lie back."

Lim lay down on his back obediently and straightened his legs. Vaarem opened up his nightgown and laid his hand on his brother's thin belly. "Where does it hurt?" he asked.

"All around," said Lim, then gasped, and turned to his side, his legs curling up, as another cramp twisted his insides.

Vaarem turned him onto his back again and straightened his legs, then started to slowly move his hand in a circular motion over Lim's abdomen, and after a while, Lim could feel magic heat emanating from his brother's hand, moving through his skin and into his organs.

"Is that better?" asked Vaarem softly.

"Yes, a bit." Nodded Lim. "Thank you." He tried to will his body to relax. "Please don't tell Mother and Father," he said weakly.

"I won't," promised Vaarem. He kept massaging Lim's belly, moving his hand from the bottom of Lim's ribs down to his hip bone, over to his other hip, and back up again.

Lim felt the magic warmth permeate through his body and start to relax him. Eventually, he managed to fall asleep again.

Vaarem woke up a little after sunrise. Lim was still asleep next to him, lying on his back, with his hands crossed over his chest. In his black nightgown, and with his pale, thin face, he looked like a corpse, and Vaarem had a small moment of panic, until he saw his brother's chest rise and fall.

Vaarem breathed a sigh of relief, then got up, careful not to disturb his twin. Lim slept so little normally, that it would have been cruel to wake him now, when it wasn't completely necessary.

Vaarem washed and dressed quietly, then he went out into the inn.

The dining room was already starting to fill with guests wanting their breakfast. They were almost exclusively human, however Vaarem spotted a group of dwarves in one corner. Apart from him, and his parents, who were sitting at a table in the opposite corner, there were no other elves.

Borla was one of the Three Countries that made up the Sirranna Region. The Sirranna Region had historically been settled by humans, but over the last few centuries, dwarves and elves had begun to settle there too. Borla was the most inclusive of the Three Countries, going so far as having representatives from all four races, even the usually elusive pixies, on its ruling council. Vaarem would have expected to see more elves this close to the Palinora border. Then again, it was winter, and elves rarely travelled for pleasure, so maybe it was completely normal that there were no other elves there.

Vaarem helped himself to some fruit and bread from the buffet, then went to sit down with his parents.

"Morning," he said, then started to eat.

"Where's Lim?" asked his mother anxiously.

Vaarem sighed, annoyed. His mother frequently made him feel invisible. It seemed that everything he did was relative to his brother, and that without Lim, he didn't exist.

"He's sleeping," he replied between mouthfuls.

"Why?" asked Garrett. "Why didn't you wake him and make him come over and eat with us as a family?"

"He had a bad night," explained Vaarem. He remembered his brother moaning and gasping in pain in a way that he'd never heard before, and he shuddered.

"What happened?" asked Zareanna, at once alert and wanting to know everything.

Vaarem hesitated. He didn't want to tell his mother that Lim was overusing his potion. That would only make her worry, and no doubt it would make his father angry, who would then accuse Lim of faking it, or of making himself sick on purpose to get attention, or any number of stupid things that he'd said in the past.

"He just didn't sleep very well," said Vaarem. "You know he often doesn't."

That was effectively the end of the conversation, and they ate the rest of their breakfast in silence.

Vaarem ran into Marla and Jessa on his way back into his room. They were carrying sheets and towels, clearly on their way to tidy up the guest rooms.

"Good morning," he said brightly, and gave them a bow as he opened the door to his room.

"Good morning," said Marla. "How are you?"

"I'm very well," said Vaarem. "Thank you for coming last night. My brother and I really enjoyed the evening."

"You're very welcome," said Marla. "We had a great time too. Where's your brother?"

"Yes, where is the lovely Lim?" asked Jessa, as Vaarem stepped into the room, and invited the girls to follow him.

Lim was still asleep on the bed. He'd moved from his creepy corpse-pose and was now lying on his side.

"He's still asleep," said Vaarem, dropping his voice, wondering whether he should have invited the girls in after all. Then again, Lim was used to being in bed when friends came over, so Vaarem figured that he wouldn't mind. He usually appreciated visitors. And hopefully he would wake up soon. Nevertheless, Vaarem kept his voice low and gestured for the girls to be quiet. "It seems that we exhausted him last night," he said, with a slight chuckle.

"Aww," said Marla. "Should we leave? We can clean up later."

"It's okay," said Vaarem, still speaking softly, as Marla and Jessa picked up their used towels and left fresh ones in their place. "He doesn't mind. He's often in bed when people come over. He downplays how ill he is," he explained, looking at his brother's sleeping form, wishing that Lim would wake up, so then he himself wouldn't need to wake him. "He tries to keep up with everyone else, and it takes a toll on him."

"Aww, the poor dear," said Jessa kindly.

"Yeah," said Vaarem, suddenly feeling guilty. Last night was not the first time that he and Lim had done something together, which had been a lot of fun at the time, only for Lim to end up paying for it for days afterwards.

Why do I keep on doing this to him? he wondered. *Why do I always guilt him into joining me?*

When they'd been younger, the other kids at school had been wary of Lim, but after Vaarem had insisted that his brother be included, the kids had always warmed to him. Lim probably didn't need him in that way anymore, but Vaarem was still scared of his brother being lonely. That, and he often felt that if he just walked out one day, Lim would be the only person who noticed. Sometime during their childhood, their roles had reversed and now it was Vaarem who needed his brother with him in order to be accepted.

"Is he going to be all right?" asked Jessa, as she swept around their things.

"Yes," said Vaarem. "At least, I hope so." He bit his lip. "We're travelling to Sirrock City to try a new treatment at the hospital."

"You sound scared," said Marla, putting her hand on his arm.

"Yes," admitted Vaarem. "I am. It's an experimental treatment. I don't know what's going to happen. Lim is not only my brother, he is also my best friend, and the bravest, and most awesome person I know. I don't know what I'd do if anything truly bad ever happened to him. He's been through so much already."

"I'm sorry," said Marla, taking her hand off and giving him a brief hug. "I hope the treatment goes well."

"So do I," said Vaarem, his voice shaking. He tried not to think about what would happen once they got to Sirrock City. The procedure that Dr Fantail had described sounded scary, and if Lim hadn't been adamant that he wanted to do it, Vaarem would have much preferred that he didn't. Still, it was Lim's choice. And Dr Fantail had assured them that it was safe, and that it had a good chance of working. Finally, Lim was running out of options.

Vaarem smiled at Jessa and Marla thinly, trying to reassure himself, as much as them.

"You'll both come and say good-bye before you go?" asked Jessa, as she emptied the dustpan into the bin by the door, and she and Marla prepared to leave the room.

"Of course," said Vaarem, smiling, looking at his brother again.

Wake up, Lim, he thought. *Show us all that you're all right and that I didn't inadvertently make you sick again.*

"I'll pack some breakfast for Lim," said Marla, as they were leaving. "Seeing as he missed it and all."

"Thank you," said Vaarem. "That's very kind of you."

"What does he like to eat?" she asked.

Vaarem shrugged. "Not much," he said with a chuckle. "But if you pack some fruit and porridge, or some bread and honey, I'm sure that he'll appreciate that. Just make sure that it's all packed separately.

He doesn't like his food to touch." Vaarem had never understood this particular quirk of his brother's, but he appreciated that it was important to Lim, for whatever reason.

"Okay," said Marla. "Now, you be sure to come and see us before you go. Both of you."

"Yes, we will," promised Vaarem, then shut the door as the girls left.

He began to pack their things, having decided that if Lim didn't wake of his own accord, Vaarem would let him sleep and only wake him up at the last possible moment. Lim obviously needed all the sleep he could get.

After packing their bags, he sat down at the dressing table and started to brush his hair. He saw Lim stir in the mirror, and turned around as his brother sat up, running his hands over his face and through his long, silky hair.

"How are you feeling?" asked Vaarem.

"Better," said Lim. He reached for his potion bottle, then stopped. He considered it for a moment, then picked it up and had a sip.

"I'll try and limit it today," he said.

"Yeah, that's a good idea," said Vaarem. "You really scared me last night. I've never heard you make sounds like that before."

"Oh no," said Lim, his face colouring, "I'm sorry."

"It's fine," said Vaarem, walking over to sit down next to him. "As long as you're okay now?"

"Yes, I'm fine. Thanks. You really helped, so thank you. I was in agony."

"Yeah, it sounded like it," agreed Vaarem.

He looked at Lim for another moment, trying to express how scared he'd been for him, when Lim said, "Did you mean what you said before? About me being brave and awesome?"

Vaarem felt himself blush. "You heard that?" he asked. "I thought you were asleep."

"I was. Kind of. I was drifting in and out."

Vaarem looked at him for a moment, then rolled his eyes. "Of course, I meant it. Every word. But I would hope that you know that anyway."

"I do know," said Lim softly. "But it's nice to hear it sometimes."

"What's the time?" asked Lim, a few moments later, as he started to get out of the bed. He felt better rested than he had since leaving home, but his chest still hurt, and he knew that it was going to be a long and difficult day.

"Mid-morning," said Vaarem. "I packed up your stuff for you. We will be leaving in the next hour or so. You missed breakfast, but Marla and Jessa said that they will pack something for you."

"Oh. That's nice of them. I hope you told them thanks from me."

"I did. But you can tell them yourself. They asked for you to see them before we left. Well, actually they asked for both of us to see them to say good-bye."

'Oh, okay," said Lim. He sat down at the dressing table and washed his face, then ran a brush through his hair.

"Here." Vaarem threw some clothes at him. "Get dressed. I have to hand it to you, at least your wardrobe is easy to coordinate."

"Not always," said Lim, catching the clothes, then removing his nightshirt and putting them on. "There is nothing worse than when your blacks don't match."

Vaarem laughed. "If only it were that simple. Now, come on, hurry up. Father is already miffed because we're surrounded by humans."

"And because I missed breakfast, no doubt," said Lim grimly.

"I didn't tell them why," said Vaarem. "I just told them that you couldn't sleep."

"Thanks," said Lim, doing up his shirt, then having to sit down to catch his breath. Vaarem sat down on the bed.

"So, did the girls say anything else?" asked Lim when he could talk again. He was starting to think that even though they'd only known them for a day, he and Vaarem were going to end up being good friends with Marla and Jessa.

Vaarem shrugged. "Just that they hope your treatment goes well, and to come and see them on our way back."

"Yes," said Lim, smiling. "I'd like that. So far, all the people we've met have been so nice. I have to say I was a bit apprehensive about going to a human hospital, but if all humans are as friendly as the ones we've met, then surely it will all be fine."

"I sure hope so," said Vaarem.

They packed the rest of their things, then put their bags out in the lobby, ready to be put in their carriage.

Lim could tell that the air outside was freezing, so he had another swig of his potion, then got his herb cloth ready to put over his face as they went looking for Marla and Jessa, finally finding them in a back storeroom.

"Hello," said Vaarem, knocking on the door.

The girls were both sitting on chairs, darning something made out of a long piece of material, most likely a curtain. Their heads were bent together, and they were talking and laughing quietly. They seemed to have the same type of close sibling relationship that Lim and Vaarem shared, which was probably why the four of them got on so well.

"Hello." Marla looked up with a smile.

Jessa finished her stitch, then looked up too, her face breaking into a smile too when she saw the elf brothers.

"We've come to say good-bye, as instructed," said Vaarem, stepping into the room.

Lim followed him. The air in here was nice and warm, and he found breathing easier. Or was it the positive energy that the sisters were putting out that did it?

Marla put down her sewing and stood up, followed by Jessa.

"We've packed you some food," said Jessa, looking at Lim. "Come through into the kitchen." She walked past them and out the door. Lim followed her, grateful that she slowed down to his pace without him needing to say anything, with Vaarem and Marla walking behind them.

"So, where are you off to today?" asked Jessa.

"We are moving ever towards Sirrock City," said Lim with a smile, trying to emulate his brother's usual enthusiasm. Vaarem grinned and raised his eyebrows at him approvingly.

"Oh yes," said Jessa. "Your brother told us. I really hope it all works out for you."

"I hope so too," said Lim, as he followed her into the kitchen.

Marla stepped around him, and she and Jessa pulled out a basket laden with food, from beneath one of the benches.

There were different types of fruit in it, as well as breads and biscuits, with a jar of honey, and a bag of leaves that Lim guessed were some kind of tea.

"Wow," said Lim. "Thank you. How much do we owe you for this?" He would have to get his coins from his bags because he guessed that the food in the basket must have been worth at least one hundred common crowns, if not more, the price of a room in an inn such as this one.

"Nothing, silly," said Jessa, walking towards him to give him a hug. He was proud of himself for not flinching when she touched him. He hugged her back, smelling her hair, which smelt of fresh bread and spices. She and Marla must have baked the bread themselves that morning.

"It's a gift," explained Marla. "From us to you. That magic show that you put on last night must be worth at least a basket of food." She smiled.

"Okay," said Lim, genuinely touched. "Thank you. Really." He hugged Jessa again and felt her rest her head on his chest. It felt nice, and he held her for a moment longer, before letting her go and smiling down at her.

"Will you write to me?" she asked him. "Tell me how it all goes?"

"Yes," replied Lim. "I will. We will." He indicated Vaarem, who was talking quietly to Marla beside them. "And we'll be back in several moons."

"That would be lovely," said Jessa.

"Hopefully I'll be better," said Lim. "And we can do more stuff."

Jessa smiled up at him shyly, and Lim hoped that he hadn't just made an inadvertent innuendo. Although hugging her just now had felt nice. Perhaps he *was* capable of a little physical intimacy after all. However, he still had no desire to ever go all the way.

Vaarem walked over to the bench and picked up the basket. Lim could tell that he was straining under its weight, and he was very glad that he didn't need to attempt to carry it himself. He hugged Jessa again, then Marla, before he and Vaarem said their good-byes and went outside into the waiting carriage.

Chapter 5

The Journey Continues

"Good morning, Limnos," said Garrett curtly, as Lim and Vaarem put their things into the back of the carriage. "You missed breakfast again," he pointed out.

"Garrett," warned Zareanna.

"What?" he asked, then turned back to Lim, "We are travelling as a family, and I expect you to participate. So, don't you dare miss any more meals, nor any other occasions when we are expected to be together, unless you literally cannot get out of bed. Is that clear?"

"Yes, Father," said Lim, hanging his head.

"Leave him alone," said Vaarem, surprising Lim. Today was the first time that Lim could recall his brother standing up for him against his father.

"Excuse me?" asked Garrett dangerously.

Lim stepped back instinctively, but Vaarem didn't back down.

"I said, leave him alone. I told you that it was me who didn't wake him. It's not his fault. He's sick."

"Is he?" asked Garrett coldly.

"Garrett," said Zareanna sharply, but he ignored her and continued,

"He was fine yesterday, but as soon as it comes to shared meals, he's conveniently sick. We are a family unit, and we will act like a family unit. Which means that both of you are expected to understand and participate. Is that understood?"

"Yes, Father," said Lim again, then coughed as the negative energy that his father was putting out hit him.

"Vaarem?" asked Garrett, looking at his first-born son.

"Yes, I understand," said Vaarem, his tone sullen.

"Good," said Garrett. "Now, I don't want to hear any more about it. Get in the carriage, both of you."

Vaarem and Lim got in the carriage and sat down, while Garrett climbed onto the driver's seat.

"I'm sorry, darlings," said Zareanna, climbing in behind them. "Your father is just stressed and anxious. Plus, you both know he doesn't do well when outside of elven settlements. Don't take what he says to heart. He doesn't mean it." She put her arms around her sons as they sat on either side of her.

"Oh, I rather think he does mean it," said Lim grimly. "He hates me."

"No, he doesn't," said Zareanna sternly. "Don't you ever think that." She kissed the side of his head. "He's just worried, and he doesn't know how to express himself. He loves both of you very much." There was a faraway look in her eyes as she said this, but then she blinked and the moment was gone.

Lim wondered what she'd been thinking.

Garrett was in a bad mood for the whole day. The bumpy road made the going slow, and the cold air made everyone generally irritable, even Zareanna, who normally had the patience of a wise elder. Lim tried to sleep, but he couldn't because his breath kept catching in his throat, making him cough.

"Would you stop that?" asked Garrett at one point. "You are driving me insane."

"Sorry," began Lim, but Zareanna interrupted him.

"We're all here, Garrett," she said. "We can all hear him, and he's not doing it on purpose, so suck it up. It's a million times worse for Lim than for any of us." She put her arm around Lim protectively and hugged him to her.

"If you really thought that, you'd stop enabling him," said Garrett under his breath.

"Excuse me?" demanded Zareanna, as Lim continued to cough.

"You heard me." Garrett turned around to glare at him and Zareanna again, then suddenly the carriage lurched, and stopped, coming to rest at an odd angle.

Lim and Zareanna were both thrown against Vaarem, who cried out in surprise.

"Fucking dragon balls!" swore Garrett.

He jumped down off the driver's seat and went to investigate.

A minute later he opened the carriage door and said, "The axle is broken. See what you made me do?" He glared at Lim.

"What?" asked Lim helplessly. Was his father really blaming *him* for this? "I'm sorry," he said instinctively. He'd learnt long ago that there was no arguing with Garrett. You just copped the blame for whatever had happened and moved on. However, this seemed particularly unfair.

Zareanna hugged Lim again. "It's not your fault, darling," she said, then she got out of the carriage to help her husband, Lim and Vaarem following her.

The back right wheel lay broken, and the horses were dancing around in confusion. Zareanna and Lim went to tend to them, while Garrett and Vaarem started to work on fixing the wheel.

Lim found that the freezing air hurt his lungs, so he took out his cloth, heated it with a bit of magic and put it over his nose and mouth, tying it around the back of his head like a mask, so that he could have both hands free. He then reached out and stroked the horses' noses gently.

"There, there," he said softly, into Sera's ear. "It's okay. It's all good." He then repeated the words to Clea, then reached over and stroked their manes, while Zareanna checked the straps and harnesses to make sure that they weren't damaged.

After a while, Garrett called Lim over to help with the wheel, so Lim left the horses and walked over to his father.

Garrett frowned at him. "Take that thing off your face," he said. "You look ridiculous."

"I can't breathe without it," said Lim weakly, knowing that he'd lost the argument, but trying nevertheless.

"Yes, you can," said Garrett impatiently. "Nobody prescribed it as a treatment for you. Did they?" He raised his eyebrow.

Lim shook his head. No one had prescribed that he breathe through a warm cloth but that didn't mean that it wasn't helping. However, his father wouldn't understand. He seemed to be completely against home remedies for some reason.

"I thought as much," said Garrett. "Now, for the last time, take it off."

Lim reluctantly took the cloth off and held it to his face with his hand, but this made it impossible for him to help, so he was forced to put it in his pocket.

As soon as the cold air hit his throat, he started to cough, as he knew he would. Nevertheless, he did his best to assist his father and brother.

After only a few minutes, he found himself drawing less and less air into his lungs, and he started to tire quickly, then black spots started to appear in his vision.

Vaarem looked at him and frowned. "Are you okay?" he asked. "You look really weird."

Lim nodded, but then the black spots grew, until they filled his entire field of vision.

Lim woke up with his head in Zareanna's lap.

"Lim darling?" she was saying, stroking his cheek gently. "Are you okay? Limmy?"

He blinked, and struggled to sit up, but his mother held him tight.

"It's okay," she said, rocking him like she had when he'd been a child. "You're okay."

Garrett was looking down at them with a frown. "He's not a baby, Zara," he said, "And you're not helping."

"He's *my* baby," said Zareanna in a voice that bore no arguments. "He's my baby and always will be, no matter how old he is."

Lim felt embarrassed at this, but he also felt too tired and sick to protest, so he lay in his mother's lap and let her stroke his hair. He put the cloth to his mouth again and breathed through it.

"Let's stop off for some lunch," suggested Vaarem from somewhere behind them. "I've nearly fixed the wheel. It will be easy from here, so let's all eat something and calm down, then we can be on our way."

His parents ignored him, as they continued to glare at each other.

"*Ah-em,*" Vaarem cleared his throat. "I *said,* let's

stop fighting and eat something so we're not snapping at each other."

Garrett and Zareanna continued to look at each other for another moment. Lim continued to breathe through his cloth, trying not to cough.

"Fine," Garrett said finally, his tone sulky, then went into the carriage to get some plates, while Vaarem took out the basket from the inn, which he set down in front of Lim and Zareanna. They'd stopped on the side of a meadow, in an uninhabited area, the same type of place that they stopped each day for their midday meal. The morning frost had melted, leaving the grass wet and cold. Garrett went and got a blanket, which he spread out in front of them.

Lim sat up slowly and with Zareanna's help moved to sit on the blanket. Garrett and Vaarem sat down too. Garrett handed out the plates and cutlery, then Zareanna started to take items out of the basket and distributing them.

She cut a piece of bread for everyone, then smeared the pieces with honey, before handing them out.

Lim stared at his food, still holding the cloth to his face.

"For the love of all the Fates, Limnos," said Garrett, "eat, or I swear if you faint again, we are going to leave you here and go home. We're doing this for you, but so far, you've done nothing except cause trouble."

"I'm sorry," said Lim miserably. "I don't mean to." He coughed again.

"Lay off him," said Vaarem, defending his brother

for the second time that day. "Why are you being so mean to him?" he asked. "Lim hasn't done anything wrong, and he hasn't caused any trouble. It was you who took your eyes off the road. It's your fault that we crashed. Not Lim's. Yours. Stop being such a bully."

Lim stared at his brother, wondering what had come over Vaarem. He was grateful for the support, but he had a feeling that this was not going to end well. He coughed discreetly into his elbow.

Garrett stared at his older son, his eyes filled with barely suppressed rage. "What did you say?" he asked with quiet menace.

"I said, stop bullying my brother."

Garrett stared at him for a moment, then he raised his hand and slapped Vaarem across the face.

"What the?" asked Vaarem, putting his hand to his cheek in shock.

"Don't you ever dare speak to me like that again," said Garrett. "I told you this morning."

Vaarem stared at his father, his hand still on his cheek. Lim stared from his brother to his father, his breath catching. Garrett had never struck either of his sons before.

Garrett stared at his hand, as if he couldn't believe what it had done. "I'm sorry," he said to Vaarem, his eyes still wide with shock, then he looked down and glared at Lim. "See what you made me do?" he hissed. "It should be *you* apologising to your brother."

Lim cringed back into his mother's arms and

coughed. He was used to being blamed for things but today was ridiculous. He coughed into his cloth.

"Argh!" said Vaarem, bunching his hands into fists. "This is exactly what I'm talking about. It's not his fault! He didn't do anything! Stop blaming him for everything!"

Zareanna looked up at Garrett with disappointed eyes. "He's right, you know," she said softly. "You're being much too hard on Lim. It's unfair. He's not Malkim."

Garrett looked up at her sharply. "Don't," he hissed. "Don't you dare." He shook his head, his face colouring. "I'm sorry," he said quietly. "I'm sorry, Lim." He looked at his youngest son with anxious eyes, but then his gaze hardened. "But I find it very hard to deal with you sometimes. One day you're walking around, acting like everything is normal, and the next day you're like," he struggled to find the words, then finally said, "this," indicating Lim sitting on the ground, being held by Zareanna. "And look, you *can* breathe without that stupid thing." He indicated Lim having put the cloth down. "I hate to see your mother so upset all the time, but *you* don't seem to care. What am I supposed to think?"

"I don't know," said Lim miserably. "I'm sorry. I'm sorry for existing."

"Oh, now you're being dramatic." Garrett threw his hands up in the air. He took his honeyed bread and an apple, then stood up and went to sit several feet away, facing away from them.

Zareanna, after making sure that Lim was all right, got up and walked over to join him. She put her arm around him, and they talked quietly together. They seemed to be comforting each other, which puzzled Lim. His parents were usually so distant.

"Are you okay?" Lim asked Vaarem, who was sitting beside him. He was still holding his hand to his cheek.

"Yeah." Nodded Vaarem.

"Does it hurt?" asked Lim, indicating his brother's face.

Vaaarem shrugged. "Stings a bit," he admitted.

"Here, let me," said Lim. He took Vaarem's hand off his face and put his own palm there. He then concentrated until he'd manifested ice energy in his core, before sending the cooling energy through his body to his hand. Like Vaarem had used magical heat on him the previous night, Lim now used magical ice to take the pain away from his brother's face.

"I'm sorry that he hit you," said Lim, as he cooled Vaarem's skin.

"Don't apologise," said Vaarem. "It's not your fault. You've never done anything wrong in your life, and it's so unfair that he seems to blame you for everything. And you should stop apologising. Because you've done nothing wrong."

"Thanks," said Lim. "But sometimes I really do feel like everyone would be better off without me."

Vaarem looked into Lim's eyes, then he held Lim's thin face in both of his hands and said seriously, "Don't you *ever* say that again. We wouldn't be better off without you. I certainly wouldn't. So, don't ever think that."

"Thanks," said Lim, hugging his brother. "I sometimes need to hear that."

"Anytime," said Vaarem, hugging him back. "I don't understand why Father seems to hate you so much sometimes. You've never done anything to warrant it."

"I do," said Lim grimly. "It's because I remind him every day that I have human blood, that we're not the perfect elf family."

"That's stupid," said Vaarem. "I have as much human blood as you. And Mother is a half-elf. She has more human blood than us."

"I know," said Lim. "Ironic, isn't it?" He picked up his bread and began to eat it. It tasted dry to him, but so did everything, and he knew that he needed to somehow fuel his body with more than just potions, so he did his best to finish the whole slice.

"What was that comment about you not being Malkim?" asked Vaarem, eating his own bread.

"No idea." Shrugged Lim. "Vada did tell me once that he used to get sick a lot," he began, only to be overcome with another bout of coughing. He put his cloth to his mouth and was shocked when it came away flecked with red. "Fuck," he whispered with a shudder, as his heart skipped a beat. He'd been coughing almost every day of his life, but he'd never coughed up blood before! Could his health have really deteriorated so much so quickly? Or was it just the bad energy that his parents were exuding? He swallowed with difficulty and went to put his cloth away, but before he'd had a chance, Vaarem was at his side.

"Is that...?" asked Vaarem, eyes round with shock.

"Yes." Lim nodded grimly.

"Oh shit," said Vaarem, putting his arms around his brother and hugging him close. "Don't you dare die on me, Lim," he said. "Please, promise me that you're not going to die."

"I don't plan to," said Lim, but he was unable to keep the fear out of his voice. He realised that Vada had never told him how exactly her father had died. "Don't tell Mother, please," he begged.

"I won't," said Vaarem, "but only if you promise not to keep anything from *me*. I'll always help you if I can. Deal?"

"Deal." Nodded Lim, then hugged his brother back. He'd always believed that he could trust Vaarem no matter what. It felt good to now know for sure.

They'd lost time fixing the wheel, so they arrived at their next inn, after a tensely quiet ride, well after dinner. Lim was glad, as he had no desire to be with his father. He was feeling extremely annoyed at being blamed for the events that had happened earlier in the day, and scared about what was happening to him.

Once again, they rented two rooms, with Vaarem and Lim sharing a small room on the ground floor. No one said anything about what had transpired earlier.

Typical, thought Lim, as he made his slow way to his and Vaarem's room, thankful that there were no stairs to climb. *This is the way we always deal with things. By pretending they don't exist. Vada leaves, and we don't talk about it. Father hits Vaarem, and it's never mentioned. And now it seems, my mere existence upsets my mother, but we can't talk about that either.* He shut the door behind him, glad to shut the world out for a while.

"Oh Fates, what a day," said Vaarem, flopping onto the bed on his back. "I believe that today has been the worst day of my life so far."

"Mine too," said Lim, then added, "Relatively speaking. The worst in a while anyway." He'd had far, far worse days than today, but he didn't want to think about those.

He unpacked his potion bottles. He'd brought eighteen bottles for the roughly two week journey, and he'd been trying to ration them by using one bottle, which had the equivalent of five doses, per day, hoping he would have enough for their entire journey to Sirrock City, with a little to spare. But because he'd been overusing it and had gone through five bottles in two and a half days, he feared he would run out long before they got to the hospital.

Could we stop off at an apothecary somewhere on the way? he wondered.

Would a human apothecary even sell his elven potion?

There are some elf settlements in Borla, he thought. *Will we maybe pass through one?*

He didn't dare get his hopes up.

"And to think that we're only a quarter of the way to Sirrock City," said Vaarem, with a shake of his head, as he began to get ready for bed.

"I know." Laughed Laarem nervously. "I fear we'll all kill each other before we're halfway there."

"Yeah," said Vaarem. "Fuck today was painful. In more ways than one." He put his hand to his cheek.

"Thanks for sticking up for me," said Lim, then he got up and started to get ready for bed too. He took a swig of his potion, then he got out some of the tea leaves he'd been given at the first inn, and made some tea. It soothed his throat, and for the first time that day, he could breathe without pain.

However, he woke up coughing at night, and when he wiped his mouth there were flecks of blood on his lips.

He tried to get back to sleep, but he slept fitfully and kept waking up. Vaarem stretched out and inadvertently ended up pushing him out of the bed. So, Lim finally gave up and got up in the early hours of the morning. He had some more potion, made himself some more tea, and sat by the window, waiting for the sun to rise.

When it finally did, he stood up and washed his face, then got dressed and brushed his hair, tying it back at the nape of his neck. There was a full-length mirror in the room, and he looked at himself critically in the dawn light. His eyes were shadowed, his cheeks hollow. He seemed to have lost even more weight, which made his clothes look like they were all too big for him.

He got his cloth and washed the blood off it, before dipping it in the herb mixture that he'd made up again. By the time he was finished, Vaarem was stirring, so Lim pulled up a chair and waited for his brother to wake up. Vaarem looked peaceful, his face relaxed, his long eyelashes resting on his cheekbones. There were no signs left on his face of the previous day's events, which made Lim smile. He'd done something useful by putting the magic ice on Vaarem's face. He sometimes needed to deliberately remind himself that he had the ability to contribute to his family, and to the world in general. That he wasn't just a complete drain on everyone and everything.

Vaarem opened his eyes and jumped a little when he saw Lim looking at him. "Whoa!" he said. "How long have you been sitting there watching me?"

Lim shrugged. "Not long."

"Couldn't you sleep?" asked Vaarem, getting up and out of the bed.

"No."

"Awww, you should have woken me."

"Why?" asked Lim, an amused grin spreading over his face. "So we would both have been sleep-deprived?"

Vaarem smiled and shook his head. He went to the bathroom to have a quick wash, then came back into the room to get dressed.

Lim watched him enviously.

I should look like that too, he thought bitterly, *but I never will.*

But when Vaarem turned around, Lim smiled at him. It wasn't Vaarem's fault that he was better-looking than his brother, and he'd never been mean or conceited about it. Neither was he falsely modest, which would have been even worse. "You look good," said Lim.

"Thank you," Vaarem smiled back, which made him look even more attractive. "Now, what time is it? I'm starving."

"I think that it's a reasonable time for breakfast," said Lim.

They went out into the inn together and met their parents in the dining room, where they all had some breakfast, then they were on their way.

All four were quiet and subdued, wary of arguing with each other. Vaarem was the only one who seemed in good spirits, however even he was quiet. Lim felt weak and sick, so he sat in the carriage with his head against the wall, his eyes closed. He kept the herb cloth to his face and managed to breathe without too much discomfort. Occasionally, he coughed, but was glad that there was no blood.

Chapter 6

The
Underground Inn

On the sixth day, they reached a dwarf settlement. It consisted of paved roads and neat lawns, but few visible dwellings. Dwarves traditionally lived underground. Garrett was tense and on edge. He seemed to dislike dwarves even more than he did humans, and he was snappy and irritable.

The inn entrance was built into the side of a small hill. Inside, there was a lobby lined with carpets and hung with tapestries. The lighting came from torches and candles, which filled the space with the scent of wax. When Lim was a child, he'd learnt that dwarf magic was earth-based; the manipulation of rock, and metal. They used their magic to sculpt their underground dwellings out of stone, the way the elves did with trees.

The dwarf at the desk squinted up at them, then his eyes widened in recognition, "Garrett Nightingale." He smiled, "It's really you. I haven't seen you for-"

"Twenty-five turns," Garrett cut him off, "I resigned my position when my sons were born." He gestured to Vaarem and Lim behind him. The tone of his voice made it clear that he didn't want to talk about it.

What position? wondered Lim. His father had always worked for the Council. It was the only thing he'd ever wanted to do. His current job as an Events Organiser didn't involve any travel, so he must've had another job that allowed him to go to Sirrock. Vada had told Lim how she remembered having met him in Sirrock City, "Your father was often up at the castle. He and my father were always yelling and arguing. It hurt my ears."

It made Lim wonder about his parents. They seemed like such an improbable couple. Half the time they didn't seem to even like each other, let alone love each other. Yet they must have, if his father, who hated to travel, had frequently taken the trip from Palinas to Sirrock to visit his mother.

Is it because of me that they no longer get on? he wondered, and his breath caught. Looking at his father's expression, Lim didn't want to ask. It did explain Garrett's growing tension, but it didn't help that he took it out on Lim.

Vaarem rubbed his back, as they went to get their things from the carriage.

Garrett was more tense than he'd been since they'd

set out. Lim coughed again, but fortunately his father ignored him, clearly lost in his own thoughts.

Despite the owner seemingly having good memories of Garrett, there were no small rooms available, so the family all had to stay together.

"I apologise," said the dwarf. "If I'd known you were coming-"

"It's fine," said Garrett curtly. He seemed uncomfortable with the attention. "I'm sorry for not calling ahead. This was kind of a last minute trip. We're not going to the castle," he said quickly, which made the dwarf nod and stop talking. He simply gave a key to Garrett, who thanked him and turned to go down the stairs.

Lim started to cough again.

Garret turned sharply towards him with a glare. "Get that out of your system now," he warned. "You better not wake us up at night."

"Yes, Father." Lim nodded, then went to stand in the corner until he could breathe again. The damp air was not doing him any favours and he dreaded having to spend the night here, but he had little choice.

They walked down a flight of earth-smelling stone stairs to the accommodation level and checked their things into the room, which was furnished with a soft green carpet, and red and green tapestries on the walls. The two beds were, thankfully, long enough to fit elves and humans. As the inn was on a main road, the owners were prepared for guests of all races.

After leaving their things, the family went to find some dinner at a nearby eatery, which like the other dwarf dwellings, was underground. The place was dim, lit only by candles, and smelt of smoke, wax, and cooking. The dwarf food was heavy on meat and cream, and Lim found himself unable to eat it. Even Vaarem struggled, although he eventually managed to get through his meal.

"This is disgusting," said Garrett, throwing down his fork. He'd eaten barely half his steak and was clearly not having any more. "Worse than human food," he added, pushing his plate away.

"Shh," said Zareanna. "Don't be rude. You never had problems with dwarf food before, but if you don't like it, you don't have to eat it. We still have some food left in the carriage."

Garrett scowled. "Whatever," he said, then sat with his arms crossed, glaring at everyone and everything in the room.

Lim's breath caught in his throat. "Excuse me," he said, getting up quickly, before his father again told him off for something that he couldn't control. "I'm finished," he managed to say before the cough overcame him.

He walked as quickly as he could, up the stone stairs and out into the fresh air. Once outside, he collapsed to his knees as he struggled to catch his breath, the cold air making his chest and throat hurt.

Eventually, just as he thought that he was going to pass out, the coughing fit eased and he leaned against the stone wall of the building, sweat running down his face and back. He looked down at his cloth and was not surprised to see it flecked with blood again. He sat with his head against the wall and waited for his family.

Eventually, Vaarem came bounding out of the door. He helped Lim to stand up, then Zareanna came out, followed by Garrett, whose shoulders were hunched, and his movements stiff, his mouth pursed into a thin line.

"The sooner we are out of here, the better," said Garrett, kicking a stone and watching it bounce down the path. Lim full-heartedly agreed.

They went down to their room and got ready to go to sleep. Vaarem and Lim were sharing a bed again, and Zareanna and Garrett the other. Zareanna tucked her sons in and kissed them both good-night, like she'd done when they'd been babies, then she got into the other bed beside her husband. Garrett ignored his sons completely. Zareanna drew the canopy around their bed, but not before Lim saw that she had her back to Garrett.

Lim couldn't sleep. He got up and had a swig of his potion, but he still couldn't breathe. He walked over to his bag, found the tea leaves he'd been given in the first inn, and made himself some tea in the dark, then sat down and drank it, but even this didn't help. The underground air was just too damp, and his family's negative energy was not helping.

As the night wore on, the air grew colder, and Lim grew more and more uncomfortable.

Eventually, he couldn't take it anymore. He'd had a whole bottle of potion that evening, but he was still coughing, and it was getting worse. His chest hurt worse than it ever had, and he was afraid that any minute now he would wake his father, and then there would be serious trouble.

He leaned over and whispered in his brother's ear, shaking his shoulder gently. "Var?" he asked. "Vaarem?"

"Hmmm?" said Vaarem sleepily, then opened his eyes and sat up, instantly alert.

"I can't sleep," said Lim, coughing into his cloth. "I can't breathe down here. I'm going upstairs, outside. It's the only thing that I can think of. Will you help me?"

"Of course," said Vaarem, looking at his brother with a concerned frown.

He got up, then put on his bathrobe. Lim did the same and grabbed a blanket and a pillow. They opened the door and stepped out of the room quietly. Vaarem picked Lim up and carried him up the stone stairs, and outside.

"What now?" asked Vaarem, setting Lim down.

"I don't know." Shrugged Lim. "I guess I'll sleep in the carriage." He coughed again.

"Lim," said Vaarem, looking his brother in the eyes, "tell me the truth. Are you getting worse?"

"I don't know," said Lim thoughtfully. "I think it's

just the bad energy from us fighting all the time. And the cold air underground."

"I sure hope so," said Vaarem, as they walked around the back of the stable, to where the guest carriages were parked.

Lim opened the door to their carriage and stepped inside. The carriage had retained some of the warmth from the day, so the air inside allowed him to breathe easier. He put his pillow down on the bench and lay down on it, bending his knees because he was too tall to stretch out.

"Do you want me to stay with you?" asked Vaarem, sitting down on the opposite bench.

"Yes, of course," said Lim, smiling at him gratefully, "but I don't know how Mother and Father will react if they wake up to find us both gone."

"Probably not as badly as they would if they find only you gone," said Vaarem with a yawn. He lay down on the bench and curled his legs up, then pulled the bench cover over himself, as he'd not brought a blanket.

"Is it just me or are Mother and Father more tense than usual?" asked Lim.

"I think they're more tense," said Vaarem. "After all, before having us, Mother did live in Sirrock City." He paused, then said, "with Vada and Malkim. I bet Father doesn't like to think about it, but he kind of has to now."

Lim didn't reply. He was still wondering about his mother's comment the other day. *"He's not Malkim."*

What had she meant? Malkim was never talked about, not even when Vada had lived with them, and after Vada had gone, the silence had encompassed her too. Was that why his father was so angry with Lim now? Because it was for Lim that they were heading to the city of Zareanna's first love, her "one and only true love" if Vada's childhood stories were to be believed, and Garrett was forced to think about the man that he most likely hated more than anyone in the world?

The twins slept for several hours, then woke up before sunrise, and went back down to their room, so that their parents didn't know that they'd gone.

They ate their food in their room, not wanting to eat in the restaurant, and were on their way early in the morning.

Despite his complaints, Garrett had slept well and he thanked the innkeeper for this as they left.

"Will we see you on your way back?" asked the dwarf. "I will set aside two rooms."

"Thank you," said Garrett gruffly, "I will let you know."

As they were getting into the carriage, Garrett looked at the map and a smile crossed his face. Lim felt his chest loosen seeing it.

"Finally," said Garrett. "Tonight, we will finally stay in a civilised place. We are less than a days' ride from Morliss."

Morliss was an elven city, the largest elf settlement

in Borla, and it was clear that Garrett was very much looking forward to being among his own kind again. "I am thinking of staying two nights there, to rest and recuperate a bit before the second half of our journey."

"Sure." Nodded Lim, knowing that he had no say in the matter but pleased with the idea, nonetheless. He looked at his dwindling medicine supply. They were barely halfway through their journey, and he'd already gone through thirteen and a half of his eighteen bottles. He hoped to be able to buy some more in Morliss, as the city was sure to have an apothecary, which was sure to stock what he needed. He found the recipe and put it in one of his books, next to the letter that he'd started writing to Marla and Jessa from the East Borla Inn.

They made good time that day, stopping for lunch near a stream, where they caught several fish, which they roasted and ate hungrily. It made a welcome addition to their bread and fruit.

They reached Morliss in the late afternoon. The sun was shining on the windows of the dwellings, which were built into the trees, as per traditional elven architecture.

They found the inn and checked into their rooms.

Lim and Vaarem had a room on the third level, but Lim was feeling rested, so he managed to climb all the stairs. He coughed at the top, and it took him several minutes to catch his breath, but he felt good about himself for having made it. Fortunately, the dining room and other common areas were on the same level in the nearest tree and accessible via a small bridge, so he wouldn't have to make the climb too many times.

After dinner, which consisted of lightly steamed grains and vegetables, Lim went into the common room and asked one of the inn staff about an apothecary.

"Yes, there is one down the road," indicated the maid, showing him the way through the window. "But it's closed now. It will reopen in the morning."

"That's fine," said Lim. "Thank you."

He smiled to himself as he went to his room. Things were starting to look up.

Chapter 7

Morliss

Being among elves again put the whole family in a good mood.

The inn had shared bathrooms on each floor, so Lim and Vaarem took the opportunity to have a proper wash.

Lim climbed into the wooden bathtub and allowed Vaarem to wash his back and hair. He looked down at his protruding ribs and hipbones and hugged his arms around himself.

"What's wrong?" asked Vaarem, combing the tangles out of Lim's long hair.

Lim shrugged his thin shoulders. "I hate how skinny I am," he said glumly.

"Aww," said Vaarem, putting his arms around him.

"Sorry," said Lim. "Once again, I bring the mood down. I'm such a party-pooper."

"No, you're not," said Vaarem, still holding him. "And hey, at least you're not fat," he said, letting go of Lim and sitting back on his heels. "Did you see that lady in the common room?" He stood up, puffed his cheeks out and waddled around the room, imitating a heavy person.

Although elves all had slender bones, they were like all the other races, and some of them were prone to run to fat.

"Really?" Lim looked at his brother coldly. "Why would you say that? She probably has as little control over these things as I do."

"You're right." Vaarem sobered up. "I didn't mean to be disrespectful."

"Yes, you did," said Lim.

"Okay, I did," said Vaarem. "I shouldn't have. I'm sorry. But I was just pointing out that you're not the only one with body image issues," he explained.

"Var," said Lim seriously, "I know that I'm not the only person in the world who has body issues that they have no control over. You making fun of someone else does *not* make me feel any better."

Vaarem's face dropped, then he nodded. "Okay," he said. "I'm sorry. I really didn't mean anything bad."

"I know you didn't," said Lim impatiently, "but intentions don't really matter if people get hurt. How would you like it if that lady's boyfriend or someone tried to console her by comparing her to me? If they told her, hey you might be chubby but at least you can breathe and you don't resemble a hunched-up skeleton like that freaky guy in black?"

"I wouldn't." Vaarem dropped his eyes. "I'd tell them off and defend you. Fuck, I really did not think that through. I won't say anything like that again."

"Good," said Lim, then smiled up at him. "Thank you."

"You're very welcome," said Vaarem, then grinned mischievously, before pouring a bucket of water over Lim's head to rinse his hair.

After rinsing himself off, Lim got out of the bath and dried himself, then helped Vaarem to wash his hair and back.

When they were finished, they walked out of the bathroom, across the bridge and into the common room. The room was empty save for Zareanna and Garrett, who had washed too and were now sitting on one of the window seats, holding hands and looking more relaxed than they had in days. It seemed that being among elves again agreed with both of them.

Vaarem and Lim said good night to their parents and went back to their room, where they talked and played cards for a while, before going to sleep. For the first time since their journey had begun, Lim slept well.

The next morning, they met their parents in the dining room for breakfast. Garrett was in a good mood and did not say anything snide to Lim, even when Lim had a coughing fit at the table, right after the family thanked the Fates for their breakfast. They'd not said the prayer since leaving home, but today even Lim felt thankful. The atmosphere was positive for once.

"Please yourselves today," Garrett told his sons. "But make sure you conduct yourselves with decorum. I will not have you embarrassing me amongst our own people," he warned them.

Vaarem and Lim readily agreed, then finished their breakfast and went into their room. Lim then told Vaarem of his intention to go to the apothecary. Vaarem had no desire to go there, preferring instead to explore the town, so the brothers decided to meet back up in the inn at lunchtime.

Lim followed the directions he'd been given the previous evening and found the shop.

He walked up the steps to the entrance, which was built into the tree trunk, then had to stop to catch his breath. He lowered his head and rested his hands on his knees for a few moments, then finally stood up and pushed the door open. A bell above the door rang to announce his presence.

The shopkeeper came out promptly. She was short for an elf, and she had small round glasses, perched on the bridge of her nose. Her skin was smooth and clear, but her eyes and her demeanour made Lim guess that she was in her mid-two-hundreds, about halfway through an elf's lifespan.

"Good morning," she greeted Lim politely. "How can I help you?"

"Good morning," said Lim breathlessly, holding on

to the door for support. "Can you please make this up for me?" He walked over to the counter and gave her his medicine recipe.

She read it carefully and frowned. "This is an awfully strong formula," she said, looking up at him.

"Yes."

"Are you sure that this is correct?" she asked.

"Yes," said Lim. "My healer in Palinas usually makes it up for me."

"Are you sure?" she asked skeptically.

"Yes," said Lim, trying not to be impatient. "Here." He took the small, now empty bottle that he carried, out of his pocket and gave it to her. He only had four bottles left, so needed to get more today.

She opened it and sniffed, then looked up at him and frowned again. "How long have you been using it?"

"Ten - eleven seasons," said Lim with a shrug. He seemed to have been using it forever. "The healers in Palinas tried several different potions until they settled on this formula."

She looked at him and frowned again.

Lim realised that he'd never before met a healer who was not aware of his condition. The healers in Palinas all knew him, and any specialists that he'd seen had been given his information beforehand. "I promise I'm not lying," he said, starting to get anxious, which made him cough again. "Why would I? I really need this."

She looked at him again and Lim had a moment

of panic. If he didn't replace his medicine, he didn't think that he'd make it to Sirrock City.

"I'm sorry," she said, "but I don't feel right giving something so strong to you without at least checking you over first."

Lim coughed, then sighed. "Fine," he said. "Check me over if it will make you feel better. But I'm telling the truth. I really need this."

The shopkeeper nodded. "Magnon?" she called out, facing the back of the shop. "Magnon. Come out here. There is a young man here who needs a check-up. My husband is the resident healer in Morliss," she explained. "He will sort you out."

Magnon was of a similar age to his wife, with soft brown hair tied back in a braid, and large green-grey eyes. He was dressed in the pale green of an elf healer, and he instructed Lim to follow him into a back room.

"What's your name?" asked Magnon, as Lim lay down on the examination table.

"Lim Nightingale," said Lim with a cough. "I'm from Palinas."

"And what are you doing in Morliss?"

"Just passing through," said Lim, then had to stop as a fit of coughing overcame him, forcing him to sit up.

"Whoa, there, there," said Magnon, patting Lim on the back. "That is one nasty cough you've got there. How long have you had it?"

"All my life," said Lim with a sigh.

"Excuse me?" Magnon raised his eyebrows.

"Apparently, I wasn't breathing when I was born," said Lim, as Magnon started to examine him. "Everyone thought that I was dead, but my sister revived me. I've been struggling to breathe ever since." He chuckled cynically. "I get lung infections all the time, like at least once every turn but recently it's been more frequent. I've had pneumonia twice, once when I was five and once when I was fifteen. The second time was really bad. What else?" He tried to think. "I recently turned twenty-five. I've tried all kinds of treatments, like herbs, and crystals, but nothing has worked. I've had lots of energy healings too, but they only had a temporary effect. I've had bad reactions to some potions, which is why I really need a refill of my current one. It's losing its effectiveness but it still works. My family and I are travelling to Sirrock City to try a new experimental human treatment. That's about it," he finished breathlessly, thinking that he'd probably forgotten some things, which he hoped were not important.

Magnon listened with interest as he examined Lim, running his hands over his body.

"My mother's half-human," added Lim, as Magnon got him to sit up and blow into a tube to check his breathing. Lim thought that he managed to get it to turn the palest hint of blue, a little better than he had back home with Dr Fantail, but he saw that Magnon made a note saying "no colour". Lim sighed glumly.

"Do you have any pain?" asked Magnon, looking into Lim's mouth.

Lim shrugged, then nodded. "Yes. Most days. It hurts when I breathe, and when I swallow. But I am used to it."

"Do you take painkillers?"

Lim shook his head. "Not regularly. Only when it gets really bad. I didn't bring any with me, so I've been doing without. It's manageable. Most of the time," he added, remembering the night he'd woken at the East Borla Inn.

Magnon nodded at that.

"I've been coughing up blood recently," said Lim, as he was doing his shirt back up. "I probably should have mentioned that earlier. It's never happened before."

Magnon frowned. "How recently?" he asked. "How much? How often does it happen?"

Lim shrugged as he considered this. "A few days ago. It's happened a couple of times since, but not for the past two days. And it's not much, just a few drops each time. Otherwise, it's just a dry cough as always."

Magnon looked into his mouth again, conjuring a tiny mage light. "Anything else you've noticed? Any more pain or anything?"

"Nothing more than the usual," said Lim. "My throat and my chest hurt more, and my ribs, but that always happens when I cough a lot." He couldn't resist a cynical chuckle at Magnon's expression, as the healer leaned back.

I have him stumped, thought Lim. *I have them all stumped.* Sometimes, when he was in a good mood, it felt like an achievement.

After finishing the examination, Magnon sat down at his desk and asked Lim to sit down opposite.

"I regret to say, Lim," the healer said gravely, "that you are a very unwell young man. Your energy is very low, and your whole body is struggling to perform its basic functions."

"I know," said Lim. Even though it had been good to talk to him, Magnon hadn't told him anything that he didn't already know. "So, can I have my medicine?" he asked, remembering that that was the sole reason for him being here.

"Yes," said Magnon, standing up to get a pad of paper, then sitting back down and writing on it. "I will give you three moons' worth, which is the most that I can dispense in one go, else we will completely run out of supplies." He chuckled grimly. "I will also give you something for the pain, and to lubricate your throat. The blood is from irritation in your throat and esophagus. So, you're not bleeding internally or anything. It is, as you suspected, from increased coughing."

"Oh, thank the Fates," Lim breathed a sigh of relief.

"None of what I give you should cause a bad reaction," said Magnon, "but I assume that you know to stop immediately if it ever does."

Lim nodded.

"How are you sleeping?" asked Magnon.

"Mmm..."

"I will give you something for that too, but bear in mind that it is addictive. So, only use it sparingly, as a last resort."

"Understood," said Lim with a nod.

"What about eating?" asked Magnon. "You are quite underweight."

Lim shrugged. "I know. I try, but I have no appetite. And I react badly to stimulants, so..." He trailed off.

Magnon nodded. "You are remarkably resilient considering all that you've told me," said the healer, which made Lim smile. This felt like an achievement too.

"However," continued Magnon, "you really need to remember to eat regularly." He kept writing the prescription. "What kind of treatment will you be getting in Sirrock City Hospital?" he asked. "I thought they specialised in treating humans only?"

"I am one-quarter human," Lim reminded him. "My local healer believes that it's my human energy that is causing my condition."

"I wouldn't be so sure about that," said Magnon thoughtfully, putting his quill away. "I treat humans occasionally, and you don't seem much like them. And while illness is rare among elves, it is not unheard of. I wouldn't be surprised if your condition has nothing to do with your human blood."

"Okay," said Lim thoughtfully. He hadn't considered this before. "Do you know what may be causing my condition?"

Magnon shook his head. "I'm afraid that I don't," he said. "I have never encountered anyone like you before."

Lim smiled, once again feeling like he'd achieved

something. He was a puzzle that no one had yet been able to solve.

They finished their session, and Lim went outside into the apothecary, giving Magnon's wife his new prescription.

She frowned at it, then looked up at Lim with raised eyebrows.

Lim shrugged. "Ask your husband if you're unsure," he said, an amused grin turning his lips up slightly. "I'm a medical anomaly."

Magnon's wife nodded, then gave him an apologetic smile, before getting him his medicines.

Lim went to pay, and was touched when Magnon came out and said, "Just pay for the medicine. The consultation is on the house. But do come back and tell me how you go in Sirrock City. I would be very interested to hear that. May the Fates be with you."

"And with you also."

Lim returned to the inn just in time for lunch. He climbed the stairs slowly and managed not to collapse when he reached the third floor.

"Did you get it?" asked Vaarem, who was already in their room, waiting for him.

"Yes." Lim nodded breathlessly, showing Vaarem the bag of potions. "And some other stuff too," he added. "They refused to give it to me without giving me a check-up first."

"You had a check-up?" asked Vaarem anxiously. "How did it go?"

"Fine," said Lim, sitting down on one of the chairs. "According to the healer, I'm "very unwell"," he put on a mock serious voice when he said this, "but in reality, apart from the fact that I've lost a pound, I am no worse than before."

"Oh, thank the Fates," said Vaarem, walking over to hug him.

"Stop it," said Lim, with a laugh, "you're crushing me."

Vaarem loosened his grip, but he kept his arms around his brother. "You have no idea how much I worry about you," said Vaarem softly.

"I think I do," said Lim. "And I appreciate it. Even though I wish you wouldn't. So, should we go out and get some lunch before Mother and Father accuse us of being an embarrassment or something?"

"Sure," said Vaarem. "Are you hungry?"

Lim shrugged. "I could eat."

They went out and sat at a table in the dining room. Garrett and Zareanna joined them soon after, and they had a pleasant meal of fruit and vegetables.

"So, did you boys do anything interesting today?" asked Garrett, as a waiter came to take their empty plates away. "Did you meet anyone in the city?"

"Huh?" asked Vaarem. "No." He looked at Lim with a raised eyebrow.

Lim shrugged. Did his father know that he'd been to the apothecary because he was running out of potions and planned to tell him off?

However, Garrett was on a different page.

"Don't think that I missed you fraternising with those human ladies a few nights ago," he said. "Why don't you try and meet some nice ladies of your own kind?"

Vaarem gritted his teeth. "We were not fraternising with anybody," he said indignantly. "And those ladies were nice."

"That may be so. But I'm sure the ladies here are even nicer. I was just wondering if you had met any-one here. You can have more than one penpal."

"What should we do for the rest of the day?" asked Vaarem, when they were back in their room.

"I don't know." Shrugged Lim, looking up from his letter. He'd taken some of the pain-killing potion that Magnon's wife had made for him, and for the first time in weeks, he was breathing comfortably. He was aware that this was only temporary, so he was determined to enjoy it while he could.

Vaarem shrugged then flopped down on one of the chairs, hanging his long legs over the armrest. "I'd like to go back into town, but I don't like being told to specifically look for friends," he said, annoyed.

Lim smiled thinly. "You can just go and walk around. You don't have to talk to anyone. Although knowing you, you probably will. You can't help yourself," he said with a grin.

Vaarem chuckled at that. "I guess," he said. "But I don't like when Father interferes." He sighed.

"I know," agreed Lim. "I don't know what's gotten into him."

They sat in silence for a moment, as they both considered this. It was clear that their father wanted them to maintain primarily elven friendships. Perhaps he was afraid that one or both of them would move to a non-elf settlement. Lim decided not to dwell on it. His father always disapproved of something he did.

"So, what should we do then?" asked Vaarem. "Are you up to coming downstairs?"

"Are you up to carrying me if I'm not?"

"Sure," said Vaarem. "See, another good thing about the fact that you hardly weigh anything."

Lim smiled thinly at that, then put his ink and quill away, tucked his letter in a book, then got himself ready to go out.

The brothers left the inn and walked down the road. Morliss was a city similar in size to Palinas and both of them felt at home walking its tree-lined streets.

They browsed some shops, which like the houses, were built into the trees. Lim looked at magic artefacts and books, while Vaarem looked mostly at clothes, but also at weapons.

"I want to train to be a soldier," said Vaarem, looking at a sword and testing its balance and weight, then giving it a couple of experimental swings. "Or a bodyguard or something. If Father really insists on me working for the Council, I'm sure I could do something in security." He swung the sword again. "Ideally, I'd like to train with Grandfather and Grandmother," he mused. Their grandfather was the Head of Security in the Royal Palace of Borla, and their grandmother was a captain in the army. "But I doubt Father would be happy with that." He shook his head.

The shopkeeper stood in the corner and looked at him warily; however Vaarem seemed to know how to handle the weapon, so after a moment, the man relaxed.

"Good luck with that," said Lim, with a cynical smile, having found a chair to sit on. Garrett was determined that his eldest son follow in his footsteps and work for the ruling city council, perhaps moving up to the post of Prime Minister one day, a dream that he'd once had for himself. Vaarem had confided that he couldn't imagine anything more boring, and father and son had had many arguments about the topic. Lim had usually started to get sick when these quarrels began, so had always left the room. Nevertheless, he knew the general gist of what they talked about.

"It's going to happen," said Vaarem seriously. "It's just a case of when. Perhaps when you're well, Father will be more open to us leaving Palinas."

"Us?" asked Lim, surprised. He'd not thought about leaving Palinas for good. Even when he considered going to the Academy of Magic, he'd always seen himself returning.

"Yes, of course," said Vaarem, swinging the sword again before putting it back on its stand. "I wouldn't leave without you."

"What if I don't want to leave?" said Lim.

"Don't you?" Vaarem seemed surprised at that.

Lim shrugged. He'd never given his future much thought, mostly because he'd never been sure if he'd live long enough to have one. He still wasn't sure, so preferred to take things one day at a time. But it looked like he would get to finish school at the end of the turn, so needed to consider his next steps. He wasn't sure what he wanted them to be.

They kept exploring the city, then returned to the inn in time for dinner. Lim was tired, but he was determined to climb the stairs all the way to the top himself. He and Vaarem took it slowly, finding an excuse to rest at each landing, and they made it to the top without incident. Lim's breath was coming to him with difficulty, but the medication eased the usual pain in his lungs and throat, so he recovered relatively quickly, with no more than a couple of small coughs.

At dinner, Lim ate hungrily. He found that he could swallow food without the normal discomfort, so he was able to eat more than he had in days.

"Did you meet anyone?" asked Garrett as they started on dessert, which was a light fruit pastry.

"No," said Vaarem with a shrug. "We just browsed some shops."

"Oh well, never mind," said Garrett, but fortunately left it alone. "There will be one more elf settlement before we reach Sirrock City," he said. "Perhaps you will meet someone nice there."

"Hmmm." Vaarem shrugged.

Lim didn't reply. He wondered again at their father's sudden interest in who they were talking to. Why did Garrett care?

Chapter 8

Sirrock

They left the next day, laden with supplies from the Morliss shops. Lim packed his potions carefully, deep inside his bags. He now had over one hundred bottles, and he didn't want his mother to see, as she was sure to worry.

As they travelled, the road became wider, and eventually started to be paved, rather than a dirt track. They reached the last elf settlement two days after Morliss. The city of Lemen was smaller than Morliss, and very quiet. Garrett and Zareanna bought some more supplies, such as food and toiletries, but otherwise they didn't linger.

The inn that they stayed in was owned by a family that had no daughters, only one son who was ten turns old. The boy talked with Vaarem and Lim, interested in what they had to say but otherwise there was no one else for them to meet. Garrett seemed disappointed but fortunately for Vaarem and Lim, he didn't make a fuss.

After Lemen, they travelled through dwarf country for two days and nights. The beds in the inns were all dwarf-sized, so for those two nights none of them slept well. They didn't eat any dwarf food and consumed most of their supplies from Morliss and Lemen. Lim bought two crystals from Regen, the last dwarf settlement. He'd been reading about the different qualities of crystals and was keen to try them out. Garrett scoffed at the idea, but he let Lim keep the crystals.

After leaving Regen, they turned north and crossed into Sirrock later that morning. The countryside was different to Borla, much wilder and windier, with fields of wild grasses, and few trees. By midday, they could clearly see the peak of Sirranna Mountain, which had been obscured by trees before.

Lim watched the mountain excitedly, hoping to catch a glimpse of a dragon. Vada's father, Malkim Blackwell, had been a dragontamer, and his daughter had inherited his talent. Soon after she'd left home, Vada had written to Lim that she'd found a dragon egg, then later she'd told him about the dragon hatching and later that it had become her familiar. Lim longed to see it.

They stayed at another human inn that night. Lim was starting to get nervous. In two days' time, they would be checking into the hospital in Sirrock City.

He hoped that when he got there, there would be a message from Vada waiting for him, or better still, Vada herself.

He couldn't sleep that night, so for the first time, he tried the sleeping potion that Magnon had given him. He fell asleep almost straight away.

Lim woke up feeling groggy and strange. Vaarem was stirring beside him, so they got up together and got ready for the day.

Lim kept nodding off as they ate their breakfast. The sleeping potion was still in his system, and he had a feeling that he would be out of it until it passed through him completely.

"Are you okay, darling?" asked Zareanna, putting her hand to his forehead.

"Yeah, just tired," replied Lim. He did his best to wake up enough to finish his breakfast.

In the carriage, he rested his head against the wall and closed his eyes. Eventually, Zareanna moved over to sit beside him, and he put his head in her lap and slept.

By lunchtime, he was a little more with it, however he slept again afterwards.

They reached the gates of Sirrock City in the early evening. The guards checked their documents and let them through without a fuss. One of them remembered Garrett, but as with the dwarf innkeeper, their father didn't want to talk about it. Vaarem raised his eyebrows in question to Lim, who shrugged.

Inside the gates, the city was like nothing that Lim had ever seen. The streets were all paved with bricks of different colours, unlike the streets in Palinas, and other elf settlements that simply had earth paths between the trees, sometimes reinforced with wood, occasionally edged with stone, but never brick. The buildings were all freestanding, made of brick and stone with slate roofs. These types of buildings, Lim had seen on their way here, but as they drove on, the buildings became taller. Until now, the tallest house that Lim had ever seen had had three floors. Here some of the buildings had five stories or more, and they were topped by domes of glass and brass. Some buildings had contraptions that looked like windmills made out of sails on the roofs.

"Most humans don't have magic," his mother explained, "so they need to use other energies to power their houses to make heat and light and to use machines. Those sails harness the wind. Those who live near the river use similar devices in the water to harness the power of the currents."

"Like pixies," said Lim excitedly. He'd only met one pixie in his life, a passing healer, but he'd not talked to him as he'd been too young. All he remembered was that the man had been smaller than the elves, and had had wings on his back, and webbed fingers. Pixies were a shy race that mostly kept to themselves. They were creatures of both land and water. Like humans, most of them didn't possess magic, and like humans who lived near rivers, they harnessed the power of water to live their daily lives.

"Yes." Smiled Zareanna. "You will find that there is a small but significant population of pixies in Sirrock. Maybe we will meet some."

"That would be great," said Vaarem, then leaned over and whispered in Lim's ear, "I hear that pixies are very liberal and fun-loving in bed." He looked at his twin with a mischievously raised eyebrow.

Lim rolled his eyes at him and Vaarem grinned, turning back to look out the window.

Lim had always felt secure inside the forest elf cities, where the dwellings were situated inside the tree trunks with only the balconies and small extensions built outside. Here in Sirrock City he felt exposed. There was not a single tree along any of the main roads. It was just brick, stone, glass, and brass. The air smelled of smoke, oil, and dust, a stark contrast to the earth and wood of Palinas. Lim put his hand over his nose and mouth, the alien smell making him nauseated.

The evening sun reflected off the domes and windows, casting the whole scene into a strange yellow-orange glow. It made Lim think of fire, only there was no heat and no smoke, which made him realise how different this place was to anywhere he'd ever been before.

In the middle of the road ran a set of parallel lines made out of metal. At first Lim thought that this was simply to mark the centre of the road. With the size-able traffic of horses and horse-drawn carriages, there were rules about which side of the street to travel on. Everyone was travelling along the left-hand side, so Lim thought that the lines marked the barrier. Therefore, he nearly jumped out of his seat when he saw a carriage, apparently not being pulled or pushed by anything, coming towards them down the two lines! His eyes widened, and he looked at the carriage in shock.

"How does that carriage go?" he asked curiously, and Vaarem looked out the window too, his eyes widening, even more than Lim's.

"Oh," said Zareanna, joining them at the window. "Wow. Those were not here when I was last in Sirrock." Lim took her hand in his. He knew that his mother had left Sirrock City for good shortly after her first husband Malkim, Vada's father, had died. It was clear that the memories pained her, and he felt his breath catch as he felt her sadness.

I will not have a coughing fit, he told himself. *This moment is not about me.*

He squeezed his mother's hand reassuringly, then, with his other hand, took his medicine bottle out of his pocket and had several long sips until he could breathe again. Vaarem took the bottle from him and closed it, then slipped it back into Lim's pocket discreetly.

All the while, Zareanna was looking out the window wistfully.

Lim followed her gaze north-west to the mountain that stood at the edge of the city; Sirranna Mountain, on the top of which stood Blackwell Castle, the ancestral home of the Blackwells, and Vada's current residence.

Lim looked up. He thought that he caught sight of a pair of large wings, too large to be an eagle or falcon.

"I think I saw a dragon," he said excitedly, opening the window and leaning out as far as he could. Lim knew better than to ask his father to stop, so he kept looking, but unfortunately for him, the dragon flew behind the mountain and out of sight. Still, he'd seen a dragon. Did this mean that Vada was coming to him?

The hospital was in the centre of the city. By the time they reached it, it was dark, so they found an inn on the next block and checked in for the night.

Once again, they rented two rooms, then they all went into the dining room to eat.

Zareanna hugged Lim closely after dinner. "Good night, darling," she said, reaching up and kissing his face. "Try and get some sleep. No matter what happens tomorrow, we will all be here for you, so don't be scared."

"Thank you, Mother." He nodded gratefully.

Garrett shook his hand. "Like your mother said," he said. "Get some sleep. All going well, the treatment will be a success, and we will be on our way home in a few days."

"Thank you," said Lim, even though he sensed a

strange undertone to his father's words. It was as if Garrett thought that the success of the treatment somehow depended on Lim's attitude and effort, that it was up to him whether it worked or not. The idea made Lim shudder, and when he closed the door behind him, he sat on his bed and hugged his arms around himself, trying to control his breathing and to slow down his racing heart.

What would happen if the treatment didn't work?

Lim couldn't sleep, but he didn't want to take any more of the sleeping potion. He needed to be alert the next day.

Vaarem, it seemed, couldn't sleep either. The brothers lay in the dark, holding hands, the way they'd done when they'd been children and scared of the dark. During those times it had been Lim who had comforted Vaarem, realising before his brother did that there was really nothing to be afraid of.

"What are you thinking?" asked Vaarem, squeezing Lim's thin fingers.

"I'm freaking out," admitted Lim. "What if it doesn't work? What if this whole trip has been a colossal waste of time?"

Vaarem squeezed his brother's hand again. "Don't think like that," he said. "Why wouldn't it work?"

"Because nothing ever has," said Lim grimly. "So, statistically, the odds are against me."

"Not necessarily," said Vaarem. "Maybe the more times that you fail, the closer you are to success?"

Lim sighed. "The healer in Morliss told me something, which I didn't think was relevant at the time, so I kind of forgot about it, but now." He trailed off.

"What did he say?" Vaarem sat up to look at his brother. Even in the dark, their elven eyes allowed them to see each other.

"That he doesn't think that it's my human blood that is causing me to be sick," said Lim.

"What?" asked Vaarem. For as long as they could all remember, everyone they'd spoken to had believed that Lim's illness somehow came from his human blood. "What made him think that?"

"I don't know." Shrugged Lim. "He just said that he has treated humans, and that I am not like them."

"That may be so," said Vaarem. "But really, you're not like anybody else. And he doesn't know you."

"If he's right, then this whole thing is not going to work."

"Not necessarily," said Vaarem. Then he lay back down and put his arms around Lim, hugging him close. "They know you're only a quarter human, so mostly elf, and they still want to go ahead. No matter what happens, we'll be fine," he said, then he kissed Lim on the cheek. "I'll always be there for you. And I do believe that it will work. And that will be awesome."

"Yeah," agreed Lim. "It *would* be awesome. If it works."

Vaarem hugged him again. "I know you're scared," he said. "I am too. But we have to trust in the Fates."

"Yeah," agreed Lim, then closed his eyes, basking in the darkness. "Hey, Vaarem?" he asked after a while.

"Yeah?"

"Do you think Vada will come down and see me? I mean, she's so close, she has to, right?"

"I'm sure she will," said Vaarem soothingly.

With that thought, Lim finally fell into an uneasy sleep.

The next day, Lim was too nervous to eat breakfast. He'd taken his usual dose of potion, as well as the painkiller, but he was still finding it hard to breathe. His hands shook, and he spilled his cup of tea on the table. Fortunately, his parents were at the breakfast bar, filling their plates, so they didn't see. Vaarem helped him to wipe it up.

"I don't know if I can do this," said Lim, forcing himself to drink the remainder of his tea. "I'm so scared. Everything in this city is so weird and alien."

"It'll be fine," Vaarem reassured him, squeezing his hand and stopping the shaking for a moment. "We'll all be right there with you. Besides, they're all healers at the hospital. It is their job to help people, to make sick people well. What can go wrong?"

"You're right." Lim tried to force a smile. "I'm just being a big coward."

"No, you're not," said Vaarem. "It's normal to be scared. Fates, I'm nervous for you. But we don't need to be. It will all be fine. You'll see. And next week you'll walk out of here being able to function like a normal person, and then you can train to do magic, or whatever you choose to do."

But despite his brother's reassurances, Lim was still scared.

The family walked down to the hospital later that morning, Vaarem supporting Lim, whose legs were shaking from what he hoped were simply nerves. Garrett led the way, striding over the coloured brick footpath confidently and making sure that the large number of pedestrians on the road made way for them. Horse-drawn carriages trundled down the roads, following groups of riders. The tracks in the middle of the road remained quiet. It seemed that the automatic carriages were not going. Lim wondered why. Did they only go on certain days or at certain times? What did they transport?

As they turned the corner, Garrett asked a passing human man for directions to the hospital, to ensure that they were going the right way. It seemed that the hospital was farther than it had looked when they'd driven past it in the carriage the previous day. The man pointed the way that they were going, and Garrett thanked him politely. Lim was surprised at his father wanting to interact with humans so much, but he let him do it. He was too nervous to speak for himself.

After walking several more yards, they saw the hospital building on the next block.

Vaarem smiled at Lim and hugged him more tightly

as they continued to walk towards it slowly, Lim doing his best to keep breathing.

The first thing that Lim noticed as he stepped inside the hospital was the smell. It reminded him of a human disinfectant he'd once smelled in his childhood, mixed with the potent solutions that human innkeepers used for cleaning their bathrooms, but much stronger, as well as the oil and dust of the city outside. It made him want to retch. He was glad he'd been unable to eat much that morning. Apart from that, it looked similar to all the other human buildings he'd been in; sterile, square, and dimly lit.

They walked up to the front desk, where Garrett announced who they were.

The young human nurse looked up at them curiously and then said, "Oh yes, the elf. Welcome. Come and follow me and I will get you checked in."

"Are there any messages for me?" Lim asked before they'd had a chance to go anywhere.

"Let me see," she said, looking through a drawer. "Lim Nightingale?"

He nodded.

"Yes, here you go."

"Thank you." He took the letters and put them in his pocket for later reading. One of them was surely from Vada, and his spirits lifted.

But only for a moment, because the farther into the hospital that they walked, the more nervous that he became. In every corridor that they passed there were strange machines. Through the windows in the doors to the rooms, he could see other contraptions, and some of these had patients strapped to them. From some rooms that they passed, his keen hearing caught sounds of moaning, and sometimes there was screaming that they could all hear.

They walked into a room that must have been right in the bowels of the hospital, where the nurse announced, "Dr Turnwall, here is your patient, Lim Nightingale, the elf." And with that, she left them.

Dr Turnwall was sitting behind a desk, looking into a microscope. He was very old for a human, and very small and shrivelled-looking. He was completely bald, with one side of his head covered in a metal plate. From beneath it, a brass ear protruded, shaped like a little trumpet, with several wires hanging out of it. On the same side, his eye was also artificial, and it swivelled to look at them from beneath the brass plate. His other eye was a normal blue, if a little bloodshot. Lim's step faltered at seeing him. *What could have happened to make someone look like that?* He reached out and gripped Vaarem's arm for support.

"Welcome," said the doctor. His voice was friendly enough but the side of his face with the artificial eye and ear seemed to be paralysed, so that when he spoke only half of his mouth moved, giving his face a sinister lop-sided expression. "Sit down," he bade them, indicating some chairs in front of the desk. "Please don't let my appearance bother you," he said. "It is the first thing that everyone notices. There was an accident in one of our research laboratories many seasons ago now. But as you can see, I survived and have been fixed, right here at this hospital. Because that's what we do here, we mend people. Now, don't worry, Lim, your remedies will not look this obvious, but I can guarantee that when you walk out of here, you will have been put right."

Lim was not sure whether he liked the sound of that, but he kept quiet and simply nodded. He was here now, for better or for worse, and he was going to go through with it.

After all, he thought, *it's not like I can get much worse.* He swallowed nervously.

"I do hope you're sincere when you say you fix people," said Garrett, with what Lim felt was a note of challenge. It seemed that even he was put-out by Dr Turnwall's appearance. "We would be much obliged if you heal our son."

Dr Turnwall looked at him with his good eye for a moment, then nodded once.

After some brief introductions, where Lim was made to sign consent forms that he was too nervous to read, and the doctor assured his parents that they wouldn't need to pay for anything, Dr Turnwall asked Lim to come through into another room.

Lim hesitated, and Vaarem immediately stood up to go with him, but the doctor waved him away.

"I need to get Lim examined and settled in," he said. "You can come back and see him later today in a couple of hours."

"It's okay," said Lim to Vaarem. Even though his mouth was dry and his hands were sweating, he was doing his best to keep it together.

"You won't need that," said Dr Turnwall, pointing to the bag of food and to Lim's potions, which he'd packed that morning. "We will look after you from here on in."

Lim swallowed and reluctantly gave his bag of supplies to Vaarem.

How did Dr Turnwall know that he wouldn't need his potions without even having examined him? Nevertheless, he followed the doctor obediently, with a last glance at his family.

The next room was an examination room, which again looked like all the human healing rooms that he'd been in, apart from the machines that stood on the sides. The machines looked like cabinets made out of metal, with dials and levers, and wires sticking out of their frames. One was the size of his dresser back home, the other a little smaller. Two nurses, both human, stood near them. They were adjusting different bits of equipment, but stopped what they were doing and looked at Dr Turnwall when he walked in.

Lim was instructed to get undressed and was given a hospital gown to put on. He was then weighed and measured, then told to sit down on the examination table so that the doctor could perform the necessary tests.

Lim swallowed and did his best not to panic. No matter how many healers he saw, he still hated to be subjected to all of their procedures. He'd tolerated seeing Magnon because he knew that it was necessary to get his potion. He put himself in the same frame of mind now.

This is a means to an end, he told himself. *It will be fine.*

First, he was asked to blow into a tube, similar to the ones that elf healers asked him to blow into, except this one didn't change colour. Instead, there was a fabric-like piece inside it, and Lim had to try and blow it from one end to the other. There were markers on the side, to show how far he'd blown the fabric. He didn't even manage to reach the first one. He couldn't read the doctor's, nor the nurses' expressions.

Next, Dr Turnwall looked into his ears, using a little electric lamp to see. The lamp emitted a buzzing noise that Lim found hugely unpleasant, but when he tried to move his head away, one of the nurses grabbed his chin roughly and held him in place. The doctor then looked into his mouth, pressing his tongue down with a metal stick and moving it so far that Lim nearly retched. But he did his best not to, because the nurse was still holding his head. Afterwards, the doctor used a stethoscope to measure his heartbeat and check his lungs. Lim had seen a human doctor once before, when he'd been younger and his human grandmother had thought that it might help, so he remembered the stethoscope and braced himself for how unpleasantly cold it was.

"Relax," said the nurse. "This doesn't hurt."

Lim didn't reply. Just because it didn't hurt, didn't mean that he liked it. As it was, he disliked being touched at all, particularly with these types of implements. But he submitted meekly because he had no other choice.

He was then asked to lie down, and the doctor strapped a couple of metal disks to his forehead. The disks were joined to wires, which were joined to a small metal box with buttons and dials, that one of the nurses had brought over.

Lim felt a jolt. He cried out, but everyone ignored him. The nurse moved a dial on the box, then Lim was jolted again. This time, it hurt less. The nurse adjusted another dial, and Lim was given another jolt. This went on for the next half an hour, with the nurse adjusting the machine, then Lim getting a jolt and the doctor making a note. Some of the jolts hurt more than others, but none were as bad as the first. Still, it was not comfortable.

Just when he thought it was all over, and the disks, which the doctor and nurses referred to as electrodes, were removed, one of the nurses strapped his arms and legs down.

"What are you doing?" asked Lim anxiously.

"We need to do a few more tests," explained the nurse. "This will prevent you from moving around."

Lim was going to ask why this was necessary, when he was wheeled into another room and the table was then put inside a strange machine. This one looked like a brass tube, with a slot at the bottom for the bed to be wheeled in.

"What's going on?" he asked, his heart pounding, and bile rising in his throat. He swallowed with difficulty, then coughed as his breath caught. His palms felt sweaty and he wiped them on the side of the bed.

"It's fine," said the nurse, a little impatiently. "This will not hurt. Now, lie still. This will help us to see your insides."

"What?!" asked Lim. His heart was beating so fast that he thought it would surely burst from his chest, and he struggled to catch his breath. He felt like he was falling, even though he knew that he wasn't. He couldn't hear anything over the blood pounding in his ears. What did she mean "his insides"? Why would anyone want to see that?

But the nurse was right, and it wasn't painful. A small metal box moved around the inside of the tube and scanned the length of his body. Lim felt its energy, but the box didn't touch him at any point. It then retreated to the end of the tube, and that was it. Lim started to relax, but the nurse came over, carrying a sharp-looking implement.

"This is a blood test," she said, then slid the sharp end into a vein in his arm.

Lim cried out, then looked down to see the barrel of the device filling with his blood. He felt woozy and blacked out.

Chapter 9

Inside the Hospital

Lim woke up in a bare, clinical room, with plain white walls and ceiling. The afternoon sun shone through a window above him. He was lying on a bed, and his arms and legs were no longer strapped down. There were several disks, similar to the electrodes, but a little softer, taped to his chest. These were attached to small box-like machines, like the ones in the examination room, by thin wires. There was a tube sticking out of his arm, where the nurse had taken his blood.

A few minutes later, the nurse walked in.

"Ah good, you're awake," she said. She came over to the side of the bed and adjusted it, so that Lim was sitting up. "You're weaker than we expected," she told him as she used a pencil to make a note in a book that she put on a shelf near the foot of the bed, "but Dr Turnwall is confident that the treatment will work."

"Okay," said Lim. "Where is my family? Where are my clothes?"

"Your clothes are over there." She pointed to a set of drawers on the other side of the bed. "And your family will come to see you later."

"There were some letters in my pocket," said Lim. "Where are they? Can I please have them?"

The nurse sighed, as if he'd asked something completely unreasonable, but she walked over to the drawers, opened one up, retrieved the letters and handed them to him.

"Thank you," said Lim.

He was about to read the letters, when Dr Turnwall came in.

"How are you feeling?" he asked Lim, after dismissing the nurse.

"Fine, I guess," said Lim. He was breathing relatively normally, and he wasn't in any pain, not even where the needle was stuck in his arm.

"Good," said the doctor. "Now, as Nurse Mela has told you, you are weaker than we expected, but I can adjust for this. She will tell you what you need to do."

"Okay," said Lim. "Do you know what's wrong with me?" he asked hopefully.

"Your energies are out of balance," answered the doctor, as if this were obvious.

"Oh," said Lim. This sounded very vague. "Do you know why?"

The doctor shook his head. "The cause doesn't matter," he said, sounding dismissive. "We treat the symptoms. Your own body will take care of the rest."

Lim didn't reply. His body had never been very good at taking care of anything.

"Trust me, it will work," said the doctor, then turned and left.

A few minutes later, Nurse Mela returned with a tray. On the tray was a large bowl of some thick white gruel-like mixture.

"You need to eat this," she said as she set it down on the bedside table.

"What?" Lim looked at the bowl doubtfully. It looked extremely unappetising.

"You need to eat this," she repeated. "You are too underweight to start the treatment as you are, so you need to eat this formula. Three times a day, until your weight increases."

"What if I can't?" asked Lim, his breath catching and his heart starting to race again. One of the machines that he was connected to, started to make a sound. Nurse Mela walked up to it and adjusted the dial until the noise stopped.

"If you will not eat it willingly, you will be force-fed it with a funnel and a tube. So, I would suggest that you eat it. It will be much easier that way all around."

He nodded, to show that he understood, and the nurse walked out.

Lim pushed the bowl of gruel away. Surely, she didn't mean that about force-feeding him. She was probably just making sure that he made an effort. And he would; a little bit later.

He looked at his letters and opened the first one eagerly. It wasn't from Vada, much to his disappointment, but it was from Jessa and Marla, which cheered him up.

"Dear Lim," it read, *"Thank you for writing to us so soon. We miss you and your brother already. We hope that this letter finds you well (or at least as well as possible), and that you had a good trip to Sirrock. We wish you all the best with your treatment. Do tell us how it all goes, and we look forward to seeing you and Vaarem on your way back. Yours with love and affection, Jessa and Marla."*

Lim smiled and re-read the letter several times. He would write to them as soon as he could. He would have to ask someone for a quill and ink. The second letter was from Dr Fantail and it was just a standard greeting that wished him well. He looked at the last letter and his heart sank. It wasn't from Vada either. It was from Magnon and his wife in Morliss, which Lim guessed was a very kind gesture. He'd only met the healer for such a short while and it was nice to know that he really seemed to care.

Lim put the letters away, then turned to the bowl of gruel. He had a tentative spoonful, and nearly spat it out. It was tasteless and gluggy, and it stuck in his throat. Nevertheless, he kept eating. If anything could make him put on some much-needed weight, then this definitely would.

He'd barely gotten through a quarter of it when Nurse Mela came back.

"I'm eating it," he told her, swallowing a spoonful.

"Not fast enough," she told him. "At this rate, you'll get through that bowl in three days. You need to have three bowls in one day. You need to be ready in a matter of days. You elves may live for centuries, but us humans need to do things quickly, and you are far too slow." She took the bowl away.

Lim stared after her, confused.

Until she came back a few minutes later, holding a nasty-looking contraption with a funnel and a tube, and accompanied by two other nurses. One of them was carrying the gruel in a jug.

"No," said Lim desperately, his breath catching again. "Please. I'll do better. Please, don't do this."

But the nurses didn't listen. Without speaking to him, Nurse Mela forced his mouth open and shoved the tube down his throat, while one of the other nurses held him down. He tried to scream and thrash, but he was restrained and weak, so they overpowered him easily. The third nurse poured the mixture into the funnel and forced it down his throat.

Lim felt the gruel fill his stomach to the point of discomfort and then pain. He felt like he was going to burst, but the gruel kept coming, and coming.

Finally, when he thought that he couldn't take it anymore, it was over. The gruel was all gone, and Nurse Mela pulled the tube out. Lim gagged.

"If you throw it up, we will come and replace it, so I

recommend that you keep it down. You will likely feel uncomfortable for a while, so don't try to move."

They walked out without another word.

Lim lay back and closed his eyes, occasionally groaning with pain. He touched his hand to his stomach, but he was so full that even that hurt. He lay his head back and a pitiful whimper escaped his lips. This wasn't how it was supposed to be. He was alone and scared, and in pain, and his sister hadn't even bothered to write to him. *Why?* he wondered. Why was he so unimportant that Vada couldn't take a few moments out of her day to write him one measly note?

For a while he lay there, feeling sorry for himself, wanting nothing more than to just go home. This wasn't worth it. If anyone had told him that the treatment would involve being shocked, stabbed with needles, and force-fed disgusting glugs on the very first day, then he would never have gone for it. And to think that he would be subjected to the glug three times a day.

Eventually, the pain in his stomach eased somewhat, and he was able to touch it. He gathered some magic heat and ran his hand along his belly. He knew that this type of thing worked better if someone else did it for him, that if he expended his own energies, most of the healing effect would be lost, but desperate times called for desperate measures.

The heat eased some of the discomfort, but his stomach still hurt.

Eventually, he fell asleep.

When he woke up, he was pleased to see his family by his bedside. His mother was holding one of his hands and Vaarem the other.

"Hey," said Vaarem, when Lim looked at him. "How are you?"

"Horrible," said Lim. "They shocked me with electricity, stuck needles in me and force-fed me some horrid glug until I thought I would burst. I hate it here."

"It will be fine, Limnos," said Garrett sternly, even now not cutting Lim any slack. "And I told you to eat when we travelled. You brought this on yourself."

"Oh hush, Garrett," Zareanna told him off. "Lim's always been underweight. I know it must be very uncomfortable, darling," she said to Lim kindly, "But it will make you better."

"But it hurts," complained Lim. He was happy that his family were here, but he was still feeling bitter about the fact that Vada had not made contact. Even if she only received half the letters he'd sent her, she would still know where he was.

Perhaps she will come tomorrow, or at least send a message, he consoled himself.

He'd told her that he'd be here for at least a week or two. Perhaps she was waiting for him to get settled in.

Eventually, one of the nurses came back and told his family that it was time to leave.

"What?" asked Vaarem. "You mean we can't stay overnight?"

"No, we can't," said Garrett impatiently. "This is a human hospital. They do things differently here. But don't worry, Lim is in good hands." He looked to Zareanna as if for confirmation.

Zareanna nodded. She didn't look very happy though. "Your father is right," she said. "Lim will be well cared for."

"But he's being tortured," complained Vaarem.

"No, he isn't," said Garrett. "He's just being dramatic, as usual."

"Your parents are right," said the nurse. "Your brother is in good hands. You can come back and see him tomorrow."

Lim suddenly realised that this was it. His family was leaving, and he would be stuck in this strange, sterile place all night, without his potions to boot. His heart began to race and one of the machines that he was attached to started to beep again. The nurse walked over to him and stuck a needle in his arm, this time injecting something into him, rather than drawing blood. He didn't have time to panic, as within a heartbeat, he felt an intense warmth wash over him, making him feel like he was floating on a cloud.

"What did you do to him?" He heard Vaarem cry, but his brother's voice seemed far away.

Lim closed his eyes.

"Just a sedative to calm him," the nurse said. "See?" She seemed to be showing them something, but Lim was beyond caring. He felt safe and warm, and he wanted to go to sleep. He felt his mother kiss his fore-head, then he was left alone.

Several hours later, the nurses came back and forced the gruel down his throat again. Again, he was intensely uncomfortable afterwards. However, this time he couldn't hold it down and was sick over the side of the bed. As soon as it happened, he got that feeling of falling again, and his heart started to race. He remembered Nurse Mela threatening him that if he threw up, they'd force-feed him again, and he desperately wanted to avoid that. He started to cough, and all the machines started to beep.

Two nurses came running in. He was pleased that neither of them was the stern Mela, but nevertheless he shrank back into the pillows.

What will they do to me? he wondered anxiously.

"Oh no, darling," said the first nurse kindly, which made Lim relax a little. At least she knew that he hadn't done it on purpose. She gave him another injection, which made him feel all warm and woozy again, then she wiped his face and sprayed something into his mouth, which made his chest loosen up and allowed him to breathe again. "There, there," she said, brushing his hair back from his face. "It's okay."

The second nurse cleaned up the mess on the floor and Lim closed his eyes for a moment, then opened them again and said in a small voice, "Please don't make me have that stuff again. Please," he begged.

The first nurse looked at him for a moment then,

when the other nurse had gone, she said quietly, "Okay, just this once, but don't tell anyone. It is your first day, and I do think it's too much for someone of your delicate disposition. But try and keep it down next time. Because you need all the nutrients in the formula. I know it's not tasty. It's not supposed to be. It's designed to be absorbed rapidly, so if you keep it down, you will only need it for a few days. There is a chamber pot under the bed if you need it. The sensor wires have enough give to let you stand up."

"Okay," he said, lying back. "Thank you."

"You're welcome, Lim. And if you need anything," she began, pointing at a button near the headboard, "just press this button, and someone will come."

Chapter 10

Eliza

Lim woke up to the feeling that someone was watching him. He was used to all manner of people watching him sleep; mostly for fear that he would die during the night or something, but the vibe that he got here was different. He sensed that the person watching him was merely curious.

He was lying in a half-sitting position to help him breathe easier, so as soon as he opened his eyes, he saw his visitor.

She was a human girl, who looked to be about his own age, which meant that she was probably in her teens (at least he thought so, as he was never quite sure about how humans matured, just that it was a little quicker than elves). She was very thin, probably thinner even than he was, and she had large grey eyes that stared at him out of her pinched, drawn face.

"Hello?" he asked, uncertainly.

"Hello," she said. "I heard there was an elf on the ward, so I wanted to meet you."

"Oh," he said, thinking that he was most likely going to get this a lot. "Right. Well, hi, I'm Lim. What's your name?"

"I'm Eliza," she said, extending her hand. He shook it. Her arm was so skinny that her wrist seemed bigger than her forearm. He'd never seen a human so frail, and immediately he felt a kind of connection to her. Humans got sick more frequently than elves, but this human seemed to be at least as sick as he was, in relative terms.

"Nice to meet you," he said. He noticed that she had a needle in her arm, like he did, and there was a tube attached to it, which was attached to a bag and a pole on wheels. He looked at his own arm and saw that he had the same set-up. Only because of the sensors and wires stuck to his chest, he couldn't walk around.

Just as well, really, he thought. He didn't think that he could have walked around even if he'd wanted to. Although he was breathing with relative ease at the moment, his chest hurt and he knew that it would get worse if he tried to stand, let alone walk. He wondered where Eliza had come from, how far she'd walked just to see him.

"Do you have an eating disorder?" she asked, looking at the bedside cabinet, on which rested the hated tube and funnel.

"What?" He frowned. "What's an eating disorder?"

"It's when you can't eat, silly," she said. "So, they make you, with that thing." She pointed to it.

"Oh," said Lim, looking at the tube with a shudder. "No. I can eat normally." *As long as my foods don't touch*, he thought, but didn't say, because everyone, other than Vaarem laughed at him for this. Even Vada didn't understand. "I just can't eat that glug." He shuddered again. "No, I think I have a breathing disorder? Although no one knows what kind." He shrugged.

"Oh right," she said. "I have an eating disorder. Or so they tell me." She shrugged her thin shoulders.

"That must be bad," said Lim kindly. He'd never before met someone his own age who was also chronically ill. Part of him felt happy, like finally he wasn't alone. But most of him felt bad for her. He didn't wish his own experiences on anyone else.

Eliza shrugged again. "I guess it is," she said. "I can't eat anything. I sometimes try, but." She shuddered. "I just can't. It's like my body and my brain won't let me." She hugged her thin arms around herself. "So, they make me drink that stuff too. It's horrible, and the worst thing is that it is supposed to make me fat, even though I really, really don't want to be, but they force me to have it anyway." She hugged herself tighter and shuddered visibly.

"You're not fat," said Lim. "But I agree, the gruel is horrible."

"Why are they making you eat it?" she asked.

He sighed. "Apparently, I need to put on weight in order to start my treatment."

"What are you having done?" she asked.

He shrugged. "I don't really know. Something experimental that uses electricity to boost your own energy. Or something," he added, wondering whether he should have read through all the consent forms before signing them. But his parents had read them, and they'd agreed to let the doctor do it to him. So, it was going to be okay. *Right?*

Her eyes widened at his answer. "They'll hurt you," she said.

"What? More than they have already?" he asked with a grim laugh. He was feeling very strange, as if he was beyond terror and was now finding everything funny.

"Yes," she said. "You should leave now, while you still can."

"What do you mean?"

"You should leave," she repeated. "They want to do it to me too, which is why they're force-feeding me." She shuddered. "But it hurts, so I won't let them."

"What?" asked Lim, confused.

She was about to reply, when Nurse Mela walked in with a jug of gruel. Lim groaned inwardly.

"What are you doing here, Eliza?" asked Mela sternly. "You should be back in your bed."

"I'm just warning the elf to run away while he still can. Before you make him fat, like you've done to me. Before you hurt him, like you've hurt me."

Lim frowned. She wasn't making sense. Was she saying that she'd already had the treatment done? But if that were so, why was she still being force fed the formula? Or had they done something to her mind to make her see and think things that were not real? He recalled Dr Turnwall saying that not all fixes were visible, and his breath caught in his throat. *What were they doing to Eliza?* He shuddered, and coughed, but fortunately only for a moment.

"Stop your lies and stories," said Mela, taking Eliza by her bony shoulders and leading her out of the room, as Lim caught his breath. "No one is trying to hurt anyone. Now leave, and don't let me catch you back here bothering Lim or any of the other patients. Do you understand?"

Eliza nodded, but before she did, Lim saw a moment of intense fear in her eyes, as if she really thought that she was in danger.

Nurse Mela started to pick up the funnel.

"Can I drink it myself?" asked Lim, desperate to avoid the tube.

"Be my guest." She handed the jug to him. "But be aware that if you don't manage, you will be made to drink it anyway. You need to make yourself ready."

Lim nodded and took the jug. He took a big gulp of it, and then another, trying to swallow fast, before his body registered what he was doing and rose up in protest.

He managed to drink half the mixture, before feeling like he couldn't do it anymore. He held the jug in his hands and tried to will himself to continue.

Mela sat on the chair and watched him.

Lim lifted the jug to his lips again, but he couldn't drink any more. His stomach was protesting already, and he felt like he was going to be sick.

"I can't," he said, desperately. "If I do, I'm going to throw up." He almost said "again" but stopped himself just in time. Hopefully, Mela didn't know what had happened the previous night.

She didn't say anything but simply picked up the funnel and tube again.

"No, please," begged Lim. "Can I have a rest? I'll finish it soon, I promise. Please?" He looked at her imploringly.

She looked at him for a long moment, her eyes hard, her lips pursed into a thin line, but then, to his intense relief, she nodded. "Fine," she said, taking the jug from him. "You can finish it in half an hour. And if you don't, you know what will happen." She looked at the funnel meaningfully. "It's important that you make yourself ready," she stressed.

"I will." he said. "I promise. Thank you." He lay back and closed his eyes, feeling exhausted from the effort.

He was still uncomfortably full when she came back half an hour later, but he drank the gruel obediently, before falling back into an exhausted sleep.

Lim woke up to the sounds of people talking around him. He opened his eyes and was pleased to see his family sitting around his bed. He was, however, disappointed that Vada was not with them.

"Good morning, sweetie," said his mother when she

saw him open his eyes. She leaned down and put her arms around him, then kissed him on the forehead. "How are you feeling, darling? Did you sleep well?"

"Hmm," said Lim with a noncommittal shrug. He didn't want to burden his family with telling them just how awful he felt.

After his family left for lunch (or so they said; they didn't look hungry, but then again, what did he know), a short man in the white coat of a human doctor came into Lim's room. The man had a long, blonde beard that was twisted into a braid, and his blonde hair was tied up in two braids that fell over his shoulders and to the small of his back. Lim thought that the style looked good, and wondered whether he could do the same with his own hair.

"Good morning, Lim," said the doctor. "My name is Dr Thorn, and I will be assisting Dr Turnwall with your treatment here."

"Okay." Nodded Lim. So far, things were not going great, but perhaps this doctor could turn things around.

"I specialise in mixed-blood medicine," said Dr Thorn. "I am half-dwarf, half-human, which is why the subject has always interested me."

Lim nodded.

"So, first things first," said Dr Thorn, "we need to get all of the potions that you have been taking out of your system so that we can start with a blank page, so to speak."

Lim nodded again, but inside he was sighing. He'd had this done before. He'd had periods of time when he'd had to wean off one potion in order to see if another worked, and so on. The withdrawal was always uncomfortable.

"I understand," said Lim, "but I was on a high dose of my potion. I fear going into withdrawal. That, and I literally cannot breathe without it sometimes."

The doctor nodded. "Yes, that is understandable, which is why you have the relaxant going into your drip."

Lim looked at the tube that was going into his arm and frowned. He'd been so freaked out about everything that he hadn't asked about the drip.

"Relaxant?" he asked.

The doctor nodded. "Yes, it is a mild herbal formula, very mild, but hopefully enough to ensure that you don't suffer any uncomfortable withdrawals. We are also hoping that it will assist you with your breathing, but we are monitoring it every hour. So far, you are doing well."

"Right." Nodded Lim. He didn't feel like he was doing particularly well. He was still full from that morning's breakfast, and he knew that the next lot of formula was coming soon. He was not looking forward to it.

"Also," continued the doctor, sitting down on the chair that Vaarem had sat on before, "because you are here as an experimental subject, you are going to be trialling some different potions."

Lim frowned. "What?" He'd trialled many potions before, but Dr Thorn made it sound very sinister.

"I am developing some potions to treat common conditions, such as pain, fever, lack of energy, but designed for people of mixed-blood. You will be trialling them so that we can measure their effectiveness."

Lim frowned again. "So, you mean you're not specifically testing their effectiveness on me? Just seeing if they work at all?"

"Yes." Nodded the doctor.

"Oka-ay," said Lim carefully. He was not sure that he liked the idea of taking a potion that no one had ever tried before. Then again, someone had to be the first so it may as well be him.

Imagine how good it would be if I were to be the first one to try something that ended up being a cure, he thought with an inward smile.

"Sure," he said. "Do I need to sign a consent form or anything?"

"You already signed them," said the doctor with a smile, "yesterday, with Dr Turnwall."

"All right," said Lim, thinking that he *really* should have read them. His parents had read them, but he was twenty-five now, which meant that he was an adult and therefore responsible for himself. He couldn't rely on his mother and father for everything any more.

"Okay." He looked up at the doctor. "I guess that I have already consented. What do I need to do now?"

"Nothing for now," said the doctor. "Just rest, and

we will start you on a new potion the day after to-morrow.

Chapter 11

Family and Friends

The nurses let Lim drink his gruel himself, as long as he finished each jug within a reasonable amount of time, which was normally about one hour. He found that going a little slower like this was not as painful, although he still felt bloated and lethargic most of the time. Because he wasn't moving much, he had little trouble breathing, which he guessed was an up-side. He was struggling to find anything else good about the whole experience.

On the third morning, Dr. Thorn gave Lim a horrible tasting potion that made him throw up and made him break out in hives. Thankfully, he drank it before breakfast, so he didn't throw up any of the formula, and the hives went away by the afternoon. The next morning, he was given a different potion that tasted a little better and had no other reactions. He kept it down and went to sleep.

His parents and brother visited every day, but he felt that he wasn't good company, being so sleepy most of the time. Vada didn't write, and she didn't visit either. This was beginning to make him angry.

Why won't she come down? he thought, annoyed. *Why won't she write me one measly letter?*

He wrote to her but was despondent that he wouldn't get a reply.

That evening, when a bowl of water was brought in for him to wash his face, he tried to scry Vada but he found that he was so tired and weak that even if she'd been there, he wouldn't have been able to reach her.

Whenever he started to get anxious the machines that monitored him would start beeping, and one of the nurses would come and inject him with a sedative. When the sedative was coursing through his system, he felt safe and warm and secure, and he had no pain. When the drug wore off, the pain in his chest and stomach, and in his arm, where the needle had pierced him, returned. When he looked down, he could see a line of bruises running down the length of his arm, and he'd start to panic, which would result in him getting another bruise. If he'd had the strength, he would have gotten up and ran away a hundred times. He hated it all so much.

His friends from Palinas, as well as Jessa and Marla wrote to him daily, which cheered him up a little, so he tried to put as positive a spin as he could on what he was going through in his replies.

But how positive can you be when you're being force-fed crap and stabbed with needles daily? he wondered cynically.

Nevertheless, he tried. In his more with-it moments, he got Vaarem to help him with the letters, his brother always having a funny anecdote to add.

The other ray of metaphorical light in his otherwise miserable existence was Eliza. She visited him in the early morning and late evening, when his family, and all other visitors to the hospital, were gone. She didn't bring up the subject of his treatment being dangerous again, so he didn't bring it up either. After all, it wasn't like she really knew anything about it. She was vague about her own, and whatever it was that the doctors were doing to her, she was still able to come and see him, so it couldn't have been too bad.

"They just force feed me that glug, then ask me what I am thinking and how I feel about things. They gave me electric shocks a few times, but as long as I don't say anything that they deem *crazy*." She rolled her eyes dramatically, and made circles with her fingers on either side of her head, "they mostly leave me alone."

"What do they deem crazy?" asked Lim curiously.

She shrugged her skinny shoulders. "Anything not normal, anything inappropriate. Like, when I say that I don't want to eat anything because I hate having gross stuff inside me, how I like to feel empty and pure, I get a painful zap, so I don't say it anymore. I try not to think it because I remember the shocks." She shuddered. "Or if I say I want to hurt someone, or myself, they get all angry and shock me. So, I don't say it anymore."

"Do you think it?" asked Lim. Vada had frequently told him that she wanted to hurt various people, most frequently girls at school who were mean to her, or teachers who didn't understand her. But he'd never believed that she actually meant it. At least, he'd hoped not.

Eliza shrugged again. "No," she said simply. "I don't really want to hurt anyone."

"That's good to know," said Lim, smiling. "I don't either."

"I do want to get better," said Eliza with a sigh. "I don't like when my brain makes me think stupid things. The shocks are supposed to help, but they don't," she said.

"Oh." Lim didn't know what to say to that.

Apart from Eliza, he saw no other patients. Or rather, he spoke to no other patients. He occasionally saw them walking past his room, some of them pushing along a pole with a drip, like Eliza, some of them with metal contraptions around parts of their bodies. They were all human as far as he could tell, and while many of them glanced into his room curiously, none of them spoke to him.

On his fifth morning, after having drunk yet

another potion, he woke up to find Eliza watching him, her eyes looking disproportionately huge in her thin little face.

"Hello, little elf," she said, as she did every time she greeted him.

"Hello, little human," he responded, which made her giggle. She really was very small. He wondered what she'd think if she saw him stand up. Would she still call him "little elf"? He figured that he was at least a foot, if not more, taller than she was.

"Are you getting fat yet?" she asked him, looking at the funnel and tube on the table. He hadn't been subjected to it, thankfully, since promising to drink the gruel himself.

"No," he replied. "I wish I was, then I could stop drinking this shit."

She laughed. "You're funny," she said.

"Not really," he replied. "My brother has always been the funny one."

"You have a brother?" she asked curiously.

"Yes," replied Lim, realising that she was the first person he'd ever met, who didn't know that he was a twin; the first person who didn't immediately compare him to his brother and find him lacking.

"Does he come and visit you?"

"Yes. Every day. Do you have any family?" he enquired.

"Not really," she shrugged. "They left me here."

"Oh no, that's awful. How terrible for you," he said, then started to cough. One of the machines went off.

Eliza watched him struggle for breath, but she didn't do anything.

Eventually one of the nurses (the nice one, who hadn't told on him when he'd thrown up on the first night) came in and sprayed the usual mixture into his mouth.

His coughing stopped, and he caught his breath. "Thank you," he said, still a little breathless.

"Eliza, what did I tell you about bothering the other patients? Go back to your own room."

"She's not bothering me," said Lim. He felt awful for her, being stuck in here all alone, without her family to support her. No wonder she was so keen to talk to him.

The nurse looked at him, then at Eliza, with a doubtful frown.

"I mean it," said Lim. "She can stay. I like talking to her."

The nurse looked from him to Eliza again, then sighed and said, "Very well. You can stay, Eliza, but only so long as you don't bother Lim. When he asks you to go, you need to go. Do you understand?"

"Yes." Nodded Eliza. "I'm not as dumb as you all think I am. I promise that I will not bother Lim, and that I will not overstay my welcome."

Lim grinned at her, and she smiled back shyly.

The nurse nodded. "I will bring your breakfast formula in a minute," she told Lim. "Perhaps you can show Eliza how you feed yourself. Perhaps she can then learn to do it too."

"Thank you," said Lim, looking at Eliza with a sheepish smile. She rolled her eyes in the nurse's direction in response.

Eliza waited for the nurse to leave, then leaned forward and swiveled her head, as if looking for something in the room.

"Where do you throw it up?" she finally asked, looking at the empty chamber pot under the bed, then around the room again.

"What?"

"Where do you throw it up?" she repeated. "The gruel."

"I don't," said Lim. "If I just lie here and don't move, I can keep it down."

She looked at him as if he'd said that he regularly dined with dragons. "You mean you let your body digest that stuff?" she asked incredulously.

"Uh, yeah," he said, wondering what he was missing. She made it sound like she was throwing up on purpose. Lim couldn't think of anything more revolting.

"Then how come you're not getting fat?" she demanded.

Lim shrugged his thin shoulders. "I don't know. Just lucky, I guess. Or unlucky, depending which way you look at it."

She laughed, then said, "You *are* lucky. If you can eat this stuff without getting fat, then you can eat anything."

"Uh, yeah, pretty much." He had no idea what she

was getting at, but it was starting to make him un-comfortable.

She looked at him for a few more moments with an unreadable expression on her face. "You're very hand-some," she said eventually.

He smiled. "Thank you. You're very pretty."

A smile broke over her face, as if he'd told her that she was the most beautiful woman in the world.

"Really?" she asked. "You mean it?"

"Yeah." He smiled, realising that he did mean it. Sort of. Initially, he'd only said it to be polite. He could feel her loneliness, her sense of rejection, her desperate need for love, and he was determined to do everything in his power to make her feel even a little bit better. He'd initially thought her quite plain to look at, and far, far too skinny to be beautiful by anyone's stan-dards. But when she smiled, he saw her kindness and gentleness, which shone through, making her appear very attractive.

Imagine being left all alone, deserted by your whole family, he thought, feeling bad for her.

The nurse came back with his gruel. Eliza took one look at it and stood up to leave the room.

Lim picked up the jug and stared at her grimly. "Cheers," he said, putting the jug to his lips.

She looked back at him with a small smile that warmed his heart. It was the first time that it had reached her eyes, and it made him think that perhaps his own lot wasn't so bad after all.

Vaarem was anxious about his brother, and he was finding the forced separation unbearable. Sure, in the past five turns or so, he and Lim had grown apart, as was natural. However, they'd always retained that special bond that they'd shared since they'd been babies. Even though they'd slept in separate rooms for the past twelve turns, Vaarem had always instinctively known when Lim had been having a bad night and had been able to be there for him. Now that he couldn't, he didn't know what to do with himself.

He was staying alone in the inn, in the room that he and Lim had shared on their first night in Sirrock City, and he was feeling lonely and out of sorts. He would wake up early each morning and wait impatiently until he and his parents could go to the hospital to see his twin.

When the family were not in the inn, and not with Lim, they went sight-seeing around the city, but they were all tense, and the conversation was more stilted and awkward than ever. Both of his parents kept glancing in the direction of Blackwell Castle, his mother's former home and Vada's current residence (or so Lim had told him), but they didn't say anything about it.

Vaarem was not enjoying himself either. Every venue, monument, and city sight that they saw between hospital visits made him feel a deep emptiness. He kept turning around to tell Lim something, to share some comment or witty observation, only to find that

Lim wasn't there. Telling him later at the hospital was not the same.

It was their fifth day in Sirrock City. After getting dressed, Vaarem walked down the corridor to his parents' room, as he did every morning, when he heard them talking. He was about to knock, to advertise his presence, but something about the tone of their voices made him pause.

They'd been tense and on edge ever since arriving in Sirrock City, and even more so since leaving Lim at the hospital. It seemed that they were finally talking about whatever seemed to be bothering them, so Vaarem didn't want to interrupt.

He went to turn around, to go back to his room, but he didn't. He wanted to listen. He knew that he shouldn't be eavesdropping, but after the stiff silence of the past few days, he was eager to hear their thoughts, even if they were not really wanting to share them with him.

"I miss him so much," his mother was saying in a choked voice.

"Me too," his father replied. "I constantly feel like I'm failing him." He too sounded like he was crying.

Vaarem frowned. His father never cried. He got angry and lashed out. Even though Vaarem had been shocked when his father had slapped him during their trip here, in a way it had been a relief. Vaarem had been waiting for something like that for a long time, it seemed. But his father wasn't angry now.

Vaarem crept closer to the door.

"I failed with Vada," Garrett was saying. "She went back to the castle, to the very place I swore to keep her away from."

His mother said something that Vaarem didn't hear, and then his father said, "And now I feel like I'm failing Lim. Fates, he's *my* child. I should be able to do *something* for him."

Again, his mother whispered something that sounded comforting, but Vaarem couldn't hear the words.

Then his father said, "And I am failing with you. I promised to make you happy, but you're not, are you? I can never compare to the great Malkim Blackwell."

"I never expected you to replace him, Garrett," said his mother softly.

"Well, that's good," said his father bitterly, "because I could never do the things he did."

Their voices moved away, as if they were going into another room, and Vaarem could no longer hear them. He turned away from the door and went back into his room.

Great, he thought bitterly. *My father thinks he's a failure because he's failing Lim and Mother, and now Vada, of all people, but there was no mention of me from either of them. It's like they don't care about me at all.*

Instead of waiting for his parents so that they could eat breakfast together, he went into the dining room alone. He got himself some fruit and porridge, then sat down and began to eat, barely tasting the food.

He thought of what he'd overheard, and wondered what Vada's father had done, that was so bad that his parents were still upset over it.

His parents arrived about half an hour later. Both of them looked tired and as tense as ever. Their previous talk had clearly done nothing to ease their mood.

"Good morning, Vaarem," said his father. "How did you sleep?"

"Fine," said Vaarem with a shrug, not surprised that neither of his parents had asked why he'd not waited for them upstairs, but disappointed nonetheless.

His mother, oblivious to his expression, leaned down and kissed his cheek, then went to the buffet to get some food. His father followed.

Fates forbid that either of them are ever alone with me, thought Vaarem with a bitter sigh.

"They're torturing him," complained Vaarem to his parents when they left the hospital, as they were asked to, each afternoon. He'd never seen Lim look quite so unwell. His brother never had rashes or hives before, he'd never complained of constant stomach aches. The pain and fear in his eyes was almost more than Vaarem could bear.

"Don't be dramatic," said Garrett, as they sat in one of the city parks. "It is admirable how loyal you are to your brother, but don't get sucked into his drama and his exaggerations. He is fine."

But Vaarem knew that he wasn't. Lim wasn't fine,

and the hospital was not helping him. Perhaps this whole trip had been a bad idea.

By the time he got back to his room in the inn that evening, he was feeling more despondent than ever, and the person he was most angry with was Vada. He'd never been as close to his half-sister as Lim had, but he still loved her and considered her family, even as he believed that his father didn't. But after over-hearing his father that morning, Vaarem had decided that everything was Vada's fault. His father had tried to be good to her, but she'd pushed him away, as she'd pushed them all away. And now his parents were both looking towards the castle where they knew that she was, but she wasn't coming down to see them. Vaarem knew that Vada must have gotten Lim's letters and there was no excuse for her silence. It was bad enough that she was ignoring them as a family, but it was especially awful that she was ignoring Lim.

On a whim, Vaarem walked to the shared bathroom down the corridor, pumped some water into a bowl, brought it back into his room, sat cross-legged on his bed, and stared into it, thinking about his half-sister, about his need to talk to her *right now*.

Despite the fact that Vada was close, there was a lot of interference from the machines and other ener-gies in the city, and because he wasn't that strong in magic anyway, it took him a long time to reach her. But finally, at around midnight, her pale thin face, with its dark blue eyes, the same as his and Lim's, swam into view.

Lim? He heard her surprised voice in his mind.

No, Vaarem scoffed, *I thought that you of all people would be able to tell us apart.*

Me of all people? She raised her eyebrow. *What's that supposed to mean? I haven't seen either of you in turns. I don't know why I should be able to tell you apart if others can't.*

I thought you believed yourself to be smarter than others, said Vaarem coldly, *But clearly you are not.*

She ignored the jab and said, *What do you want?*

You know damn well what I want.

She sighed. *Vaarem, I am not a mind reader.* She rolled her eyes. *Even a mind as small as yours is a mystery to me. So, I ask you again, what do you want?*

Why haven't you replied to Lim's letters?

She didn't reply, but instead asked, *How is Lim?*

If you had bothered to answer his letters, you would know, he said impatiently. He'd been hoping that perhaps something had befallen her, and that was the reason for her silence. But it seemed that she was simply ignoring them as she always did. He wondered whether he should tell her that his parents had talked about her that morning, that despite what she thought, they both seemed to care about her, even his father. But what would be the point? Vada knew that *Lim* cared about her, yet she was ignoring him anyway.

I'm busy, she said impatiently, *I can't be expected to know everything all the time.*

What are you so busy with? he demanded.

Nothing that you would care about nor understand, she said dismissively.

Did you get Lim's letters? Vaarem tried a different tack.

Yes. She nodded.

Then you know that we're in Sirrock?

Yes. What of it?

So, why are you ignoring us? he demanded. *Why are you ignoring Lim? He is so miserable, and yet you still stay away.*

I didn't know, said Vada impatiently. *As I keep telling you, I can't be expected to know everything all the time. Besides, you're his twin. Isn't it your job to cheer him up? You with your endless jokes and stories and constant shenanigans. I cannot possibly compete with all that.*

Does it hurt to have your head that far up your arse all the time? demanded Vaarem, *It is not a competition and you know it. It never has been. He loves you for you. Fates know why, but he does, and you know it, even if you pretend that you don't. And you* know *that our little brother is very sick, and yet you still stay away. I am starting to run out of excuses to try and justify your behaviour.*

Excuses? She frowned.

Vaarem sighed. *He asks about you all the time. I keep assuring him that you will write, that you will come, but I am running out of possible reasons why you don't. Why are you so cruel?*

Vada sighed and looked down, as if embarrassed.

It seemed that he'd finally gotten through to her. *I'm sorry,* she said finally. *I did mean to write back. I always do. But I never know what to say. I do miss you, and Lim especially. I miss him so much that it's just too painful.*

Vaarem scoffed at that. *Too painful for you. Right. Well, just imagine how painful it is for him. At least you can breathe.*

Is he really that bad? asked Vada, her mind voice small and scared.

Yes, said Vaarem. *I don't know what they're doing to him in that hospital, but it doesn't seem to be working. Please come and see him. I'm begging you.*

Oooh, begging are you? She smirked. *You must be desperate.*

I am, sighed Vaarem. *I don't care what you think of me, or Mother, or Garrett. It is not about any of us. It's about Lim. Please, Vada. Even if you don't care, Lim does. Please.* He sighed, running out of steam. This had been a bad idea.

Okay, said Vada finally. *I'll come. If it really means that much to him, I'll come,* she sighed. *I promise. Tell Lim that I will come.*

I'm not going to tell him anything, said Vaarem. *Because I don't trust you. If I tell him you'll come and then you don't, I'm afraid the disappointment will kill him. So, come. Or don't. But if you care about Lim at all, about any of us, I really recommend you come.* He broke off the connection before she could say anything else. He wondered again whether he should have told her that it appeared that his parents cared more about her than she thought, more than they appeared to care about *him*. But what would have been the point of that?

Lim drank the, by now familiar, hated gruel, then lay back with a groan. No matter how many jugs he drank, his stomach still hurt afterwards. And as far as he could tell, he was still as thin as he'd ever been, so he wondered how long they were going to make him do this.

The nice nurse, whose name he still didn't know, came to pick up the empty jug. "How are you feeling?" she asked, leaning down and checking him over.

"Horrible," he said.

"Aww, dear," she said kindly. "What's wrong? Your vital signs all seem well."

Lim sighed. "I just feel generally horrible. And I have a constant stomach ache."

"Oh no," she said. She lifted the blanket and put her hand on his still-bloated belly. "Your poor tummy is not used to all this, is it?"

"No," said Lim in a small voice, grateful that somebody finally acknowledged this fact. Everyone else had sternly told him to stop being so dramatic.

"I'll get you something that will help," she said. "And hopefully you won't be subjected to this for too much longer. Your weight is nearly high enough to start the treatment, so hopefully you only need to do this for one more day."

"Really?" asked Lim, with hope in his voice. "How much weight have I put on?"

"About half a stone," she said. "Another pound and you will be eligible."

"Oh," he said, pleasantly surprised.

"So, all this pain will be worth it in the end," she told him. "Wait here," she instructed, which Lim thought was funny. Where was he going to go?

She came back a few minutes later with a water skin, which she'd filled with hot water. She then put it on his stomach, instructing him to hold it. "Is that a bit better?" she asked him.

"Yes," he said, surprised again. "Thank you." The idea was the same as magic heat, only now that he wasn't expending his own energy, the heat was able to soothe him. He fell asleep again and was woken by his family talking around him.

"Oh, my poor baby," said Zareanna, looking at the bruises on his arm. "What have they done to you?" She leaned down and kissed his cheek, then brushed his hair away from his face. He realised that he hadn't brushed his hair since coming here, and his head felt disgusting. He wondered whether he would be given a brush if he asked for one. But would he have the strength to use it? It was exhausting to even think about it.

"It's how they administer some of the medicine," said Lim, following his mother's gaze along the length of his arm. "Through a needle and straight into your blood."

"That's barbaric," gasped Zaareanna, hugging him to her. "No wonder Vada's father refused to ever come here. If I'd known they would do it to you-"

"It's fine," said Lim. He didn't want to think about it.

"Does it hurt?"

"Surprisingly little," he replied.

"That's good to hear," said his father, taking his usual seat in the corner, "How are you really doing, Limnos? We've been here for nearly one week and your treatment hasn't even started. Are you really doing all that you can to make yourself ready?"

"Yes, father," said Lim meekly. "I've put on half a stone apparently, which means that I am nearly there."

"Good," said Garrett. "And I do hope that this experience teaches you some better habits."

"Yes." Nodded Lim.

What better habits? he wondered, but didn't say anything.

Vaarem was strangely subdued. Lim longed to talk to his brother alone, but he didn't feel right asking his parents to leave. Zareanna was particularly anxious, and she had not let go of his hand since coming in that morning.

"What's wrong, Var?" Lim asked his brother, then lifted his other hand and took Vaarem's in it.

"Nothing." Smiled Vaarem. He had dark rings under his eyes, and he looked more wretched than Lim had ever seen him. "I'm just tired," said Vaarem, squeezing his hand. "I can't sleep, I'm so worried about you," he explained. "But other than that, I'm fine," he gave Lim a tired smile.

Lim felt like there was something that Vaarem wasn't telling him.

Why do we always avoid talking about everything? he thought, annoyed and anxious in equal measures. He desperately hoped that this attitude had not rubbed off on Vaarem, that his brother was *not* keeping things from him, the way that his parents always seemed to.

The family made small talk for the remainder of their visit. At lunchtime, they had to leave, while Lim drank his gruel, but were able to return in the afternoon.

Lim lay back with his eyes closed, holding Zareanna and Vaarem's hands, wishing that Vada was there. She'd still not replied, nor come to visit, and his parents and brother avoided talking about her. Fortunately, he was too tired to be too upset about it. For a while at least.

That evening, he received a letter. Marla and Jessa had been writing to him most days, and Dr Fantail, Fen, and a couple of other friends from Palinas occasionally, so he thought that it would be from one of them.

He was beyond excited when he saw that it was from Vada.

She'd finally written to him!

He tore the envelope open, careful not to rip the

letter in his excitement, then he began to read. *"Dear Lim, I am sorry that I haven't written earlier. I really am. I am not ignoring you, so please don't think that I am. I miss you so much that it hurts, and every time I try to write, my mind freezes up. I can't express my feelings in mere words. Please know that I think about you every day. I hope that you are being well looked after and that your treatment is a success. And even though the idea of seeing you, only to have to leave you again, is almost too painful to contemplate, I will come and see you in Sirrock. I promise. I wish you all the Blessings of the Fates. Your ever-loving sister, Vada."*

He read and re-read the letter so many times that he nearly memorised it by heart, then for the first time since being admitted, he took off the sensors and got out of bed, then went out of his room. He was so excited that he needed to tell someone, so he went looking for Eliza. He walked through the hallways, pushing his drip stand, the way that he'd seen her do, as he searched for her. His breathing soon started to come to him with difficulty, and several times he was grateful for the chance to lean on the drip stand as he caught his breath.

He saw some of the other patients as he walked past their rooms. Most of them were lying in their beds, but some were sitting up, either reading, writing, or chatting with others. These ones looked at him curiously as he passed, but didn't try to talk to him. Most of the patients were human, however he saw two dwarves, and out of one bed stuck out a wing, indicating a pixie. As far as he could tell, he was the only elf.

He walked up and down the hospital, stopping frequently to cough and catch his breath, until he finally found Eliza's room. It was very far from his own and he wondered at her frequent visits. Why did she come all the way to him? Was she merely curious to see an elf? Or did she feel somehow connected to him personally? He hoped that it was the latter.

Eliza was asleep in her bed, so he sank on the chair beside and waited for his breath to return, then he watched her as she'd previously watched him. She looked small and frail, and his heart went out to her. He'd never seen anyone sicker than himself and he wondered whether people felt the same pity for him as he did for her now. She seemed so vulnerable, and he felt an overwhelming urge to protect her.

He saw on her bedside table a necklace with a charm. The charm consisted of a circle with a spiral inside it, the symbol of The Faith, the same symbol that was carved above the doors in his house in Palinas.

The Faith was the main religion that was practiced by most members of the four races living on the continent of Jaanis. It was a worship of the forces of nature, which people called The Fates. Priests and priestesses of the Faith would lead daily prayers for those who cared to join in, as well as officiating major life events, such as namings, weddings, and funerals.

Lim and Vaarem had been given similar charms to

the one on Eliza's table when they'd been born, and Lim wondered now what had happened to them. His mother had even told him that when he'd been a baby, and everyone had been afraid that he was going to die, his parents had asked a priest to bless and heal him. It hadn't worked, of course. Or perhaps it had, because he was still alive.

He wondered about the charm on Eliza's table. Did she believe that The Fates could be influenced some- how? Lim wondered whether he thought that him- self. After all, the Council of Magic used the spiral as its symbol too, which had always made him wonder whether The Fates that the priests worked with were the same Fates of the Universe that mages used. If so, surely they could influence them?

He was contemplating all this when Eliza opened her eyes.

"Hi." He smiled at her.

"Hello, elf," she said, sitting up with a groan, her movements stiff. "What are you so happy about?"

"I got a letter from my sister." He beamed. In the past few days, he'd told her about his family, about Vaarem and Vada. Eliza found it difficult to believe that he and Vaarem were best friends, rather than hating each other. She apparently had a brother too, but they didn't get on.

"That's so great for you." She tried to smile, but she looked pained. He suddenly realised that his excite- ment may have seemed like he was gloating, rubbing it in that he had two siblings who loved and cared about him, while she had none.

"I'm sorry," he said. He was used to people's displeasure and disappointment always somehow being his fault.

"Don't be," she said. "I'm happy for you. Really."

"I like your necklace," he said, indicating the charm on the table, trying to change the subject.

She picked it up and held it between her fingers. "My father gave it to me," she said, sounding sad. "He doesn't like me much, you know."

"I'm sorry," he said. "My father doesn't like me much either."

"How can anyone not like you?"

"How can anyone not like *you*?" he countered, and meant it. How *could* anyone not like her? She was like a little lost kitten, all big eyes and innocence.

She smiled sadly, then continued, "My uncle is a Priest of the Fates. He blessed these charms for all his niblings, including me, infusing each one with good energy, saying that it would help and protect us. My father brought my one to me the last time he came to visit. Then he left me here. If the charm ever had any positive energy, it's long gone, so I don't wear it anymore."

"How long have you been here?" asked Lim curiously.

"Four, nearly five moons," she said with a dismissive shrug. "No one comes to visit me."

"Oh, that's awful," said Lim. He stood up, then

leaned down and put his arms around her. She felt like a baby bird in his embrace, all tiny, fragile bones. He held her lightly, careful not to crush her. Again, he wondered whether people felt like this when they tried to hug *him*. But surely, he'd never been quite this frail.

He held her for what seemed like a very long time, until she pushed him away. "Wait," she said, then got up off the bed and walked towards a chair that was standing under the window. She climbed the chair, opened the window, and leaned over the sill. For a moment Lim was scared that she was going to jump, but then he saw her thin body convulse and heard her throwing up into the garden outside. He watched in fascinated horror until she straightened up, wiped her mouth, and climbed down, looking at him with a defiant expression on her face. "Are you going to tell on me, elf?" she asked challengingly.

"What?"

"Are you going to tell that I threw up my disgusting gruel?" she asked, climbing back into her bed.

"No, of course not," he said. "But why did you do it?"

"Because I told you, I can't handle that stuff rotting inside me." She shuddered.

"It doesn't rot," said Lim but suddenly he felt rather ill himself, so he stopped talking. He held his hand over his mouth until the nausea had passed.

In a bid to change the subject he asked, "How did your uncle bless your charm?" He was genuinely interested. This seemed a lot like magic, and he was fascinated. He'd never heard of something like this being done. It reinforced the idea that the Fates that the Faith used and the Fates of the Universe of the mages were one and the same.

"I don't know." Eliza shrugged, clearly not finding the topic anywhere near as interesting as he did. "I think he just said some prayers and poured some energy into it."

"But it's worn off?"

"Yes," she said impatiently. "I could feel it when I first got it. And then when my father first brought it to me here. It felt all warm and." She paused, trying to find the words. "It had a sort of vibration to it. You know what I mean?"

"Yes," he said. "I know exactly what you mean. It sounds like simple magic. I could re-energise it for you," he offered.

"Really? You can do magic?"

"Yes. Well, sort of. I can do simple magic like this. I can't do big, powerful magic though," he said sadly. "I'm not strong enough. Big magic is very physically demanding, and I'm afraid I just don't have it in me. That's why I'm here," he added. "I am hoping that this new treatment will heal me once and for all, so that I will finally be strong enough to do what I want to do. Here," he said. "Give me your charm. I will energise it for you. Hopefully, it will make you feel a bit better."

"Okay," she said, and handed him the necklace.

He held the charm in the palm of his right hand and

with his left hand, he held Eliza's. He sat down on the edge of her bed and concentrated. In his experience, this type of magic worked best when done by a family member or a close friend of the recipient, as the magic user needed to be on the same energy wavelength as the person who would receive the object in question. However, Lim was a powerful empath, which meant that he could read and connect with almost anyone's energy. Furthermore, because he was working with someone else's force, he didn't get exhausted the way that he did when using his own energy.

He concentrated.

Eliza's energy was a puzzle to him. She was sweet and gentle, but there was a deep-rooted self-hatred within her that he didn't understand. He hoped to cure her somehow, to make her happy. He poured all of his love and good-wishes, as well as her own positive energies, into the charm.

Eventually, it was done. He opened his eyes, took his hand away from hers, and gave her the necklace.

"Here you go," he said. "Put it on."

She pulled the chain over her head and let the charm fall on to her thin chest. She looked up at him, an expression of wonder on her face. "Thank you," she said, putting her hand over the charm, feeling it. "Thank you," she said again. "I can feel it working. I can feel the warmth, and the love. Oh, elf, thank you so much." She threw her arms around his neck and hugged him to her. He hugged her back, feeling good at her happiness. She needed all the positivity that she could get, and he'd given some to her. He felt good about that.

"Wear it," he told her. "The more that you wear it, the more energy it will have. I think that it wore off last time because you took it off too much. Wear it and remember that you are loved and cherished."

He talked to Eliza for a while longer. She seemed genuinely happier with the charm, and he hoped that things would start going better for her now.

When he returned to his room and was weighed and checked over, he was informed that he was finally ready for the procedure the next day.

Because he'd put on enough weight, he was only given half the usual amount of gruel for supper.

"You'll be happy to know," said the nice nurse, whose name he finally found out was Ariella. She was a middle-aged human with blonde hair tied back in a bun, and she reminded him a little of his mother.

"Happy to know what?" asked Lim, feeling happier than he had since setting foot inside the hospital. He'd gotten a letter from Vada, he'd helped Eliza to feel better, and now he only had to drink half the usual amount of glug. What other thing was going to make him even happier?

"This is the last time that you will have to drink this formula for a while. After this, you will have water only overnight, then you will need to fast for several hours before the procedure tomorrow. When you're going through it, you won't be forced to eat if you're not hungry."

"Oh, okay," he said, smiling. This all sounded very good.

However, the more that he thought about the actual procedure, the more nervous he got.

"It will be fine," said Ariella, stroking his hair back from his brow and behind his pointed ear. "You'll see."

Nevertheless, he couldn't sleep.

Chapter 12

The Procedure

The next morning dawned bright and sunny. Lim looked out of his window and watched the light change, as the sun rose.

Dr Turnwall came in about an hour later to check him over and to do some measurements, and then Lim was left alone. He found that he was surprisingly hungry, but he knew that he would not have been able to swallow anything, even if he'd been allowed to, because he was so anxious.

His family came to visit, as they usually did, and they all sat around, subdued. Garrett was excited that Lim was finally going to be treated, but even he seemed nervous. Eventually, they were asked to leave.

As soon as he was left alone, Lim's heart started to race, and his breath caught in his throat. He started to cough. The nurses had taken the sensors off him that morning, so the machines didn't alarm anyone to come. Lim finally remembered the button that Ariella had asked him to push if he needed anything, so he pushed it and waited.

Ariella and Mela came running in, their faces creasing with concern when they saw him struggling to breathe.

"There, there," said Ariella, spraying the usual stuff into his mouth and down his throat. His breathing eased, but his heart was still racing. Ariella held his hand and squeezed his fingers, while Mela checked his pulse on his other hand, then made some notes in a pad she carried.

"Look at me, Lim," said Ariella, as Mela left the room.

Lim looked at her.

"Breathe," she said, which he thought was funny. He'd never been very good at breathing.

Ariella squeezed his fingers again and stroked his face with her other hand. "It's okay," she said gently. "Shhh."

Lim stared at her, still terrified.

"You're fine, dear," she said. "I know you're scared, but it's going to be okay, I promise. Now, take some deep breaths," she instructed.

He did as she asked and felt himself calming down a little.

"I can't give you a sedative, as it's too close to the procedure. We don't want it to interfere. So, just look at me and breathe, okay? And if you get anxious, just squeeze my hand, yes?"

"Okay." He nodded, his voice so soft that he barely heard himself.

Ariella was true to her word and stayed with him. Any time that Lim felt his anxiety rising, he would squeeze her hand like she'd told him to, and she would squeeze back reassuringly. After a while she started to talk to him, to distract him from what was coming.

"What's your home like?" she asked.

"I come from Palinas," he said. "It's a big elf city, but it's nowhere near as big as Sirrock City. There are lots of trees everywhere. The houses are built in them. The roads are made of earth and stone. There are no machines like here," he told her. The more he talked, the more he realised how much he missed his home.

"Well, you will be back there very soon," said Ariella.

At midday, Mela came back, wheeling a bed. Lim swallowed, knowing that the time had come.

Ariella squeezed his hand. "It's okay," she reassured him, as she took the drip out of his arm.

He was given a pair of loose white trousers to change into, as they needed the top half of his body to be exposed.

Lim shivered as he stepped back from behind the screen that the two nurses had put up beside his bed to give him some measure of privacy. He hugged his arms around himself as he stood and waited for instructions on what to do next.

"Lie down here." Mela pointed to the bed on wheels, "so that we can take you to the operating room."

Lim wanted to protest that he could walk, but then remembered how much he'd struggled when looking for Eliza the previous evening, so he lay down obediently. Mela covered him with a sheet then wheeled the bed out. Ariella found his hand again and held it as they made their way through the corridors. Mela rolled her eyes when she saw this, but she didn't comment.

Lim was almost delirious with terror. His heart was hammering in his chest, his palms were sweating, and his mouth was so dry that he could barely swallow. He had that feeling of falling, as he was wheeled into the operating room. The room was lit by many lamps, so that it was very bright and very hot. Lim felt his whole body begin to sweat under the sheet.

Dr Turnwall greeted him, then explained what he was doing as he hooked up several disks, similar to the sensors that Lim had been hooked up to before, to Lim's chest and temples. Lim was too terrified to take any of it in. When the doctor was done, Lim had three disks stuck to each side of his ribcage, and one on each temple.

Dr Turnwall then picked up a leather strap and placed it in Lim's mouth, like a gag. "This will be uncomfortable," he explained. "Bite down on this when you need to."

What? thought Lim, beginning to panic again.

Ariella was still, thankfully, holding his hand, so he

squeezed her fingers so hard that he feared he might break them. She didn't complain though, only stroking his sweat-beaded brow with her other hand and murmuring reassurances.

Finally, when everything was set up, Dr Turnwall placed a blindfold over Lim's eyes. Again, Lim's heart started to race with panic, and Ariella reassured him.

"It's to protect your eyes," she told him gently. "Don't be scared. Now, I will have to step away, as I can't touch you during the procedure, but I will be right here, don't you worry."

"Okay, Lim, here we go," said Dr Turnwall. "It will hurt, but it's only temporary. Now."

Lim felt an electric current go through him, and his body convulsed. He tried to scream but couldn't because of the gag in his mouth. The pain was like nothing that he'd ever experienced. It felt like a million hot needles stabbing him repeatedly. He felt, and smelt, his skin burning beneath the disks, and he felt like his blood was literally boiling. He gasped as the current ran through him again and again.

He felt a sharp pain in his chest and found himself unable to breathe. He coughed, which made the pain worse. This wasn't the same chest pain he'd suffered every day of his life. This was sharper and radiated all the way to his shoulders, and it increased with each attempt to draw breath. He tried to cry out, but his mouth didn't seem to be working. He heard the panicked voices of Dr Turnwall and the nurses. He couldn't make out the words, as his brain was too fuzzy, but he could read the tone. Something had gone wrong.

"Lim!" He heard someone say. He couldn't tell which one of the nurses was talking. "Lim! Stay with me." The blindfold was taken off and he blinked in the suddenly bright light, before his oxygen-starved brain shut down.

Vaarem had never been the type of twin that could feel his brother's physical pain. Although he felt guilty when he thought about it, he was very glad of this. He didn't think that he could have handled it. However, when he suddenly felt like something had slammed into him, and he staggered against his mother, he instinctively knew that something was very wrong.

"Vary?" asked his mother anxiously. "Are you okay?"

The family were sight-seeing in a museum, looking at all sorts of strange and wonderful sculptures made of glass and other delicate materials. Vaarem couldn't recall a single sculpture, and he didn't think that his parents could either. It was as if their bodies were going through the motions, while their minds were somewhere else.

"Something's wrong," said Vaarem, holding his hand to his head, as the world swam in front of his eyes. "We need to get to the hospital now! Something's happened to Lim."

"Surely not," said Garrett, his eyes wide. "Lim is in good hands. They assured us he was safe."

"No," said Vaarem, shaking his head. "This is

different. We must get there now. They're killing him."
He ran out of the room before his parents had time to respond.

"What happened?" called the museum attendant as he ran past her and out the door. "Is everything all right?"

He didn't have time to respond, but just ran out.

Vaarem ran down the street, barely looking where he was going. People stopped what they were doing and stared at him, but he hardly noticed and didn't care. He heard his parents calling out behind him.

"Vaarem! Stop! Wait for us."

But he couldn't wait. They knew where he was going, and they would catch up in their own time.

He ran across the street, in front of one of the horseless carriages.

"Oy!" called the driver and rang a bell.

A little further down, a horse was startled by the commotion and reared on its hind legs, jerking its carriage. Vaarem barely gave them a second glance and ran ahead heedlessly. "Sorry," he called behind him.

He had to stop on a corner to catch his breath. He had a stitch in his side, but he ignored this, holding his hand to his ribs, and continued running. When he reached the hospital, he took the front steps three at a time and ran into the foyer.

"Where is my brother?" he demanded, panting, looking at the startled nurse behind the desk. The hospital all seemed to be in a panic and there was a commotion everywhere, with people running in all directions, calling frantically to each other.

"He is in the operating room," said the nurse, looking up at him with wide eyes. "There was a complication with his procedure, but the doctor is trying to stabilise him."

"What?" asked Vaarem. "What does that even mean? I need to see him. Now."

"You can't see him. The doctor is working on him. You can come back and see him later."

Vaarem had heard enough. He ran past the reception desk, and into the hospital, as the nurse called after him. He ran into Lim's room, only to find it empty. He stopped in the doorway, then looked up and down the corridor, picking a direction at random and running that way. He opened every door that he found, but his brother was not behind any of them. Eventually, a couple of nurses and orderlies caught up with him and escorted him back into the front foyer.

He leaned against the wall, and slid down, sinking down to the floor, his head in his hands.

A few moments later, his parents ran in.

"Vaarem," said his mother anxiously, crouching down in front of him and taking his hands in hers. "What happened?"

He looked up at her, feeling despondent. "I don't know," he said helplessly. "They won't let me see him."

His parents looked down at him, then at each other, their expressions shocked and helpless.

Lim woke up in his room. His mouth was horribly dry, and every fibre of his body was crying out in pain. He felt like he was still being burned and shocked.

"Lim?" Eliza's voice asked anxiously.

He opened his eyes and looked at her. It was the first time that she'd called him by his name.

As his consciousness returned, he looked around. He was lying propped up, so that he could breathe. His body was covered in a sheet. He risked a look beneath it, noticing that the drip was again in his arm.

He gasped when he saw himself.

His chest was burned and scarred where the disks had been attached to his skin, and beneath them there were two tubes sticking out of either side of his ribcage. He couldn't tell what they were attached to or where they went, but he could see blood and pus, and who knew what else, dripping through them. He shuddered, and the movement sent waves of pain running through his body.

"Aaah," he said, with another shudder. "What happened to me?"

Eliza took his hand in hers. A jolt of static electricity coursed between them, making Lim jump and cry out again.

"They did it wrong," explained Eliza. "They miscalculated something, and your lungs collapsed. But they managed to fix them. You nearly died."

"Oh," said Lim, trying to take this all in. It seemed so surreal.

"Do you want some water?" asked Eliza, picking up

a glass, and pouring in some water from the jug on the bedside table."

"Yes, please," he managed to say. His mouth and throat were so dry.

He tried to take the glass from her, but his hand shook too much.

"Here, let me," she said, bringing the glass to his lips and tipping it slightly.

Lim drank gratefully, starting to feel better after a couple of sips. "Thank you," he said, and she put the glass down.

"I was scared for you," said Eliza. "I am so glad that you didn't die. You must not let them try it again."

Lim promised Eliza that he had no intention of allowing anyone to try the procedure on him again. However, this turned out to not be so straightforward.

Dr Turnwall came to see him and explained what happened. "It looks like your elf energy is more powerful than I accounted for. However, now that I know what went wrong, I can adjust for this. We will let your lungs heal for a few days, then we can attempt it again."

"I don't want you to attempt it again," said Lim.

He was feeling weaker than ever. He couldn't do anything for himself because his hands shook so much, and every time he touched anything he would get an electric shock from the residual static electricity in his body. Dr Turnwall explained that all of these things were temporary and that they would pass.

Lim's family were not keen on Dr Turnwall attempting the procedure again either.

"He nearly died," said Zareanna, holding Lim's shaking hand between both of hers.

Garrett however, was of a different opinion. "If I counted all of the times that Limnos has nearly died, I would run out of fingers and toes. Isn't the whole point of this exercise to stop that happening?"

Zareanna couldn't argue with that, however she was still reluctant.

Dr Turnwall had another reason. "You consented to one treatment," he told Lim, but addressed his whole family. "We had to abort it part of the way through, so technically you are obliged to stay until at least one round is completed. Besides, this is an experimental procedure, and the consequences of leaving it unfinished are unknown. It would be safer to attempt it again and finish."

In the end, Dr Turnwall won, and Lim consented to stay. He really didn't want to, but he was scared of the consequences of leaving the procedure unfinished. He decided that this scared him more than going through it again.

He was allowed to rest and recuperate for three days. During this time, he was given regular sedatives to help him sleep. He couldn't feed himself, so the nurses brought back the hated tube. Fortunately, he was only ever given half the previous volume of the gruel, so he wasn't too uncomfortable afterwards.

Jessa and Marla wrote to him, as did Fen, but he was too sick to reply to any of them. His hand still shook when he held a quill and his brain was too foggy to think, so Vaarem wrote to them all on his behalf.

On the evening of the second day after the failed procedure, the tubes in his chest were taken out, which allowed him to at least sit up and lie down more comfortably. His sedatives were reduced, so that they would not interfere with the procedure the next day.

Lim was hugely anxious, but he was also immensely tired. Even though he couldn't fall into a comfortable sleep, he did keep dozing off, before waking up again. This meant that he didn't have a chance to freak out too much, which was a small blessing.

The next morning, he was weighed and measured as usual, then he was left alone for several hours while Dr Turnwall got the operating room equipment ready.

Lim's family sat with him and tried to make conversation. Vaarem tried to tell him about some of the sights they'd seen in Sirrock City, but it was clear that his heart and mind were not in it. At one point, Lim stopped him to say, "Yes, I know, you said that three times," before laughing nervously.

"Sorry." Vaarem tried to smile. "I am so scatter-brained. How many hours did you sleep last night?"

Lim thought about this. "Perhaps a total of two hours. In five to ten minute naps. What about you?"

"Same," said Vaarem. "It's not very restful, is it?"

"No, it isn't," agreed Lim. "At least I don't have to do anything," he said, trying to force a laugh again.

In the early afternoon, Nurse Ariella came in and told Lim's family that they had to leave. They did so reluctantly, promising Lim that they would be waiting in the foyer. After the last time, they didn't want to leave the premises.

Vaarem squeezed Lim's hand, then gave him a big hug. "Hang in there," he said. "I will be praying to the Fates that it all goes well this time." He then kissed Lim on the cheek, before hugging him again, until Zareanna told him to stop, so that she could have a turn. Vaarem reluctantly let his brother go, but not before whispering in his ear, "Don't you dare die."

Zareanna then leaned over and kissed Lim's face and head so many times that he started to feel em-barrassed, even though there really was no reason to, as Nurse Ariella had momentarily left the room. "Be safe, my darling," said Zaareanna, hugging Lim so hard that he had to tell her to stop. "Good luck, Limmy," she said, kissing his forehead again. She had tears in her eyes.

Garrett merely shook Lim's hand, saying, "Good luck, Lim. Don't let us down."

And then they were gone.

Nurse Ariella came back with the bed on wheels and helped Lim to get on to it. He hadn't realised just how weak he'd become, and he wondered whether this would be a problem. Last time, they'd delayed the procedure for a whole week, until he was strong enough. But, he'd been examined and measured so many times that he figured they knew what they were doing and would have told him if something was wrong, or at least delayed the procedure once more.

Again, the sensor-disks were placed on his chest, beside the marks left by the previous ones.

"I am going to have to adjust for the placement," said Dr Turnwall, then adjusted one of the dials on the machine.

Again, Lim's arms and legs were strapped down, and the gag was put in his mouth. Nurse Ariella put the blindfold over his eyes, then stroked his cheek briefly. "Here we go," she said softly. "Good luck."

The first jolt was not as intense as the previous time, however it was still extremely painful. Lim bit down on the gag and tried not to scream. The second jolt was stronger, and he felt his whole body convulse, his wrists and ankles pulling at the bindings. The third jolt hit him like a runaway carriage and knocked all the wind and breath out of him, so that he blacked out.

Lim woke up in agony. His chest felt like he'd been run over by a herd of unicorns, and his wrists and ankles stung where he'd been strapped down to the operating bed.

He looked around and saw that he now had a drip coming out of both arms. His mother sat on a chair beside the bed. Her eyes were red and puffy, her face streaked with tears. On his other side sat Vaarem, looking as pale as the bed sheets. His father sat on a chair in the opposite corner of the room, his arms and legs crossed, looking furious.

Without anyone saying anything, Lim immediately knew that something had gone wrong again.

He longed to lift the sheet that was covering him, to look down at his body, but his hands and arms shook too much when he tried to move them. Vaarem saw him wriggling his fingers and looked up into his face. The relief in his eyes was so obvious that it made Lim want to cry. It seemed that something had gone very wrong indeed.

"Lim," said his brother, taking his hand. "He's awake." He looked at his mother.

"Oh, thank the Fates," said Zareanna. She leaned over and went to put her arms around him, but stopped, as if scared that she might hurt him. Instead, she ran her finger over his cheekbone, then kissed his forehead. "Oh, my poor Limmy," she said, her voice choked. "My poor darling."

"What happened?" Lim managed to ask, his voice weak and croaky.

"They fucked up again," Vaarem spat out the words. "That's what happened."

"Vaarem, there's no need for that kind of language," said his father with a shake of his head. His whole body looked tense.

Vaarem glared at him sullenly from beneath his hair. Lim realised that his brother was looking dishevelled, and not like his usual well-groomed self.

"There was another complication, darling," said Zareanna gently. "Your heart stopped in the middle of the procedure, apparently. It was completely un-expected. But they managed to re-start it, thank the Fates, and you are going to be fine." She took his hand, the one that Vaarem wasn't holding, and kissed his fingers.

"So, it didn't work," said Lim, with a sigh.

"We don't know that," said Garrett. "They are going to let you recover, while they work out what went wrong, and then they are going to attempt it again."

"No." Lim shook his head, a moan escaping his lips. "I don't want to."

"You have to," said Garrett. "You signed up for one treatment, and you are going to get one treatment from start to finish. Besides, you heard the doctor the first time, it would be more dangerous to leave it unfinished. Please, Lim, you have to try."

As the afternoon wore on, Lim found out a bit more about the extent of the procedure. It had, apparently, been going well, when his heart had inadvertently stopped. No one could work out why. To re-start it again, the doctor and the nurses had worked on him for several minutes and had ended up breaking most of his ribs. The second drip was a strong painkiller, which would be taken out when the worst of his injuries were healed. His lungs had, fortunately, not collapsed again, which was the one bit of good news that had come out of the procedure. It seemed that they'd successfully fixed *that* problem, so there was no danger of it happening again.

Later that night, when his family had gone, Lim found himself feeling more despondent than ever. He was feeling worse than he ever had in his life. He'd never broken a bone before, and the mere idea freaked him out.

After a while, he stopped feeling sorry for himself and began to feel angry. He'd travelled halfway across the continent to be healed. The treatment had been meant to take up to one week. Yet here he was, nearly two weeks in, and instead of healing him, they had gagged and bound him, shocked him with electricity, stabbed him with needles, poking painful holes in his skin, and now they had broken his bones! The worst thing was that now he *couldn't* leave. He'd walked in here, not very well, but he'd walked in like a normal person. Now he couldn't even sit up, let alone stand or walk.

I'm going to die in here, he thought desperately, and the thought filled him with such anxiety that the machines that he was once again attached to went off.

A nurse, whom he'd never met before entered. She was younger than Mela and Ariella, with dark hair and dark eyes. He noticed that she moved a little awkwardly, and when she got closer, he could hear one of her feet making a strange clicking sound against the floor. When he looked down, he could see that under her long skirt, one of her legs was made of metal.

He shuddered. He didn't want to get any part of his body replaced with an artificial material. He would rather be sick and whole than healed but broken.

"There, there," said the nurse. She had a kind voice. "It's okay, little elf. Here you go." Instead of the usual needle, she gave him something to drink.

He couldn't hold the cup, as his hands were still shaking, so she held it to his lips. It tasted bitter, so after a few sips he tried to turn away, but she held his head, albeit gently, in place.

"No, dear," she said. "Drink it all. It'll do you good."

He had another sip. She didn't rush him, but she held the cup to his lips until he'd drunk it all.

"There you go," she said, patting his shoulder, as she put the cup down on the bedside table. "You're okay. Just breathe."

"I'm not good at breathing," he said with a bitter laugh, which hurt his ribs. "And it really hurts because my ribs are broken."

"I know," she said kindly. "I know. But just take it easy. Concentrate on taking slow breaths. There's a good boy."

Lim did as she asked and began to feel a little calmer.

"You gave us all a big scare today," said the nurse after a while.

"Really?" asked Lim, surprised. Did the whole hospital know his business? Not that it mattered.

"Yes," she said. "We thought you were going to die

for sure. But you pulled through. You are surprisingly resilient for someone so otherwise frail."

Lim smiled cynically. "That's me," he said. "Resilient. Or stubborn maybe. I promised my brother that I wouldn't die, so I didn't."

She smiled at that, then asked, "You and your brother are identical twins?"

"Yes," said Lim. "Although you probably can't tell right now," he added bitterly.

"Oh, you can tell," she said. "We can all tell. And it may give us an insight into finding out how to treat you."

"Huh?"

"Dr. Turnwall was saying that we can observe your brother to get a good idea of how your body functions."

"I wouldn't be so sure," said Lim cynically. "His body actually works the way it's supposed to."

"Exactly," said the nurse. "If we could see how his body works, we can see how yours is supposed to work."

"Hmmm," said Lim thoughtfully. "Maybe."

"Yes," she said. "Dr. Turnwall will talk to you and your family about it tomorrow. One way or another, he is determined that when you walk out of here, you will be healed."

The next morning, when Lim's family were, as usual, sitting around his bedside, trying to make awkward conversation, Dr Turnwall came in. The morning light from the window shone on his metal headplate, giving him a strange kind of halo from certain angles. Lim couldn't decide if this made him look more or less sinister.

"I have to say that I am stumped," the doctor told Lim. "And I don't often say this. I cannot for the life of me work out what went wrong yesterday. However, I have a proposition which may shed some light on how to proceed with your treatment."

Lim remembered what the nurse had said the previous night about Vaarem, and his blood ran cold. Last night, it had all seemed so surreal and far away. But in the clear light of day, he could tell that the doctor was serious.

Before Lim could start voicing any objections, Dr Turnwall turned to Vaarem and said, "You are Lim's identical twin, yes?"

"Yes." Nodded Vaarem.

"I would like to do some tests and measurements on you," said Dr Turnwall.

"No," said Lim, but no one was looking at him, everyone's attention focused on his brother. Lim could tell that his parents were both shocked at the idea.

"Yes," said Vaarem. "If it will help my brother, then yes. I am happy to let you do whatever tests you need on me."

"No," said Lim again. "Var, you don't know what you're saying."

"Yes, I do," said Vaarem. "Having tests done can't possibly be worse than what you've been going through. And if it will help you, I would do anything. So, yes," he turned to the doctor. "Where do I sign?"

Their parents were not exactly pleased with the idea, but they were all running out of options. They had planned for a maximum stay of two weeks in Sirrock City, thinking that the whole treatment couldn't possibly take that long. But here they were, one week and four days in, with no end in sight. If Vaarem could help in any way, surely it was worth it.

Chapter 13

Twins

Vaarem was checked in that very day.

The nurses wheeled in a second bed into Lim's room, so that the twins could be together. This was at least one good thing, as far as Lim was concerned.

Vaarem went behind the screen to change into a hospital gown, then came out, twirling like a ballroom dancer and leaping around. Lim started to laugh. He'd missed Vaarem's funny antics so much. Today was the first time since they'd arrived that Vaarem was acting like his usual self.

Garrett and Zareanna then left for a few hours. They needed to have something to eat, they said, as well as wanting to spend some time alone. Lim wondered whether they meant alone alone, or alone together. They were both constantly tense, so Lim hoped that whatever they chose to do would make them both feel better.

Vaarem sat in his bed and looked around, as if gauging the feel of the place.

"It is not a luxury inn," he remarked, "but it will do. What's the service like?"

"Oh, the service is wonderful," said Lim with a laugh that made his ribs hurt, but he didn't care. Having Vaarem with him was the best thing that had happened since they'd arrived in this wretched city. "They feed you thick gluggy gruel three times a day," he continued, "and then for dessert, you get a needle in your arm."

"Ugh," said Vaarem. "Are there no other options?"

"Oh, but there are," said Lim. "They also give you a lovely selection of potions to drink, each one more horrid than the last." He laughed, then added, "Seriously, it's so gross. I've had a constant stomachache since I got here. I'm afraid that when I leave, I'm going to have more problems than I had coming in."

"Don't say that," said Vaarem anxiously. "They're experts here. They know what they're doing."

"Everything I have experienced since coming here leads me to the opposite conclusion. But who knows. Perhaps studying you *will* help them work out how to fix me. I wonder why nobody ever thought of it before."

"Because humans think differently," said Vaarem.

Their lunch was brought in soon after.

Lim was most disappointed to see that since Vaarem wasn't sick, he was given normal human food to eat, while he himself was again given the horrid formula.

"That's not fair," he told the nurse with the metal leg, whose name he didn't yet know. "Why doesn't he have to drink this?"

"Because your brother doesn't need to keep his weight up," she replied matter-of-factly. "And because even after everything, he still weighs nearly a stone more than you do. So, drink your formula, Lim, because you don't want to be force-fed again, do you?"

"No," admitted Lim grumpily, picking up the jug and looking over at Vaarem's filled bread and fruit enviously.

"Here," said Vaarem, ripping the bread in half when the nurse had left, and giving Lim a portion.

"Thank you," said Lim, taking the piece of filled bread and bringing it to his mouth. His hands were still shaking, but not as badly as the previous day, so he could at least feed himself without too much hassle. He savoured the flavours and textures of the bread and the filling. He'd never cared much for food, but after ten days of nothing but tasteless gruel, the bread with meat and relish was very welcome.

He lay back when he finished it, looking at the jug of gruel with a sigh. He would wait for a short while before attempting to drink it but drink it he would.

After several minutes, he decided that he better start on the gruel.

He picked up the jug and had a sip, grimacing as always at the lack of taste and the gluggy texture.

"Do you want to try?" he asked, holding the jug out to Vaarem.

"Not really," said Vaarem, "but I am morbidly fascinated." He took the jug from Lim's shaking hand and brought it to his mouth, taking a tentative sip. He swallowed it, then considered the experience.

"Well, it is not a taste sensation," he declared. "And the texture reminds me of mud mixed with pigswell. So, overall, I wouldn't recommend this eatery. But seriously," he added, "it's tolerable. Here." He handed it back to Lim.

"Don't let them catch you holding my formula." Laughed Laarem, taking the jug and taking another gulp. It was very filling and after the bread and meat, he had even less desire to drink it than ever, but nevertheless he forced himself to finish it. He didn't want Vaarem to see them using the tube and funnel, for fear that his brother would jump to his defence and end up assaulting someone.

"Vada wrote me a letter," said Lim, after both brothers had finished their meals.

Vaarem's eyes lit up. "Really?" He sounded pleasantly surprised.

"Yeah," said Lim, smiling. "She said that she will come and see me."

"Okay." Nodded Vaarem, smiling thinly.

"What?" asked Lim.

"Nothing." Vaarem shook his head. "Mother and

Father are just so tense. I heard them talking about Vada and Malkim. But," he added quickly, "they seem to miss Vada too. I've never heard them talk about her before."

They were silent for a moment. Lim recalled his mother's comment on their way to Sirrock after his father had blamed him for the carriage wheel breaking. "*He's not Malkim.*"

"Var?" asked Lim after a moment. "Do you know how Malkim died?"

Vaarem shrugged. "I don't know. I can't say I've ever given it much thought, but I kind of always assumed that Father killed him."

"What?" Lim sat up, aghast. His breath caught and he coughed, but managed to stop after a moment.

Vaarem shook his head and chuckled. "Not like that, but in a duel over mother's hand or something." He shrugged. "It would explain why they never talk about him. Why?" He looked at Lim curiously. "Why are you suddenly so obsessed with Vada's father?"

Lim shrugged, then closed his eyes for a moment as he considered this. "Vada told me that he used to get sick," he said carefully, "and then, when Mother compared me to him." He trailed off. "What if his death had nothing to do with Mother and Father? What if he just got sick and died because of that? What if?" He swallowed, "What if that happens to me?"

Vaarem sat up on his bed and looked at Lim with a thoughtful frown on his face. "Malkim was old," he began.

"No, he wasn't," said Lim. "He was not yet fifty."

"That's old for a human."

"I don't think so." Lim shook his head. "Not old enough to die, anyway."

Vaarem looked at him for a few moments, then said, "I don't think that that's what happened. If he'd been sick and died, wouldn't Mother have mourned him for longer? And if Malkim had been making himself sick, like Father accuses you of doing, wouldn't Father have seen that as a good thing? As in, if Malkim essentially killed himself, then that would work out well for Father, right? And he wouldn't have hated him so much that no one is allowed to mention him. But like I said, I don't think that that's what happened. I think it was a duel over Mother's hand."

Lim shrugged. He didn't agree with his brother's assessment, but there was no point in discussing it because he had no better ideas. In any case, even if Vada's father had died due to illness, he'd been human, thus weaker than an elf. Surely Lim, weak as he was, was still more resilient than the average human?

Yet, his mother's comment still haunted him. *He's not Malkim.* Why would she say that? Why would his father think that? When he'd been younger, Lim had once wondered whether Malkim may have been his real father, however he'd gotten that notion out of his head almost straight away. For a start, he was an elf. If he and Vada had had the same biological father he would have been as human as her. Plus Lim looked like Garrett. Finally, after he'd done the maths, he'd calculated that there was more than a whole turn between Malkim's death and the birth of him and Vaarem. While elven gestation could sometimes be as long as thirteen moons, there were more than fifteen moons between the day that Malkim had died and the days that Vaarem and then Lim had been born.

So, why had his mother said it? *"He's not Malkim."* Of course I'm not, thought Lim anxiously.

He needed to ask Vada when she came down.

Lim soon started to feel tired and sleepy again. The formula had that effect on him, so he found himself nodding off. Vaarem started to tell him jokes, but Lim was too tired to listen.

"Oy," said Vaarem. "Am I boring you over here or something?"

"No," said Lim, "quite the opposite, your voice is soothing me to sleep." He opened his eyes and looked at his brother. "No, really, this always happens. This stuff always makes me sleepy. I think because it's so difficult to digest. And the painkillers probably don't help. So, I'm sorry if I am not going to be very good company."

"You're always good company," Vaarem assured him. "And to be honest, I haven't been sleeping that well myself recently. I really miss having you around. And Mother and Father have been so strange, it's making me nervous. I keep expecting them to either start yelling, or crying. So, maybe we should take advantage of the calm and both take a nap now."

"Sure," said Lim, closing his eyes again.

Vaarem got off his bed and pushed it closer to Lim's, so that the beds were about two feet apart. He climbed back in and reached over to take his brother's hand. "Sweet dreams," he told Lim. "Let's hope we get some good news later this afternoon."

Vaarem woke up about an hour later. He was feeling surprisingly well-rested and calm. Being with Lim, and away from his parents' constant tension had done him good. He'd started a letter to Marla and Jessa the previous day, at Lim's request. The letter read,

"Dear Jessa and Marla, I am writing to you again, because Lim is still too sick to do it himself. His hand shakes when he holds a quill and he is too tired to think of the right words. Or so he says. I am really worried actually. It seems that everything they try here just makes Lim feel worse. Send us your good wishes because I don't know what else to do." He was now thinking of getting up to add something more positive. Perhaps that he was now helping.

He opened his eyes to find that his parents had returned. Zareanna was sitting on the chair near Lim's bed, and she had an extremely tender and loving expression on her face. Vaarem realised that he and Lim were still holding hands and that this was what she was looking at. Apparently, they'd slept like this, holding each other's hands for the first eight or so turns of their lives, until they'd started sleeping in separate beds. But sometimes, if their beds were close, they would still do it, often unconsciously.

Vaarem let go of his brother's hand and sat up. His mother looked at him and smiled. Even his father, who was sitting in his usual spot in the corner, had a tender smile on his face.

"Oh, you two boys are so sweet," said Zareanna. She smiled at Vaarem, then stroked Lim's sleeping face. "You always look after each other. It is so beautiful to see."

Vaarem smiled. It felt good to finally be noticed, and to do something to assist. He hoped to all the Fates that his input would finally allow Lim to get better, and that they could then put this whole nightmare behind them.

"Thank you for doing this for your brother, Vaarem." His father came over and told him. "The sooner that we leave here, the better. This is no place for elves."

Vaarem wondered whether his father meant the hospital, or Sirrock City in general. In either case, he was right.

Lim woke up a short while later, and the family spent the afternoon together, until his parents had to leave again. With Vaarem here, Lim was feeling a lot better. Not physically. Physically, he was still in pain and felt generally ill, but his brother's presence made it all bearable, the way that it always did. So much so that he wanted to try writing to Jessa and Marla again, as well as to Fen and other friends in Palinas, and possibly also to Vada, as he'd not replied to her note. However, his hands still shook too much, and he ended up spilling the ink all over his hospital gown and sheets.

"Trust you to try and colour your hospital bed black." Laughed Vaarem.

Lim laughed too, as Vaarem got up out of his bed and helped him to clean up the spillage.

"I don't know," said Lim, examining the spillage of ink, "I rather like it. What do you think would happen if I dyed my sheets black at home?"

"I think," said Vaarem, in a mock-serious tone, "that Mother would literally kill you, which would make this whole trip a complete waste."

"Oh yes," said Lim, remembering the time that he'd forgotten to wash out the pot after dyeing his clothes black. His mother had used it, and her laundry had all come out grey. It had been the only time in his life when she'd truly been angry with him. While Garrett always blamed Lim for everything that went wrong, his wife was the opposite and whenever the twins had done anything bad, it was always Vaarem that she'd told off. Apart from that one time. That time she'd known that Lim was to blame, and she'd been furious. She'd not only made him clean the pot out properly, but she'd also made him re-wash all the laundry until all the dye was out. He'd had to wash everything three times, as the dye had been strong, and he had been exhausted by the end of it. If he'd really been the type of person to play up his illness for attention and sympathy, like his father constantly accused him of doing, he would have done it then. But he hadn't. He remembered the incident now and laughed. He missed home. He missed his normal everyday life that he'd complained about before.

When I get home, I am not going to take anything for granted, he promised himself.

For some reason, he didn't imagine himself healed. He realised that even now he was not hopeful about the treatment working.

That night, after Vaarem had spent the day being submitted to various tests, Lim held his hand again as they slept, and both he and Vaarem woke up feeling well-rested the next morning. Vaarem was measured and tested again throughout the day. Lim was anxious for him, as were their parents, but after each round of tests Vaarem returned with a smile on his face and a spring in his step. Whatever they were doing to him obviously didn't put him out too much. Lim, meanwhile, was still being given different types of potions. Most of them either made him feel nauseated (although luckily he didn't throw up again), or gave him a stomach ache, or made him itch, or most frequently, a combination of all three. He didn't complain though. There was no point. He knew that they were all clutching at straws.

Vaarem was discharged the next morning, the doctors having completed their tests. Lim was sad to see his brother go. He was still too weak for the doctors to do the procedure again, and in any case, they had to wait at least forty-eight hours for all of the potions to leave his system before they could even attempt it. Lim knew that he had at least three more days here before he would get the procedure done again. And no one knew what would happen when it was done because it was experimental. Even if it worked it was most likely that Lim would still have to stay for some time afterwards.

After Vaarem had left with their parents, Lim realised that he hadn't seen Eliza in a couple of days. He'd been wanting to introduce his brother to his new friend, and he felt a little bad that when Vaarem had been here, he'd forgotten all about her. That afternoon, after the painkiller drip and the sensors were removed and he could walk around again (albeit still very painfully), he went to visit her.

She was lying in her bed, with sensors attached to her chest like they had been to him until recently.

"What happened to you?" he asked her, sitting down on the chair next to her bed.

She looked at him and curved her lips up into a smile that didn't quite reach her eyes. "I collapsed," she said matter-of-factly, as if this type of thing happened to her all the time.

Lim frowned. He had collapsed himself on more occasions than he cared to think about, but he'd never been so blasé about it. "How?" he asked. "Why?"

She shrugged her thin shoulders. "I was leaning over the sill like I do, you know, to smell the flowers." She laughed. Lim didn't. "And when I straightened up, I suddenly felt really strange and fell off the chair. I broke my arm."

Her left forearm was bandaged from her hand to her elbow. "Ouch," he said, wincing at the sight. "I'm sorry to hear that. I'm sorry that I didn't visit. My last procedure didn't work. I don't know if you heard. They broke my ribs."

Her eyes widened at that. "I told you not to do it."

Lim sighed. "I didn't have much of a choice. Anyway, I just wanted to say hi. I've missed you."

She smiled at that and took his hand in her right, un-injured hand. "Really?" Her eyes filled with tears. "No one's ever missed me before."

"I'm sure they do," said Lim. "Sometimes people just find it too painful," he explained, remembering Vada's note. He hoped that she would come, as he'd not heard from her again.

Chapter 14

Vada Blackwell

The procedure was scheduled for three days after Vaarem's discharge. The doctors needed this time to make the necessary preparations after studying Vaarem's data, and Lim needed this time to recover from the previous attempt, and for all of the experimental potions to leave his system, in case they had been part of the problem before. He was given nothing but gruel and water to eat and drink, but he did his best to remain positive. Finally, there was an end in sight.

He visited Eliza daily, as she was still not able to leave her bed. She gave him a book on the second day.

"Here," she told him. "My uncle gave it to me for my last birthday. I've never read it, but it might interest you."

Lim looked at the book. It was a medium-sized

book with a green cover. On the front was the Spiral of the Faith. The title was *"How to Utilise the Fates for Love and Success"*. It was a cheesy title, but looking inside, Lim could see that it spoke a lot about using magic, so he took the book gratefully.

He found out that The Worship of the Fates was something that he'd been unconsciously doing all his life. He remembered the prayers that he'd said, concentrating his will on making something happen, such as passing a test at school, or having Vaarem do well in a tournament. Each time, the thing he'd wished for had come to pass. As a child, he'd imagined the Fates as anthropomorphic spirits, like the goddesses of the Remmet tribes of the northern deserts, that took pity on him and granted his wishes, but now he wondered, and the more he read, the more he realised how magic played into it. And this type of magic didn't leave as much strain on the body as traditional magic, because it didn't involve the magic user expending their own energy, but rather manipulating the energy around them. It was intriguing, and Lim spent most of his time reading, to the point that both his family, and Eliza, accused him of making them feel neglected. Lim would then put the book down and talk to his family or friend, but his mind was still on the book and its contents.

The day before the procedure, Eliza came into his room in the morning.

"Hey," said Lim brightly, glad to see her up and

about. She still looked as thin and ill as ever, but there was something more alive about her eyes.

"Hey, elf," she said. "Did you hear the news?"

"No." Lim sat up. Each day his ribs hurt less and less. He could almost move normally now. "What news?"

"Vada Blackwell is in the hospital. She must be visiting a patient."

"What?" asked Lim, sitting up straighter.

"Vada Blackwell," explained Eliza. "She's a mage, and she lives in the abandoned castle on the top of the mountain above the city. They say that she rides dragons, and she is very powerful and dangerous."

"I know who Vada Blackwell is," said Lim, trying not to let his impatience show. She was finally here! "She's my sister".

"How can that be?" Frowned Eliza. "She's not an elf."

"She's my half-sister," Lim explained. "Our mother is a half-elf. Her father was human, while my father's an elf. Where is she? Who told you she was here?"

"I heard the nurses talking," said Eliza. "Is she *really* your sister?"

"Yes," said Lim, getting out of the bed carefully, as he was still fragile. "Come on, I'll introduce you to her."

"Oh," said Eliza, suddenly shy and reluctant.

"It's fine," said Lim. It would be better if he and Vada caught up alone first. He hadn't seen her in so long. "I will go and find her," said Lim, "and I will come and see you after. Or, you can stay here," he said, seeing that she'd made no move to stand up.

"Thank you," she said softly.

Lim smiled at her, then walked out of the room slowly, heading towards the front foyer.

He was halfway there when he saw her walking down the corridor towards him. "Vada!" he called, waving to her, using his other hand to hold on to the wall to keep his balance.

At the sound of his voice, she turned towards him. Her eyes widened and her face broke into a smile as she recognised him. "Lim!" she cried, then ran to him and threw her arms around him.

"Ow," he said, hugging her back. "Be careful. I've still got broken ribs."

"What?" asked Vada, shocked. "Why? What happened?"

"Long story," said Lim, then put his arms around her again.

"Oh, Limmy," she said. "Look at you, all grown up. When did you get so tall?" she asked, her eyes wide with shock. He was shocked himself to realise that he stood a couple of inches taller than her. It had been so long. "Probably about six or seven seasons ago," he said, leading her back into his room.

"You're looking well," she said as they walked.

Lim frowned and raised his eyebrow questioningly.

"No, I mean it," she insisted. "I don't know what I was expecting, but..."

They walked into Lim's room. Which was empty. Eliza must have left. Lim sat down on the bed and Vada sat on the chair beside, the one that Vaarem usually occupied.

They looked at each other, studied each other's faces, so familiar and yet so different. Vada had been gone for sixteen turns; more than half his life. Her face was thinner than it had been, her eyes more shadowed, her black hair longer. But her expression was still the same; smart and determined, with a hint of humour that she reserved only for him. It was all still there.

"I've missed you so much," he told her. "You have no idea."

"I really wish that you wouldn't," she replied. "I got all your letters. I'm sorry that I haven't replied. I tried many times. I think about you often, but when it comes to writing, I never know what to say." She sounded guarded, but it was okay. Lim knew how difficult she found it to open up to people, to be vulnerable. Just the fact that she was here meant everything.

"It's okay," he said. "You're here now, and that's all that matters."

They made slightly awkward small talk for a few minutes, then as they became more comfortable, they started to talk more freely, like they had when they'd been younger. Lim found himself forgetting about his physical discomfort, and he poured his heart out to Vada, like he'd done in the past. He told her how scared he was, and how lonely, about how this whole trip seemed to be destined for failure. Vada listened, interested. She offered advice when she could, and simply listened when she couldn't. She answered his questions about her life but volunteered little information herself.

"I spend most of my time studying magic up in the castle. Some of our old servants are still there but I don't talk to them any more than I have to."

At one point, Vada saw the book on his bedside table. "I didn't know you were religious," she remarked.

"Neither did I," said Lim. "But it's actually just a different way to channel magic. Like, instead of channelling your own energy, you use the essential energies of whatever you're working with. It's really interesting. For example, depending on different factors, the energy of a certain thing may be more auspicious at one time or place than another. It's why crop blessings are always done at the same time each turn. It's not just tradition, but because the underlying energies in the earth and plants are fundamentally different in spring, and most auspicious on the first day. It's why it's the first day. It's the same for the whole calendar," he told her excitedly. "I'm thinking of studying more when I get back home, maybe training to be a Priest of the Fates."

"Really?" She seemed surprised.

He was quite surprised himself. He'd never really considered it before saying it just now.

"Sure," she continued thoughtfully. "If you want. But you know that they discourage personal unions, right? Like, you're not forbidden from getting married, but it's better if you don't."

"So?" asked Lim. "It's the same with mages. I'm not planning to get married. It's never been something that I've even considered. Besides, you're not married, nor romantically involved with anyone, are you?"

She shook her head.

"So, if it's good enough for you, why not me?" he challenged.

She shrugged. "I've never been interested."

"Neither have I."

She raised her eyebrow at that. "Don't you have some human girlfriends that you write to? And one right here in the hospital?"

"No." Laughed Laarem. "They're just friends. Fates, what do you think I am? Vaarem?" He laughed again.

"How is Vaarem?" asked Vada, changing the subject.

"Fine," said Lim. "He's still always the life of the party."

Vada smiled thinly. "He really cares about you," she said softly.

"I know," said Lim. "Why?"

"No reason," said Vada. "I guess I just always assumed that he was really shallow and selfish. But it seems that I was wrong."

Lim frowned, but didn't say anything, as he had no idea what she was talking about.

Soon after, Lim's family arrived. Zareanna's eyes lit up when she saw Vada and she ran towards her, throwing her arms around her daughter's waist. Lim couldn't help seeing how strange and uncomfortable they looked together, how different. Vada was tall and thin, with straight black hair that she'd inherited from her human father, while Zareanna was shorter and curvier, with wild curly light-blonde hair, features that she'd inherited from her own human mother (apart from the hair colour, which was most definitely elven).

Vada hugged Vaarem just as awkwardly.

"I'm really glad you came," said Vaarem, looking into her eyes for a moment. Vada gave him the slightest nod. Lim wondered what had transpired between his brother and sister. Whatever it was, he was glad that they were getting along because they didn't always.

Vada and Garrett greeted each other the most awkwardly of all.

Garrett nodded to his step-daughter. "Vada."

"Garrett." She nodded back. She'd always called him by his first name. Now that she was an adult, it didn't seem so awkward.

"Thank you for coming," said Garrett softly. "I know that Lim appreciates it."

Vada nodded in response.

They all took their usual seats, which meant that Vada was forced to sit on the edge of the bed. Lim shifted over to give her space, and she put her arm around his shoulders, allowing him to lean against her, the way he'd done so often when he'd been little. Lim rested his head on her shoulder, although he had to slouch down a little to do so, as he was too tall other-wise. Vada put her arm around him protectively.

"How have you been?" Zareanna asked Vada.

"I've been well, Mother," said Vada stiffly. "Thank you for asking."

Garrett sat with his arms crossed, and refused to meet Vada's eyes, looking at Vaarem instead. "Did you tell your brother about the art gallery?" he asked, then when Vaarem shrugged, he looked at Lim and said, "We went to the Sirrock City Art Museum. They have some really lovely sculptures. Perhaps when you're well we will go again. I forgot how much art and culture this city has. Have you been, Vada?" He looked at Vada, and there was an accusing undertone to his question, like he expected her to say no and to admit that she'd in fact been doing something that he disapproved of. Lim swallowed with difficulty. His father and sister had always been like this, and it seemed that time and distance had done nothing to mellow their attitudes.

"Not for a long time," said Vada, then turned to Lim and said, "So, you're studying the Faith?"

"Really?" Zareanna asked curiously.

"Yes," said Lim, then told his family about what he'd read in the book so far, and how similar the practices of the Faith were to those of mages.

Everyone listened with interest, until Vada said, "My father told me that he'd felt his magic was augmented after attending a Temple service."

Garrett frowned at the mention of Malkim, and he said, "Don't-"

Lim began to cough, but managed to catch his breath after Vaarem gave him some water to drink. His family were all looking at him, but he could still feel the tension between his father and sister, so he turned to Vada and said, "Tell me about your dragon. Did you fly down on it?"

"Her," said Vada. "Her name is Amber, and yes I did." She smiled at him. "I left her on the outskirts, and she is probably flying around the mountains, scaring the livestock." She chuckled. "Although, she only hunts wild animals. She knows not to actually touch the farms."

Garrett sat with his arms crossed and looked at Vada and Lim disapprovingly from beneath his eyebrows, but thankfully, he didn't say anything.

A short while later, Dr Turnwall came in and asked the family to leave, saying that he needed to run some tests and measurements on Lim for the procedure the next day.

Vada hugged Lim and got up off the bed.

"Please come back this afternoon," he said to her, worried that this was it, and that when she left the room she would be gone for good. His father had done his best to make her feel unwelcome.

"I will," she told him, kissing his cheek. He hoped that she meant it. She left without looking at any of them.

"Good luck, Lim," said his father, then his mother hugged and kissed him.

Vaarem hugged him, then said into his ear, "Told you Vada'd come. Now, good luck. I have a good feeling." He smiled, then hugged Lim tightly again, until Lim yelped, then laughed. Having his family all together had been wonderful, despite the awkward vibe.

After his family left, Dr Turnwall consulted his notepad, then looked at Lim. "How are you feeling?" he asked.

"Fine, I guess," replied Lim with a shrug. "As well as can be expected."

"Good," said Dr Turnwall, making a note. "I'd like to run some tests before we do the procedure tomorrow," he said. "I want to compare your readings to your brother's, to make sure that all the settings are correct. I do apologise for what happened during the last two attempts, but you must understand that those were truly unforeseen events. It was not done on purpose, nor due to lack of care. I want to avoid anything else going wrong."

"I understand." Lim nodded. He could tell that the doctor was telling the truth, and that he felt extremely frustrated at the failure of the last two treatments.

"Can you walk?" asked the doctor, after making another note.

"Yes," said Lim, standing up carefully. When he was upright, Dr Turnwall's head barely came up to his chest.

Dr Turnwall looked up, clearly put out by the sudden height difference, but he didn't say anything.

Lim followed the doctor through the hallways, until they reached a room that he didn't recall being in before. He was asked to lie down on the table, which he did obediently. A couple of nurses walked in, and they wheeled some machines towards the table. Dr Turnwall then opened up Lim's gown and attached some sensors, similar to the ones on Lim's first day, to his chest, careful to avoid the areas that were still marked from the failed procedures. He attached some more sensors to Lim's forehead and temples. "You will feel a mild current," he said. "It may feel uncomfortable, but it shouldn't hurt. If it does, yell out."

"Okay," said Lim, his heart speeding up and his palms beginning to sweat. However, these sensors were clearly not the usual ones, as none of the machines made a noise, nor reacted in any way.

As Dr Turnwall had said, the test was uncomfortable, but not exactly painful. Lim was subjected to different currents running through his body. He could sometimes tell which ones were more magic, and which were more electricity. The magic felt more fluid, while the electricity was more abrupt. The electricity stung, the magic merely feeling alien, but not painful. Occasionally, the doctor would stop and check in to make sure that Lim was still conscious, and still okay. Each time, Lim gave a small nod and tried to smile. Inside, he was freaking out, but he did his best to remain calm. The more that he was around Dr Turnwall, the more he realised that despite his freaky appearance, the man did genuinely want to help.

When the tests were over, Lim was weighed and measured again. He was not surprised that his breathing capacity was as bad as it had ever been. Despite this, he was hopeful that this time the procedure was going to work, that with Vaarem's help, he would finally be better.

When his family came back that afternoon, Vada wasn't with them, but she came in about an hour later. She sat on the bed and put her arm around him like she had before.

They made small talk again, Lim asking Vada about Amber, trying to avoid any topics that would upset his father.

Then, Vaarem and Lim compared their experiences with the tests. Vaarem had not been able to differentiate between the magic and the electricity as well as Lim had, telling Lim that all the jolts had felt the same to him, but otherwise his experience had been similar to his brother's.

"I'm scared," Lim admitted when there was a lull in the conversation.

Vada and Vaarem both leaned over and hugged him, one from each side. Lim let them hold him, soaking up their positive energy. His mother was looking at her children tenderly and even his father gave him a small smile.

"We're all anxious for you too," said Vaarem "And

we know, at least, I know, that it's not going to be much fun for you, so we all want you to know how loved and cherished you are."

"Thank you," said Lim, leaning his head on Vaarem's shoulder. He was feeling extremely exhausted. He recalled saying the exact same words to Eliza recently. He hoped that they had had the same effect on her as his brother's had on him, which was to make him feel very good inside.

In the evening, after his family had gone, Dr Thorn came into his room. Today he was wearing his long hair in a tight braid that fell to his waist. "As you are no doubt aware," he said to Lim, sitting down on the chair next to the bed, "your ribs are fractured. It normally takes about six weeks for such an injury to heal."

Lim nodded. He'd been wondering whether his broken ribs would be a problem.

"Luckily, modern medicine and modern magic have come up with a way to help bones heal a lot quicker. With your permission, I would like to attempt the procedure on you today."

"Okay," said Lim. "Sure. Permission granted. But what's the catch?"

"The catch," said Dr Thorn, "is that the procedure can be painful. Very painful in fact. However, once it's over, the pain stops. So, it is up to you."

"What happens if I don't do it?"

Dr Thorn gave an almost imperceptible shrug. "As the procedure tomorrow is still in the experimental stages, there is no long-term data to go on. I don't believe that broken bones will interfere with tomorrow's procedure, and if successful, the procedure may even lead to your bones healing quicker naturally."

Lim nodded, thinking that this all sounded pretty good.

"However, if there is a complication again, then your ribs may be a serious problem."

Lim considered this.

"Is the bone-healing procedure guaranteed to work?" he asked.

"As much as anything can ever be guaranteed," replied Dr Thorn. "It is an established procedure, with an almost universal success rate."

"Right." Nodded Lim. "What would you recommend?"

Dr Thorn again gave that almost imperceptible shrug, "I would personally recommend that you get your bones healed. However, like I said, it's painful, and I know that tomorrow's treatment will not be exactly comfortable either, so it depends on how much pain you can handle. Painkillers are, unfortunately, not an option, as they dull your overall energy, which needs to flow freely in order for any kind of energy healing procedure, such as the bone-healing and the one you're having tomorrow, to work."

Lim nodded again. He could handle pain, so it seemed that his choice was clear. "I'll do it," he told Dr Thorn resolutely.

"Good." Dr Thorn nodded, then left the room.

Lim picked up his book, but he couldn't concentrate. He hadn't written to any of his friends recently. Neither had he replied to Dr Fantail's latest letter to him either. He really wanted to go home. And to think that he'd voluntarily signed up for an extra procedure that promised to be painful.

Am I going insane? he wondered with a sigh. He hadn't been outside for two weeks, had not been anywhere beyond the few rooms in the middle of the hospital.

He was thoroughly over it.

An hour or so later, Nurse Ariella came into his room. "How are you, Lim?" she asked him kindly.

"Fine." He looked up from the book that he'd picked up again.

"I'm glad that you're getting your ribs healed," she told him. "If you had left before they were fully mended, you would have been at risk of pneumonia, which can be dangerous, especially for someone with your particular condition."

"I know," said Lim. "I've had it before. Twice. Nearly died both times."

Recalling those instances confirmed that he'd made the right decision to get his bones healed. The way that things were going, he was due for a bout of pneumonia, and he really wanted to avoid it. He feared that the next time he got it would be his last.

Nurse Ariella measured his vital signs, then gave him a very small jug of gruel.

He raised his eyebrow in question.

"You shouldn't eat too much before the procedure," she explained. "But you don't need to fast completely before this one."

"Can't I have some real food?" he asked, drinking the gruel. He'd learned that the sooner he drank it, the sooner he could forget about it for the time being, and the less time he devoted to thinking about it.

"I will bring you something after the procedure tonight," she promised him. "But you still need to drink your formula, as you still need to keep your weight up."

Lim rolled his eyes. "Yes, I know. But why can't I do that eating real food?"

Nurse Ariella smiled at him kindly. "The doctors are afraid that you cannot consistently eat enough of that while you're in here. The formula has sufficient calories, so you don't have to eat so much of it."

"Not so much of it?" Lim laughed incredulously. "Even with the smaller portions I feel uncomfortably full afterwards."

"Precisely," she replied, still smiling. "Imagine how much normal food, as you call it, you would have to eat for the same amount of calories."

"Really?" He frowned. "I never thought about it like that. I've never been a big eater. Not sure why. I've never had much of an appetite."

"That's probably another symptom of your condition," she said. "Hopefully it will also disappear after your next procedure and you won't struggle so much to maintain your weight."

"Hopefully," said Lim, drinking the rest of his gruel.

Half an hour later, Nurse Ariella returned with Dr Thorn. Lim was once again asked to change into the hospital trousers, leaving his top half bare. It appeared that this procedure would be done right here in his room. He sat down on his bed and Nurse Ariella wrapped a bandage around his ribs. After she'd done this, Dr Thorn asked him to lie down, and wet the bandage with a solution that smelled of herbs and minerals. He then took a brush and drew some symbols on the bandage with ink. Lim couldn't see what exactly the symbols were, but he could see the standard circles, spirals, and other geometric shapes that mages often used. It appeared that this procedure would use magic too. Lim hoped that it would work.

Dr Thorn asked Nurse Ariella to stand by Lim's head and put her fingers on his temples. Finally, Lim was given a piece of leather to bite on.

"Close your eyes," instructed Dr Thorn, then he placed his hands on Lim's chest, and began the procedure.

At first, it didn't hurt, and Lim was wondering what all the fuss was about. His bones fusing back together felt strange, like they were all vibrating at different frequencies, but it wasn't painful. But then he started to feel hot, as if his body was heating up inside. Then it started to burn. Lim felt like there was a fire burning inside his chest, and then it was like firecrackers going off inside him. He felt like his bones were melting, then hardening to reform, then melting again. He was afraid that if he opened his eyes, he would see fire and steam rising off him, so he kept them shut tight.

He bit on the leather with all his might, ignoring the strain this put on his jaw.

Nurse Ariella held his head in place, else he would have thrashed around like he was convulsing. "Stay with me, Lim," she said. "You're doing really well. That's a good boy. We're nearly done. Just a little bit more. Hang in there."

Lim hung in there.

He thought about Vada having come to see him, and hoped that she would return. The thought that he was likely to see her again soon kept him going.

Finally, after what seemed like hours (but turned out to be a little less than half an hour), it was over.

Lim gasped when Nurse Ariella finally took the leather out of his mouth. His jaw hurt from being clenched so much, but otherwise he was feeling surprisingly well. His ribs no longer hurt, and the burning had been replaced by a pleasant warmth.

"You did really well," said Nurse Ariella, stroking his hair.

"Now, you can rest for a while," said Dr Thorn. He had dark rings under his eyes, and he looked exhausted. "Don't try to sit up. Just lie back. One of the nurses will come and remove the bandage soon."

"Okay," said Lim softly, then closed his eyes again. He was feeling quite tired himself.

It's amazing how tired one can get just lying in bed,

he thought, and wondered whether he was really that sick, or whether the forced inactivity was making him lethargic. In any case, he was too tired to care at that moment.

Eventually, someone came and removed the bandages, but Lim was only half-conscious, and went back to sleep straight away. Nurse Ariella (or someone else) brought him the promised food, but he was too tired to eat it.

The next morning, when he woke up, there was a wilted fruit salad and two pieces of day-old bread with filling, on the bedside table. He sat up, wondering at the lack of pain, and ate it all hungrily. He didn't care that it was stale. It was still a lot better than the formula gruel he'd been having for the past two weeks.

After eating the food, he found his quill and ink, as well as some paper, and started to write. He wrote to Jessa and Marla first, as he felt that he'd been neglecting them since first Vaarem and then Vada had been with him.

"Dear Jessa and Marla," he wrote, pleased that his hand was no longer shaking, and he could write neatly, like he usually did. Having been forced to spend a lot of time indoors as a child, he'd had a lot of time to practice his fine motor skills, so now he was very proficient at writing and drawing. It was one of the only things that he was better at than Vaarem. *"Today is the day."* he wrote, *"I'm sorry that I haven't written for so long, but as Vaarem has probably told you (unless*

he didn't write to you and just told me that he did, haha, did he?) things have not been going very well for me here. But, it seems like things are finally falling into place. Today, the doctors will attempt the procedure for the third time (third time lucky?). I am actually feeling quite positive about it, so hopefully it's a success (or at the very least, not a complete and utter failure like the last two attempts). In other news, I got my broken ribs healed by magic last night. (Vaarem wrote to you about how that happened, didn't he?) The procedure hurt like the bastard son of a goblin, but now the bones seem to be completely healed, so all in all, I think it was worth it. Anyway, I hope that this is one of the last letters that I write to you from here, and that I finally get to see you both soon. I am so desperate to leave this hospital. It is so boring. Anyway, I hope that by the time you read this, I am all better and on my way to see you. I miss you both. Love, Lim"

He then sent a bit of magic heat to his hand and held it over the letter, starting from the top and moving down to his signature, to dry the ink, then folded the letter and put it in an envelope, ready for someone to send it off. He then wrote to Fen and to his friends in Palinas, and finally to Dr Fantail, because he knew that his usual healer would want to know how he was doing.

He was finishing addressing the letters when Vaarem walked into the room, followed by Zareanna and Garrett.

"Did they really heal your ribs?" asked Vaarem excitedly.

"Yes," replied Lim, just as excited. His top half was still bare, so he showed his brother the lack of bruising.

"Wow," said Vaarem, impressed. He ran a tentative finger down Lim's side.

"You can touch me if you want," said Lim. "It doesn't hurt."

"That's really great, darling," said Zareanna, walking over and putting her arms around him. Now that she knew she wouldn't hurt him, she hugged him tightly. He hugged her back, feeling good in her embrace.

"I'm glad you're feeling better," said Garrett, then sat down in his usual spot in the corner. Lim couldn't tell what his father was thinking, but he didn't seem angry, nor was he projecting any other negative emotion.

Perhaps deep down he does care about me, Lim dared to hope. Even after all this time, he was still desperate for his father's approval.

"How are you all doing today?" Dr Turnwall surprised them all by walking in unannounced.

"Good," said Lim.

Dr Turnwall walked over and examined him. "Good," he said approvingly, running his hands along Lim's sides and chest. "The bones are all healed nicely. This will make today's procedure easier," he said, then walked out of the room, leaving the family alone again.

"Let's hope the procedure goes well this time."

Vaarem voiced what Lim was thinking, "and that they don't do you any more damage. Because so far, they seem to have broken you more than they have fixed."

"I know," Lim sighed. "I know."

"So far," said Vaarem, "they have broken your lungs and your heart, and your ribs. I don't think that you have any other vital organs in that area?" he asked.

Lim laughed bitterly. "Don't forget my stomach. It's still mostly painful since they first gave me that horrid stuff."

Vaarem smiled thinly and his parents looked uncomfortable. Lim wished that he hadn't said anything. Then again, it was his body, and if he couldn't laugh at its failings, what could he do?

The uncomfortable silence was broken by Vada walking into the room. She was dressed in different clothes than she'd worn the previous day, and her hair was pinned up in a knot at the top of her head. It seemed that she'd returned to her castle overnight and came back down this morning.

"Vada!" cried Lim happily. "I was so afraid that you wouldn't come back."

"And miss seeing you after the procedure?" she asked, walking over to hug him carefully.

"You can hug me," he said, putting his arms around her. "My ribs are healed."

"That's wonderful, darling," she said, and drew him to her. He rested his head on her shoulder, feeling happy beyond expectations that she'd come back. Perhaps today's operation would be a success after all.

Chapter 15

Third Time Lucky?

The family left at midday, as they always did.

Lim was feeling excited and anxious in turns. This was it. If today's procedure didn't work out, then there was nothing else to do, except to go home.

I am going home soon, he thought, feeling excited at the idea, despite himself. He was so homesick.

He decided to visit Eliza, hoping she would distract him.

He stood up slowly. Despite his ribs being healed, he was still weak and had to move carefully.

His top half was still bare, so he got a sheet and draped it over his shoulders, feeling too self-conscious to walk around topless, even though as well as the bruises, the marks left by the two failed procedures had also faded. The only scars that were left were the two small marks from where the tubes had been in his lungs, but these were very small.

Eliza was sitting on her bed, writing. He noticed that like him, she used her left hand, and like him, she wrote in neat, small, precise strokes.

"Hi," he said, walking in and sitting down on the chair next to the bed.

"Hi." She looked up. She was wearing her necklace and holding the charm in her right hand. "I am writing a letter to my family," she explained. "Hearing about you and your family has made me realise that I don't want mine to forget me. So, I am going to ask them to come and visit me."

"That's great," he said, smiling. "I'm sure they will. Why did they stop coming?"

"I told them to," she replied with a shrug. "But now I realise that I miss them."

"Yeah," said Lim. "My family drive me crazy, but if they weren't around, I would miss them."

"Yeah," she agreed. "My brother used to tease me," she said wistfully. "He always told me that I had thin mousy hair, that no one would ever want to marry me because my hair was too ugly." She shook her head with a cynical chuckle.

"That's so mean," said Lim. He couldn't recall anything like that happening to him.

"My brother and sister were always kind to me," he said carefully, thinking how fortunate he was for this. "They used to tease each other though," he said.

"My sister used to call my brother a flaky airhead and she'd tell him that he was so stupid that he couldn't even get dressed. The next day, he came to breakfast wearing his underpants on his head." He laughed, remembering the day. It had been so ridiculous, that even his father had chuckled.

Eliza laughed too. "Yeah," she said. "I used to wear my hair in silly braids just to show my brother how 'ugly' I was." She held her hair up in two bunches on the top of her head, and bobbed up and down.

Lim laughed.

Eliza let her hair fall back down. "Then he got lice and my mother shaved his head," she said. "Served him right. Although," she added soberly, "when it grew back, he never teased me about mine again. I miss him. I never really thought that I liked him, but I miss him. How stupid is that?"

"Not stupid at all." Lim put his hand on hers. "People are complicated, and you can both love and hate a single person."

"Yes," Eliza nodded in agreement. "I think my family love and hate me at the same time."

Lim smiled thinly. "I'm sure they love you, but sometimes hate some of the things you do." He recalled her leaning out the window to throw up. "But that happens to everyone." He thought of his father. Garrett loved him, but hated some of the things he did; even if Lim had little control over said things. It wasn't fair, but that was the way it was.

They talked for a while longer, then Lim went back

into his own room to wait for Dr Turnwall and for his final procedure. He picked up the book that Eliza had given him, and said a small prayer, wishing that the procedure that afternoon would go well.

His family came back after having had their lunch in the city. Once again Vada had left them, promising to come back, but not returning with them. Zareanna sat next to Lim on the bed and put her arm around him. It seemed that she was taking her turn to hold him, the same way that Vada and Vaarem had done the previous day. Lim slouched down and put his head on her shoulder.

"My poor baby," said Zareanna, hugging him closer and kissing his head.

"I'll be fine, Mother," he told her, embarrassed. He didn't like it when she called him "baby" around others, even if the others were only his family. He saw his father roll his eyes, and chuckled inwardly.

Eventually, Vada returned, and sat on Zareanna's usual chair. "How are you feeling, Limmy?" she asked anxiously.

"Hungry," said Lim with a grin. He was doing his best to keep his mind off the upcoming procedure. He really hoped that there would be no further complications.

Eventually, two nurses came in, Mela wheeling the operating bed, and the nurse with the metal leg, whose name he'd learned the previous day was Silveia, walking beside her. Silveia asked him how he was feeling, then they both did the usual measurements, assuring him that he would get a supper of "real" food after the procedure. Then, they asked his family to leave. His family all took turns giving him a hug and a kiss (or about twenty kisses in Zareanna's case, which prompted Lim to say, "Enough, Mother, it's fine, please," in an embarrassed tone), with Garrett squeezing his hand.

After his family had left, Lim got on the operating bed and lay down, and the nurses wheeled it out of the room.

Dr Turnwall was already in the operating room, adjusting the dials on the machines. He greeted Lim, then, when the table was in position, he strapped Lim's wrists and ankles to the table, then placed the sensor-disks to Lim's chest and head. Lim noticed that the placement of the disks was slightly different to the last two times, and that as well as on his temples, the doctor also placed two on his forehead.

Finally, the leather strap was placed in Lim's mouth, and his eyes were covered.

"You've got this, Lim," said Nurse Silveia, squeezing his left hand, before letting go.

"Here we go," said Dr Turnwall, then the procedure began.

Lim had forgotten how uncomfortable it felt. The first few jolts were bearable, but as they progressed, they grew stronger and more painful.

Eventually, Lim couldn't take it anymore, and screamed.

One of the nurses adjusted the leather in his mouth and instructed him to bite down on it, which he did. But he eventually forgot, and he screamed again.

The leather slipped, and when he bit down on it, he bit his lip painfully.

He felt blood running down his chin. Someone wiped it off and readjusted the leather. Lim bit down on it again. And again.

"Stop!" he cried at one point. "No more." But the jolts kept coming, and someone readjusted the leather again, so that he couldn't talk.

He bit down again, so hard that he thought he might bite straight through it.

It slipped again, and he bit his lip again, and then he screamed again.

At one point, he thought that he might have passed out, only to be woken up by another jolt.

The jolts kept coming. He passed out again, only to be woken up again. And again. And again.

He screamed so much that his throat was hoarse, and his lip was bruised and bloody, so much so that the nurses couldn't keep up, and the blood ran down his chin and into his ear.

Finally, when Lim thought that he would rather die than be subjected to another minute of this torture, it stopped; it was over.

His wrists and ankles were unstrapped. Lim felt the skin around the bonds start to bruise.

The blindfold was removed, as were the sensor-disks, and the strip of leather. Lim ran his dry tongue over his lips to find them bruised and bleeding. He kept his eyes closed, because the lights seemed unnaturally bright.

"You did really well," said Nurse Silveia, patting him on the shoulder.

Lim didn't reply. He didn't feel that he'd done well at all, what with the thrashing and screaming. He was too exhausted to speak or move in any case.

Someone lifted his head and gave him something to drink. The liquid tasted sweet, and it eased the pain in his raw throat. Someone applied some salve to his lips, then he was covered up with a sheet, and wheeled out of the room. He was so exhausted that he fell asleep before they reached his room.

In the hospital foyer, Vaarem hugged his mother, snuggling into her, the way he'd done when he'd been a child.

This is so bad, he thought, as he found himself shaking.

As always, he couldn't feel his twin's physical pain, but he felt a great sense of tiredness and discomfort. Then again, as he looked around the foyer, he saw his feelings reflected on everyone else's faces. Even his father had gone pale.

"What are they doing to him?" sobbed Zareanna.

The nurse on duty, an ancient-looking human with dark skin and white hair tied back in a tight braid, looked pained too. "This is all normal," she reassured them. "The procedure cannot be used with any kind of anaesthetic," she explained. However, even she winced when she heard Lim's piercing shrieks coming from within the hospital.

Vada sat in the corner by herself, not meeting anyone's eyes. Vaarem couldn't tell what she was thinking, but out of all of them, she seemed the most calm.

Dangerously calm, thought Vaarem, but he was too worried about Lim to analyze Vada.

Finally, after nearly two hours, the procedure was over. The electricity in the hospital stopped buzzing, and everything was silent.

A few minutes later, Dr Turnwall came out to see them. He looked tired, his one eye shadowed. But he also looked excited. "The procedure went well," he told them, and they all breathed a collective sigh of relief. "Everything went as planned. The rest is up to Lim. Let's hope that his body grasps on to the energy and starts to heal itself."

"So, there is still a chance it might not work?" asked Vaarem, standing up, desperate to see his twin.

"Yes, there is always that *possibility*," said Dr Turnwall. "But we will cross that bridge if and when we come to it. Right now, Lim needs to rest and allow the energy to work its way through his body. We will know in a couple of days how well it took."

"Can we see him?" asked Zareanna anxiously.

"Yes, of course," said Dr Turnwall.

They all stood up, apart from Vaarem, who was standing already, and followed him into the hospital.

"He is sleeping," said Dr Turnwall, as they walked. "And will be for some time."

When they entered Lim's room, one of the nurses was tucking a sheet around him, then she checked his pulse before saying to Dr Turnwall, "He's stable."

"Good." Nodded Dr Turnwall, then turned to the family. "You can stay as long as you like but let him rest."

"How long will he stay asleep?" asked Vaarem, sitting down on his usual chair, and looking at his brother's face. There were a couple of marks on Lim's forehead and temples from the sensors, and his bottom lip was bruised and swollen, but apart from that, he was sleeping peacefully. His arms were out on top of the sheet and there were no drips in them, the bruises from the previous needles starting to fade. He looked peaceful for the first time since coming here and Vaarem allowed a small smile to cross his face.

"Hopefully all night," said Dr Turnwall, "He will likely wake for a few minutes here and there, before going back to sleep, so don't try and talk to him yet. He will need to rest for at least two or three days. During that time, his body will be working to incorporate the new energy, so he may look more tired and drawn for a while, but that is normal and will pass." With that, he left the room.

Zareanna sat on the other side of the bed and

picked up Lim's hand, running her fingers over his frail wrist. "I can't believe how thin he still is," she said, her voice choked. "I hope he's going to be okay." She brought Lim's hand over to her lips, as tears filled her eyes.

"He'll be fine, Zara," said Garrett, walking over to put his arm around her shoulders. "He's turned out to be one tough little nut. Who'd have thought," he said, with something akin to grudging admiration.

Vada stood in the doorway awkwardly. She looked like she was about to leave, so Vaarem stood up and went up to her. She hadn't said anything since they'd been ushered out of the room prior to Lim's procedure.

"I can't deal with this," she said under her breath. "That was the single worst experience of my life."

Vaarem frowned. "It's not about you," he told her coldly. "Because I highly doubt that Lim was enjoying himself either. We're all handling it. I would have thought that you'd be holding up the best out of all of us."

She glared at him from beneath her eyelashes. "Don't you dare tell me how to feel, Vaarem," she hissed.

"I'm not telling you how to feel. I'm telling you to hold it together for our brother's sake."

"I'm holding it together," said Vada coldly. "I am holding it together more than you will ever know. And you can be damn sure that if they actually hurt him, I will not allow them to get away with it."

Chapter 16

Revelations

When the family came back after dinner, Lim was still asleep on the bed. He was covered by a sheet, but his arms and shoulders were visible, and Vaarem saw that the bruises, which seemed to have been fading before, were now looking darker and more prominent. There were also dark patches that looked like bruises on his temples, and his lips were scabbed and swollen. He looked worse than he had a mere hour ago.

Zareanna gasped and ran over to the bed. She picked up his limp hand, as tears filled her eyes.

"What's happened to him?" she whispered.

"The doctor said he might look worse before he gets better," said Vaarem carefully. Was this what was happening? Lim was looking *a lot* worse.

"Fuck," sighed Garrett, taking in Lim's form and shaking his head. "Not again. This is all so unfair," he whispered, looking at Zareanna with serious eyes. "It's not fair on you. It's not fair on anyone."

"What do you mean?" asked Zareanna, narrowing her eyes suspiciously.

"You know what I mean," said Garrett quietly, sitting down in his usual spot. "I feel like we're with Malkim all over again. I feared that nothing good would come of this." He shook his head.

Vada, who was standing in the corner of the room, with her arms crossed, frowned down at him.

Vaarem sat down on his chair and picked up Lim's other hand, looking from his half-sister to his father. Garrett was looking up at Vada with a strange expression that Vaarem couldn't read.

"Typical," said Vada, looking at Garrett with narrowed eyes.

"Excuse me?" He frowned. "What's typical?"

"You," she spat. "You always hated my father so much that even now you can't handle talking about him. That's why you've always hated me too, isn't it? Because I am a constant daily reminder that my mother loved *him* best, not you. Admit it."

Vaarem sat still, his eyes wide. He'd always known that his father felt tense about the subject of his mother's first marriage, but it had never been spoken about.

Garrett looked at Vada, with a confused frown. "What?" he asked. "What do you mean? I never hated your father. He was my friend." He was looking at

Vada with a pained expression now. "Do you not remember?" he asked quietly.

"I remember that you two were always fighting," said Vada.

"When?" Frowned Garrett.

"Every time you visited," said Vada. "You two were always yelling. I had to cover my ears."

"Oh," said Garrett, looking down. "I'm sorry if you thought we were fighting. We did have some animated discussions on the state of things in Jaanis." He chuckled wistfully. "Some of the news that I brought him was not what he'd hoped for, and we disagreed on how to respond, but it was never bad intentioned. Would he have really let you stay if we had truly been fighting? Would he have let me teach you elf magic if he didn't trust me? Fates, Vada, he carried you in his arms all the time, and then when he got tired, *I* would hold you." He looked up at her with a hurt expression.

Vada looked down at him thoughtfully. "Well, if he was truly your friend, why did you take us away as soon as his ashes had been scattered?"

"Because he asked me to," said Garrett quietly. "Everything I've done is to honour his wishes, to honour his memory."

"What?" Frowned Vada, and Vaarem frowned too.

"So, you didn't kill him in a duel over Mother's hand?" asked Vaarem quietly.

Everyone looked at him with shock and he realised that he'd had it all wrong for all this time.

"*What?*" demanded Garrett, and Zareanna and Vada echoed his question.

"Sorry," mumbled Vaarem, "I just thought-"

"You thought what?" demanded Garrett. "That Malkim and I fought over your mother like she was some kind of object? Is that what you really think of us, Vaaremill?"

Vaarem shook his head and dropped his gaze, wanting to get away from his father's sudden anger. He felt Lim's fingers tighten around his own, indicating that he was conscious, but his twin had the good sense to remain quiet.

"Your mother loved Malkim," said Garrett seriously, "so for that reason alone, I would have never hurt him. But as I said, he was my friend. Sure, I was jealous of him at first, but when I got to know him and saw how happy he made your mother." He trailed off. "Well, he grew on me, especially after he gave me the job of official envoy between Palinora and the Three Countries. I'm still grateful for that opportunity, even after resigning from the position. And he was not possessive, so the idea that he'd fight a duel over a woman is, quite frankly, insulting. He was a good person."

"He was," said Zareanna quietly. "And your father is right. Malkim didn't want me to be alone after he died. He planned it all."

"Yes," sighed Garrett bitterly. "He certainly did." He looked up at Vada. "Everything I did, your father asked me to do," he told her. "He knew that you and your mother would outlive him, so he asked me to take care of you both. I thought that he simply meant the differing lifespans of humans and elves." He shook his head, "I never dreamed that he was deliberately planning to end things the way he did, and I guess that I am still angry. I feel like he tricked me. If I hadn't agreed, would he still be with us?" He looked up and sighed.

"He was very weak towards the end," said Vada quietly. "He was physically and emotionally spent. *You* had nothing to do with it."

Garrett nodded at that. "I like to think so, but I'll never know for sure," he said, his voice breaking, "I loved him. I still do," he said wistfully. "That's why I don't like talking about him. It's still too painful." He shook his head again. "And every time Lim gets sick, it just reminds me of Malkim, and I fear that one day he'll decide to end it too, and I won't be able to do anything. I know I'm too hard on him." He sighed.

He was silent for a long moment, he looked up at Vada again, "In any case," he said, "your father asked me to look after you and your mother, which is what I have been trying to do all this time."

"Then why did you take us to Palinas? Why did you take *me* away from Sirrock, from my home?"

"Because your father asked me to," said Garrett, beginning to get impatient. "He knew that his mother and her cronies, the Blackwell Loyalists, as they call themselves, would swoop in and try to use you and manipulate you the way they'd done to him. They were going to use your grief to twist you to their side. I could not let that happen."

Vada looked at him for a moment, and something in her demeanour changed. She was still standing with her arms crossed and her chin raised, but her face had softened a little. She looked at him and said, "I didn't know that. Thank you, I guess." She dropped her eyes.

"You're welcome," said Garrett. "I am glad that they haven't gotten to you the way he feared they would. I guess that I haven't failed him after all."

"If Malkim was your friend," Vaarem found the courage to speak up again, "then why did you take all his pictures down at home? Why did you take Vada's down?"

"You took our pictures down?" Frowned Vada, back on the defensive.

Garrett sighed again. "When you left to go back to Sirrock City." He looked up at Vada, "I felt that I'd failed. I thought you would join your grandmother for sure. I couldn't look at your father, even a picture of him. He loved you so much, and I couldn't handle seeing him and you together when I had thought that you'd betrayed him."

"I would *never* betray him," spat Vada. "And I would never join *them*."

Garrett nodded. "I know that now," he said. "I'm sorry. It seems that we both underestimated each other."

"Yes," said Vada. "I am sorry for thinking badly of you too." She looked down at the ground, before looking up again, "So, why did you have sex with my mother, then?" She glanced at Vaarem and Lim as if pointing out the evidence of her statement. "Did he ask you to do that too?"

"Not exactly," said Garrett, and Vaarem saw his face colour. "Although he did mention several times that your mother wanted more children and that if he was unable to give them to her." He trailed off, then looked down.

Zareanna, who had been quiet until that moment, looked up, "That is private, Vada," she said sharply. "Your father, Garrett, and I had a special understanding." She dropped her eyes too.

Vaarem looked down, his own face colouring. Lim squeezed his hand, but Vaarem couldn't look at his brother. He now understood why Lim had been uncomfortable when Vaarem had told him about his sexual escapades. Picturing his family's sex lives was not something that he wanted to do.

"It only happened once," said Garrett, looking back up at Vada. "I would never deliberately disrespect either of your parents."

Vada looked at him for a moment with a hard expression, then she sighed and said, "I believe you."

Garrett nodded in acknowledgement, then stood up and walked over to put his arms around Zareanna. She buried her face in his chest.

"I still miss him," she said softly.

"I know." Garrett kissed her head. "I miss him too."

Vada continued to frown, but then Zareanna stood

up, lifted her arm and beckoned her over. Vada stepped forward and let her mother and stepfather embrace her. She put her arms around them both.

Vaarem sat in the chair, feeling awkward, like he was suddenly not a part of the family. His parents and Vada, all held each other, united in their memories. Memories that Vaarem was not part of. He squeezed Lim's fingers under the blanket.

Lim opened his eyes and looked at Vaarem for a moment, before closing them again, indicating that he'd heard everything.

Vada stepped away from her mother and step-father's embrace. Then Garrett and Zareanna took a step away from each other. All of them had tears in their eyes, and were wiping them away, Vada and Garrett surreptitiously, as if they didn't want anyone to see, Zareanna, openly. She looked down at Vaarem and Lim, as if just remembering that they were there. She walked over to Vaarem, then leaned down and put her arms around him.

"I'm sorry about what you just heard, Vary, but your father is right. We should have said it all earlier. Know that your father and I love you and Lim and Vada very much. Even though it hurts, I do not regret anything in my life."

Vaarem smiled at that, his own eyes beginning to fill with tears. He remembered a passage he'd read in the Book of the Fates, when there had been a lesson about the Faith at school, "To know joy, one must

know pain, for one cannot exist without the other,"
and he finally understood.

Chapter 17

Recovery

Lim woke up in the early hours of the next morning. It was still dark, and the hospital was very quiet. He recalled the conversation that his family had had at his bedside and wondered whether he'd dreamt it.

His father and Vada's father had been friends? His father and *Vada* had gotten along? Their parents had had an "understanding"? All his life he'd felt like his parents had been hiding something and now that he knew, he felt like a weight had been lifted off him.

But was it enough for him to actually heal? He'd always suspected that bad energy made his underlying condition worse but had never voiced this suspicion to anyone other than Vaarem, for fear of being labelled dramatic and being accused of blaming others for his problems. He wondered now whether the improvement in his family's energy would help him to finally get well.

He moved his body experimentally. There was no pain, but his muscles all felt exhausted, like he'd been running great distances, or climbing trees, or something. He sat up slowly and had a drink of water from the jug on the bedside table. There was also a bowl of fruit there, so he picked it up and examined its contents, trying to decide whether he was hungry or not.

Well, of course he was hungry. But what did he feel like eating?

After some deliberation, he ended up selecting a pear and an apple, mostly because the other types of fruit would have required peeling, but he couldn't see a knife nor anything else to do that with.

After eating the apple and pear, he was still hungry, so he ended up peeling the orange and peach with his fingernails, depositing the peels as neatly as he could beside the bowl.

After a while, he took the remaining two pieces of fruit, a mandarin and a mango, out of the bowl and ate them, then put the peels, seeds, and cores in it, feeling a little annoyed at not having been given a bin.

Or did they not expect me to actually eat anything?

His throat felt raw, but the juice of the fruit eased it, and when he ran his tongue over his bottom lip, he felt that it was swollen, but it was not too tender.

He lay back and closed his eyes because it was still too dark to read or write, or do anything else.

When he woke up again, Vada was sitting on the chair beside the bed. Her expression was anxious, and Lim frowned when he saw her.

"How are you, Limmy?" she asked, her voice as anxious as her eyes.

"Fine, I guess," he said. "Tired. I heard everything yesterday."

"Oh," she said. "Sorry about that. But thank the Fates that you're okay." She leaned down and kissed him between the eyes. "I was so scared. You sounded like you were in indescribable agony."

"Oh," said Lim, remembering the procedure with an involuntary shudder. "You heard that?" he asked, feeling embarrassed.

"Everyone heard it," she said. "I think people in Palinas heard you. I felt like running in there and making them stop."

"Oh crap," he said. "I didn't realise I was so loud."

Vada took his hand and sat up again. "Are you okay?" she asked.

"Yeah," he said, sitting up. The sheet fell away, so he looked down at his body and examined himself.

There were marks on his chest from the sensor disks, but there were no burns like there had been the previous two times. "It was horribly painful," he admitted, "but it's over now." He wondered whether the procedure had been successful, and whether once he recovered, he would actually be able to breathe properly, climb stairs, and have the ability to walk and talk at the same time. Regardless of the outcome, Vada was here, and his parents were talking, so the whole thing had been worth it, no matter what happened now.

"Are you okay?" He looked up at her.

"Yes, I am fine," she said. "I had been so angry at being taken from my home that I had forgotten the good things about your father. But it doesn't change anything, Limmy. The Blackwell Loyalists are wanting to use me the way they tried to use my father, but I can look out for myself. One day, I will make them pay for what they did. I will mend all the pain that my ancestors caused. And if anyone ever hurts *you*, or any other innocents, I will make them pay, too. I will set things right."

Lim didn't know what to make of that. Instead, he opened his eyes and looked at his sister seriously. "Vada?" he asked, remembering the previous day's conversation. "How did your father die?"

Vada sighed. She closed her eyes for a moment, then opened them and looked at Lim, "People say he starved himself, but that wasn't the reason. It was the Blackwell Loyalists. It was their doing."

"What?" he asked. "I thought you said that he was sick?"

She shook her head. "He was, but not sick like you. It was sorcery sickness. They drove him to it. He was forever trying to work magic to get away from them, to stop their influence, and it made him sick. Then he became weaker because he wouldn't eat anything. Sorcery sickness makes you lose your appetite, but

my father never seemed to have one to begin with."
She sighed.

"Like me?" asked Lim, equally curious and anxious,

Vada shrugged. "I don't think so. I don't think he
was born with it. He did it to himself. He was always
despondent, angry and sad, and would experiment
with complicated magic, which overwhelmed him in
the end. They wore him down completely and he was
working on a last-ditch spell that he thought would
rid the world of their influence, *'Make everything right
with the world and rid the world of pain'*, according to
his notes. It was a dangerous and volatile magic."

"So, it was an accident?"

Vada shook her head, "For a long time, I wanted
to think so, but I know it was deliberate. I found his
notes and it appears that the spell he was working on
required a great blood sacrifice."

Lim shuddered. Blood magic was illegal. It was the
reason the Blackwells had been overthrown. Hadn't
Malkim rejected all that?

Vada saw his expression. "He thought that by sac-
rificing himself he wouldn't be breaking any laws. He
knew what he was doing." She held Lim's hand, and
he saw a tear roll down her cheek. She wiped it away
with her other hand. "I know that his mother, and
the other Blackwell Loyalists drove him to it. I often
think of recreating the spell myself, and wiping them
out, wiping out their influence. But not until I find a
better way to do it. I do not intend to sacrifice myself
nor any innocents."

Lim stared at her. What did she mean by "wiping them out and wiping out their influence"? Using magic to kill was the single worst crime on Jaanis, blood magic or not, and he couldn't believe that Vada would ever seriously think it.

Vada looked at Lim and bit her lip. It looked like she was trying to decide what else to tell him, what to leave out.

"Tell me," he said. "I want to know. I am so tired of all these secrets. They serve no purpose."

She sighed. "You're probably aware that there is still a faction of people wanting to unite the Sirranna region under the rule of the Blackwells. My father signed a peace treaty, giving up the Blackwell throne, which the Blackwell Loyalists were not happy with, so they tried to get him to reverse it. They threatened my father, our mother, me. After my father died, I was the Blackwell heir, and it seems that they wanted to use me for that. Your father took me away to prevent that. I could've handled myself, as even as a child I could have taken them on, but I guess it was good to be away from them. They are still plotting, trying to convince me to take up their cause." She sighed angrily. "I hate them all." She looked at him, her eyes filled with venom.

He shrank away from her expression.

"And one day, I will make them pay".

Lim's breath caught for a moment, but then he managed to exhale. "How?" he asked quietly.

"What?" She looked down at him, as if he'd interrupted her thoughts.

"How will you make them pay?" he asked quietly. "Aren't they all old, anyway? Won't they eventually die out, along with their influence?"

She sighed again. "Oh, Limmy." She reached out and stroked his hair behind his ear. "It is so much more complicated. They are always recruiting new followers, promising them positions of power, promising them riches. They've been doing it for generations, ever since the Blackwells were first overthrown." She shook her head. "I am going to find a way to recreate my father's spell, but without the need for blood sacrifice," she said. "The spell that will set everything right. You can be sure that when I'm done, the continent and all of Zemia will be at peace for good."

"How?" asked Lim. "What can such a spell do?"

Vada sighed impatiently. "Like I said, I'm still working through my father's notes, that I found in the castle," she told him. "But when I've worked it all out, I will avenge him. I will make the loyalists pay," she said, and he saw the anger blazing in her eyes. "No matter how long it takes, I will make them pay, and I will also take away the pain of all those who are suffering, all those who are ill like you. I promise," she told him, her expression momentarily feverish.

He lay back down and closed his eyes, his breath catching for a moment again. Vada's ideas sounded benevolent, but he was anxious about her earlier words, "wipe them out", "make them pay", "hate them all". But surely, she knew better than to actually do anything destructive?

"I'm glad you're okay," said Vada carefully after a few moments.

"Oh no," said Lim, sensing the sudden change in the air. "You're not leaving?"

She looked down at his hand, still in hers, and sighed. "What did you think was going to happen, Lim?" she asked. "With me, I mean."

"What?"

"This is why I didn't want to come," she said. "Because I knew that I would have to leave, and you'd make me feel bad."

"I'm not making you feel anything," he said, lying back down again. Vada was right, of course. What *had* he expected? He closed his eyes. "It's fine," he said. "Leave if you want."

"Lim," she said desperately. "Please don't do this. I have my own life here. You know that I can't go back."

"Can I stay with you?" he asked, opening his eyes again.

"What about Vaarem?" asked Vada. "What would he do without you?"

"I don't know," said Lim with a frustrated sigh. "We're not talking about Vaarem. I'm talking about me. And you. Can I come and stay with you? Please?" He looked up at her and tried to stop his lip from quivering.

Vada closed her eyes and bit her own lip. "Don't do this, Limmy," she said. "Please don't do this."

Lim closed his eyes again. He bit his swollen lip and sighed. The pain felt distant. Of course, he'd known that it would be like this. Why had he ever thought that it could be different? "It's fine," he said. "I understand." Even though he didn't and didn't think that he ever would.

Vada sat by his bedside for a while, not saying anything.

Lim lay with his eyes closed, trying to will himself back to sleep.

"Lim?" asked Vada eventually. "Are you all right?"

"Fine," he said. "But I'm really tired. I don't want to talk anymore."

Vada was silent for a while, then tried again. "Lim,"

"I mean it, Vada," said Lim. "I am really tired. I'm going to go to sleep now. Thank you for coming. Thank you for visiting me. I really do appreciate it. But I want to sleep now."

"Okay, darling," she said, sounding sad, but also relieved. "I love you. I hope you feel better soon." She sat with him for a while longer, then she stood up, kissed his forehead again, and left.

Lim wasn't asleep, but he pretended to be, because he didn't want to make this any more painful or awkward than it needed to be.

When she was finally gone, he fell asleep for real.

He woke up again after another hour. Nurse Mela was checking his pulse. He opened his eyes and looked around. It was fully light now.

"How are you feeling, Lim?" asked Mela.

"Fine," he said. "Tired and sore, but fine."

"Yes, that's to be expected," she said. "You will probably be a little off for the next two or three days. So, get plenty of rest during this time. It will increase the chances of the treatment sticking."

"Okay." Nodded Lim, sitting up and having another drink of water.

"Are you up to eating anything more substantial than fruit?" she asked, as she listened to his lungs with the stethoscope.

Lim considered this. He was satisfied from having eaten six pieces of fruit earlier, but he felt ready for something else. "Sure," he said. "Yes, please."

"Good." She nodded. "I will bring you something. Do take it easy on the food though," she warned him. "Don't try and eat too much too fast. It's not so imperative that you keep your weight up right now, so eat as much as you want, but don't feel obliged to finish everything that you're given."

"No worries there," he assured her. "That is not going to happen."

He went back to sleep after that, and when he woke up, his family were sitting around his bedside again.

"How are you, darling?" asked his mother, stroking his hand.

Lim sighed. He was going to get asked this question a lot over the next few days, so he thought that he ought to get used to it. "Fine," he said, sitting up.

Zareanna went to help him, but he waved her away. "I'm fine, really," he insisted. "I can sit up on my own. I may not be able to do much more, but I can at least do that."

She smiled indulgently at that and left him alone.

"Vada's gone," said Lim, when he was sitting comfortably. He looked at the bedside table, but the promised food had not materialised. Typical.

"Did she at least say good-bye?" asked Vaarem.

"Yes," replied Lim.

"Good."

There was an awkward silence for a few moments.

"What are you thinking, darling?" asked Zareanna, stroking his hair behind his ear.

"I can't wait to get out of here," he said. That seemed to sum up his thoughts nicely.

"You will soon," his mother reassured him.

Lim lay back down and closed his eyes.

"Are you okay?" asked Zareanna. "You look very pale."

"I'm fine," said Lim. "I'm just tired. They said that I would be for a while. Although if you really want to help, you could ask someone to bring me something to eat." He opened his eyes and looked at his mother hopefully. "I'm kind of hungry."

"Of course," she said, patting his hand and going to stand up.

"I'll do it," said Garrett, standing up from his usual seat in the corner. "I need to stretch my legs anyway," he explained, and left the room.

Lim closed his eyes again, then pulled the sheet up around his shoulders, as he was starting to feel cold.

"Are you warm enough?" asked Zareanna anxiously.

"I am now."

Zareanna held his hand and stroked his hair. He found it soothing, so he allowed her to continue.

"My poor, sick baby," she said softly.

"I do wish that you'd stop calling me that, Mother," he said wearily.

"I'm sorry, darling," she continued to stroke his hair. "I just worry, and I feel so bad for you. It's so unfair."

"I know," said Lim with a sigh. "Life isn't fair. But I am fine, really. Now, please let me sleep."

"Of course."

"You can keep on doing that," he said, referring to her stroking his hair. "That feels nice."

"I'm glad." She leaned down to kiss his cheek.

Lim allowed himself to drift off to sleep again.

He woke up about once every hour. Sometimes his family were there; other times, they weren't. Sometimes there was a snack on his bedside table. When there was, he ate it hungrily, before going back to sleep.

On the morning of the third day after the last procedure, Dr Turnwall came to see him. "How are you feeling?" he asked.

"Fine." Shrugged Lim. He was still feeling very tired and sleepy, and much as he wanted to go home, he didn't yet feel up to it.

Dr Turnwall examined him carefully, his face looking anxious, his natural eye wide.

"What?" asked Lim, putting his head in his hands as he sat up on the bed. He hadn't done more than eat or sleep for the past three days, so he was very shaky on his feet when he had to stand up. Dr Turnwall continued the examination, before asking Lim to sit down again.

Lim sat down on the bed.

He knew what was coming. He'd seen the same look on the face of every healer who had ever examined him. "It's bad, isn't it?" he prompted.

"It's not good," agreed Dr Turnwall, sitting down on the chair.

"Shit." Lim put his head in his hands again, letting his hair cover his face.

"Your body seems to be rejecting the treatment."

"Oh?" Lim looked up from under his hair. "How?" Of course, deep down, he'd known that it probably wouldn't work. Nothing ever did. But "rejecting" sounded ominous, even to him.

"Instead of incorporating the new energy, you seem to be working to get rid of it. I mean, your body is. Obviously, you're not doing this consciously. Your attitude has got nothing to do with it. That's why you're so tired, and why you're losing weight."

"What?" asked Lim. "How can I be? Losing weight, I mean? I've been eating everything I've been given."

"You've lost over a pound in the last three days," said Dr Turnwall gravely. "It seems that your body is working hard to rid itself of the foreign energy. Once this has happened, you will go back to normal, and by that, I mean, your normal, how you were before, when you first came here."

"So, I'm going to still be sick?" asked Lim grimly. *Why did I get my hopes up?* he berated himself.

"Yes, I'm afraid so."

"Right," said Lim, hanging his head.

"However, I do have a little bit of good news for you," said the doctor after a moment.

"Yeah?" Lim looked up again, doing his best not to get his hopes up, but hoping, nonetheless.

"Several of the potions that Dr Thorn gave you seemed to help with your breathing and your energy. This means that you will no longer have to rely solely on your previous medication, which I understand was losing its effectiveness."

Lim nodded.

"You will now have several options, so you won't need to worry about overdosing on any single thing, as you can take these new medications as well as your old one together."

"Right." Nodded Lim, "So, I'm not going to get better, but now I have a greater range of potions to manage my condition?"

"Yes, precisely," said Dr Turnwall, not realising that Lim was being sarcastic. "I am so sorry," continued the doctor. "I don't know why it's not working on you. This has never happened before."

"Yeah, yeah," said Lim. "I know." And then, because

he realised that he probably sounded rude and ungrateful, he said, "Thank you for trying, anyway. I'm sure the new medicines will help." Then he lay back down, feeling really low and disappointed. Furthermore, he felt like he'd let everybody down, not just the doctors and staff, but also his family and his friends. He hated the thought of writing to Jessa and Marla and telling them the bad news. He dreaded telling Fen and his other friends back home, and writing to Dr Fantail, and then to Magnon, because he knew that the healer from Morliss would want to know what had happened, regardless of the outcome.

"I'm sorry," said Dr Turnwall again, "but there is nothing more that we can do for you. We'll keep you here until your condition stabilises, then you will be able to go home."

"How long before that happens?" asked Lim. Today had been meant to be the day. Every time he thought that this horrid experience was coming to an end, the finish line got moved.

"It's hard to say. Perhaps another week."

"Great," said Lim with a sigh.

Dr Turnwall patted his hand awkwardly, then apologised again, before leaving.

When he was alone, Lim felt like he wanted to cry, but no tears came.

Fucking excellent, he thought. It'll probably happen when everyone is here, when my father tells me what a useless disappointment I am.

He closed his eyes and drew the sheet over his

shoulders, suddenly feeling cold again. He couldn't help hating himself even more than he ever had before. Everyone had had such high hopes, but his stupid body had, as usual, said "nope" to all that.

Lim continued to eat and sleep for the next few days. He had no energy, nor any desire to do anything else. He lost another three pounds in weight by the end of the week but steadied out after that. When his weight was stable for three days, Dr Turnwall told him that he would be discharged in three more days, barring any other complications.

Lim breathed a sigh of relief. The end was finally in sight.

He decided to get up and see Eliza. He hadn't seen her in days and was wondering what she was up to. He'd made peace with the fact that his treatment had failed, and he was ready to tell her, ready to listen as she said, "I told you so".

When he got to her room, he found that she wasn't alone. A man and a woman, as well as a boy of a similar age to her, were sitting around her. Lim figured that they were her family and was about to leave when she caught his eye. He smiled at her and was turning around when she said, "Wait!"

He turned back towards her.

"Come in, Lim," she said, using his name for the second time since she'd met him.

He came in, feeling suddenly shy.

"Mum, Dad, this is Lim. He's the elf that I was

telling you about. He recharged my charm. And convinced me to write to you."

"Hello, Lim." Eliza's father stood up to shake his hand.

Lim smiled down at him, as the man was about a head shorter than he was. Eliza's mother then stood up and hugged him. The boy stayed sitting and looked up at him curiously, before giving a small nod of greeting.

"Thank you," said Eliza's mother, looking up into Lim's face for a moment. "We were so worried about our Eliza, and she seems so much happier than the last time that we saw her. Thank you for giving us all hope."

"Um, yeah, sure," said Lim awkwardly. "You're welcome."

He sat down on one of the offered chairs.

"Eliza tells us that you want to be a Priest of the Fates," said Eliza's father, looking up at him.

"Yeah." Nodded Lim, wondering what exactly Eliza had told her family about him.

"I think you will make a great one. I can tell that you have very positive energy. That's rare," said Eliza's father.

"Thank you," said Lim, feeling touched. It seemed that Eliza's father was one of those rare humans who were sensitive to magic. Lim smiled at him awkwardly.

The vibe in the room was generally good. Lim could sense that Eliza's family were genuinely happy to see her. Currently, that was the overwhelming emotion. There was no blame, no guilt. It was nice.

However, he felt like he was intruding. "I better go," he said, after what he deemed was a polite amount of time. "My own family will probably come to see me soon. I just came to say hi."

He left the room, after saying good-bye to everyone, while also conveying to Eliza that he would be back. He wanted to talk to her alone. So, with a final smile and a wave, he left Eliza's room and walked back to his own, where he got into the bed and lay down. He was feeling extraordinarily tired again.

When he woke up, Vaarem was there, but no one else.

"Hey." Smiled Lim, sitting up. He'd missed talking with Vaarem. No matter how much he loved his mother, she was still his mother, and there were things that he didn't want to talk about in front of her.

"Hey," said Vaarem brightly. "I told Mother and Father to buy us some food, and they left. They seem a lot better than they were before, but Mother is still worried about you, so I assured them that you were sleeping. So, when they come back, please pretend that you just woke up."

"Okay," said Lim. "But why? Also, is there anything to eat? I'm starving."

Vaarem looked at the bedside table. "No," he said. "That's why I sent Mother and Father out. Did they not give you anything?"

"Obviously not." Shrugged Lim. "Unless I already ate it. Or," he added cynically, "they want to find another reason not to let me go."

"Huh?"

"Haven't you heard?" said Lim. "I am supposedly meant to be getting discharged in three days' time. Provided that I don't lose any more weight. It would be just my luck if I did because they deliberately didn't feed me." He laughed, but there was an edge to it.

"They wouldn't do that," said Vaarem, although he sounded unsure.

Lim wondered why. Had Vaarem been talking to Eliza?

"Probably not," agreed Lim. "Although I am quite hungry, so I hope someone brings me something soon. I don't want my body to get any ideas. I am sure that it hates me."

Vaarem didn't reply for a moment, but then said, "I wish you wouldn't say stuff like that. I never know what to tell you."

Lim chuckled. "Oh, I'm sorry that me venting about always being sick inconveniences you." He wasn't angry at Vaarem. In fact, he found the whole thing quite amusing. He was aware that his illness affected his brother too, as well as his family and anyone that he cared to get close to.

But them's the breaks, he thought. If you can't laugh, you'll go insane.

Vaarem grinned. "Oh, you can vent all you want.

Just don't expect me to say anything to make you feel better."

Lim was about to say something witty about Vaarem being an airhead who was incapable of thinking up an appropriate comeback to make anyone feel better, but instead said seriously, "Var, you should be aware that just knowing that you're always there for me is enough to make me feel better. You don't have to say anything, ever."

Vaarem looked at him for a moment, then leaned over and put his arms around Lim's shoulders. "Thanks," he said. "I'm glad you know, because you really are my favourite person in the whole world."

"And you're mine," said Lim softly, holding on to Vaarem.

They were interrupted by Nurse Silveia walking in with a lunch tray. The click-clack of her step warned of her coming, but the brothers didn't care and kept holding each other for a while longer.

"Hello?" said Silveia cautiously, as she tried to manoeuvre the tray around Vaarem.

Vaarem let go of Lim and sat back in his chair, allowing the nurse to put a tray down on the bedside table next to him.

Lim looked over at it. There was a bowl of soup and some bread, as well as a salad.

"Thank you," said Lim, picking up the bowl and a spoon.

"You're very welcome," she said. "I hear you will be leaving us soon."

"You hear correctly," said Lim between spoonfuls. "In two and a half more days."

She smiled at him, a little sadly. "Well, we will sure miss you. But I am sure you won't miss us."

Lim smiled at her. "I will miss some of you," he said, smiling warmly at her. She and Nurse Ariella had been particularly nice to him, and he imagined that he would probably miss them sometimes. And Eliza. He would have to make a plan to write to her, as she'd become one of his best friends.

Silveia smiled at him again, then left the room, leaving the elves alone again.

"Oh, guess what?" said Vaarem after a while.

"What?" asked Lim, between spoonfuls again. He was surprised at how much he was enjoying eating food.

"I got a letter from Marla and Jessa. They wrote to me at the inn."

"Oh?" asked Lim. He hadn't realised that Vaarem had taken to writing to the sisters on his own too. He was glad of this, as it had been Vaarem who had introduced them all to each other and Lim had always felt a little strange thinking that the sisters somehow preferred him over his brother. He was happy that this wasn't the case. "What did they say?"

"Well, they are very worried about you and hope that your treatment is going well. I have not yet told them otherwise."

"Thanks," said Lim. "I am gearing up to tell them. What else?"

"There is some human winter lights festival or something in a couple of weeks' time, and they would really like it if we could time our journey to be there for it, and to accompany them to the party, as their dates."

Lim smiled despite himself. "Dates? They really said that?"

"Well, they didn't use that particular word. I can't remember their exact wording, but that was the implication. What do you think?"

"Sure," said Lim. "Why not? Sounds like fun." He'd never been on a date before.

"Great," said Vaarem. "I was afraid that you wouldn't be discharged in time, but if you're getting out of here in three days." He trailed off.

"Barring anything else stupid happening," said Lim.

He put the half-eaten bowl of soup back on the bedside table, then picked up the salad and had a forkful, before lying back down. "I'm full," he told Vaarem. "You can have some of the leftovers if you want."

"You're full already?" asked Vaarem incredulously. "Half an hour ago you were going on about being starving, and now you're full after half a bowl of soup? No wonder you struggle to keep weight on. Sheesh, that wouldn't even be a snack for me."

Lim shrugged in response. "I guess because I only lie around in bed, I don't get that hungry." He wondered whether he should try and eat more now, but he really hated the feeling of being stuffed. It was so uncomfortable. "I'll try and have some more later," he said. "Fuck, I'm so tired again." He closed his eyes.

"It's okay," said Vaarem, reaching over and stroking his hair. "Didn't they say that you will get your energy back eventually?"

"Eventually," conceded Lim. "I will get back *my* energy levels, which have always been laughably small. Fortunately, my current lack of energy extends to my brain, and I am just too tired to give a crap at the moment." He closed his eyes again, but a moment later, he heard his parents walking into the room.

"Here you are, Vary." Lim heard his mother say. "I got you some bread filled with chicken and salad. And we got some for Limmy too. Has he been sleeping all this time?"

"Thanks," said Vaarem, obviously taking the offered food, but Lim couldn't be sure because he had his eyes closed. "He woke up before," said Vaarem, "and had some food, and then he went back to sleep."

"Awww," said Zareanna, sitting down on her usual chair and taking Lim's hand in hers. Lim wondered whether she would still do that if he slept with his hands under the blanket. He resolved to find out the next day. If he remembered.

Although he was tired, he couldn't sleep, so eventually he opened his eyes and lifted himself up on his elbows.

"Did you sleep well, darling?" asked Zareanna, her tone, as always, anxious.

Lim was conscious of how worried his mother was

about him, and he longed to somehow reassure her. He hated seeing her with a tear-stained face and puffy, red eyes, especially hearing about how she'd fretted over Malkim the same way.

Well, I will not die, he resolved. I will not do that to her, nor to anybody else. "Yeah," he said.

He sat up, trying to make himself comfortable. He was starting to realise just how narrow and creaky the hospital bed was. Even being as skinny as he was, he found that there was not enough space to ever be truly comfortable. Once again, he thought of how he longed to go home.

"Did the doctors give you any more updates?" asked Zareanna.

"Yes," said Lim. "I will be ready to be discharged in three days, well, two-and-a-half days' time from now. Provided that nothing else bad happens and that I don't lose any more weight. I seem to be steady there for the past three days."

"That's wonderful, darling," said Zareanna, sitting on the side of the bed and hugging him to her again. He slouched right down so that he could rest his head on her soft breast, the way he'd done when he'd been little. She held him and stroked his hair, not saying anything else. Vaarem sat on Lim's other side, eating his filled bread quietly. Garrett sat in his usual spot in the corner, his arms crossed. He looked at his wife holding their youngest son with an unreadable expression on his face.

Lim couldn't help thinking that his father was

disappointed in him, as usual. He closed his eyes, wishing, not for the first time, that there was something that he could do to make his father care about him the way that he did about Vaarem. He wished that he hadn't been cursed with a body that refused to function properly, no matter how much help and assistance it was given. He kept his eyes closed and allowed his mother to hold him, pretending that he was once again a small child, and that everything was going to be all right.

"My poor, sweet Limmy," said Zareanna, kissing the top of his head. "It will be good to have you home again."

"Yeah," agreed Lim. It *would* be good when they all finally got home.

A little later that afternoon, while Lim's family were still with him, Dr Thorn came in. Having exhausted all topics of conversation, the family had decided to play the card game that Vaarem had brought along for the trip. They had played three rounds and Lim had won them all.

"How are you feeling today, Lim?" asked the half-dwarf. Today, his hair was done up in two braids, as was his beard. Lim thought that he looked rather stylish and resolved to attempt the style with his own hair one day soon, as well as momentarily lamenting elves' inability to grow facial hair.

"Fine," said Lim, putting his cards down on the bedside table.

"Good," said Dr Thorn, checking Lim's vital signs. "Everything seems to be in order." He smiled when he'd finished.

Lim smiled back uncertainly.

"Are you sleeping okay?" asked Dr Thorn.

"Yes." Nodded Lim. "But I'm still constantly tired." He felt the need to add.

"That's to be expected," said the doctor. "But your energy will return. I will start you on your new course of potions this afternoon. You should see some improvement in your energy levels after that," he told Lim, as he made some notes. "In the meantime, keep on resting and don't over-exert yourself. And make sure you keep eating regularly."

"Thank you," said Lim. "I will."

When Dr Thorn had gone, the family played another round of the game, with Lim winning again, then Garrett winning the round after. The vibe in the air was cautiously optimistic.

Lim picked up the filled bread that his parents had brought in for him earlier, and bit into it as his father shuffled the cards. He ate about half of it, before putting the remainder back on the plate because he was full.

Garrett frowned at him. "Didn't the doctor tell you to eat, Limnos?"

"Uh, yes," said Lim. "That's what I'm doing."

"Well, make sure you eat enough," said Garrett. "I really have no desire to stay in this wretched city any longer just because you're too lazy to look after yourself."

"I have no desire to stay here any longer either," protested Lim.

"I'm glad to hear that," said his father coldly. "Because it's up to you. As we are finding out each day, no one can help you. So, please, for the sake of all the Fates, look after yourself so that we can all get out of here once and for all."

"Yes, Father," said Lim, dropping his gaze. He wished that he had as much control over his life and his body as his father seemed to think that he did.

They played another round, but Lim's heart wasn't in it anymore, so Vaarem ended up winning. He was extremely proud of himself and jumped up to do a victory dance around the room. Lim laughed until his sides hurt, but in a good way. He was so glad that out of all the brothers in the world, Vaarem was his brother. His twin always made every situation better.

Later that evening, when his family had gone, Lim went to visit Eliza.

She was sitting on her bed, making notes on a piece of paper. As he got closer, Lim saw that she was drawing pictures of dresses.

"Hello, elf." She looked up and smiled. She seemed so much more alive recently, so much more vital. It was beautiful to see.

"Hello," he said, sitting down on a chair next to her. "What are you doing?"

"Just drawing," she said. "My mother is a seam-stress. When I finally get out of here, I am going to help her in the shop."

"That's great," said Lim. "Do you know when you will be getting out of here, then?"

She sighed and shook her head. "No," she said. "Not yet."

"Oh," said Lim. "I hope you get an update soon."

"Yes," she agreed, then said, "I'm sorry that your treatment didn't work." She patted his hand. "But I told you, didn't I?"

"You did," he agreed. "But I guess it could have been worse. At least they didn't damage me the last time like they did the first two times."

"Small mercies," she said with a chuckle. "So, what's going to happen to you?" she enquired. "Are they going to try again?"

"No," said Lim seriously. "There is nothing more they can do for me. However, even if they wanted to try, I wouldn't let them. I want to go home."

"So, what's going to happen?"

"They're going to discharge me in two-and-a-half days. Provided that I don't lose any more weight," he added with a sigh.

"Oh yes," she said. "That reminds me. I have taken your advice and have started to eat a bit. I figure that if you can eat normally and stay so skinny, then I should be able to as well, right?"

"Yes," said Lim carefully, "Although if we're on the topic, I often wish that I wasn't quite so skinny. Then again, that's the least of my problems." He shrugged and gave her a grim smile.

"Well, like I told you, I think you're absolutely beautiful," she said, "and not just because you're an elf. You're handsome even by elf standards."

Lim felt his face colouring, feeling strange at the compliment, but nevertheless he smiled at her and said graciously, "Thank you. And like I told you, you're lovely too. So, I am very glad to hear that you're start-ing to eat normally. Because eating is kind of impor-tant," he said with a chuckle. "And I'm sure that you'll stay skinny too. You've got a very slight build for a human."

She looked at him with that same wonder in her eyes that she gave him whenever he said anything that she deemed a compliment. "You mean it?" she asked.

"Of course, I mean it. Why would I say it if I didn't mean it?" he asked, even though he was aware that he'd said many things in his life that he didn't mean to avoid hurting people. But this was not one of those times. "Will you write to me when I leave here?" he asked her. "I would really like it if you did."

"Of course," she replied. "I am going to miss you."

"I am going to miss you too. Perhaps when you're better, you can come and visit me in Palinas."

"Perhaps," she said. "And when I learn to sew, I will make you a coat or something. Would you like that?"

"Yes," said Lim. "I really would. Very much."

"Great." She clapped her hands. "What colours do you like to wear?"

"Black," he said, realising that she'd never seen him in anything other than the hospital gown, and vice versa. He wondered what she normally wore.

"Any other colours?" she asked.

He shook his head. "No. Maybe very, very dark grey or something."

She laughed at that. "Okay. That was something I didn't expect. I like to wear pinks and yellows and lavenders. All the colours of the rainbow."

"I'm sure you look lovely in them," he said, picturing her in a pastel-coloured dress, twirling around in a field of flowers.

"I don't know about that," she said.

"I think I do," he said, not knowing how it was that he knew this, but knowing that he did.

He gave her his address in Palinas, before leaving to go back to his own room. He was feeling tired again.

When he got to his room, Dr Thorn was waiting for him.

"Good to see that you're up and about," said the doctor.

"Thanks," said Lim. "I'm sorry to keep you waiting. I didn't know you were coming."

"Not to worry." Dr Thorn waved Lim's concern away. "I wasn't waiting long. Come and sit down and I'll take you through your new prescriptions."

Lim sat down on the bed. Dr Thorn checked his

pulse, then did some other checks and made some notes, before sitting down on the chair facing the bed. Lim saw that on the bedside table there was a tray stacked with small bottles and jars. Dr Thorn picked one up. "This is the formula that you were taking before. From what I understand, it was becoming less effective, but you were already taking the maximum dosage?"

"Yes," agreed Lim glumly.

"Now you will be taking it once a day only, in the mornings when you get up. So, you will take your full dose in one go."

"Okay." Lim nodded.

Dr Thorn picked up another bottle, explaining what it was, and instructing Lim to take it each day with his midday meal. Lim nodded in understanding.

"This one," Dr Thorn continued, picking up yet another bottle, "you will be taking at night, before you go to bed. It is not a sleeping potion mind you, it's just to assist you with your breathing."

"Okay." Nodded Lim again, thinking that he should probably be writing this down, as he feared that he wouldn't remember it all.

"Don't worry," said Dr Thorn, as if reading his mind, "I will write all of this down for you. I will give you several moons' supply, and I will also give you the recipes, so you can get your local healers to make these up for you."

"Okay." Nodded Lim again.

"Now," said Dr Thorn, taking two little bottles off

the tray and putting them directly on the bedside table, "it is important that you take your medications each day. Do you understand?"

"Yes." Nodded Lim.

"Because hopefully you will start to feel better within a week or so of starting this routine. But you must not stop. Once the levels build up in your system, you need to maintain them. If you stop the potions, you will get very sick very quickly. These are not a cure for your condition, it's all just to help you manage it. Do you understand?"

Lim nodded again. "Trust me, I understand," he said. He knew better than to think he'd been cured.

"Now," the doctor continued, picking up one of the small jars, "there will be times when you will inevitably feel worse, despite this regime. So, if that happens, you can take this. Pour boiling water on the leaves and make a tea. You can drink it as often as you need, however if you still need it after using it every day for longer than a week, then go and get a check-up. So, if you feel bad, don't increase your doses of these ones here." He indicated the first three bottles. "Just use this." He put the jar next to the three bottles.

"Sure." Lim nodded.

"Finally," said Dr Thorn, indicating the remaining jar and bottle, "you have these. This one." He picked up the jar, "is a sleeping potion. Take this if you can't sleep, but use it sparingly, as it is very strong. So, only as a last resort, yes?"

"Yes," said Lim, remembering the last time he'd

used a sleeping potion. He wouldn't use one again unless he was extremely desperate.

"And this one is a painkiller." Dr Thorn picked up the last bottle. "Again, like the sleeping potion, it is very, very strong, so again, use it sparingly, and only as a last resort. Understood?"

"Yes," said Lim. "Understood."

"Good." Dr Thorn smiled. He got up off the chair and instructed Lim to take some of the evening potion from the third bottle. "It also goes without saying that you need to remember to eat regularly. You need to fuel your body regardless of what else may be happening. The potions are all more effective when taken with food, too."

Lim nodded.

Dr Thorn smiled. "Good," he said. "Sleep well. I will come and check in on you tomorrow morning."

Lim slept better than he had in days. He wasn't sure if this was due to the new medication, or because the failed energy treatment had finally left his system, or perhaps because he was finally on the home-stretch. It didn't matter, because he was going to be leaving soon regardless.

He spent his last two days in the hospital writing letters.

He wrote to Vada, then to Fen, then to Marla and Jessa, and later to his other friends in Palinas, and finally to Magnon and Dr Fantail, telling them all that while the treatment had failed, and he wasn't cured, he'd at least gotten some new potions to manage his condition. To his friends and sister, he also wrote about his hopes for the future, about how even though he would never be a mage like he'd wanted to, he'd found a great consolation prize and was excited to start studying to become a Priest of the Fates. After that, he wrote to the Temple of the Fates in Palinas, asking for permission to train with them.

Chapter 18

Discharge

On the last morning, after Dr Turnwall and Dr Thorn had both given him his final check-up, Lim started to pack his things. He hadn't started getting ready to leave earlier, in case this tempted the Fates somehow and the doctors found a reason to keep him in longer.

As it turned out, his examination went well. His weight was steady, and his overall energy levels had increased. His breathing was as good as it had ever been. He managed to blow the piece of fabric almost to the first marker, which was a little further than when he'd been admitted.

He said good-bye to the doctors and nurses, thanking them all for their care, then he went to see Eliza.

Her eyes widened when he walked in. She'd never seen him in his street clothes before.

"Well, I guess this is good-bye," he said, walking over and hugging her. "I will write to you, and hopefully we will see each other again one day. I hope you get better soon."

"Thank you," she replied, hugging him back. "Thank you for everything. I wish you all the best."

Lim was happy to finally leave the hospital. He rode the horseless carriage back to the inn in wonder. His family had seen all this every day for the past four weeks, but Lim hadn't, so he gaped at everything in awe, ignoring his family behind him. They were all much more relaxed than they'd been on the way here. This in itself made Lim feel better, even as he still struggled to walk and talk at the same time and got winded when walking up a single flight of stairs. The smell of dust and oil still made him a little nauseated, but not as badly as before. By the time he got off the carriage, he barely noticed it anymore.

When arriving at the inn, the first thing he did was to visit the stable. He'd missed Clea and Sera and was very glad to see them again and stroke their soft noses and manes. The horses seemed happy to see him too, and he spent a good half hour sitting with them and telling them about everything that had happened. He also spent some time talking to the other horses in the stable, finding their presence calming, until Vaarem, who was with him, started to get bored and bade him to go to their room.

As soon as the twins got back to the suite in the inn, the tension started.

It appeared that Garrett and Zareanna were arguing with each other over the hospital staff. Zareanna had wanted to get them all a little token of appreciation, to say thank-you for looking after Lim, but Garrett had been adamant that they'd done nothing, so didn't deserve it.

"He's not cured," said Garrett, rolling his eyes. "They only fixed what they themselves broke. None of us are better off, especially not Lim."

Vaarem rolled his eyes. "They've been at each other all day," he said with a sigh. "You would think that that breakthrough with Vada after your last procedure had never happened."

"Don't worry," said Lim. "I'm here now, so Father will soon realise that he has someone else to yell at."

Garrett didn't yell at Lim, nor say anything spiteful or nasty. "I am sorry that the treatment didn't work, Lim," he said simply. "I must admit, my hopes were never high, but still." He shook his head. "I've been thinking recently," he continued, looking at Lim with an expression that Lim couldn't quite read. If he'd had to guess, he would have said that his father looked regretful, and he wondered why.

"Yes?" Lim asked carefully.

"Your mother is right," said his father, "I *have* always been too hard on you. But you've got to understand. You remind me of Malkim so much and I really fear that you will suffer the same fate."

Lim looked at his father. "How am I like him?" he asked. No one had ever explained this to him.

Garrett sighed, then said, "He was an empath like you, sensitive to the energies around him. He was very, very smart but quiet, and thoughtful like you are. He was very powerful. He had more magic talent than anyone I've ever known, with the possible exception of Vada, but he overused it." He looked away wistfully, as if remembering. "He was the best," he said, "But he was also the worst. He was the most self-destructive individual I'd ever met. He was frequently ill, but he pretended that he wasn't, and would push himself beyond his limits, like I've seen you do. He'd refuse healers. He refused to go to the hospital." He shook his head. "He refused to eat," he said, and Lim saw the obvious anger in his father's eyes. "That was the worst thing. He never ate anything, and if he ever did, he'd throw it up as soon as he could. It was like he wanted to be empty."

Lim was reminded of Eliza. "Malkim had an eating disorder?" he asked curiously.

"What?"

"There was a girl at the hospital," Lim told his father about Eliza.

Garrett listened carefully, then was silent for a long moment. "Fuck," he said softly, "I had no idea. So, it's an actual condition?"

Lim nodded.

"Shit," said Garrett, "And all this time I thought that he was just being deliberately difficult."

"Well, I never knew him, obviously," said Lim, "but Eliza did tell me that she *couldn't* eat anything. Not wouldn't, but couldn't. It made her feel sick," he tried to explain.

Garrett nodded, "Malkim used to say the same." He sighed. "I didn't believe him."

"I'm sorry," said Lim, "That must've been hard for Mother and for you." It had been difficult enough watching Eliza's obvious pain, and he'd only known her for a few weeks. He didn't want to imagine seeing someone he cared about going through that for turns upon turns.

"It was," said Garrett, "It was awful. But your Mother." He paused as if considering what to say next, "had different ways of dealing with it." He shook his head and looked down. Lim could tell that he was struggling to keep his emotions under control. He was sad and angry, and just generally upset. Lim wanted to reach over and comfort him but held back. His father had never been one for being comforted; he would normally lash out in anger.

"That's why I want you to eat," said Garrett, looking up. "I don't want you to get so weak that you can't take care of yourself. Malkim," he began, then shook his head. "I was really scared when your procedure was delayed. I blamed you, like I blamed Malkim. I'm sorry. I know now I didn't help. But at the time." He trailed off, and Lim couldn't tell if his father was talking about him or Malkim, or probably both of them.

"I know," said Lim softly, "but it's different. Eliza, at

the hospital, told me that she had many issues, many reasons as to why she couldn't eat. She didn't like the idea of the food "rotting inside her" as she said. She was afraid of getting fat, even though she was bone thin. She complained of stomach pains when she did eat. She saw it as a way to control her body and by extension her life," Lim tried to explain, "But I'm not like that. I don't think any of that. I'm certainly not afraid of getting fat." He chuckled.

Garrett nodded, listening intently, for the first time that Lim could recall, actually paying attention to him, and taking his words seriously, "It sounds like your friend has the same disorder that Malkim did. He too complained of stomach pains after eating, but I thought it was an excuse. He once mentioned that he'd been teased for being plump in his youth, so was deathly afraid of putting on weight." He sighed. "Fates, if only I'd known."

"I don't know if you could've done anything," said Lim. "Eliza told me that she was making a conscious effort to start eating, but I don't think it's that simple," he said sadly. "She wants to get better, but she feels like she can't. Like her brain and body won't let her. It sounds like an awful disease, and it seems like something that doesn't just have an easy cure," he said with a thoughtful shrug of his shoulders. He wasn't the only one with problems, and this made him feel better about himself. He may have been a freak, but he wasn't the only one. Everyone had something they struggled with, whether it was physical, or emotional.

"It sounds awful indeed," Garrett shook his head once more, "Fates, I feel like such an arse. I couldn't help him, and now I can't help you either."

"But you can," said Lim, "You are helping me. You brought me here to Sirrock City, even though I know you didn't want to. And even though I'm not cured, I now have better ways to manage." He smiled at his father. "And I think that this trip has brought us closer as a family, which is helpful too."

Garrett smiled back, then reached over and threw his arms around Lim, drawing him into a tight hug. Lim yelped at the unexpected gesture, but promptly hugged his father back.

"I still worry about you," said Garrett, as father and son dropped their arms and looked at each other.

Lim bit his lip. It always came down to this. Everyone *worried* about him, and he felt helpless when it came to trying to reassure them. "I am not like Malkim and Eliza," he said firmly, "I have no problems with the idea of eating or controlling my body or anything, I just have no appetite, but I do think that I am getting better at eating regularly."

"Not that I've seen so far," said Garrett, then when Lim felt his face fall, he said, "Fates, Lim, I'm sorry. I'm doing it again, making it your problem because I can't fix it. What I meant was that I haven't noticed you eating more, but I will do my best to trust that you're telling the truth."

"I am," said Lim earnestly, "I really do feel that my appetite has increased a little. Perhaps I haven't been eating more as far as you've seen, but it's not as much of a chore as in the past. You will see a visible improvement soon, I hope." He smiled, and Garrett smiled back.

"Fair enough," said Garrett, "but do look after yourself, Lim because it's not just the eating thing, it's everything." He lifted his hands up, as if encompassing the whole world. "And your mother does worry, but." He bit his lip, then he said quickly, "Sometimes I feel like she enables unhelpful behaviour because she doesn't want to cause you any more pain, and I am just really, really scared to where that may lead. Please don't misunderstand, your mother is doing her best, and she did her best with Malkim. No one loved him more than she did, but sometimes just loving someone is not enough. Sometimes people need help and other times they need to be called out if they are doing something dangerous, even if it's painful in the moment. Do you understand?"

"Yes." Nodded Lim, "I do," he said, "and for what it's worth, I'm sorry."

"It's not your fault," said his father. "However, I do expect that you will take your new potions as prescribed. You need to look after yourself, Lim. And if you so much as think about missing a meal, I swear that I will personally ram it down your throat. Now that I know that you *can* eat, you *will not* starve yourself on my watch. There are things that you can do to help yourself, so you *need* to do them. This has been hard on all of us, but especially your mother. She worries about you so much and gets so upset. You need to do all that you can to take care of yourself, for her sake as much as your own."

"Yes, Father." Lim hung his head. *I know that it's hard on everyone. Fates, why do you think that I don't try?* But he didn't say anything else because there was no point.

Zareanna was in the living room, packing. She looked up when Lim walked past and saw his expression. "What happened, darling?" she asked, standing up.

Lim simply shook his head. He couldn't talk, as he was afraid that he would burst into tears. As always, he'd let everyone down.

Zareanna took his hand and led him out of the room, through the corridor and into the suite next door, where Vaarem and Lim would be spending the night.

Lim put down his bag. Dr Thorn had given him a large satchel to keep his potions in. He opened this now and took out the bottle with his midday dose, then had a swig, before sitting down on the couch. Zareanna sat down with him.

"What happened, darling?" she asked, putting her arm around his shoulders and using her other hand to stroke his hair.

Lim shrugged. "Just the usual," he said with a sob, as a tear leaked out of his eye. "I feel like I've let every-one down, especially you. I don't want you to always have to worry about me."

"You haven't let anyone down," she assured him, "Especially not me. I am so proud of you and how bravely you handle yourself. You could never let me down, sweetie," she kissed his head.

"Yes, she's right," said Vaarem, walking in from the bedroom and sitting down on Lim's other side. "You have not let anyone down. It wasn't under your control." He patted Lim on the shoulder, then stood up and said, "Come on. Let's go and do something." He took Lim's hand and pulled him to his feet. "We've got one more day left in the city," he explained. "You haven't seen the sights, so let me show you."

"Okay," said Lim. It sounded better than sitting in this room, feeling sorry for himself.

Zareanna smiled, then she stood up too. "Be careful," she said. Lim didn't know whether she was talking to him or to Vaarem, or possibly to both of them in general.

"We will," said Vaarem, before Lim had a chance to respond. "I'm going to take Lim to the museum, and the park, and maybe the library." He looked at Lim questioningly. Lim nodded. "Then we can have dinner somewhere, so you and Father can spend some time together," he suggested. "You must be sick of me tagging along with you all the time." He grinned.

Zareanna nodded. "That would be lovely," she said, "but don't stay out too late," she warned. "We will see you both for breakfast tomorrow, and then we will check out and be on our way home."

"Yes," said Vaarem. "Thank you." He leaned down and kissed his mother on the cheek. Lim did the same.

"Have fun, sweetie," said Zareanna to Lim. "And don't overdo it. Vaarem, you'll have a care for him, won't you? Come back if Lim looks like he's getting tired or something. And, Limmy, you too. Don't try and do too much. We will return to Sirrock City another time if you want, so don't feel like you need to do everything today."

"Yes, of course," said Lim, letting her hold him for a few moments. He then kissed her on the cheek again and went to follow Vaarem outside. At the last moment, he turned around and picked up his medicine bag. He picked the bottles that he thought he might need and put them in his coat pocket.

Chapter 19

Out in Sirrock City

Vaarem led Lim out of the inn. The afternoon was cool, but the sun was shining. There was a hint of the coming of spring. Lim breathed in carefully, enjoying the fresh air (or as fresh as it was in the city, which was still better than the stale chemical-scented air in the hospital).

"Where do you want to go?" asked Vaarem.

Lim shrugged. "I don't know. The museum sounds good. And the library."

Vaarem chuckled, as they made their way towards the horseless-carriage stop. The line of carriages, Vaarem had told him earlier, was called a tram. "Trust you to actually want to go to the library," he said, rolling his eyes.

Lim shrugged again. "I like to read," he said simply.

"I know." Vaarem smiled, then put his arm around Lim's shoulders.

Many people turned to look as the two of them walked down the street. Vaarem took it all in his stride and strutted his stuff proudly. Lim followed him, hugging his arms around himself, looking down at the ground, too shy and awkward to meet anyone's gaze, even as he heard some appreciative mutters and felt positive sentiments. His breath came to him with difficulty, but his lungs didn't hurt as much as previously. He pushed his hair behind his pointed ears, not liking how greasy it felt in his fingers. He would wash it that very night, he decided, as he hadn't washed his hair since coming to Sirrock.

Vaarem put his arm around Lim's shoulders again, as if to shield and protect him from all the attention.

They got on a tram and rode it all the way to the museum, which was situated in the north-west of the city.

"How are you really?" asked Vaarem, as the tram made its way through the streets. "I know you get asked that all the time but tell me."

Lim smiled at his brother, then rested his head on Vaarem's shoulder. "It varies from moment to moment," he admitted. "Physically, I feel fine. Or, as fine as I ever get. I can breathe. My chest and stomach don't hurt. But emotionally?" he shrugged. "I don't know. I do feel like I've let everybody down." He sighed.

"Oh man," said Vaarem, drawing him in closer.

"That's not true. Really. Like I keep saying, it's outside your control. And despite everything, I think this trip has been good for Mother and Father."

Lim smiled thinly. The trip *had* been good for their family as a whole, and it was because of him that they'd all come here. But he still felt let down by his own body. Why did it refuse to function properly?

They got off the tram and walked the short distance to the Museum of Art.

"You're back." The young human woman at the entrance desk smiled at Vaarem, as he paid their entry fee.

"Well." He grinned at her, "I had to show my brother. We are leaving Sirrock City tomorrow. I also wanted to see you again before leaving. We hardly got a chance to talk last time."

The young woman blushed. "I know," she said. "You didn't even ask me my name."

"I apologise," said Vaarem. "I was not in a great state of mind. My brother was in the hospital, undergoing an experimental procedure and I was very worried."

Lim felt his face colour, and he stepped behind Vaarem. He looked down at his feet and kept his eyes down.

"Oh no," the young woman said to Vaarem kindly, "I am so sorry to hear that. How did it go?"

Lim kept looking at his shoes and at the ground beneath them. The floor was made of stone, with a mosaic pattern of circles, stars, and diamonds in blue, grey, and gold.

"He's here with me," said Vaarem, ushering Lim forward.

Lim looked up.

The young woman smiled up at him. "I am so glad to hear that you are well now."

Lim smiled thinly. "Yeah," he said, praying to all the Fates that Vaarem wouldn't go into details.

"What is your name by the way?" asked Vaarem, smiling.

"Melissa, what's yours?"

"I'm Vaarem. This is my brother Lim."

"Well, lovely to formally meet you, Vaarem, and nice to meet you, Lim," said Melissa. "The artworks in the main gallery have all been created by artists from the Sirranna Region. The media includes glass, stone, wood, and metal. In the far rooms, there are some paintings and drawings created by artists from all over Zemia."

"Oh," said Vaarem, "I didn't know that."

"Well, it's a good thing that you returned." She grinned. "Enjoy the art, Vaarem, and you too, Lim. I will see you on the way out."

"Thank you," said Vaarem, giving a small bow.

"Thank you," said Lim and followed his brother.

They walked through the rooms and looked at the sculptures. Many were of animals and of people: humans on winged horses, elves on unicorns, dwarves on lindwyrms, pixies on hipponixies. Then there were trees made of gold and silver, flowers made of glass, dragons carved from wood. Some of the sculptures were more abstract: a coloured glass tunnel that people could walk through, a group of wooden spheres and pillars of varying sizes.

Lim found it all very soothing. He'd never created visual art like this. His preferred medium had been music, and he thought back to his violin, which was still in the bottom of his wardrobe. As with most things, he'd eventually gotten too sick to play it, and then his father had threatened to sell it to pay for Lim's medical treatments, so Lim had put it in the wardrobe and not touched it again. That had been more than five turns ago.

As they walked into the last room, the one with the paintings, Lim thought of his mother. One day, she'd stopped painting. Just like he'd stopped his music, she'd stopped her art. He wondered why.

The first paintings that they looked at were water-colour landscapes. There were paintings of forests by elf artists, mountains by dwarves, rivers and lakes by pixies, cities by humans. Then there were portraits. The first portrait was of a tall, slender elf with auburn hair and aqua-coloured eyes. The caption read *"King Feanarill Flamewind, also known as Feanarill the Fair"*.

"The previous king of Palinora," said Vaarem, and Lim nodded, leaning forward to read the rest of the caption.

"He was the king of all elves," said Lim, "of Palinora and Talinda. It was after he died with no heirs that the two countries split up."

Vaarem nodded.

Lim sighed at the thought. Vada's human ancestors had also been kings and queens, and after their deposition, the land of Sirranna had been split into the Three Countries. It seemed that some family dynamics had great consequences. But all families had consequences that were important to their members.

The next portrait was of a dwarf woman with black hair streaked with silver, and bright blue eyes. She was Queen Vermana of the Mountain, and she'd ruled the country of Gidean a century ago.

On the far wall hung a large portrait of a human man. He was tall and thin, dressed in high black boots and a dark blue riding coat. His arm was raised towards a silver dragon that flew along the top of the frame. Lim recognised the style as his mother's and he stepped closer. The man in the portrait had long black hair, and a neat black beard and moustache. His face was very thin and angular, his cheekbones high and sharp, his eyes dark and shadowed. Even though his eyes were dark brown, not blue, the resemblance to his daughter was uncanny.

"Wow," said Vaarem, looking up at the painting, "did Mother paint it?"

Lim nodded. "I think so," he said quietly, his voice full of awe. Did his mother even know that her painting hung in the Museum of Art in Sirrock? "It's her style," said Lim, reading the caption. *"Malkim Blackwell, also known as Malkim the Great, and Malkim the Mediator, he officially decreed that the Three Countries remain independent, giving up the throne for good, stating that the Blackwells would not rule, but merely protect and advise. Portrait painted by Malkim's wife, Zareanna Bluebell."*

"Wow," said Lim, looking up at his brother with wide eyes.

Vaarem read the caption. "That must've been what Father meant," he said.

"What?"

"I overheard Mother and Father talking," explained Vaarem. "Mother said that she never expected Father to be like Malkim. Father said, "Good, because I could never do the things he did." I thought he meant something bad, but he must've meant this. Officially giving up his throne to secure peace," he said. "That must have been hard. Now I feel so bad for thinking bad things about him. And about Father."

Lim nodded. The Blackwells had had a very bad reputation before Malkim, and he'd sought to change this by giving up their rule, but still giving those loyal to them positions of influence and respect. This had appeased most people, but the fanatical loyalists, those who wished to reinstate the rule of the dragontamers at any cost, still called Malkim a weakling and a traitor to their cause, so they were giving the family a bad name again.

"Poor Vada." Lim shook his head. "No wonder she's too busy to write to me. She probably has her hands full, trying to keep the fanatics in line."

Vaarem, nodded in agreement.

They looked at the painting of Malkim for a long

time, then had a brief look at some of the others, before making their way back to the cafe in the front of the gallery.

"Would you like to join us for a cup of tea?" Vaarem asked Melissa.

"I would love that," she said. "I just need to close up for lunch. I will see you shortly."

Inside the cafe, they ordered a cup of tea each and Vaarem ordered a plate of biscuits for the both of them. Lim rolled his eyes. It seemed that even his brother was going to be at him to eat.

But that is a good thing, he reminded himself. Hopefully, if he ate more and fueled his body better, he would get stronger; even if it was only relative to himself.

After a few minutes, their teas and biscuits arrived, and a few minutes later, Melissa came and joined them. Lim noticed that she was quite tall for a human, not as tall as Vada, who stood tall amongst both humans and elves, but taller than their mother. She sat down and helped herself to a biscuit when Vaarem offered her the plate.

"It's so nice to finally talk to some elves," said Melissa.

"Oh?" Vaarem raised his eyebrow, smiling slyly.

"My grandmother was half-elf," she said, "so I am an eighth elf, I guess. My grandmother died giving birth to my father, so I never knew my elf ancestors."

"Oh," said Vaarem, "I'm sorry to hear that. Our mother is half-elf, half-human."

"Really? She looked like an elf to me when I saw her, although I remember that she wasn't very tall by elf standards."

"No." Smiled Vaarem, "But elves, like humans do come in all shapes and sizes. However, a more interesting thing about our mother is that she painted one of the portraits in your gallery. She never told me that."

"Maybe she wanted to show you," said Melissa. "I do remember that you ran out rather abruptly. I was wondering what happened."

Lim frowned at Vaarem, even as he felt warned by his brother's actions. "You shouldn't have." He chuckled.

Vaarem smiled and patted his knee, but he didn't say anything.

"So, which painting did your mother paint?" asked Melissa curiously, tucking her wavy brown hair behind her ears. Despite her elf ancestry, her ears were completely round and human. Then again, so were Vada's, and she was more elf than Melissa.

"The portrait of Malkim Blackwell," said Vaarem.

Melissa considered this, as if trying to recall the paintings. "Oh yes, the big one on the far wall."

"Yes." Nodded Vaarem.

"Wow." Smiled Melissa. "She is very talented."

"Thank you," said Vaarem, "She is."

"Can either of you paint or sculpt?" asked Melissa, "I've always liked to play around with clay but alas, I am not very good."

"I'm sure you're better than you give yourself credit for," said Vaarem, "but as to us no, not really." He looked at Lim, "You used to draw, didn't you?"

Lim shrugged. He'd done a little drawing in his childhood, but it hadn't been for art, more to illustrate the things he'd been writing about.

"My art form was music," he said instead, "I used to play the violin. Var would sing and our father played the tambourine."

"Yeah." Vaarem's eyes lit up at the memory. "I remember that we used to have fun." He trailed off and Lim knew that like himself, Vaarem was remembering that their mother had been absent in those moments. Where had she been?

"I love to sing too," said Melissa. "If you guys like music, there is a club in the south-east quarter where they play music each evening and people can dance. Do you like to dance?"

"Yes," said Vaarem excitedly. Lim merely smiled. He'd never been fit enough to dance, but his brother loved it, so he was not going to say anything disparaging.

"Oh." Melissa's eyes lit up. "There is a really good band playing tonight. Do you want to go?"

"Okay." Vaarem nodded enthusiastically, and Lim smiled too even though he was reminded that his treatment had failed and all the things that he'd been unable to do he still couldn't do; such as dancing. But Vaarem and Melissa were obviously keen, so he smiled more widely and nodded. "Sounds great," he managed to say. Vaarem got the address and the time from Melissa and Lim wrote it down in his notebook.

After saying good-bye to Melissa and arranging to meet up that evening, the brothers walked to the library, which was on the next block

"How are you holding up?" asked Vaarem when Lim's step fell a little behind.

Lim nodded and smiled. He was feeling reasonably good overall. His chest didn't hurt as it usually did when he did a lot of walking, but he still didn't have enough breath to walk and talk at the same time. Vaarem put his arm around him and led him into the library building.

The library of Sirrock had a good collection of books, so the twins looked at books on animals and plants, and decided to go to the botanical and zoological gardens next. They got the next tram, Lim grateful for the ability to sit down without having to make an excuse. Although his midday medication was still holding him, he was tired, so welcomed the rest. They walked through the botanical gardens slowly, Vaarem considerately allowing Lim plenty of time to look at the different trees and flowers, which Lim knew was an excuse to let him rest periodically.

The zoological park was like nothing that Lim had ever seen before. There were dozens of enclosures that housed different animals from around Zemia. Lim felt the magic that controlled the habitats, which ensured that the wyverns from the south were cool enough and the phoenixes from the north were warm, and that all of the animals in between, such as the ador-able shturkas, which resembled large winged mice, of central Jaanis, were comfortable.

There was a large lake in the centre of the park where hipponixies splashed around. Hipponixies were the preferred transport method of pixies as they travelled through lakes and down rivers. They were known to save pixies from drowning during floods and storms. Looking like a cross between a horse and an eel, they swam around the lake, allowing visitors to feed them specialised fish bits that could be bought for the purpose.

Lim and Vaarem bought several pieces of fish to feed the water mammals, and Lim smiled as a small foal licked his hand after eating the offered snack.

"She likes you," said the pixie who worked as the hipponixies' keeper. "Wild hipponixies are normally very shy. These ones are tame and friendly by com-parison, but I have never seen them get so close to a visitor before."

Lim smiled at the woman, feeling warm inside. He'd always liked animals and it always made him feel good when they liked him back.

After the hipponixies, they went to see the enclo-sure of lindwyrms. Lindwyrms had first been tamed by dwarves several centuries ago, and they were now used as a mode of transport underground. They re-sembled large lizards with two front legs and a tail that they used to move their back half. Living in caves, they were almost completely blind and navigated by smell and sound. The information board said that tame lindwyrms were very protective of their owners and had been known to look after injured dwarves, by sharing their food, and carrying them to safety as needed. Like the hipponixy foal, the two young lindwyrms came up to Lim and allowed him to stroke their pale-green snouts, which shocked their keeper.

"I have never known them to do that before," said the old dwarf, looking up at Lim with wide eyes. "They can tell who means them harm, and who is merely curious, but they are not normally curious themselves. You must exude some strong, friendly vibes."

Lim, again, felt warmed.

"Do you think that I can get a companion animal when we go back to Palinas?" wondered Lim aloud.

Vaarem shrugged. "Maybe."

Elves didn't often keep pets, however the twins were aware that their grandfather's family had kept a salamander in their home, and their mother's cousin had kept a shturka, so it was not unheard of. Lim had never thought that he would be strong enough to look after an animal. He could barely look after himself, and he was fairly sure that he could never live alone and would always need someone to care for him. But after reading how some animals cared for their owners, it made him wonder. What if he got some kind of animal that could help him, and as he looked after it, the creature would care for him too?

"What are you thinking?" asked Vaarem as they walked through a forested enclosure that housed birds from different parts of the continent. The enclosure was cold at one end to mimic the climate of the south, then got gradually warmer until the other end mimicked the heat of the northern jungles.

Lim marvelled at the fact that he'd walked through the cold part of the enclosure without needing to breathe through a cloth. His lungs had hurt when the cold air had hit them, but they'd continued to function. Even so, he knew that there would be times when they wouldn't.

"Having a companion animal might allow me to safely live on my own," he told his brother.

Vaarem looked at him with a puzzled expression. "Why would you live on your own?" he asked.

Lim shrugged. "I don't expect you, or anybody else, to give up your life for me," he explained. "As I do not plan on getting married or anything, it follows that I would live alone. Lots of people do it, Var." He smiled. Their mother had often lived with one of their aunts when her parents had been away. Naria Bluebell was a mage, and now that she was no longer caring for Zareanna, she lived on her own.

Vaarem frowned curiously. "I don't know," he said. "I am not sure if I like the idea of you being on your own."

"Why?"

Vaarem shrugged again. "I really can't say. All I know is that I cannot imagine us being separated long-term, like I don't think that I would like it if you moved away like Vada did."

"Really?" frowned Lim, "You were supportive of me going to the Academy of Magic. Or did you only say that because you knew that it would never happen?"

"No." Vaarem shook his head. "What? Why are you suddenly so angry with me? I *wanted* your treatment to work. I *wanted* for you to go to the Academy. But I always thought that you would return home at the end of it, that's all."

"Sorry," sighed Lim. His breath caught and he coughed into his elbow. He spotted a bench near the unicorn enclosure and went to sit down on it. Vaarem followed him and sat down next to him. He patted Lim's back until the coughing fit eased. Lim drew a shuddering breath, then hugged his arms around himself as his ribs ached. He contemplated taking some of his new painkiller but decided against it. This pain would ease on its own.

"Are you okay?" asked Vaarem, his eyes wide with concern.

"Yeah." Lim nodded. "Sorry," he said, "I don't know what came over me. I'm not angry with you. I'm." He paused, as he considered what he was actually thinking and feeling, "I never thought that I would have a future," he said finally.

Vaarem frowned, his brow so creased, it looked comical.

"Not like that," chuckled Lim.

Vaarem tilted his head, his brow still creased.

"It sounds morbid, but I was never sure if I would get to grow up at all," Lim tried to explain, "It was all an abstract concept, which I guess it is for everyone to a certain extent, but." He trailed off again.

"But?" asked Vaarem patiently.

"But," said Lim, "I never thought of my future in practical terms. I am now starting. Father told me that I need to look after myself."

Vaarem nodded.

"I don't want anybody to give up their life to care for me," said Lim, "but I also know that I can't always care for myself. I am thinking that some kind of companion animal may be a good compromise."

Vaarem put his other arm around his twin and hugged him close. "Oh dude," he said, "I know what you mean, but I would never think of looking after you as giving up my own life. We are twins and we've always looked out for each other. I will always care for you when you need it. It will never be a chore."

Lim smiled despite himself and allowed himself to relax into his brother's embrace. He put his own arms around Vaarem's slim form and held his brother close. "Thank you," he said softly, unbidden tears coming into his eyes. He'd always known that Vaarem would look out for him, but he'd never heard his twin say it out loud the way he just had. "I love you, Var," he said quietly. "You are the absolute best brother anyone could hope for." He recalled Eliza's brother sitting awkwardly in her room and he appreciated Vaarem all the more. "But." Lim raised his head. After a while he dropped his arms and Vaarem did the same.

Vaarem raised his eyebrows in question.

"One day you will have your own family," said Lim. "You'll get married, and I don't want you to feel obligated to ever neglect your future wife and children because I need you."

Vaarem looked at him for a moment, "That will never happen," he said, "Anyone I marry will have to understand my obligations to you."

Lim nodded, then dropped his eyes. "This is what I mean, Var," he said, "I don't want to be an obligation."

Vaarem bit his lip. "Wrong choice of words," he said quickly, "but, Fates, Lim you know what I mean."

"Yeah." Lim nodded, but he still felt like an obligation.

When it got dark, they found a small, intimate restaurant, where they decided to have dinner.

They were taken to a table for two, and when they were seated they looked at the menus and ordered a bowl of soup each, neither of them wanting to eat anything too heavy.

"Very good choice, Sirs." the waiter smiled, then left with their order.

Lim took one of his potion bottles out of his pocket and had a sip. He was starting to get used to this new routine and so far, it seemed to be working. He was starting to feel consistently better on a day-to-day basis. But he remembered Dr Thorn's warning that this was all due to the medication. If he stopped taking it, he would get sick again.

"What are you thinking?" asked Vaarem, as they waited for their food to arrive.

"That I can probably manage to live a fairly normal life, as long as I carry an apothecary around with me at all times," said Lim with a grim laugh.

Vaarem laughed too. "Oh, my Fates, you really have a way of saying things to make them sound so dramatic."

"Well," said Lim, "Father does always say that I am overly dramatic. So, why not do something that I am only going to be accused of doing anyway?"

Their food arrived promptly and Vaarem tucked into his meal enthusiastically. "Mmm, this is very good," he said, savouring his tomato soup.

"Mine is good too," said Lim, swallowing a spoonful of his soup, which was made of potato and leek.

Vaarem looked at his brother, trying not to make it obvious that that was what he was doing. He knew that Lim hated people watching him eat so was very pleased to see that Lim finished his entire meal, even mopping up the last bit with a piece of bread and eating it with apparent enjoyment.

"Are you serious about doing the priest training when we return home?" asked Vaarem as they waited for their dessert.

"Yep." Nodded Lim. "I've already written to the Temple in Palinas, asking for entry. It is a type of magic that I can do. I don't know why I've never thought of it before."

Vaarem shrugged. "I don't either."

"Yeah," said Lim. "So, for this reason alone, that I have had this idea here and now, this trip was worth it, in my opinion at least. Father probably wouldn't agree, but then again, he never agrees with my ideas," he added bitterly.

"Yeah," said Vaarem, "Then again, ever since talking to Vada, and telling us about Malkim, Father, and Mother too, have been a lot less tense, so this trip has been good for them too. Although for my part, I still feel mostly invisible." He sighed.

Lim nodded but didn't reply.

Lim was having one of the best days of his life, or of his recent life, anyway. He and Vaarem had seen the sights of Sirrock City and were currently finishing up a most pleasant dinner.

Lim had the last bite of his fruit pastry and pushed the plate away. Vaarem had eaten his own dessert some time ago and had been waiting for Lim to finish.

"What do you want to do now?" asked Vaarem. "Is it time to go dancing?"

Lim looked at the clock that hung on one of the walls. "Yes."

Vaarem raised his eyebrow. "Are you sure?"

Despite the fact that he was not a good dancer himself, as he'd frequently missed lessons due to illness, Lim knew that Vaarem loved dancing and was desperate to go. He was not going to deny his brother the opportunity.

"Yeah," said Lim. "I know you're dying to dance. If I get too tired, I'll just sit and watch."

"Thanks," said Vaarem, standing up and indicating that they were ready for the bill. "You're the best."

"Thanks," said Lim. "So are you." He was feeling good and hoped that this would continue.

Chapter 20

The Nightclub

They walked into the club together, following a group of young humans down the stairs into a dimly lit room.

The air was smoky, and Vaarem turned to Lim with an anxious frown. "Can you breathe?" he asked.

Lim nodded. "Yeah. I have my emergency meds if I have any problems," he said, patting the little jar in his pocket.

They found a table in the corner of the room and sat down. Lim was pleased to see that they were not the only elves. Although the vast majority of the clientele were human, there were a couple of groups of elves, as well as several dwarves and pixies.

"May I have this dance?" asked Vaarem, standing up and extending his hand.

"I would be delighted to," said Lim, taking his brother's hand and letting Vaarem pull him up.

They walked over to the dance floor and joined in with the group of people who were already there, dancing in a circle. Lim did his best to follow what everyone else was doing and to keep up. Being as tall as he was, made it easy for him to see what every-one was doing, and his keen elf eyes also helped him to watch where he was putting his feet and ensure that he didn't step on anyone's toes. It was surpris-ingly fun.

He managed two dances before feeling the need to sit down.

He told Vaarem that he was going to have a rest, but that Vaarem should keep going for as long as he wanted, then made his way back to their table, where he leaned his head back against the wall and watched the dancers.

The elves towered over the humans, who towered over the dwarves, but they were all respectful of each other's spaces. A pixie extended her wings and per-formed a graceful glide from one end of the room to the other.

Out of the corner of his eye, Lim saw someone sit down on the chair next to him. He turned his head to see Melissa from the art museum. She smiled at him.

"Hello," she said. "You made it. I see your brother is already into it." She indicated Vaarem, who was now dancing in the middle of the room. The other danc-ers were standing around and clapping. Occasionally, one of them would go into the centre and dance with him, before moving back and letting someone else have a go. Vaarem danced with both the men and the women, with the elves, humans, dwarves, and pixies. He seemed to have an unending supply of energy and Lim tried not to feel jealous.

"He's such a show off," chuckled Lim good naturedly.

"He is a bit." Melissa laughed. "But he's very good."

"He is," agreed Lim. "He's been wanting to dance for over a moon," he explained, "so he's clearly making up for lost time."

Melissa laughed at that. Lim turned to look at her. Her dark brown hair was piled up on the top of her head in an elaborate braid, and she was wearing an orange and white embroidered dress with a fitted bodice, a full skirt, and puffed sleeves trimmed with lace. He felt scruffy in comparison, with his loose greasy hair and plain black clothes.

Melissa smiled at him again. "Would you like a drink?" she asked him.

"No, thank you." He shook his head. "I don't drink," he explained.

"Fair enough," she said. "Would you like to dance?" she extended her hand to him. "It looks like your brother is otherwise occupied." She chuckled, looking over at Vaarem, who was once again dancing alone in the centre of the room, doing a series of graceful pirouettes.

"Um, sure, but I'm not very good," said Lim

awkwardly. He looked over at Vaarem, who was now dancing with one of the human women, twirling and twisting her around as expertly as he'd spun himself before. Lim had never danced with a girl, let alone done anything like Vaarem was currently doing. If Melissa was expecting him to be similar, she was going to be sorely disappointed. "I mean it," said Lim, "I'm really not good."

"That's okay," she said. "I am. I'll teach you."

"Okay," he said, unable to come up with a decent excuse.

He let her lead him to the dance floor. She held his hand and put her other hand on his shoulder.

He flinched a little, then looked down and smiled at her uncertainly.

"Sorry," he said. "I wasn't expecting that." It sounded better than admitting he didn't like being touched by strangers.

She smiled back up at him, confidently. "Put your hand on my waist," she said, guiding his hand up over her hip. "Now, follow my feet. Do a step forward, then to the side, back, other side, and then repeat. Got it?"

"I think so." He nodded, looking down at their feet. Melissa was wearing delicate silver satin slippers, and he did his best to ensure he didn't step on them with his sturdy boots. Even though he'd packed his dress boots, he'd never worn them.

"How much longer are you going to be in Sirrock City?" she asked.

"We're leaving tomorrow," he replied.

"Oh," she said. "That's a shame. There are several other clubs which I'm sure that your brother would enjoy visiting. Next time?"

"Sure" he said, wondering whether he and Vaarem would ever visit Sirrock City again. After having seen Vada and having heard his parents reveal their history, he felt a sense of closure himself, and he didn't know if he wanted to come back.

"What's wrong?" she asked, clearly sensing his sudden tension.

"Nothing," he said. "I think I need to sit down." He swayed on his feet and would have fallen had she not caught him. He held onto her for a moment, then, with her help, made his way back to his seat.

He put his elbows on the table and rested his head in his hands.

Melissa hovered around him anxiously. "Lim?" she asked. "Are you okay?"

"Yeah." He nodded, his breath coming to him with difficulty.

Suddenly Vaarem was beside them. "Lim?" he asked anxiously. "Are you okay? Hi." He nodded to Melissa, who nodded back in acknowledgement.

"Yeah." Lim nodded. "Can you please get me a glass of water?" he asked his brother. "Hot water, or warm if that's not possible. Thanks."

"Sure." Vaarem nodded and walked over to the bar, leaving Lim alone with Melissa.

Melissa sat down next to him and put her hand on

his shoulder. He didn't flinch this time. "Are you really okay?" she asked again.

Lim nodded, then he popped open the lid of the jar and put some leaves in the water that Vaarem brought over to him. He stirred the mixture with his finger as he'd not thought to ask for a spoon, then drank it down in one gulp. It tasted bitter but it went down without too much difficulty.

He felt his chest loosen as the mixture worked through his body.

He smiled wearily at Melissa. "I'm fine," he said. "This happens to me all the time. It's why I was at the hospital. Unfortunately, they couldn't cure me," he explained.

"Oh," she said awkwardly.

"Yeah," he shrugged, hoping that he hadn't made her uncomfortable. Then again, this was his life. He had no control over what others thought, and he couldn't censor himself all the time just because hearing about his experiences may make someone else feel bad.

"I'm sorry to hear that," she said after a moment, "But I guess we all have our challenges."

"Yeah," agreed Lim. The idea made him feel better.

"How are you feeling?" asked Vaarem, on Lim's other side. "Do you want to go home?"

Lim shook his head. "I'm fine. We can stay for a bit longer because I know you want to. I'll just watch though."

"Okay," said Vaarem, clearly grateful. "If you're sure," he added.

"I'm sure," said Lim. "I doubt we'll be back in a hurry, despite what Mother says, so have fun. Go," he waved his brother away. Melissa hovered uncertainly, so Lim smiled at her, and said, "I think I'm all danced out for the moment, but I know that Vaarem is dying to dance with you."

"Thank you." She smiled, then allowed Vaarem to lead her on to the dancefloor. Lim watched as she danced with Vaarem, then with another elf, then with a human, and finally with Vaarem again, before waving to another human woman whom she clearly recognised, and going to sit with her at the bar. She waved to Lim as she passed him, and he smiled at her.

A few people gave Lim curious looks as they walked past and some asked him whether he was okay, before moving on, but for the most part he was left alone.

I seem to cause a scene wherever I go, he thought with a sigh. Perhaps Father is right, and I *am* dramatic.

He leaned his head back against the wall and watched the dancers, then he turned to watch the band, who were playing on a small dais in the corner of the room. They were all humans, and they were all playing different types of stringed instruments, with a drummer sitting behind them.

Lim recalled his days when he'd played the violin. He'd done it quite well, but as with everything else, he'd eventually gotten too sick to continue and had had to stop. He wondered whether he could try it again now. With his new routine of daily medications, Melissa's comment about everyone having different strengths and challenges made him think about his realistic options. Yes, there were some things that he couldn't do, that he would in all likelihood never be able to do, but he wasn't the only one who had issues. Vaarem, for example, had the physical strength to do the type of high magic that Lim longed to do, but he lacked the patience and the raw talent. Lim wasn't the only one who was unable to do every single thing that he may have wanted to do. And there were so many things that he *could* do; there always had been.

He decided that when he got home, he would take his violin out and start to play it again. After that, he would try something else. There were so many things that he'd given up on. He owed it to himself to try again.

Eventually, Vaarem had danced himself out and the brothers decided to head back to the inn. Melissa and her friend had left half an hour ago.

When they got outside, they found out that the trams didn't run at night.

"Shit," said Vaarem. "We're gonna have to walk home."

"Okay," said Lim. "I think I can manage that, as long as we take it slow."

They put their arms around each other's shoulders and started walking in the direction of the inn.

They walked two blocks before Lim had to stop. He crouched down and put his head in his hands, waiting for his breath to return. He didn't cough, which was a pleasant change, so after a few minutes, he allowed Vaarem to help him to his feet and they kept going.

After walking another block, they saw a horse and carriage, so Vaarem hailed the driver, and they rode back to the inn.

"Thanks," said Lim, as Vaarem paid for the ride. He'd been paying for everything all day. "I'll pay you back my share when we get inside."

"Don't worry about it," said Vaarem. "It was my treat. Father has been giving me money since we got to Sirrock City, to "entertain myself", but this is the first time that I've spent anything."

"Okay," said Lim, "thanks." His father had never given *him* money, apart from the regular allowance that he and Vaarem got each moon. Then again, he hadn't been going anywhere. He tried not to dwell on it.

When they got to their room, Lim went into the bathroom to wash his hair. He'd told Vaarem that he hadn't had a chance to wash it since arriving in Sirrock City, so was now taking the opportunity, despite the late hour. Vaarem packed his things, in readiness for leaving in the morning, which was only a couple of hours away.

Half an hour later, Lim came out of the bathroom, wearing his black nightgown, his wet hair falling over his shoulders. He was drying it, strand by strand, using his magic.

Vaarem clicked his tongue in admonishment. "Here," he said. "Let me. Sit."

Lim sat down on the bed obediently and Vaarem put his hands on his head, concentrating on creating gentle heat.

"I see you warmed the bath using magic," said Vaarem, with a shake of his head. "I can see dark rings forming under your eyes already."

"It was quicker than the mundane way," said Lim with a shrug.

"Yes, but I could have helped. Seriously, Lim, you shouldn't do these things. I know you want to be as independent as you can, and I know that you're capable, but you shouldn't exhaust yourself when there's no need for it. In this one instance, I agree with Father. You need to look after yourself."

Lim sighed, as Vaarem finished drying his hair and leaned down to look into his face. "I know," he said softly. "I'm sorry. I just don't want to be a burden, you know? There's so much that I can't do."

"Like what?" asked Vaarem.

Lim considered this but couldn't think of an example. Many people couldn't do high magic, so it seemed like a petty excuse.

"Everyone needs help sometimes, Lim," said Vaarem seriously. "That's what families and friends are for. And for the last time, you're not a burden and you never have been."

Lim smiled at that, as Vaarem picked up a brush and ran it through Lim's long, shiny hair.

"Now, go to bed," said Vaarem, putting the brush away, then tucking Lim into bed.

He went into the bathroom and had a quick wash before coming back into the bedroom in his night-shirt. He brushed his own hair, turned the lamp off and climbed into bed. He put his arms around Lim and drew his brother's thin body towards him.

Like his twin, he was looking forward to going home.

Chapter 21

Homeward Bound

Lim woke up with Vaarem's arm tight around his chest. He went to move it, but his brother's grip was too strong. "Var?" he said softly, then more loudly when his brother didn't stir. "Vaarem? Move your arm. You're crushing me."

"Mmm, sorry," said Vaarem sleepily. He let go of Lim and turned over, still dozing.

"Thanks," Lim stretched, then got out of the bed. He washed his face, then got dressed. It was strange to think that they were finally going home. It seemed unreal.

He sat at the dressing table and started to braid his hair, trying out the style that he'd seen on the half-dwarf doctor a few days ago. Vaarem got up and got dressed, then sat down next to him.

"How did you sleep?" asked Vaarem.

"Good," said Lim with a shrug. "You?"

"Good." Vaarem shrugged back. "It's good having you by my side, knowing that you're safe." He smiled at Lim tenderly.

"Thanks," said Lim. "It's good to be back with you too. I didn't realise how much I missed you."

"Yeah." Nodded Vaarem. "By the way, did you have your medicine last night? I forgot to ask."

"Yes," said Lim, tying up his first braid with a black ribbon and starting on the second one. "I had it at the club, remember? And at the restaurant."

"Okay." Nodded Vaarem. "I need to learn your new routine. So, I can help you if you need it."

"You mean if I become incapacitated and can't look after myself," said Lim cynically, tying up his second braid and turning his head this way and that in the mirror.

Vaarem chuckled. "Sheesh, you *are* dramatic," he said. "But I suppose, yes. It could happen to anybody."

"Okay," said Lim with a laugh. "I'll show you." He stood up and went to his medicine bag, then showed Vaarem his potions, the same way that Dr Thorn had shown Lim in the hospital.

They met their parents in the inn's restaurant. Vaarem and Lim were already sitting at the table when Zareanna and Garrett arrived, dressed in their travelling clothes, ready to leave.

"Good morning," Zareanna kissed both of her sons on the cheek, then sat down next to Lim. "Your hair looks nice, darling," she said to him.

"Thank you," he replied, then took another sip of his coffee.

Garrett sat down opposite. "Did you boys have a good time last night?" he asked, looking at Lim with a raised eyebrow.

"Yes," said Lim. "We did. Thank you."

"Where did you go?"

"We went everywhere," said Vaarem. "To the museum, and the zoo. Where else?" he asked Lim, trying to remember.

"The library," said Lim. "And the botanical gardens. We saw one of Mother's paintings in the museum," he added.

"Really?" asked Zareanna, "Which one?"

"It's the one you did of Malkim," Garrett answered. "I was going to show you, but then Vaarem ran out."

"Oh," Zareanna was taken aback. "Really?"

"Yes." Nodded Garrett. "It's been hanging there for a long time. I never got the chance to tell you."

Zareanna smiled. "I'm glad," she said quietly. She looked wistful for a moment, then looked at Vaarem and Lim again. "What else did you do?" She clearly didn't want to discuss the painting.

"We went dancing," said Vaarem enthusiastically. "It was fun." He looked at Lim as if to confirm.

Lim nodded. "Yes. It was."

"Did you dance?" asked Zareanna curiously.

"Yes," said Lim shyly. "A little bit. I mostly watched. Vaarem danced."

"It seems that your treatment was at least a bit

successful if you had the energy to go dancing the very night that you were discharged from the hospital," said Garrett approvingly. "Make sure you keep on looking after yourself."

"I will."

Their breakfast arrived, which consisted of bread, porridge, honey, and eggs.

Lim noticed that his father watched him carefully as he ate. He immediately lost his appetite and went to push his plate away.

"I don't think so, Lim," said Garrett. "You're going to finish that. And you're going to finish every meal from now on. You just said that you will look after yourself, which includes eating properly."

"Fine," said Lim, picking the plate up again. "But don't watch me. I can't eat when you look at me like that."

"I will look at you however I want. And no one else has a problem being watched, so there is no reason for you to. Now, finish your breakfast because we're not going to leave until you do."

"He's right, Limmy," said Zareanna. "You need to eat."

Lim sighed and did his best to finish his breakfast.

As they were checking out, the innkeeper gave Vaarem an envelope. "Are you Lim Nightingale?" asked the man.

"No," said Vaarem, "but I'm his brother. I can give it to him."

He gave the letter to Lim, who put it in his pocket, then the family went into the stables to get their horses and carriage.

Garrett and Zareanna had decided to drive the carriage together, with Lim and Vaarem sitting inside. Lim smiled, his breath coming to him easily for once.

As soon as the carriage drove out of the city, Lim opened the letter. It was from Vada, and he read it excitedly.

"Dear Lim, I miss you already. I wanted to tell you that you gave me an idea, when you talked about the Fates, and the seasons and the forces of the universe being stronger at certain times than others, and it got me thinking. Surely this extends beyond Zemia. They are the Fates of the Universe after all. So, I studied the stars, and guess what? The stars align too, to give powers to Zemia. There is an event that the scholars of old called The Great Alignment, where all the stars and planets align with the powers on Zemia, giving maximum power to our world. This event is real, and it will happen, likely within the next ten turns. So you see, Limmy, I will heal you, and the world. I will rid the continent of the Blackwell influence for good. I will free the world from pain, and it is all thanks to you. I love you and miss you, and hope to see you again. Your sister Vada"

The letter made Lim feel cold, and he coughed.

Vaarem turned to look at him.

"Vada is talking about doing some powerful magic," said Lim. He gave Vaarem the letter to read.

Vaarem raised his eyebrows as he read, then gave the letter back to his brother. "So what?" he said with a shrug. "She was always excitable, when she had a new idea. I'm sure that nothing bad will come of it." He smiled and put his arm around Lim's shoulder. "And if she does end up doing something good, then she says right here that you inspired it."

Lim smiled thinly. "Yeah," he said, "but doesn't that sound a little unbalanced? She says she will rid the world of pain, but the Book of the Fates says that pain and joy go together, that you can't have one without the other."

Vaarem shrugged. "I'm sure she's exaggerating."

They planned to return home along the same roads that they'd taken to get to Sirrock City, however on the first evening, the keeper of the inn they were staying at, told them of a hot spring that was meant to be therapeutic, one day's ride north, so they decided to check it out the next day.

The medicines that Dr Thorn had given Lim seemed to be working, because he found that he could do more things than he'd ever done before without getting out of breath, and he hadn't coughed since leaving the hospital, apart from that one cough after reading Vada's letter. Overall, he was feeling cautiously optimistic.

They arrived at the hot spring in the early afternoon,

just in time for their midday meal. They unhitched the horses and let them graze, then Zareanna laid out a blanket on the grass, overlooking the water. The water bubbled and steamed, and smelt slightly of sulphur. Lim put his hand over his nose, wondering whether he wanted to get into the spring after all, but Vaarem urged him on excitedly.

"Ooh, it looks so nice and warm," said Vaarem, running his hand through the steam that was coming over the top of the spring and on to the grass. The air around the spring was warm too. Lim breathed in and realised that for the first time in his life, the cold air was not bothering him. He could breathe just as easily over the hot water as further away. Zareanna put out some food, and after tending to the horses and securing the carriage, the twins and their father joined her. Garrett still watched Lim closely as he ate, but Lim was starting to get used to this and found himself able to ignore it.

After eating, they rested for a while, then after half an hour, they decided to go in the water. Vaarem was the first to stand up and get ready. Lim looked down the stream and saw a family of pixies enjoying the water too. The pixies were all naked, which was probably the best way to swim here, but Lim knew that there was no way that he was going to get naked in front of his parents. In fact, it was going to be bad enough going in wearing just his undergarments, which was what Vaarem had decided to do.

"Come on in," said Vaarem from the water, steam

billowing around him. "It is beautiful." He pushed himself away from the edge and swam over to the other side, making sure to keep his head above the water.

Zareanna put her hair up in a bun on the top of her head and walked into the water in her undergarments too, followed by her husband.

Lim hesitated, then put his hair up in a bun too and slowly got undressed, suddenly feeling very, very self-conscious. He put his clothes down near the carriage, then walked over to the spring, his arms crossed over his chest, conscious of his protruding ribs and hip-bones.

He looked up to see his father gazing at him with a frown.

Lim looked down again, as he walked into the water. Vaarem was right and the heat did feel wonderful, so Lim quickly crouched down, immersing himself up to his shoulders.

But not before Garrett said. "I can't believe you do that to yourself, Limnos."

"Do what?" asked Lim with a frown.

"Let yourself get so thin. It is not healthy."

"I know," said Lim. "But I don't do it on purpose."

"You weren't always like this," said Garrett, still frowning.

"Yeah," countered Lim. "I used to be even thinner." He hugged his arms around himself, suddenly feeling really bad.

"Leave him alone, Garrett," said Zareanna, coming over and putting her arm around Lim protectively.

"Stop punishing Lim for Malkim's perceived mistakes. It is not Lim's fault. He's doing his best."

"Well, his best is not very good, is it?" said his father. "Or do you want him to fall down the stairs one day and hurt himself beyond repair?"

"It's not like that and you know it," said Zareanna quietly.

"Do I?" said Garrett. "It looks freakishly similar to me."

"Well, it isn't," snapped Zareanna.

Lim bit his lip and looked down into the water. The heat was relaxing his muscles and easing the tension in his shoulders and neck that had developed from his sleeping upright in the carriage. But any physical pleasure he may have felt was counteracted by his father's words.

I'm a freak and a failure no matter what I do, he thought miserably.

He moved away from his mother's embrace and swam a few metres upstream. Vaarem followed him.

"Don't worry about what Father says," said Vaarem kindly.

"Easy for you to say, Var," said Lim bitterly. "You've always been perfect. You don't know what it's like to be a dud."

"You're not a dud," said Vaarem, rolling his eyes. "Fates, Father keeps comparing you to Malkim Blackwell, who was most definitely *not* a dud. Come on, come back."

Lim didn't feel like coming back, so he kept his back to his brother.

"Come on, Lim," said Vaarem, swimming away a little to give his twin some space. "Don't be like this. I'm so sorry that Father is being such an arsehole. But whatever his problem is, it's not actually with you. So, don't give him the satisfaction."

Lim turned around and sighed, keeping his arms crossed across his chest. "It doesn't matter what his motive or reason is. I hate myself enough without him having to point out all my flaws all the time. He's only saying what I'm thinking anyway." Despite himself, he began to cry and bit his lip to try and stop it.

But Vaarem saw, not only because he was obser-vant, but also because he was in tune with what his twin was feeling. "Oh man, I'm sorry," he said awk-wardly, swimming over and putting his arm around Lim's bony shoulders. "I don't know what to say, other than that I feel really bad. For you, and just in general. It's not fair. It really isn't, and I wish that I could say or do something to make it better, but I can't. Perhaps that's my failing."

"Hmpf," Lim snorted. "It's not your failing. I still sometimes think that I shouldn't even exist. I always bring the mood down and ruin everything. Nobody needs me."

"Don't say that," said Vaarem, hugging Lim closer. "It really shits me when you say that. Because *I* need you."

"Thanks, Var," said Lim. "But realistically, if I'd

never been born, or if I had died at birth, the way that everyone thought that I would, you'd still be fine. Everyone would still be fine. In many ways, you'd all be better off without me. No one would need to do any of this for example," he waved his arm, indicating their whole situation.

Vaarem held his brother close, letting the warm water soothe their bodies. He hated it when Lim went on these downers, where he went on and on about what a useless failure he was. It made Vaarem feel bad, not only because he had a lot of empathy for his twin, but also because in what he said, Lim was insulting him. Because if Lim was useless, then Vaarem, who thought the exact opposite, was a bad judge of character, and stupid to boot. Not to mention that without Lim, Vaarem would be completely ignored by everyone.

"Come on," said Vaarem, giving Lim a tight hug that made his brother squirm, then letting him go and swimming further upstream, away from their parents. After a while, Lim followed him. When he was closer, Vaarem splashed some water on him, to which Lim responded by kicking his feet to make an even bigger splash that wet Vaarem's face and hair. Vaarem laughed, and for a while the brothers chased and splashed each other, playing like they had when they'd been children.

Even further upstream, the water was deeper, so that they could climb the banks and jump and dive in, seeing who could make the biggest splash, or do the most impressive-looking jump. Vaarem, of course, "won" all of these competitions, but Lim nevertheless had fun copying him.

It had always been like this when they'd been young. Vaarem would do something, then Lim would copy him until he could do said thing himself. Their mother had once told them that she'd worried about Lim not meeting the usual baby milestones, but that she needn't have fretted, because every single achievement that Vaarem made, Lim would achieve within twenty-four hours. Now, as Vaarem jumped and somersaulted into the water, Lim watched and copied him, by the end of the day even achieving a complicated double-somersault into the pool himself.

By the time their mother called them back, they were both exhausted and were glad that their father had hitched up the horses and gotten the carriage ready, rather than waiting for them and making them do it themselves.

Vaarem helped his brother climb into the carriage, before shutting the door behind them. Lim closed his eyes as soon as he sat down next to Zareanna while Vaarem sat in the opposite corner, resting his head against the wall. As the carriage took off, Zareanna put her arm around Lim and drew him to her. He rested his head on her shoulder. She stroked his hair, then moved his legs so that they were hanging over her lap.

She rested her head against his. Lim let her hold him, or was too tired to care, because he didn't protest.

"Did you have fun, Limmy?" asked Zareanna, stroking her youngest son's face.

"Mmm-hmm." He nodded, his eyes still closed.

Vaarem tried not to feel bitter. For the past few weeks, he'd constantly felt even more invisible than usual. His parents had persistently talked and argued about his brother, or about Vada, or Malkim even, ignoring Vaarem almost completely.

Malkim is dead for Fates' sake, he's been dead for over a quarter of a century and yet they pay more attention to him than to me, he thought. Why does no one see *me*?

"How are you feeling, darling?" asked Zareanna.

Vaarem looked up, but of course, she was talking to Lim.

"Mmm," said Lim.

"You're looking so much better," Zareanna stroked his hair again.

Vaarem sighed. Can't you see that he doesn't want to talk? he wanted to say. But you can talk to me, he thought.

But she didn't talk to him, so after a while he dozed off.

When he woke up a short time later, Lim was lying on his back, his head on his mother's lap, his hands resting on his belly. She had her hand on his chest and was looking into his face with an almost teary expression.

Vaarem was immediately awake. "What happened?" he asked. "Is Lim okay?"

"Shhh." Zareanna looked up at him. "Look," she said softly.

Vaarem looked.

His brother was sleeping peacefully, his chest moving up and down rhythmically, his breath not rattling in his lungs the way it frequently did.

"He hasn't slept this peacefully for a long time," said Zareanna wonderingly. She then extended her other hand and beckoned for Vaarem to come over. He moved across the carriage and sat on his mother's other side, allowing her to hold him too. He rested his head on her shoulder, feeling good.

Lim was still asleep when they reached that night's inn in the evening. Vaarem had dozed off too, as had Zareanna.

The carriage door opened. "We're here," said Garrett.

Vaarem opened his eyes and blinked. "What?" he asked, as his mother stirred next to him.

His father rolled his eyes impatiently. "We have arrived at our destination," he said slowly, as if to make sure that they got it. "I am glad that you all seem to have had a restful trip. I, however, am exhausted. So, let's check in. Vaarem, wake your brother and help with the horses and carriage. Zara, come with me and let's get some rooms."

Zareanna lifted Lim's head off her lap. "Wake up, Limmy," she said. "We're here."

Lim opened his eyes, then promptly shut them again. Vaarem thought that he was looking strangely pale, worse than he had since leaving Sirrock City.

Zareanna stood up and allowed Garrett to take her hand and help her down from the carriage, and into the inn. It was a dwarf settlement, however instead of being underground, it was a stone building built into the side of a hill.

When their parents were gone, Vaarem shook Lim's shoulder. "Come on," he said. "We're here. Come and help me."

Lim sat up slowly, holding his hand to his head. He took a breath and coughed.

Oh shit, thought Vaarem. Not again. His brother had been doing so well. What was happening now?

"Are you okay?" asked Vaarem.

"Yeah." Nodded Lim, as he struggled for breath. "I can't breathe," he said, holding his hand to his chest. "Shit." He coughed again.

"Do you have your potion?" asked Vaarem, looking around for Lim's coat. Didn't his brother keep his medication in his pocket?

"I forgot to take it," said Lim. "At lunchtime," he explained.

Vaarem rolled his eyes. "Dragon dung," he said. "What now?"

"I don't know." Shrugged Lim, coughing again. "Dr Thorn told me to not miss a dose. He never told me what to do if I ever did. Fuck. I guess I'll take it now?"

Vaarem shrugged. "If you think it's best," he said.

He remembered on their way to Sirrock City when Lim had overused his potion. He didn't want a repeat of that. But what else could they do?

"Where's your coat?" asked Vaarem.

"Over there," Lim pointed to the corner of the carriage.

Vaarem picked it up and brought it over to him. Lim took his coat from his brother and fumbled around in the pocket. His hands were starting to shake.

Fuck, he thought. *The doctor was right in that if I stop taking my meds, I'll get very sick very quickly.*

He just hadn't counted on how quickly.

He finally found the right bottle, but he couldn't open it, so had to ask Vaarem for help. Vaarem frowned but opened the bottle obediently and handed it back to Lim.

Lim had his dose, then closed the bottle and put it away, back into his coat pocket. "Right," he said. "I hope it starts to work quickly. I feel really horrible," he added, with another cough.

He remembered starting to feel bad when they'd been swimming earlier that day. He'd thought that that was due to his father's unkind words, but now wondered whether it had actually been his body trying to tell him something.

He stood up carefully, holding his hand to his head, then allowed Vaarem to help him step down from the carriage.

The sun was starting to set, and Lim had to put

his hand to his eyes to stop the glare. He stumbled after his brother, as Vaarem unhitched the horses and allowed one of the grooms from the inn to rub them down and feed them.

After the horses had been seen to and the carriage had been wheeled away into a safe area, Vaarem and Lim went inside the inn. This place was more grand than the other places they'd stayed in until now. It was more of a hotel than an inn, and both brothers looked around in wonder. The lights in the hall were most definitely powered by electricity, and they buzzed softly. Lim shuddered, remembering his treatments. But it seemed that electricity was becoming all the rage, as even dwarves were using it here.

Garrett and Zareanna were standing at the desk, talking to the innkeeper, or rather, arguing.

"I'm sorry, sir," the dwarf was looking up at Garrett, clearly intimidated by the much taller elf, "but we only have one room available. It is a very popular time of season, and you did not write to book ahead."

"I find it difficult to believe that every room in your vast establishment is full. Payment is not a problem," said Garrett, putting down a pile of gold coins on the desk.

"I'm sure it isn't, sir," said the innkeeper. He was a middle-aged dwarf with grey-brown hair and a full beard that fell past his waist, so was looped through his belt. "But the fact remains that we are full up. I can give you a room on the second floor. It is not large, but you can sleep the four of you in there."

"Fine," said Garrett through gritted teeth. He picked up half of the coins and put them back in his purse. The innkeeper gave him a key, which Garrett took, rather ungraciously, in Lim's opinion.

"I can sleep in the carriage," offered Lim, remembering the time that he and Vaarem had done that on the way to Sirrock City.

Garrett turned to him and scoffed. "Oh, don't try and play the martyr, Limnos. As long as you don't spend all night coughing, you will sleep in the same room as the rest of us." He then looked at Lim and frowned. "What happened to you?" he asked. "Or should I ask, what have you done to yourself now? You look terrible."

"Thank you for your assessment, Father," said Lim coldly. "I haven't done anything. I'm just tired."

"Well, go and get some rest, then," said his father, throwing the key to him. Lim had not been prepared for that, but he caught it nevertheless, then turned to walk down the hallway, up the stairs, and into their room.

He took the stairs very slowly, Vaarem's arm around his waist, and managed to climb to the first level without running out of breath completely.

As long as I am careful, and don't forget my potions, I can pretend to be normal, he thought with a bitter smile.

He unlocked the door and walked into the room, which had one large, canopied bed, and several armchairs and couches along the walls, which were hung with coloured woollen tapestries.

He walked over and threw himself down on the couch in the furthest corner. Then, he remembered that he'd left his potions bag in the carriage and that he didn't have his evening dose in his pocket.

Shit.

He thought about asking Vaarem to go and get it, but his parents had come into the room, and he didn't want to draw attention to himself and his forgetfulness. His father would have a field day if he found out that Lim had forgotten to take his medicines up to the room.

Instead, he stood up slowly, and walked out of the room, hoping that no one would take his couch.

"I need to get something from the carriage," he explained.

There were many carriages parked behind the hill that housed the inn, and Lim could tell that they belonged to people of all four races. The dwarf carriages were squat and sturdy, usually pulled by ponies. The human carriages had metal trim around the doors, windows, and wheel rims. The elf carriages, like his family's, were made of wood and were decorated with nature-inspired carvings and solderings. The pixie carriages were small and delicate, similar to the elf ones but in miniature. Lim saw that one of them was being pulled by two goats with curling horns. He looked at them all curiously as he looked for and found his family's carriage. He went in and got his medicine bag, then went back out.

On his way back inside, he ran into the groom, who had been tending to the goats before. The young dwarf looked up at Lim and gave him a friendly smile. "Hello," he said, smoothing his silky auburn beard over his chest. "How can I help you?"

"What's happening?" asked Lim. "Why are there so many people here?"

"Tomorrow is the Festival of Diamonds," said the dwarf, sounding surprised that Lim didn't know.

"What's that?" asked Lim curiously.

The groom looked up at him. "There is a diamond mine in this area," he explained. "Every turn, in the last week before spring, we celebrate diamonds. I thought that you and your family were here for it."

"No," said Lim. "I've never heard of it."

The groom nodded, accepting that. "I guess it is not that well known outside of this region. Anyway, there is going to be a bit of a party after dinner tonight, and tomorrow morning we celebrate by giving each other diamonds. Just small ones, mind you. Nothing elaborate. Here." He took a tiny diamond, about the size of the top of a pin, out of a small box that he carried in his breast pocket, and gave it to Lim.

"Thank you," said Lim, taking the little stone and wondering what he should do with it. Diamonds were not particularly valuable on Zemia, as they had no healing nor other magical properties. Large diamonds were sometimes used as precision tools, but small ones like this were purely decorative. Still, it was a very nice gesture, so Lim smiled gratefully.

"Here." The groom took a small drawstring bag out of his other pocket and gave this to Lim too.

"Thank you," said Lim again, putting the diamond in the bag.

"By the way, I'm Terry," said the groom.

"Thank you, Terry. I'm Lim."

Terry smiled up at him, and it was warm and genuine. "Well, lovely to meet you, Lim. May this stone bring you luck," he said.

"Thank you," said Lim, for the third time. "I don't have anything to give you, I'm afraid."

"That's okay," said Terry. "Not everyone does. I hope that you and your family enjoy your stay."

"Thank you," said Lim yet again. "I'm sure that we will."

"I'll see you after dinner tonight?" asked Terry hopefully.

Lim smiled. "I'll try and make it," he said. "I'm really tired, but I'll try."

He walked up the stairs slowly, crouching down to rest on the landing, then went into his family's room and collapsed on to his couch, which no one had touched in his absence.

After a few moments, he pushed himself up onto his elbows and looked around. His parents were sitting on the bed, talking softly, their heads bent. Vaarem was sitting cross-legged on one of the other couches, playing a game, several rows of cards laid out in front of him.

"I found out why there are so many people here today," said Lim.

"Yeah?" said Vaarem, as everyone turned to look at his twin.

"Apparently tomorrow is the Festival of Diamonds," said Lim. "There is a diamond mine nearby," he explained, "and tomorrow is the day that the people around here celebrate, by giving each other diamonds. I got given one by the groom." He took the little pouch out of his vest pocket and showed his family the diamond inside.

"Wow," said Vaarem.

"What a lovely idea," said Zareanna.

"Pfft," said Garrett. "Dwarves have some strange traditions."

Lim put the diamond away and put the drawstring bag back in his pocket, before lying down on the couch again and closing his eyes.

His family went back to what they'd been doing, until Garrett announced that it was time for dinner. Lim put his hand on his stomach. He'd been feeling a little strange after taking his last dose of medicine. He remembered now that he was supposed to take this potion with food, but he'd had it on an empty stomach, which was, no doubt, the reason that he was feeling so odd now.

"I'm not really hungry," he began, then realised that

his father would not allow him to stay upstairs while the rest of them went down to the restaurant.

"I don't think so, Lim," said Garrett. "I told you before. You are not skipping a meal on my watch. Now, let's all get ready and go down. If there is a party happening in this place, then we are going to dress and act accordingly."

Chapter 22

The Festival of Diamonds

It took the family all of twenty minutes to get ready for dinner. Zareanna put on a lilac-coloured dress with short sleeves, a full skirt, and a sheer-lace-trimmed over-skirt on top. She piled her curly blonde hair on top of her head in an elaborate bun. She then put lilac shadow on her eyelids and painted her long lashes to make her eyes stand out.

"You look beautiful, Mother," said Lim, his voice filled with awe. Of course, he'd always known that his mother was beautiful. She was his mother, and the loveliest, gentlest woman that he'd ever known. But at times like these he realised that even apart from her loving nature, she was stunning to look at too, with delicate features .

"Doesn't she just," said Garrett, for once agreeing completely with his youngest son.

Garrett wore a shirt in a similar shade of lilac to his wife's dress, teamed with cream-coloured trousers and a matching waistcoat. His hair was brushed back from his face and hanging loose over his shoulders.

Vaarem was wearing a crimson shirt with gold cuff-links. He had on dark-green trousers and a matching vest that hung to his mid-thigh. His hair was up in its usual top-knot.

Lim was the last to get ready. He was dressed in his customary black; black slim-fitting trousers, a black silk shirt that laced up at the front and tied up with ribbons at the cuffs, and a black velvet vest which was fitted at the top then flared out over his hips finishing just above his knees. His hair was up in the two braids that he'd been wearing for the past couple of days.

They went down into the restaurant and found an out-of-the-way table in the corner.

The restaurant served three different types of meat dishes, as well as soups and salads. Garrett ordered the chicken for all of them before Lim had had a chance to decide what he wanted. In hindsight, his father ordering for him was probably a good idea because Lim, as usual, didn't feel like eating anything. He picked at his dinner when it came, trying to ignore his father staring at him.

When dinner was over, the lights dimmed and a curtain opened on the far side of the room, revealing a small stage. As the lights on the stage brightened,

Lim could make out several people standing, or sitting and holding musical instruments.

Once again, he was reminded of his violin and how much he longed to play it again.

Eventually, Lim saw the band. There were three humans, two of whom were playing guitars and one playing the drums. The fourth person, he realised, was an elf. She wasn't very tall, and she was quite plump, but when the lights shone on the tips of her pointed ears and on her slanted eyes, there was no mistaking her heritage.

And then she began to sing.

Her voice was deep and powerful, and she crooned about eternal love and undying passion. Lim found himself entranced, not by her words, nor the sway of her body, but by the power in her voice.

She was weaving a spell of calm and unity over the audience. Lim turned to see his father take his mother's hand and look into her eyes. They smiled at each other and exchanged a brief kiss. Lim had never seen them do that before. They occasionally kissed each other on the cheek, but never on the mouth.

As Lim watched, the rest of the audience also seemed to relax. Animosities died away and everyone seemed to be at peace, with themselves and each other. Lim turned to Vaarem on his other side. Vaarem was staring at the singer with a glazed expression on his face, his lips curved into a lazy smile. Lim seemed to be the only one unaffected. Although, he realised that he too was feeling relaxed; he was just aware of it.

The singer finished her song and looked into the audience as they erupted into thunderous applause.

"Thank you," she said in a husky voice. "Thank you so much."

She then began the next song and continued to weave her spell.

By the end of the set, all couples in the room that Lim could see were holding each other's hands, or embracing each other, any quibbles they may have previously had, forgotten. All singles were also smiling, either thinking of an absent love, or looking around the room for a potential partner. Lim surprised himself by thinking of Eliza and wishing for a moment that she could have been here and experienced this evening with him. But the thought was brief, and he soon snapped out of it and started to look around the room curiously.

Vaarem had gotten up off his seat and was standing at the other end of the room, talking to a young elven woman that Lim had not noticed before. She was smiling at Vaarem, her hand on his arm, as she listened intently to what he was saying. Garrett and Zareanna had walked over to the bar and were now drinking glasses of wine, their eyes still on each other.

Lim saw Terry the groom standing in the doorway. The young dwarf's eyes met Lim's and he smiled, then raised his hand in greeting. Lim raised his own hand, but then became aware of someone sitting down on the chair next to him. He turned to see the singer sitting beside him. She had dark brown hair, the top of which was pulled back, letting the rest flow over her shoulders and down her back. She was dressed in a green dress with a tight-laced corset accentuating her curves.

"Hello," she said, extending her hand. "I'm Milia."

"I'm Lim," he replied, shaking her hand.

"Did you enjoy the show?" she asked. He felt that there was an edge to the question.

"Very much," he said. "But I am curious as to what you were doing?"

"What do you mean?" she asked, tilting her head and looking at him curiously. "I was doing what I am paid to do. Sing and entertain."

"What about weaving the love spell?" he asked, looking straight at her.

She sat up, clearly taken aback. "So, it was you," she said. "I could feel some resistance in the audience."

"I wasn't resisting," said Lim. "I was just aware. What were you doing?"

She sighed. "It's nothing sinister," she said, a little defensively. "I just get people to recall their feelings of love and joy. I don't coerce."

"I never meant to imply that you were doing anything bad," said Lim quickly. "I'm just curious."

"You must be very sensitive," she said. "I do try to be subtle. No one has ever picked up on it before."

Lim shrugged. "Sorry," he said, feeling a little bad. He hadn't meant to make her feel exposed. He was just genuinely interested.

"I'm not paid to do the love spell, as you call it,"

she told him. "I am just paid to sing. But, if people feel loved, they are more likely to stay out longer, and order drinks and things, so it is good for the inn when I do it. But it's nothing sinister as I told you. It's not coercion or anything. I don't make anyone do anything that they wouldn't do anyway. I just help people to get in touch with themselves and their positive emotions."

"I see," said Lim thoughtfully. "It's basically just a reminder of your positive feelings and sentiments, of how much you love your significant other. If you have one that is," he added.

She smiled. "Exactly," she said. "I sometimes officiate weddings, and when I do, I always throw a little bit of a couple's positive energy back at them."

Lim smiled. "That sounds really lovely. I'm reading a book about this type of magic. I've decided that I'm going to study to be a Priest of the Fates, to work with this kind of magic full time. I will have to remember that when I officiate a wedding."

She returned his smile. "Please do," she said. "And you know it isn't just about romantic love. Love for your family and friends, and even special places, or just special ideas can be accessed and enhanced too. It could also work with other ceremonies such as baby namings, or even funerals."

"Funerals?" He frowned. "How?"

"Well," she said, "like getting people to recall positive memories of their departed loved ones. Making peace with a loved one's death, that sort of thing."

"I see." Nodded Lim thoughtfully, "I think that is a lovely idea."

She smiled at that. "I think you'll make a wonderful priest," she said, patting his hand. "I can tell that you're very sensitive to this type of magic, and likely very powerful, if you put your mind to it."

"Thank you," said Lim. No matter how many people told him that he was good at this type of thing, it always made him feel warm inside when he heard it.

Eventually, the hotel guests dissipated and went back into their rooms. Milia went back to her bandmates. Lim followed his family upstairs and into their room, needing to stop only once on the landing.

"That concert was lovely," said Zareanna, undoing her hair as she sat on the bed.

"It was very impressive," agreed Garrett, helping her unlace her dress.

Lim was glad to see his parents getting along. Even now, they were often tense, and it made a nice change to see them relaxed. Milia was right in that she was enabling people to remember their affections for their spouses and loved ones. He wondered whether his parents were thinking of Malkim, or each other? Whichever it was, they seemed happy.

Garrett helped Zareanna to get comfortable inside the bed, then he drew the curtain around the canopy. "Good night, Vaarem. Good night, Lim," he said to his sons. "Sleep well and don't make too much noise. See you in the morning." He climbed into the bed and secured the curtain around it, leaving Vaarem and Lim essentially alone.

"Good night, Var," said Lim, sitting down on his couch and looking around for his medicine bag. He found it under the couch, took out his evening potion bottle and had his dose, before putting the bottle away again and getting ready for bed.

Vaaren caught Lim's eye as he was getting into his own bed, and grinned at him.

"What did you and the singer talk about?" asked Vaarem curiously.

"Just about magic," said Lim dismissively.

"Oh," said Vaarem.

"What?" Laughed Lim. "What were you expecting?"

Vaarem shrugged. "I really don't know," he admitted. "Aren't you going to ask me who I talked to?"

"Who did you talk to, Var?" asked Lim obediently.

"Her name is Ninetta, and she's from Morliss," said Vaarem. "She's here with her family for the Festival of Diamonds. They're leaving tomorrow and we were hoping, as in, me and her, that our families could travel together for a few days until we reach Morliss. What do you think?" he asked expectantly.

"Sure," said Lim. "Have you asked Mother and Father?"

"Not yet," said Vaarem. "But I'm sure they'll agree."

"Yeah," said Lim. He was feeling strangely resistant to the idea. He didn't know why. He'd never been possessive of Vaarem. Vaarem had always been the more outgoing one of the two, so he'd always had more friends. This had never bothered Lim, so he wondered what the problem was now.

As usual, Lim couldn't sleep. The dark room was eerily silent without the soft buzz of the electricity in the air. His stomach hurt; most likely from having had his two doses of potion so close together. No matter which way he turned, he found that he couldn't get comfortable.

"Ow," he said quietly, as he tried to draw his knees up to his chest. "Ow, ow, ow," he lay on his back again, his legs straight, his hands on his belly. He tried to soothe the ache by calling the magic heat to his hands, but this only made him exhausted, without making any significant difference otherwise, so he rolled over onto his side again and drew his legs up to his chest once more. He curled up, then stretched out again, trying every possible position, before finally giving up.

He sat up slowly, being as quiet as he could, then stood up and walked out of the room. He went downstairs, into the empty foyer, where he found some paper, some ink, and a quill on one of the shelves, then went through into the empty dining room.

The place had been cleaned up from the night's event and there were fresh tablecloths on all the tables. In the centre of each table, there was a vase with a single white rose. On closer inspection, he saw that the roses were made of silk, and inside each flower there were tiny diamonds, like the one that

Terry had given him earlier. The whole effect was very festive, and he smiled, before walking over to the corner table, the one that his family had sat at before, and pulling out a chair. He sat down and gasped as another cramp ran through him.

"Ow," he said to himself, as he put the writing implements on the table, then crossed his arms over his stomach as the cramp passed through him. When it was over and he could move again, he laid the paper out, opened the ink pot and dipped the quill in.

It was dark in the room, but the moonlight coming in through the window was enough for his elven eyes to see what he was doing.

He began to write a letter to Eliza. He'd been unable to stop thinking about her since the previous evening. He wrote about their journey home so far, about their day at the hot springs, about the hotel that they were currently at, and the Festival of Diamonds. He took a tiny diamond out of the nearest rose, with the intention of including it in the letter.

Eventually, he started to get sleepy.

He put his quill down and closed his eyes, resting his head on his hand.

He was woken up by someone shaking his shoulder. He sat up, startled, and in doing so, tipped the ink bottle with his hand. The black ink started to spill all over the white tablecloth. Lim quickly picked up his letter, before the ink had managed to touch more than its edge.

He realised that the writing was all smudged any-way. He must have slept with either his hand, or possibly his face on it.

Dragon shit, he thought, annoyed with himself.

"Hey." He heard someone say.

He turned around to see that the speaker was Terry. The dwarf was carrying a small candle, which he set down on the next table.

"Oh Fates, I'm so sorry," said Lim, looking down at the spilled ink. "I can help you wash it," he said. "I know how to get black out of white. Trust me."

"It's okay," chuckled Terry. He'd picked up the ink pot and had taken the tablecloth off the table, so that there was no further spillage. "What were you doing?"

Lim looked down at himself, at his ink-stained hands and nightshirt, and was suddenly embarrassed. "I couldn't sleep," he explained. "So, I came down to write a letter. And then I ended up falling asleep." He sighed, feeling really stupid.

Terry smiled, the corners of his eyes crinkling. "Oh no," he said. "Isn't that always the way?"

Lim shrugged. It seemed to always be the way when he was involved.

"Like I said, don't worry," said Terry. "No harm done. Why don't you go upstairs and get ready for breakfast? It's nearly sunrise."

"Okay," said Lim, getting up, still holding his smudged letter.

"By the way," said Terry. "You have some ink on your face. Here, let me."

Lim leaned down and let Terry use the edge of the tablecloth in his hands to wipe his cheek.

"Oh crap," said Terry. "I'm sorry. Now I made it worse."

"It's okay," said Lim, holding his cheek and laughing slightly. He thought that he must look absurd. "I'll go upstairs and wash up."

"I like your nightgown," said Terry, as Lim turned to walk away. "Where did you get a black one?"

"I dyed it myself," said Lim. "To hide all the ink stains." He laughed. It wasn't the primary reason that he chose to wear all black all the time, but it certainly helped.

"Good idea," laughed Terry. "Now go. I'll see you soon."

Lim turned to go, and his movement made the candle on the next table go out.

"Sorry," he said, then quickly lifted his hand and re-lit the candle with magic. He could see in the dark himself, but he knew that Terry couldn't, hence the candle.

"Thanks," said Terry. "Once we switch the lights off for the night, they stay off until the next evening. It's unusual for dwarves to use electricity," he explained, "but my mother was half-human, so she liked to sometimes do things the human way, if that makes sense."

Lim nodded.

"It's due to her that we've opened up this inn." Terry smiled a little sadly, "She always wanted to ensure that I didn't forget my human ancestry. So we are here, halfway between the dwarf and the human settlements. And then we get elf and pixie guests too. Well, pixies not so much, but elves, yes."

"It's very nice," said Lim, looking around, "Very impressive."

"Thank you." Smiled Terry.

"My mother is half-human too," said Lim conversationally.

"Oh wow," said Terry, "That's nice. I mean." He paused, looking down awkwardly for a moment, before looking back up at Lim. "I don't meet many people of mixed blood. It's nice when mixed-race unions work out. It gives you a good feeling, like the world is a good harmonious place."

"Yes," agreed Lim. He'd never thought of it like that, but Terry had a point.

"Anyway," said Terry, "you should get going and wash up. I will see you later. Happy Diamond Day."

"Happy Diamond Day." Lim smiled.

As he made his slow way back up to his room, he pondered the idea of mixed-race unions showing that the world was in harmony.

There is a balance in all things, thought Lim. *The bad is always counteracted by some good. In turn, we recognise the good as good because we know what is bad.*

To know joy, one must know pain.

There was also a curious balance to his family that he'd never considered before. His mother was half-elf, half-human, and she'd married a human and produced a human child, and then she'd married an elf and produced elf children. Three children, three parents. It was all in balance.

Again, he thought of Eliza's book. The magic used by the Faith was exclusively focused on keeping this balance, this harmony in the world and the universe.

This is my calling, thought Lim, as he stopped on the landing to catch his breath.

He opened the door quietly, hoping against hope that his family were still asleep and that his absence had gone unnoticed.

But of course, that was too much to ask for and everyone was already awake.

"Lim!" said Vaarem, as Lim walked in. "Where were you?"

"Downstairs," said Lim.

"What happened to your face?" asked Garrett with a disapproving frown.

"I got ink on it," said Lim, putting his hand to his cheek, wondering just how bad he looked.

"Why? What were you doing?" demanded his father.

"I was just writing a letter," said Lim. "To Eliza."

"To your human girlfriend?" Garrett frowned.

"She's just a friend," said Lim with an irritated sigh.

"Whatever," said Garrett. "Wash your face. You look ridiculous." He rolled his eyes and shook his head scornfully.

Lim went over to his couch to get his things, then

went into the bathroom area of the suite to wash up. When he looked in the mirror, he saw that his right temple and cheekbone were smudged black, as well as the tip of his nose. He also realised that he'd lost the little diamond that he'd planned to give to Eliza.

Damn, he thought, as he washed his face, then got dressed and braided his hair. He came out of the bathroom to his family all ready to go, waiting for him. He took his morning potion dose, then followed his family out of the room and down the stairs.

The dining room was already full when they got there. The tablecloth on the corner table where Lim had slept, had been replaced, and the family made their way over to it. They sat down, then looked around the room curiously. Lim realised that this was the first time they'd seen the festive set up.

A short while later, waiters came in and handed out glasses of sparkling water. Then, the owner of the inn stood up on the stage and made a welcome speech. He talked about the local diamond mine and the significance of diamonds. In this area they'd come to symbolise everlasting love and beauty. Like Milia the singer had mentioned the previous evening, the love represented was not limited to romantic love, but to anything and anyone that one found valuable. He made a toast, and everyone raised their glasses and drank.

The water tasted clear and refreshing, and Lim

drank it with pleasure. It was the best water that he'd ever tasted, and he wondered where it had come from.

Then, breakfast was served, which was a selection of fruits, porridge, bread, eggs, fish, meats, and pastries. Lim got himself a bowl of porridge and fruit and watched the people around him.

Ninetta and her family were seated at a table across the room. Vaarem caught her eye and smiled. She seemed to be travelling with a young woman of a similar age, and two older ladies. Lim looked over in their direction too, but none of them looked at him.

When everyone had finished their breakfast, the innkeeper stepped on the stage again and announced that it was time for the gift exchange. For those, like Lim's family, who had not brought gifts, there were the tiny diamonds inside the roses, which they could give to each other. Lim took a couple of the diamonds to give to Marla and Jessa, then a couple for his friends back in Palinas, and finally he took another one for Eliza. He wrapped these all up in tissue and put them inside the drawstring pouch. He didn't want to get these stones mixed up with the one that Terry had given him.

Garrett took the biggest diamond out of their rose and presented it to Zareanna. She gave him a small one in exchange. Vaarem walked over to Ninetta's table and presented her with a diamond, and she gave him one too. Lim noticed that Ninetta's companion was sitting at their table alone. No one seemed to have given her anything and she had a sour expression on her face.

Garrett nudged Lim with his elbow. "Look, there is a nice elven lady over there. Go and talk to her. I'm sure your human wenches won't mind."

Lim frowned at his father and wanted to say something to defend his friends, but he didn't want to piss his father off and then have Garrett forbid him from joining Jessa and Marla at the festival in their inn. So, he stood up and walked over to where Vaarem and Ninetta were talking, and seemingly, ignoring Ninetta's companion.

As he walked across the room, Lim scanned the gathered faces, looking for either Terry, or perhaps Milia, but neither of them seemed to be there.

He had to stop and catch his breath when he reached the table, but soon straightened up and smiled. "Hi, I'm Lim," he extended his hand, then sat down on an empty chair.

The girl shook it shyly. She had pale blonde hair, similar to his own, and bright green eyes. He saw that she wore jewels in both of her delicately pointed ears, as well as on her slim wrists and slender fingers. Overall, she was very pretty, but there was something about her that gave Lim an apprehensive feeling.

Perhaps she's just shy, he reasoned.

"I'm Pelleata," she said. "Named after the city of Pelleas."

"Oh, that's beautiful," said Lim politely. "Have you been to Pelleas?"

"No," she said dismissively. "Why would I want to go there?"

Lim shrugged. "I hear it's a nice place," he said with a thin smile. "Happy Diamond Day," he said, giving her one of the small stones that he'd brought over for this purpose.

"Thank you," she said, taking the diamond, then putting it on her empty plate. It seemed that she wasn't going to keep it, nor was she going to offer him one back.

Well, who cares? thought Lim to himself. *It's not like any of this means anything.* Yet, he was a little annoyed at how dismissive Pelleata was of him; until he remembered that his father had made him talk to her and he had no vested interest in the conversation.

"So, who are you travelling with?" asked Lim, trying to start up another conversation.

"My cousin." She pointed to Ninetta, who turned around and smiled at them, "and my aunts." The two older elven ladies were deep in conversation at the other end of the table and didn't turn around. One of them seemed very old for an elf, with white hair, while the other one looked to be of a similar age to his parents.

"Oh," said Lim. "That's nice. And you're here for the Festival of Diamonds?"

"Yes," she said with a sigh. "It's such a let-down. I thought I'd get some real jewels, but no one's given me anything."

Lim didn't point out that he had in fact given her

something, because it was obvious that that wasn't what she meant.

"Yeah," said Lim. "We didn't come prepared either. As in, my family and me didn't even know about this festival until yesterday. We're just passing through."

Pelleata didn't say anything to that, just looked at him quizzically.

He stared right back at her, then coughed into his elbow. Despite having taken his potion, he was feeling a little off.

"What's wrong with you?" she asked after a moment, her tone making him feel like she thought him somehow unpleasant.

"What?" he asked, frowning.

"What's wrong with you?" she repeated. "You're always coughing, and you're so skinny and strangely pale. Are you sick or disabled or something?"

He closed his eyes and sighed. This was the worst thing about his condition, he sometimes thought. Worse than constantly feeling like crap and being unable to do anything, were people's constant enquiries about what was wrong with him, like he was some freakish curiosity. It seemed awfully rude, but if he responded with, "Nothing. What's wrong with *you*?" he was the one that came off like a dick.

He was trying to think of how to reply, when Vaarem came to his rescue, and putting his arm around Lim's shoulders, said firmly, "He's fine."

"Oh." Pelleata pursed her lips with distaste. "Well,

don't touch me," she shifted away from Lim. "I don't want to catch anything from you."

"Trust me," said Lim through gritted teeth, "I have no desire to touch you." He wondered now about his bad feeling the previous night when Vaarem suggested the two families travel together. Could it have been a premonition of unpleasant things to come? He'd read about this in Eliza's book and wondered whether he could hone his intuition to recognise these things. Perhaps he could use it to prevent disaster, or at least prepare for it?

He looked up, just to avoid having to look at Pelleata, and was gratified when he saw Terry moving through the tables, picking up empty plates and glasses.

"Excuse me," he said, standing up carefully and walking over to Terry. "Happy Diamond Day," he said to the dwarf, taking the rose off the nearest table and giving it to him. He hoped that there were still some diamonds inside it.

"Thank you." Terry took the rose, then put it in his breast pocket.

"I just had a conversation with one of the most unpleasant people that I've ever met," said Lim, indicating Pelleata with his eyes.

Terry looked over, then turned back to Lim. "The young lady in the pink?" he enquired.

Lim nodded.

"Yes," sighed Terry. "She was not very nice at check-in. Very entitled and demanding. But, many of our guests are entitled and demanding, and it's our job to meet their demands," he said with a laugh. "Fortunately, they are balanced out by the genuinely pleasant guests, such as yourself." He smiled. "Now, I need to clean this up, but I will hopefully see you later, yes?"

"Yes."

As Terry walked away, Lim looked back into the dining room. His parents had walked over to Ninetta's table and were now talking to the two elven ladies. They were all talking and laughing amiably.

Lim sighed and went back up to their room to pack. He had a bad feeling about all of this.

Chapter 23

Pelleata

A few minutes after Lim had gotten his things together, Vaarem bounded into the room.

"Guess what?" he asked, standing in front of Lim and hopping from foot to foot excitedly.

"What?"

"Mother and Father agreed to let the girls ride in with us to Morliss. Or, should I say, Ninetta's mother and aunt allowed them to ride with us. So long as Mother chaperones, but hey, that's all fine, we don't plan to be physically intimate yet," he said with a grin.

Lim rolled his eyes and sighed. "Great," he said, without enthusiasm.

"Why? What's wrong?" Vaarem was instantly alert.

"I don't know if you noticed, but Ninetta's cousin is not exactly pleasant. I don't relish the thought of being stuck with her for three days."

Vaarem's face fell, and Lim sighed again. "Fine," he said. "I'll give her a chance. For you."

Vaarem smiled a dazzling smile and threw his arms around Lim. "Oh, thank you, thank you, thank you!" he cried. "You are the best brother ever."

"I know," said Lim, then turned back to his packing.

Lim helped Terry and Garrett to hitch up the horses, then, when his father went back inside to get their things, Lim continued to talk to Terry. He was feeling reasonably good overall, and he told the groom about Palinas and about the Winter Lights festival that he and Vaarem had been invited to. Terry listened with interest, and when Lim was about to climb into the carriage, asked to keep in contact.

"Sure." Lim smiled, then gave Terry his address in Palinas. He'd made more friends during this trip than he ever had in his life.

"Ugh," said Pelleata, as Lim sat next to her in the carriage. "Are you really going to write to a dwarf?" she asked, crossing her arms and looking at him sideways. "And not only a dwarf, but a servant?

"He's not a servant," said Lim. "He's the son of the innkeeper." *And even if he* had *been a servant,* he thought, *what difference would it have made?* "And, yes, I am going to write to a dwarf. Why not? He's nice." *Unlike you,* he thought, but didn't say.

"You're strange," she told him.

"So they tell me" he said with a shrug, then looked out the window as the carriage took off.

Vaarem and Ninetta sat across from Lim and talked and laughed amiably. Occasionally, Vaarem would meet Lim's eyes and smile. He seemed smitten and Lim was happy for him. He did his best to ignore Pelleata, who had nothing positive to say, not even when Zareanna tried to engage her in conversation.

"What do you like to study at school, Pelleata?" his mother asked her.

"Nothing." The girl crossed her arms even tighter. "School is boring."

Zareanna smiled thinly, then looked away.

They stopped mid-morning near a waterfall. Ninetta's mother and aunt (who turned out to be a great-aunt) joined them for the quick snack. Their carriage was pulled by a single winged horse, therefore was a little slower. Lim was fascinated with the winged stallion, and helped the two women to tend to him. He stroked the horse's mane and was pleased when Ninetta's mother said, "He likes you. He is usually very standoffish." Lim smiled, as he sat down to eat. He found the two older ladies pleasant to talk to and wondered where Pelleata got her attitude from. Her family were all lovely.

As they were sitting on the grass and looking at the water, Vaarem leaned over and said into Lim's ear, "Pelleata is grumpy because apparently, she recently got dumped by her boyfriend. He left her for someone else."

"Gee, I wonder why," said Lim under his breath.

Vaarem punched his arm softly. "Be nice," he said.

"I'm trying," said Lim, through gritted teeth. The revelation did not make him feel any warmer towards his unwanted companion, who was sitting across from him, and picking at the grass, looking bored and annoyed.

As the day grew hotter, Lim took off his coat and put it in the carriage, before returning to sit with his parents and the older ladies. He had no desire to be around Pelleata any more than necessary.

A short while later, they packed up the food and went to get back into the carriages. Pelleata grumbled about everyone's coats and jackets taking up too much space, and rearranged the Nightingales' carriage, moving everyone's things to make herself more comfortable and moving all of her own luggage into her aunts' carriage. Lim wished that she would move herself there, but he did his best to remain civil as the carriages took off again.

A couple of hours later, the weather turned cool. Lim looked around for his coat, but he couldn't find it.

"Where's my coat?" he asked, hugging his arms around himself to try and stay warm.

Vaarem and Zareanna began to look around for it too.

"Oh, I put the coats in my Auntie's carriage," said Pelleata dismissively. "There was no room for them here."

"Fuck," swore Lim.

"Lim," Zareanna told him off. "Language. Here, you

can use this." She took the cover off her seat and gave it to him to wrap around his shoulders.

"Thank you," said Lim. However, he soon realised that he still had a problem. His potions were in his coat pocket. He hoped that they would meet up with the other carriage before he needed them.

But when they stopped for their afternoon meal, the other carriage was nowhere in sight.

Lim ate his meal anxiously, wondering whether he should unpack the carriage to find his medicine bag, or whether he could wait a few more hours. He was feeling reasonably fine, so he decided to wait.

As the afternoon wore on, he began to feel ill. He closed his eyes and leaned his head back against the wall, trying to keep his breathing even.

A short while later he began to cough.

"Ugh," said Pelleata, moving away from him dramatically. "Don't do that. I don't want to catch something off you."

Lim glared at her. "I can honestly say that you make me sick," he told her in disgust, then coughed again, and again into his elbow, unable to draw a breath. "Mother," he gasped, looking at Zareanna, who was looking out the window, seemingly lost in her thoughts. "I need my potion. I'm sorry, but we need to stop and unpack."

Zareanna immediately asked Garrett to stop the carriage, and they all got out. Lim all but fell out the door, then rushed around to the back and opened the luggage compartment. He searched for his medicine bag but to his horror, he couldn't find it. "No," he gasped, then choked, and fell to his knees. "It's not there."

"What do you mean?" said Vaarem. "It must be. I saw you put it in." He stepped past Lim and looked. However, neither Vaarem nor his parents, who searched after him, could find it. They searched the entire luggage compartment, as well as the inside of the carriage, but the bag was not there.

"I don't understand." Garrett shook his head. "It was right there."

Ninetta hugged her arms around herself anxiously, unable to do anything to help.

Then Pelleata said, "Was it the green bag with the gold clasp?"

"Yes!" gasped Lim, sitting down and putting his head in his hands. He was still wheezing and felt like he might pass out at any moment.

"Oh, I put that in Auntie's carriage too," she said dismissively.

"You what?" demanded Lim, while the rest of his family stared at her.

"There was no room," she said defensively.

"Why didn't you say?" gasped Lim. "Why didn't you ask?"

Zareanna knelt down next to him and held him, staring up at Pelleata in shock.

"I'm sorry," said Pelleata, not sounding sorry at all. "I didn't know it was important."

"Well, it was," said Vaarem angrily. He went back

into the carriage, then came back with a bottle of water, which he gave to Lim. Zareanna helped to hold it to his lips, and he took a couple of grateful sips, but he still couldn't catch his breath, and coughed again, spitting out the water.

"Eww, gross," said Pelleata, but everyone ignored her.

"I'll scry my mother," said Ninetta, taking a crystal out of her pocket and running around to the other side of the carriage, most likely to have some quiet. She came back several minutes later, saying, "They're coming. They'll be here soon. Are you okay, Lim?" She knelt down beside him and Zareanna.

Lim was leaning against his mother, still coughing, trying to not pass out. His chest and throat burned with pain, and he hugged his arms around himself, as he gasped for air.

After what felt like an eternity, but was in fact barely twenty minutes, the carriage came into view, the stallion's wings spread as he ran as fast as the carriage allowed, and a few moments later, the carriage stopped beside them.

Ninetta's mother jumped off the driver's seat and asked anxiously, "What happened, Nin?"

"It's Lim," said Ninetta. "He's sick. Le put his medicine in your carriage," she added accusingly.

Vaarem had jumped into the carriage, and now emerged with Lim's coat. "What do you need?" he asked, kneeling beside Lim and his mother.

"The jar," Lim managed to gasp. "And some water. Please. In a glass."

Vaarem got a glass out of their own carriage, filled it with water from the bottle, then warmed it with his magic. He gave it to Lim, who put some leaves from the jar into it, stirred it with his finger, then drank it down in one gulp. He put the glass down and leaned back into Zareanna's arms.

"What did you do, Le?" Ninetta asked her cousin accusingly. "He could have died."

Pelleata didn't respond and refused to meet anyone's eyes.

Lim lay back in his mother's arms, feeling sore, weak, and most of all stupid, but also angry, both with himself and with Pelleata. How had he allowed her to take his things? How had he not noticed?

Eventually, Lim felt well enough to resume their journey. He allowed Vaarem to help him back into the carriage, where he lay down on one of the benches and closed his eyes.

None of them wanted Pelleata to ride in their carriage after that, and to Lim's surprise, his father was the most adamant that she stay away, telling her sternly, "You have shown that you have no respect for my family or our possessions. You are not welcome in our carriage." So, she went back to her aunt's carriage, sulking and muttering about how unfair everyone was being to her. Her aunts apologised to Lim on her behalf, which Lim accepted. It wasn't their fault..

Vaarem got Lim's medicine bag, as well as all of their other things that Pelleata had inadvertently put in her aunt's carriage, and with Garrett's assistance, packed them into their own.

Garrett, who was usually the first to blame Lim for any problems that arose, was angry with Pelleata and for once didn't say anything disparaging to Lim, simply asking, "Are you all right?"

Lim nodded, and hugged his arms around his chest, trying to get comfortable. The prolonged coughing and wheezing had had an impact on his body and now he felt tender and sore whenever he tried to move. Fortunately, Vaarem had put the medicine bag under Lim's seat, where it should have been in the first place, so they didn't have to stop the carriage for Lim to get the painkiller out. He'd never used this potion before and had therefore not put it in his coat pocket. Zareanna got the bottle out of the bag for him, then helped him to sit up as he drank his dose, then she put it away afterwards, letting Lim lie down on the bench again.

Ninetta kept looking at him with frightened eyes. Lim tried to reassure her, but his throat was too dry and raw, so he couldn't talk.

When they reached that night's inn, Lim realised that after all the day's commotion, he'd once again forgotten to take his usual lunchtime medication. No wonder he was still feeling so bloody awful despite everything.

When Garrett and Zareanna had secured them a

room for the night, Vaarem helped Lim to get out of the carriage and into the inn.

Their room was, fortunately, on the ground floor, so with Vaarem's assistance, Lim was able to make it all the way there without having to resort to being carried. He felt tired, and sore, and embarrassed, and he just wanted to go to sleep and to put the whole day behind him.

He lay down in the bed, while his family unpacked around him, then when they'd settled in for the night, he called his mother over weakly and told her that he was not going to come out to dinner. There was no way that he was up to it, and he hoped that his father would understand.

"Of course, darling," said Zareanna gently, sitting down next to him. "I'll stay here with him," she told Garrett. "Can you get someone to bring us some dinner please?"

For once, Garrett agreed without any malice or other negativity.

"Lim, I'm so sorry," said Vaarem, crouching down next to the bed, so their faces were level.

"It's fine," said Lim, his voice still weak. "You weren't to know. But hey, I was right, wasn't I?" He laughed a little, before coughing again.

Vaarem reached over and rubbed his back. "I will never doubt your judgement again," he said seriously.

Lim smiled weakly. "For what it's worth," he said, "Ninetta seems really nice. You can keep seeing her if you want. Just keep her cousin away from me," he added with a grim smile.

"You can be sure of that," said Vaarem. "I am so mad at that girl, and Nin is too. She feels really, really bad about the whole thing."

"I know she does," said Lim. "And, hey, at the end of the day, she was the one who saved me by scrying her mother and getting her to come. I have no problem with her at all."

"You really are the best," said Vaarem, leaning over to kiss Lim on the cheek.

"Hey," said Lim with a shrug. "I learnt it all from my older brother." He laughed softly, managing not to cough this time.

Vaarem and Garrett went out into the dining room and soon after, there was a knock on the door. Zareanna opened it and came back with a tray of food. She brought it over and put it on the bedside table. She lifted the lid to reveal bread, meat, and cheese, as well as some fruit, and a bowl of salad.

Lim turned his face away, as the smell of it made him feel nauseated.

"Get up, darling," said Zareanna. "You have to eat. I know that you don't want to, but you need something after today."

Lim sat up with a groan, then reached over and took a grape off one of the plates on the tray. The painkiller was making him feel all warm and woozy. He remembered the feeling from the hospital, so he simply sat back and let the drug course through him, doing its work.

He tried to think of what to do about his other medication. He'd missed his midday dose and he wasn't sure about taking the evening one without the earlier one, but he also knew that if he took them too close together, he risked a stomachache.

In the end, he decided to go without, and to start the routine again the next morning. He was going to feel sick tonight regardless.

He took another grape, then Zareanna gave him some bread filled with cheese, which he ate slowly. She pulled a chair over and sat down next to him, taking some filled bread for herself. "How are you feeling, darling?" she asked, touching his forehead.

"Like I'm floating on a cloud," he replied with a laugh, then stopped because laughing hurt.

Zareanna smiled at him tenderly. "But you're okay otherwise?" She brushed a strand of hair behind his ear. Sometime during the course of the day his neat braids had gotten all messed up. He pushed the hair on the other side of his face behind his ear and ran his fingers along its length, trying to get the knots out.

"I can't believe that girl," said Zareanna, taking a bite of her bread. It seemed that she wasn't hungry either, but she was forcing herself to eat because if she didn't, then he wouldn't either. "I am so angry."

"Don't be," said Lim gently. "It's not worth it."

"But you could have died," she insisted, tears forming in her eyes.

He put his hand on hers. "But I didn't," he told her. "And everything's fine now." He lay down, closed his eyes and held his mother's hand.

"Are you okay?" she asked him after a while, seemingly out of the blue.

"Yeah," he opened his eyes. "Why?"

"You're holding your side," she said. "Does it hurt?"

"No." He looked down at himself. He'd crossed his arm over his body the way he usually did. If he hadn't been holding his mother's hand, he would have probably crossed his other arm over it too. "Really," he said, lifting his hand up. "I was just resting my hand. Sheesh." He rolled his eyes, putting his arm down on his other side, suddenly feeling strangely self-conscious, like his mother was scrutinising every little thing he did. "Really, Mother, there's nothing wrong," he told her. "See for yourself." He let go of her hand and lifted his shirt, so that she could see for herself that there really was nothing wrong with him. She lifted her hand and ran it down his ribs tentatively, past the small scar from when his lungs had collapsed, then down his waist to his hip bone. He looked at her with raised eyebrows. She returned his gaze, then dropped her eyes, adjusting his shirt back down.

"Satisfied?" asked Lim, half-laughing, half-challenging. He really couldn't be mad at his mother, no matter how much her unwanted attention may have irritated him.

"I do worry about how thin you are," she said softly.

Lim rolled his eyes and sighed a long-suffering sigh.

"Well, what do you want me to do about it?" he asked. "It's not like I do it on purpose." He briefly thought of Malkim, and of Eliza, who he knew, *had* been trying to make herself as thin as possible on purpose. He hoped that she was okay. He'd not heard from her since leaving the hospital, as he'd only given her his address in Palinas, and that of the East Borla Inn. He then remembered that he'd still not finished the letter he'd started writing to her the previous night.

"I'm sorry, darling," said his mother softly. "I know you do your best. And I know that you manage very well most of the time. But I'm your mother and it's my job to worry about you." She leaned over and put her arms around him, then kissed his head. "I love you so much," she said softly.

"I know," he told her. "I love you too. But please don't worry about me. I'm fine. Really. Worry about Vaarem for a change. Who knows what trouble he's getting into?"

"What?" she asked. "What's he done?"

"I don't know." Shrugged Lim. "Doesn't that worry you?" He laughed.

She smiled, then kissed his head again. "I really do love you so much, Limmy," she said. "I really, really dislike it when these things happen to you."

"Well, it's not exactly much fun for me either," he said. "But so far, I am managing. Although, I am really tired. I might go to sleep now, if it's okay? Can you find my nightshirt, please?" he asked, lying back down and closing his eyes.

A few minutes later, she came over and gave him his black nightgown. "Do you need any help getting changed?" she asked.

"No thanks." He shook his head. After her earlier comment, he was not about to undress in front of her, so he sat up carefully, then stood up and went over to the bathroom, where he washed himself with cold water (he was too exhausted to heat it with magic and too impatient to use mundane methods), then got changed into his nightgown and came back into the room.

Zareanna brushed his hair, remarking on how lovely it was, then she tucked him into bed as if he were still a little boy, and kissed him on the forehead.

"Can you please pass me my medicine bag," he asked after a moment.

"Of course." She passed it to him. He took out the bottle with the sleeping potion, then took a sip and put the bottle back in the bag, before putting the bag under the bed, where he could reach it.

"I am never letting this out of my sight again," he said, lying back down and letting his mother tuck him in once more.

"Don't worry, darling," she assured him. "No one is ever going to take your medicines away from you again." She kissed his forehead once more, then sat back down on the chair and began to sing softly, the way she'd done when he'd been little.

The sound of her voice, coupled with the medication, began to work on him almost straight away and soon he drifted off into a deep, relaxing sleep. He dreamed of Eliza, and of Vada, and magic.

Vaarem was feeling terrible. It was him who had insisted that Pelleata ride with them after all.

His father's face was grim as they sat at the table, waiting for their dinner.

"I can't believe that girl," said Garrett angrily. "How dare she move our things without telling us? Lim could have died." Today was the first time in his life that Vaarem had heard his father voice any real concern for his brother, and it brought home to him just how serious the situation was.

"I'm sorry for asking them to ride with us," said Vaarem. Then he felt bad for saying "them", because Ninetta was just as upset and distraught as he was. He really liked her, only now he couldn't think of her without seeing her awful cousin standing callously by as Lim struggled to breathe.

"It's not your fault," said his father. "I'm the one who insisted that you two meet some elven ladies." He shook his head and sighed. "I'm sorry. I never imagined anyone would do something like that. I hope that Lim is okay. If anything happens to him, I am going to kill that girl."

"How's Lim?" asked Vaarem, as he and his father walked into their family's suite. When they'd been walking down the corridor, Vaarem had heard his mother singing, but she stopped when he opened the door.

She was sitting on a chair by the bed. "He's asleep," she said quietly.

"That's good?" said Vaarem, but it came out as a question.

"Yes." Nodded his mother.

"Did he eat anything?" asked Garrett.

"Yes," said Zareanna. "He had some filled bread and some fruit."

"Good," said Garrett, sitting down on the other bed and starting to take off his boots. "That boy really needs to eat. I know he's not Malkim, and I am going to make sure he doesn't end up the same way."

"I know," said Zareanna quietly.

"Good." Nodded Garrett. "I can't believe that girl," he said, standing up again and starting to get undressed. "I can just about understand Limnos being careless enough to forget his potions. But someone else taking it away? I never even considered that someone could do that. I felt like slapping her."

Vaarem walked over and sat on the other side of Lim's bed. Lim was lying on his back with his hands crossed over his chest in that creepy way he did. Vaarem took one of his brother's hands and held it for a few moments, before laying it back down on Lim's side.

"He took some of his sleeping potion," said Zareanna. "So, we don't have to worry about waking him."

"Okay." Nodded Vaarem.

He went into the bathroom, where he had a quick wash and put on his nightshirt. When he came out, his mother was still sitting beside Lim, watching him sleep.

Vaarem got into the other side of the bed. "Can you please sing again?" he asked his mother.

"Of course, darling," she said, then began.

Vaarem looked over at his brother. Lim's face was pale, and he had dark rings under his eyes, but his breathing was regular, and his chest didn't rattle. He looked peaceful. Vaarem put his arm around him and let his mother's voice lull him. Just before he fell asleep, he heard his father's voice join in the song.

Lim woke up to the sound of movement around him. It was still early, but his family were already up, getting dressed and ready for the day ahead.

He sat up slowly, feeling strangely disorientated. This, he knew, was due to the sleeping potion still running through his system, so he moved slowly and deliberately, careful not to knock anything over, nor to fall over himself.

"Good morning, Limmy," said his mother, when she saw that he was up. "How did you sleep?"

"Good," he said, putting his hand to his head, and heading for the bathroom.

When he was finished, he washed his face, ran his fingers through his hair, then put on his clothes, which he'd left on the floor the previous evening.

When he was dressed, he stepped back out into

the room, holding on to the door-frame, as he was still unsteady on his feet. He walked back over to the bed and got his medicine bag out, then took his morning dose quickly before his fuzzy brain made him forget. He then got the rest of that day's potions together and put them in the pockets of his vest. The bottles made the material bulge out, the vest having been designed to carry nothing bigger than a handkerchief or a small purse, but Lim wasn't prepared to risk being separated from his medicines again. When he got home, he would have to somehow get himself a small carry-bag or something.

My personal, portable apothecary, he thought with an inward laugh, then stood up and followed his family out of the room.

Ninetta and her family were already sitting at one of the tables. Lim and his family looked in their direction awkwardly.

"What should we do?" asked Zareanna as they looked around for somewhere to sit. The table next to the other elf family was empty.

"We can't avoid them forever," said Lim with a sigh. He had a feeling that his family were waiting for him to decide what to do, so he started to walk towards the other elves' table. Ninetta and her mother, whose name Lim had learned was Lyanna, looked up at them and smiled. Lim smiled back, then took a seat at the empty table.

Zareanna greeted Lyanna warmly and Vaarem

greeted Ninetta. Pelleata kept her eyes firmly on the table and didn't say anything.

A few moments later, the food arrived, so everyone focused on their plates. That day's breakfast was eggs and bacon with bread and fruit on the side. Lim ate one of his eggs, as well as the bread and the fruit, but his stomach revolted at the thought of the bacon, so he gave his share to Vaarem when no one was looking.

"I should give you something off my plate to compensate," said Vaarem out of the corner of his mouth. "Otherwise, it's like you're giving half your meal away."

"It's hardly half," said Lim. "Although if you insist, I will have your strawberries. Oh, wait, you already ate them." He laughed. Vaarem's food was all mixed up on his plate, and Lim couldn't imagine eating any of it.

"Well, you could have asked earlier," said Vaarem. "Like when you first offered me your bacon."

"You could have offered earlier," replied Lim, "and not as an afterthought." He laughed again. "Before you made everything touch." He stifled a shudder.

Their back and forth was interrupted by someone coming to stand behind them.

They both looked up to see Pelleata. She had her hands in front of her and her fingers were fidgeting nervously. She was dressed in a sheer pale-yellow gown, with a sunflower clip holding up her pale blonde hair. As always, she looked very pretty.

"Hello," said Lim carefully.

Vaarem put his hand on Lim's elbow, in a show of support.

"Hello," said Pelleata, looking down at her hands awkwardly. "I just wanted to say that I am very sorry about moving your bag and coat yesterday. I was only trying to make the carriage more comfortable for us all, but it was your bag, so I shouldn't have moved it without telling you. I apologise for any inconvenience that my actions may have caused you." She looked up at Lim, then at Vaarem, then back to Lim, her expression expectant. It was clear that one of her family members had made her say what she'd said and that she really didn't want to be there.

"I forgive you," said Lim, putting his hand on Vaarem's, to stop his twin saying anything.

"If it's okay with you, Ninetta and I would like to ride with you in your carriage today," she continued, her eyes still downcast, her hand now fidgeting with the laces of her bodice.

"Yeah," said Lim. "Fine."

"Thank you," she said flatly, then walked back to her own table.

Chapter 24

Companions

"You don't have to ride with her if you don't want to, darling," said Zareanna, as the family were back in their room, getting all of their things.

"It's fine, Mother," said Lim. "If she doesn't ride with us, then her aunts don't want Ninetta to ride either, and Ninetta is nice and I know that Vaarem likes her. And I have my potions in my vest today." He showed her the bulges in his pockets.

"I know," she said with a gentle smile. "And I know that she didn't try to hurt you on purpose. It's her dismissive attitude that I don't like. She does not seem to care about how serious the consequences of her actions could have been."

"I know," said Lim, walking over and giving his mother a reassuring hug. "It pisses me off too. But it's all fine. Var does so much for me, I am happy to do this one thing for him."

As soon as they had set out, Pelleata started to complain. Lim was not feeling up to talking, so he sat in the corner of the carriage, with his head against the wall, his arms crossed, and his eyes closed. Vaarem and Ninetta were talking quietly together, while Zareanna, after Lim had assured her that it was okay, was sitting out the front with Garrett, leaving the young people alone.

"Talk to me," complained Pelleata.

"What do you want to talk about?" asked Lim, opening his eyes.

"What do you like to do?" she asked him.

"Magic," he replied after a thoughtful pause.

"Pfft," she scoffed. "You're too weak to do magic."

"Not the kind I want to do," he said. "I am going to study the Faith, and use magic the way that the priests do."

She rolled her eyes. "As if any temple would accept you."

"Why do you think that?" he asked, suddenly anxious. He believed that she was only trying to antagonise him, but what if she was onto something?

"Because," she spoke to him like he was a moron, "everyone knows that you need concentration to do magic. How can you concentrate on anything when you can't even breathe? And everyone knows that potions interfere with your energy, which you need to flow freely to do magic."

"No," said Lim, shaking his head, "that's not right." *Was it?* He'd used potions all his life and it was never a problem. But what if the sheer number of medications he was using now *did* cause issues?

"Anyway," she said, with a dismissive shake of her head. "Magic is boring. I like to dance and sing. I love music. Although that singer the other night was so fat," she remarked. "Ugh. It really ruined the performance."

"Seriously?" asked Lim, glad to change the topic. "I thought she was wonderful."

"You would."

"What's that supposed to mean?"

She shrugged. "Well, it figures. You're so skinny, so you like fat chicks to balance things out." She laughed spitefully.

"Do you have to insult everyone and everything all the time?" demanded Lim, his patience wearing away quickly.

She drew back, as if surprised by his outburst. "Well, you're not perfect either," she told him.

"I never claimed to be."

"But you think you're better than me," she insisted. "Everyone is so mad at me about what happened yesterday, but no one has addressed the fact that you were very rude to me too."

"When?" He frowned. He'd been careful to *not* say anything rude. "What did I do?"

"You told me that I make you sick. That was very hurtful."

"I'm sorry for saying that," said Lim with a sigh. That had just slipped out. "I didn't mean to offend you. I was feeling ill and lashing out. I'm sorry," he said again.

She smiled triumphantly at that, as if she'd won somehow.

Lim sighed. It was going to be a long drive.

They stopped for lunch soon after. Vaarem and Ninetta sat on the grass outside the carriage and made small talk. The more he talked to her, the more that he enjoyed her company.

"You're so sweet how you look after your brother," she told him, touching his hand briefly.

Vaarem smiled. "He's my best friend," he said. "And he looks out for me too."

"I'm sure he does," said Ninetta with a soft smile. "I'm an only child," she told him. "You're so lucky to have a brother who is a friend. Le is one turn younger than me, and after her father died, my mother took her in." She smiled sadly. It was clear that she and Pelleata did not have as amicable a relationship as Vaarem and Lim did. Vaarem felt lucky to have a brother who was also a best friend. Despite his family's problems, overall they were doing pretty well, it seemed.

Lim was happy to see Vaarem and Ninetta getting on so well. His brother had had several casual girlfriends in his life, but none of them had made him smile the way Ninetta did. He smiled at them both when they caught his eye, as they ate their midday meal. They both smiled back, making him feel good. However, his own patience for Pelleata was dwindling by the minute.

Because Vaarem was with Ninetta and his parents were talking to the older ladies, Lim was stuck eating with Pelleata. He had no appetite, as he was still feeling very weak from the previous day, so eating with her was proving extremely difficult.

His father glanced over at him and frowned. "Eat, Limnos," he told him sternly. "We won't leave until you're finished, so don't hold us up."

Lim sighed and took another bite of his filled bread. He'd already had his midday medication, so he knew that he should eat, in order to avoid feeling sick again afterwards.

"You're so boring," remarked Pelleata, as she chewed and swallowed her own filled bread.

"I'm sorry you feel that way," said Lim flatly. "What would you have me do?"

"Talk to me, duh." She rolled her eyes.

"I'm sorry." He sighed, "but I'm eating, in case you can't tell. I can't really talk and eat at the same time, what with it being bad manners to talk with your mouth full and all that."

"Hmpf," she said, crossing her arms and staring at him. She'd already finished her meal.

"You know," he told her between bites, "you can

talk to me if you want. A conversation goes both ways. And if you think that I'm so boring, why don't *you* say something interesting?"

"Hmpf," she said again. "I never had this problem with Randall."

"Who's Randall?"

"My boyfriend," she explained.

"Right," said Lim. He recalled Vaarem telling him that Pelleata's boyfriend had left her, but didn't mention it. What could he say?

He finished his bread and started to stand up, but he was still weak, so he stumbled and fell down again. "Ow," he said, rubbing his elbow that he'd landed on.

Pelleata looked at him like he was some abnormal oddity. He was getting utterly sick of her looking at him with that expression. His only consolation was that she looked at everyone in a similar way.

"You're such a freak," she said under her breath, but he heard her, nevertheless. He had a feeling that she'd meant for him to hear.

"Well, no one is forcing you to talk to me," he said wearily. "You're welcome to ride with your aunts."

She turned up her nose at that, as if he'd told her something hugely offensive.

He put his hand to his head, waiting for the dizziness to pass.

Vaarem was almost instantly at his side. "Are you okay?" he asked.

"Yeah," Lim looked up at him and smiled. "Sometimes when I stumble, it is simply because I'm being clumsy, and not a sign of anything sinister."

"Well, considering you're naturally not clumsy, perhaps it is," said Vaarem, but seeing that Lim was genuinely okay, he smiled and dropped it.

Lim tried to stand up again and managed it without problems this time.

When they were in the carriage again, he decided to try writing his letter once more. There was still one full day of riding before they reached Morliss and he really needed something to take his mind off Pelleata and her horrid attitude. However, Pelleata seemed determined to get under his skin.

"Who's Eliza?" she asked, reading over his shoulder.

He lifted the letter so that she couldn't see it. "She's my friend," he said, surprised at how defensive he felt.

"Is she your girlfriend?"

"No," said Lim with an irritable sigh. "She's just a friend."

"Of course," said Pelleata with a smirk. "You don't have a girlfriend. No one would go out with *you*."

"Aha." He nodded, coughing into his elbow.

Lim was exhausted by the time they reached the inn that they would be staying in that night. The owner remembered them from their previous stay and offered the family a couple of very nice rooms on the first floor.

Soon after Vaarem and Lim had unpacked their

things in their room, they heard voices in the corridor. Lim was on the bed, his hands beneath his head, his ankles crossed. He sat up, as did Vaarem beside him.

"I'm going to tell your mother." Lim heard Pelleata shout. "I'm going to tell her what a rude little bitch you are, and how your nasty boyfriend and his freak brother make me feel so unwelcome. Just you wait." There was the sound of a shuffle, then a knock on the door.

Vaarem got up and let Ninetta in.

Lim took a deep breath (or at least, as deep as he could) and looked up, plastering a pleasant smile on his face.

"Hello," he said.

"Hello," said Ninetta, trying to smile. He could see that her face was blotchy, as if she'd been crying. "How are you feeling?"

"Tired," he said. "But otherwise fine. How are you? What happened?"

"Are you okay?" Vaarem asked her, ushering her into a chair.

Ninetta looked up at him and nodded. She lifted her sleeve and rubbed her arm. There was a bruise beginning to form on her skin. Lim saw that she also had several other visible bruises.

"Ouch," said Lim empathetically, getting up off the bed and walking towards her. Vaarem was standing behind her. He started massaging her shoulder with his hand. "That looks painful," said Lim, bending over to examine her wrist. He put his hand on her bruise and concentrated on sending cooling energy into the area. He felt her relax as the soothing vibration entered her skin.

"It's okay," she said softly. "Thank you. She grabs me all the time. I'm used to it."

"She shouldn't do that," said Lim, then bit his lip and looked at her, realising that he'd just stated the blatantly obvious.

Ninetta shrugged. "She's always been like that," she said. "Ever since her father died, she's been living with me. Her mother died giving birth to her. I don't think that my mother ever got over that. They were best friends."

"I'm sorry to hear that," said Vaarem. "Losing family can be hard. Our mother's first husband died before Lim and I were born and our parents are still not over it," he said softly.

Lim nodded and smiled at Ninetta sadly.

"Oh no," said Ninetta. "I didn't know. It is hard. I think my mother still misses her brother, that's Le's father, as well as Le's mother, so she spoils Le and lets her do whatever she wants. It's really annoying. But it's only recently that Le's started actually hurting me. This was supposed to be a holiday, but she has been making my life miserable every single day. I can't wait to get home and be free of her." She looked up and smiled sadly.

Lim let her wrist go. She looked at it, then ran her hand along the area that was now no longer bruised.

"Thank you for that," she said. "You're really good at this. Have you ever thought of being a healer?"

Lim laughed grimly. "That would be the ultimate irony," he said. "The healer who is always sick himself."

"I thought that your brother said that you were better now?" she asked, with a slight frown.

Lim sighed and sat back down on the bed, putting his head in his hands. He was already feeling the toll of having used that tiny amount of magic on her. "Better is relative," he said, looking back up at her. "I'm better than I was, but that's only due to the new medication. I'm not cured, and as far as I know I probably never will be."

"Oh no, I'm sorry to hear that." She leaned forward and patted his knee.

He looked up at her and smiled. "I'm okay," he said. "But even just doing that now has made me tired. I couldn't do it for a living. But I do help if I can."

"Thank you," she said again, then looked up at Vaarem and touched his hand, which was still on her shoulder. "And thank *you* too," she told him. "These past few days have been the most fun that I've had in a long time. I mean, with the both of you," she corrected herself, looking from Vaarem to Lim.

"It's okay," said Lim. "I know you've mostly been with Vaarem. But thank you for not forgetting me," he added with a small chuckle.

"I could never forget you," she said with a smile.

"Now, should we go down to dinner? I'm kind of hungry."

"Yes," said Vaarem. "So am I. Great idea."

"Let's sit at a small table, so that Le can't join us," said Ninetta, with a mischievous glint in her eye. She seemed much happier and more animated without her cousin around.

Lim grinned at her. "Sure. Just as long as *I* don't need to sit next to her." He laughed. "Because I'm not exaggerating when I say that she makes me sick. I can hardly stomach the food here as it is."

"You don't like human food?" asked Ninetta curiously.

Lim shrugged. "Not particularly."

"Lim claims that his tastebuds are broken," said Vaarem. "That's why he doesn't eat much."

"Yeah, he's not wrong," grinned Lim.

"Oh, I don't think there's anything wrong with your tastebuds," she said. "You've just never had really good food. Which, I admit, a lot of this stuff being served at these inns is not great. But when we get to Morliss I will invite both of you for dinner at my house. I will cook. And I promise you, Lim, it will be the best thing you've ever eaten."

"Okay." Smiled Lim. "You're on." His mother's food was considered "good" by everyone he'd talked to, but perhaps Ninetta was an even better cook. He was game to find out.

"Your parents will be invited too, of course," said Ninetta. "We will hopefully arrive sometime in the middle of the afternoon. So, you and your family can find an inn or somewhere to stay for the night. I'd offer to put you all up, but I'm afraid we only have one small guest room, so you will not all fit. Anyway," she continued, "while you and your family find somewhere to stay for the night, I will go home and cook. And then you can all come over in the evening. How does that sound?"

"That sounds great." Smiled Vaarem, putting his arms around her and hugging her close.

"What about your cousin?" asked Lim, standing up. "Will she be there?"

Ninetta's face dropped. "Yes. She lives there, so she'll have to be. But I'll make sure to give her something bad on her plate." She laughed.

"Don't do that," said Lim gently. "Don't stoop to her level. Negativity only breeds more negativity."

As he lay in bed that night, Vaarem sleeping beside him, Lim considered the past day's events. Pelleata had left a (metaphorical) bad taste in his mouth. He was feeling horrible and was unable to shake off the bad energy that she'd thrown at him, and he was anxious about her saying that his potions would interfere with him working with magic.

I will *get into the Temple training,* he told himself. *I will help keep the balance in the world. My potions will* not *interfere. They never have. It's not a problem.*

He ended up rolling right over towards Vaarem and putting his head on his brother's shoulder, his arm around Vaarem's chest. Feeling his brother's steady breathing and rhythmic heartbeat finally allowed him to relax enough to get an hour's sleep.

He woke up feeling tired and sore. Vaarem was immediately concerned.

"I'm fine," Lim reassured him. "I just couldn't sleep."

Nevertheless, he put his arm around Vaarem's shoulders and allowed his brother to support him when they went downstairs for breakfast.

They sat down at an empty table and ordered their food in companionable silence. When they were halfway through their porridge, their parents arrived to join them.

"Are you taking your medicine, Lim?" asked Garrett, frowning.

"Yes," said Lim. "I just didn't sleep well."

"Don't you have medication for that?" asked his father.

"Yes," said Lim, "but I didn't think that I needed it."

"Well, you clearly thought wrong," remarked Garrett. "You look terrible. I really don't want you to get sick again before we return to Palinas."

"I won't." Lim promised meekly.

As usual, Pelleata insisted on riding in their carriage. Because her aunts seemingly had no idea how unpleasant she was to them, they were happy with the idea. Lyanna asked Zareanna to ride with her, but Zareanna politely declined, saying that she needed to be near Lim. He was still looking and feeling very weak and tired, so the other two ladies accepted her explanation graciously, especially since Ninetta had told them that when they arrived in Morliss the next day, she would cook dinner for them all, so they would still have a chance to catch up.

Lim was grateful to his mother for staying with them. It felt good to know that there was at least one mature adult to witness Pelleata's antics.

Perhaps Pelleata will actually behave herself and leave the rest of us alone, thought Lim.

As soon as the carriage began to move, Lim dozed off, as he was still tired. Vaarem and Ninetta talked amiably. Pelleata complained of being bored, but Zare-anna firmly, yet politely, told her to keep quiet and let Lim sleep. After that, Pelleata crossed her arms and looked out the window sulkily, but she didn't say anything else.

At lunchtime, when they stopped at another picturesque spot, Pelleata tried to antagonise Lim again.

"How does it feel to be a legal adult and have your mummy still look after you like you're a baby?" She laughed.

"She doesn't," said Lim wearily. He was aware that Pelleata's mother had died when she'd been a baby, so he was careful not to say anything hurtful. He was not going to stoop to her level. He'd meant it when he'd told Ninetta the previous day that negativity breeds more negativity. He was not going to add to it; at least not intentionally.

"You are so thick you don't even see it," Pelleata scoffed. "It's embarrassing. I am *so* glad that none of my friends can see me now. Imagine if they thought that we were actually friends, that you're my preferred company." She shudder dramatically.

"I'm sorry you feel that way," he said, and went back to eating his meal. He wasn't hungry, as usual, and Pelleata's presence was putting him off his food even more, but he did his best to ignore these feelings and kept eating until he thought that he'd consumed a reasonable amount to not only keep his father happy, but to keep himself from keeling over.

If I pass out, Pelleata will have a field day, he thought grimly. She will probably also quite literally kick me when I'm down.

Lim did his best to finish his filled bread, but the crust was too tough, so he threw it into the grass behind him.

He saw movement near where it landed.

Pelleata saw it too, and he saw her eyes widen in alarm. "What's that?" she asked, grabbing his arm, then looking down and dropping it quickly. She rubbed her hands as if to clean them.

Lim sat up slowly and carefully. He looked over and saw movement in the long grass again, leading towards a small bush.

Pelleata had stood up, and he felt her fling a

magical punch at the spot where the movement had stopped.

Lim heard a squeak, as if she'd hit something.

He looked up at her. She was smiling triumphantly.

Something moved in the grass again, and Pelleata took a tentative step towards it. She raised her hand, as if to throw another magic punch.

"Don't," said Lim, standing up carefully, his hand to his head.

She rolled her eyes and threw another magic punch at the spot in the grass.

There was another squeak, as if of pain, then the movement and the sound stopped.

Pelleata smiled again. "Can you check that it's dead, whatever it was? Are you man enough to at least do that for me?" she asked scornfully.

Lim walked over, then crouched down, and looked into the grass.

A pair of large black eyes blinked up at him. He didn't need to be an empath to sense that the creature was in pain.

"Hey," he said softly, extending his hand. "It's okay."

A furry leg, ending in a claw, touched his hand. Lim stroked the creature's soft, furry head with his other hand, and the animal chirped cheerfully.

"Come here," said Lim softly, kneeling down in the grass. "It's okay."

"Is it dead?" called Pelleata. "Can you kill it?"

"Shush," he replied irritably, then looked back down.

He extended his hand, and the animal stepped onto it.

It was about the size of his palm, with eight legs, each one the length and width of his finger. Two large, black eyes looked up at him with three smaller eyes beside each large one. A pair of tiny fangs extended from the animal's mouth, which was situated below its eyes. Its two front legs ended in a set of pincers, like those of a crab, while the six back legs, each ended in one sharp claw.

Lim stroked the animal's head and back. The creature was covered in soft black fur, with purple markings on its abdomen.

Pelleata had walked over to stand behind him.

"Eugh," she said. "What is it?"

The creature looked up at her, raised its front legs and hissed.

Pelleata drew back and screamed.

"It's okay," said Lim to the creature, still stroking it, "I won't let her hurt you."

Vaarem and Ninetta had run over to see, and the adults, who were further away, began to walk over too.

"Aww," said Ninetta crouching down beside Lim. "It's a gargantula. They live in the fields and forests of the Sirranna Region. They're normally very shy."

"Yes." Nodded Lim, stroking the gargantula again.

Lim had heard of gargantulas, and he knew that they were rare, and, as Ninetta had said, very shy. They resembled spiders in shape, because they had eight legs and eight eyes, but were actually egg-laying mammals. They were known to be intelligent, and the females raised their young for about a turn before the youngling left to live on its own. Unlike spiders, who were carnivorous, gargantulas were herbivores. They built webs to protect the grasses and weeds that they ate. Lim had never seen one before, as there had been none at the Sirrock City Zoo. He stroked the gargantula's soft fur now. When he touched one of its back legs, the animal flinched. "Sorry," said Lim. When he looked at the leg more closely, he saw that the claw was torn, likely from Pelleata's attack.

"Aww," he said softly. Then he gently touched the injured claw and sent a little of his own energy to relieve the pain. He wondered whether he could use magic the way the priests did to heal, to get the animal's own energy to speed up its mending, but he didn't know how to do it, so just used his own. It was only a tiny bit, and he hardly felt it.

"There you go," he said, and went to put the creature down.

But the gargantula looked up at him and chirruped, not wanting to leave.

"I think she likes you," said Ninetta.

"She?" asked Lim. "How do you know?"

"The markings on her back," she said, reaching out to stroke the purple lines with her finger. "Females have purple or red markings. Males are green."

"Oh," said Lim, as the gargantula began to climb up his arm to settle on his shoulder. It chirped and snuggled its soft head into his neck. He lifted his other hand and stroked it.

"Well, you wanted a companion animal," said Vaarem. "Looks like you have one."

Lim smiled, as the gargantula chirruped again and snuggled into his neck once more. It seemed that she understood, and was happy with the arrangement

"Well little one," he said, turning to look at the little critter on his shoulder, "do you want to stay with me?"

The gargantula snuggled into his neck again.

"Ewww," said Pelleata, as the adults came over to see what was happening.

"Lim found a pet," said Vaarem, pointing to the gargantula on Lim's shoulder.

"Oh," said Zareanna, her expression uncertain.

"You can't take it into the carriage," said Pelleata.

"Yes, I can," said Lim. "It's my carriage."

Garrett looked at Lim and the critter and said, "It's a wild animal, Lim."

"I know," said Lim, "but she climbed on to me and wants to stay,"

Garrett nodded. "Well, if she wants to stay with you." He chuckled. "But if you want a pet, you have to look after it, understood?"

"Yes," said Lim. "Of course."

"Aww," said Sereanna, walking over to look at the gargantula. "I haven't seen one in so many turns. There was one who lived in our garden when I was a little girl. They are quite cute. And they eat weeds, so good in the garden. You're lucky, Lim, they don't normally like people, but like I said, beneficial in the garden if you can get one."

After Sereanna's words, Lim's parents agreed that he could keep the gargantula. They lived for about five turns, so it wouldn't be a hugely long-term commitment. Zareanna also told Lim that it would be good for him to take care of an animal, as it may help him remember to look after himself.

Pelleata whined that the gargantula was gross and that she didn't want it in the carriage, but as it was not her carriage, there was nothing that she could do. It was either ride with the animal or with her aunts, and for some reason, she wanted to stay with the young people.

"What are you going to call it?" asked Vaarem, as they got back into the carriage. The gargantula hissed at Pelleata when she got too close. It seemed to know that she'd tried to hurt it.

"I will call her Isha," said Lim, "after the sound she makes when she's annoyed. It's a reminder not to annoy her," he said, not looking at Pelleata.

They were glad to reach that night's inn. The going had been slow because of the recent rains, so they arrived after dinner time. Lim wanted nothing more than to just go to bed, so he was happy about this. Isha was sleeping on his shoulder.

Tomorrow, they would be in Morliss, where he'd decided he'd re-stock his potions.

"Why?" asked Vaarem. "I thought the hospital gave you several moons' worth of stuff."

"I seem to be going through it quicker than anticipated," said Lim with a shrug. The main thing that he was going through quickly was the "emergency" meds, the herbs that he used between his three main potions. He'd been given three jars and had gone through a whole one already. He had no doubt that Pelleata's bad energy was contributing to this, but he needed what he needed.

The family got two rooms again, with Lim and Vaarem sharing as usual. Lim had put Isha in his pocket, just in case there were rules about animals.

"I can't wait to leave Pelleata behind," said Lim, as they got ready for bed, Isha curling up on the bedside table on top of a cloth that Lim had laid out. He hadn't needed to breathe through it since leaving the hospital. He hoped that this was a sign that he was getting better, although it was more likely due to the weather being a little warmer. He tried not to dwell on it.

"Yes," agreed Vaarem, taking out some bread and cheese, and making a quick meal for himself and Lim. "Although I feel bad for Ninetta. She's so sweet. It's so unfair how Pelleata treats her, and her family seem oblivious."

"Sometimes people only see what they want to see when it comes to family," said Lim thoughtfully.

"What's that supposed to mean?" asked Vaarem suspiciously.

"Nothing sinister." Lim shook his head. "I mean, for example, until this trip, you never defended me against Father. Every time I complained that he was treating me like shit, you gave some excuse about tough love or whatever else. Mother is the same."

"True." Vaarem nodded thoughtfully. "And sometimes people are blind to how their own actions affect others. Mother and Father have been so cut up about Malkim for so long but never told us, which, I don't know about you, but made me feel like shit about myself, like I wasn't good enough."

"Oh, Var," said Lim, "You are most definitely good enough." How could Vaarem ever think that he was anything less than wonderful?

"Thanks," said Vaarem, "I also recently realised that I guilt you into doing things that you shouldn't be doing. Like that night of Jessa and Marla's visit, I felt so bad." He trailed off.

"You don't force me to do anything that I don't want to do," said Lim firmly, "and I know that you care and that you'd never deliberately do something to hurt me. But I do know what you mean. I need to speak up if I feel that I'm not up to something, rather than pushing myself beyond my limits to avoid disappointing others. So, yeah, Pelleata's aunts want to like her. Her parents, whom they no doubt loved, are dead, and she is the only one left. They want to see something of them in her. They don't want to believe that she's a nasty little brat. So, they make excuses. Nin herself does."

"I know." Nodded Vaarem. "It can be so complicated sometimes. Like, people are so desperate to not forget their departed loved ones that they can forget about those who are right in front of them."

"Yes," agreed Lim. "Sometimes we get so wrapped up in ourselves that we forget how we affect others."

Vaarem nodded in response, then gave Lim some bread and cheese and watched until his brother began to eat it.

Lim sighed. It seemed that Vaarem was going to be on his case about eating more too. His initial thought was, Bloody dragon balls, will they never leave me alone? But then he realised that this was precisely what they'd been discussing. Vaarem was only doing what he believed was best for his twin, and it was Lim's own behaviour that was making Vaarem act the way he was.

Lim ate without complaint, resolving to take better care of himself all around. There was more to it than just taking his potions.

Chapter 25

Return to Morliss

The next morning, Pelleata started on Lim almost straight away. Zareanna was sitting out the front with Garrett, so the four young people were alone inside the carriage.

"You look so dumb with all those things sticking out of your pockets, and that wild animal on your shoulder." Pelleata laughed. "You look like a homeless bum."

Vaarem heard her and frowned, then said, "He is not a homeless bum. Fuck, why are you intent on trying to upset him? You're the biggest bitch that I've ever met."

"Do you kiss your mother with that mouth?" asked Pelleata haughtily, then turned to Ninetta and said, "I don't know what you see in him, Nin. He's a complete loser, just like his bum brother."

At that, Ninetta put her head in her hands and began to cry. "Why do you always do this?" she sobbed. "Why is it that whenever I like a boy, you always either steal him or drive him away?"

"She won't steal me," said Vaarem, looking at Pelleata with hard eyes, "because I'm not a thing to be stolen. And she won't drive me away either," he said more gently, putting his arm around Ninetta's shoulders and giving her a warm smile.

"Of course not," said Pelleata mockingly. "He's going to get his mummy to come and defend him. Like she had to do yesterday, to make sure that poor little Limmy got his beauty sleep." She laughed nastily. "And as for steal you, I'd rather kiss a goblin."

Vaarem was about to say something else, but Lim reached over and touched his knee, then shook his head, indicating for Vaarem to be quiet.

Pelleata laughed nastily again. "What? No comeback, Limmy? Because you know that it doesn't matter how much beauty sleep you get, you're still a pale, skinny freak with dark rings under his eyes, that nobody likes or wants to be around."

Isha lifted her front legs and hissed, making Pelleata draw back in alarm.

Lim simply looked at her and said, "You're a sad, petty girl, aren't you, Pelleata?"

She frowned at him. She was clearly annoyed that she wasn't getting a rise out of him, and she didn't know what to do.

"Why are you being so mean?" demanded Ninetta. "What have Vaarem and Lim done to you?"

Pelleata smiled nastily, then laughed. "Well, they're both rude and obnoxious," she said. "They've been rude to me right from the start, which you so conveniently failed to notice."

"When?" demanded Ninetta.

Pelleata rolled her eyes. "All the time. How about just now, when Limmy here called me a sad, petty girl, eh?"

"Well, he only said that because you've been repeatedly calling him a freak when he's not a freak. He's perfectly nice and you're being horrible. Not to mention that you nearly killed him that first day."

"Oh, I did not." Pelleata rolled her eyes. "He's just dramatic. Even his own father says so."

Lim closed his eyes and crossed his arms in front of his chest, as Isha snuggled into his neck.

Oh, my Fates, she actually hates me, he thought and was surprised at how anxious this made him feel. No one had ever outright hated him before. Sure, his father was often annoyed with him, and many people were wary of him, but no one had ever purposefully directed this much negative energy at him.

He felt his throat begin to tighten up and he coughed. Isha dug her claws into his shoulder to stay on. Fortunately, his coat was thick enough for it not to hurt.

Pelleata smirked. "Are you okay, Limmy?" she asked mockingly.

Lim couldn't talk. He felt like he was choking.

Isha chittered loudly and looked at Vaarem.

Fortunately, Vaarem knew Lim well enough to know when he needed help, even without Isha's alert, so he immediately got the bottle of water and poured some into a glass. He used his magic to heat it up, then gave it to Lim, who got his herbs and poured them in.

The carriage went over a bump and Pelleata took the moment to knock the glass out of Lim's hand. The hot potion spilled all over his hand and leg.

"Shit," he managed to gasp. "Ow." He immediately applied magic cold to the affected areas so he didn't end up burned, but the effort made him so weak and dizzy that he could barely sit upright. And he still couldn't breathe.

Isha chittered loudly in alarm, then hissed at Pelleata and bared her fangs when Pelleata took a swipe at her.

"You stupid little bitch!" cried Vaarem, lunging at Pelleata and grabbing her arms. "What did you do? Lim?" he turned to his brother. "Are you okay?"

Lim couldn't speak. He kept coughing and looked up at Vaarem with bleary, fear-filled eyes, as his vision threatened to black out. He got the jar of herbs out of his pocket and with his last strength handed it to Vaarem, hoping that his brother would know what to do.

The next thing he knew was that Vaarem was supporting his head and putting a glass to his mouth, Isha snuggling her head into his neck. Lim drank the potion obediently, then when it was empty, he collapsed into his brother's arms.

Vaarem held his twin's frail body to him, all the while glaring at Pelleata. He'd never hit a woman in his life; he'd never hit anyone. But it was taking the utmost effort not to punch her in her smirking face.

Ninetta sat on his other side, holding one of Lim's limp hands, as if she wanted everyone to know whose side she was on. Isha sat on Lim's shoulder and would occasionally look at Pelleata and hiss.

Vaarem was so angry that he couldn't think. No one had ever deliberately tried to hurt him or his brother before, and he couldn't understand Pelleata's motivation.

Pelleata looked at him again and smirked. "What are you going to do, Vary? You look like you're about to explode. Are you going to hit me?" she asked, then she fluttered her eyelashes mockingly.

"You'd like that, wouldn't you?" asked Vaarem through gritted teeth. He felt Lim shift and sigh beside him, so he relaxed a little. It seemed that Lim was going to be okay. He always was. His brother was a fighter, and much stronger than he looked, but it still scared Vaarem when these things happened.

"Hmph," said Pelleata, crossing her arms and looking at her cousin. "Looks like your *boyfriend* here only cares about himself and his dumb brother. He's no good for you."

"What?" asked Vaarem. "Why am I supposedly not good?"

She scoffed at that. "Where do I start? You're rude and vain, and you only seem to care about yourself and your brother. Do you guys fuck each other at night or something?" she smirked.

Vaarem's breath caught in his throat, and he was literally speechless. No one had ever insulted him like this before.

"Why would you say something like that?" asked Ninetta softly.

Pelleata shrugged. "I've heard it's the kind of thing twins do." She laughed nastily. "Is it?"

Vaarem glared at her. "No," he said. He'd seriously had it with her, and he didn't know how much more he could take. He felt Lim shiver in his arms, and he looked down to see a thin layer of ice forming on his brother's sleeve and trousers, where Pelleata had spilled the potion.

"Is he okay?" asked Ninetta, having felt Lim's movement too, "He's so cold." She indicated Lim's hand that she was still holding.

"Yeah." Vaarem nodded. "He'll be fine." He used his magic to warm Lim's shivering body and was gratified when his twin started to relax.

"I'm so sorry," said Ninetta, stroking Lim's hand. "Why do you deliberately hurt him?" she asked Pelleata accusingly.

Pelleata shrugged her slim shoulders. "Why not?" she said dismissively. "I didn't realise that you wanted to fuck *him* too." She laughed nastily, then stuck her tongue out at Ninetta.

Vaarem hugged Lim closer to himself, then looked at Pelleata and said through gritted teeth, "When we stop for lunch, you are going to leave this carriage, and you are going to stay away from my brother, or I will make you sorry."

"Ooh, so now you're threatening me." smirked Pelleata. "Very nice. Just you wait until I tell my aunties how awful you and your brother and *you*," she glared at Ninetta, "have been to me. They will ground you again, and they will be oh so nice to me and give me things," she smirked.

Vaarem closed his eyes and slowly counted to ten in his head. He was afraid that if he wasn't careful, he would do something exceedingly stupid. He had a suspicion that if he punched Pelleata in the face, like he really, really wanted to, no one would be sympathetic, even if he told them everything that had gone down. So, he sat as still as he could, with one arm around Lim, and the other around Ninetta, and looked down at the floor.

Pelleata continued to taunt him, but he did his best to block her out.

"You want to hit me, but you don't have the balls." She laughed. "You'll have to get your mummy to do it. I bet she's so embarrassed to be related to you. No wonder your real father killed himself. Just like Nin's."

"What?" frowned Vaarem. "My father is alive. He's

driving the carriage," he said in a tone that implied she was an idiot.

"No." She laughed. "I heard your mummy telling my aunties."

Vaarem gritted his teeth and looked down at the floor. His mother must have been talking about Malkim. It made sense, given that Ninetta's father was dead too. Their mothers had likely bonded over a shared experience of grief. It was beyond insensitive of Pelleata to say anything, given that she'd meant to upset Ninetta too. He held Ninetta, as she sobbed next to him, doing his best to comfort her. At one point he whispered, "It's okay," reassuringly to her, only for Pelleata to tell him off for being rude.

"You should not whisper when there are other people around," she said accusingly.

He ignored her and kept looking at the floor.

At one point, Lim opened his eyes and said, "Ow, you're holding me too tight," before going back to sleep.

"Sorry," said Vaarem, loosening his hold. He was so angry that he hadn't even realised that he'd been doing it.

"Thanks." Smiled Ninetta, as he loosened his hold on her too.

"Sorry," said Vaarem again. "I didn't mean to crush you. You should have said something."

"It's okay," she said. "It didn't hurt. But it was getting a little uncomfortable." She rested her head on his shoulder.

He snuck a glance at Pelleata and saw her staring at the three of them, her eyes seething.

What in the name of all the Fates is wrong with her? he wondered.

Finally, they reached Morliss. It had been a hard ride, as they'd not stopped for lunch, only for a quick bathroom break. Pelleata and Ninetta got out of the carriage. Ninetta thanked Garrett and Zareanna politely for letting her ride. Pelleata smiled and did the same, which left Vaarem seething again. But he didn't say anything. It was finally over.

Lim stayed in the carriage, where Ninetta said goodbye to him and apologised for her cousin's actions. Then, she came out and gave Vaarem her address, making him promise that he would come to dinner with his family, which he agreed to do.

"Where's Lim?" asked Zareanna, when Ninetta and her family had driven away.

"He's in the carriage," said Vaarem. "She did it again."

"Pelleata?" asked Zareanna. "What did she do?"

"She was antagonising Lim again, and when he was having his potion, she knocked it out of his hand. It was bad. She then said some really awful things, trying to deliberately upset us, and Ninetta too." He didn't feel the need to specify what Pelleata had said, and simply added, "I really, really hate her. It was all that I could do not to slap her."

Zareanna shook her head angrily.

"What happened?" asked Garrett, coming around to see them.

"Pelleata hurt Lim again," said Vaarem, still annoyed.

"What? How?" demanded Garrett.

Vaarem explained again what had happened, and Garrett shook his head. "I don't know what that girl's problem is. I've never known an elf to behave like that. But she's gone now. Are you okay, Lim?" he asked, looking into the carriage.

Lim nodded but didn't open his eyes.

"Good," said Garrett, "Let's just go to the inn." He got back onto the driver's seat.

Zareanna, who had been riding with him earlier, got into the carriage with Vaarem. Lim was still sitting in the corner, his arms crossed, his head back, and his eyes closed, Isha on his shoulder. He appeared to be asleep, but he opened his eyes when his mother and brother came in. He was looking very pale and there were pronounced dark rings under his eyes, but when he saw Vaarem and Zareanna he smiled, which lit up his face and made him look less wretched.

"Is she gone?" he asked, his voice weak.

Vaarem hated Pelleata more than ever, hearing his brother's quiet voice. Lim had seemed so well that morning, but all it had taken was a couple of hours with that stupid bitch to make him sick again.

"Yes, darling," said Zareanna, sitting beside him and putting her arm around his shoulders, careful to not hurt Isha, who rubbed Zareanna's hand with her head, then snuggled into Lim's neck again. "She's not going to bother you anymore."

"Oh, thank the Fates," he said with a sigh, then rested his head on his mother's shoulder.

Zareanna drew him to her, careful not to squash Isha, and kissed the top of his head. "I forgot to tell you this morning that your hair looks really nice," she said.

"Thank you," he replied, closing his eyes again.

Vaarem sat across from them and slumped in relief.

They reached the Tree-Top Inn soon after.

"Are you up to walking up the stairs?" asked Vaarem, as he and Lim stood at the bottom of the staircase. They'd been assigned rooms on the second floor.

"Yes." Nodded Lim.

He managed it but collapsed onto the bed when he got to the room. Vaarem thought again of how much he hated Pelleata.

"Ugh," said Lim, turning over to lie on his back. Isha was sitting on the bedside table, chirruping, as if wanting to comfort him. "I feel awful."

"What's wrong?" asked Vaarem, coming to his side and sitting on the bed beside him. "Anything I can get you? Do you need your potion?"

"Yeah," said Lim. "Probably. I haven't had my mid-day dose yet. But I need to have that with food, else my stomach's going to hurt. Fuck, I'm such a mess," he put his hands over his eyes.

Vaarem stood up and returned a moment later with an apple. "Here," he said, giving it to Lim. "Eat this. I'll get us something more substantial later."

"Thanks." Lim sat up and bit into the apple. When he'd eaten it, giving a bit to Isha, he threw the core across the room and into the rubbish bin, then took his potion out of his pocket and drank some.

"Well, your aim is as good as ever," said Vaarem, sounding and looking impressed that Lim had got the core into the bin from such a distance.

Lim smiled cynically. "Thanks. Good to know that I'm not *completely* deficient."

"You're not deficient," Vaarem reassured him. "But you do look really tired. Why don't you get some sleep while I go and get us more food? Ninetta still wants us to come over for dinner. Will you come?"

"Yeah," said Lim, lying down on his side and putting his hands under his head. "I'll come. I feel bad for her. It must be hard living with Pelleata's attitude around her all the time." He closed his eyes. "Although I kind of feel bad for Pelleata too. She's clearly hurting."

Vaarem rolled his eyes. "So? That's no excuse for being such a bitch. Father was an arsehole to you for so long because he was hurting, but it still sucked. And he still does it sometimes, even after acknowledging everything and apologising. Everyone hurts sometimes. *You* hurt more than anyone I know but you've never taken it out on anyone else."

Lim smiled thinly, "Different type of hurt, Var," he said, "When you feel secure in yourself and your loved ones, physical pain is easier to bear. Most of the time," he conceded. "But I think that emotional pain is worse. I count myself lucky to have never experienced it before. Like, I used to say that Father hates me but deep down I know he doesn't. Pelleata actually hates me. It's not nice."

"No," agreed Vaarem.

"But she needs to learn to deal with whatever is hurting her," said Lim thoughtfully, "Because no one can help her if she doesn't help herself."

"Yes." Nodded Vaarem.

"What are you thinking?" asked Lim after a moment.

Vaarem was looking at him thoughtfully. "If you ever need to talk about anything, no matter what it is, you can talk to me, and I will listen," he said.

"Thanks," said Lim, "But why? I mean, why mention it now?"

"I heard Mother and Father talking, and Mother mentioned that you and me remind her of Father and Malkim. Father said that he hopes that we don't come to resent each other the way they did. I don't ever want you to-"

"Yes." Lim held up his hand. "Don't say it. I promise that I will never do what Malkim did. I see what it did to Mother and Father, and Vada too. Perhaps." He looked up at Vaarem, "the Fates deliberately give us lessons so that we can learn, and not repeat the mistakes of the past."

"How did we get onto this topic? We were talking about Pelleata," chuckled Vaarem.

"Maybe the Fates don't want us dwelling on her," said Lim, "Seriously, the more I read this book." He lifted Eliza's book for Vaarem to see, "the more I see how everything and everyone is interconnected. It's really interesting, but also reassuring, you know? Like, no matter how many mistakes you make in your life, you'll always find your right path, and all mistakes are just lessons."

"I hope Pelleata learns her lessons without hurting anyone else," said Vaarem grimly.

Lim smiled. "Me too."

They sat on the bed in silence for a while, each lost in his own thoughts. Lim lay down and closed his eyes. He thought of Vada and of her saying that she wanted to recreate the spell her father had been working on, a spell that would "rid the world of pain and negative influences".

But how can that be? he wondered. *How would we know the positive without the negative to contrast it?*

Vada is not stupid, he consoled himself. *She is a fast learner and would not repeat her father's mistakes. Would she?*

Lim slept for nearly an hour, then Vaarem came back with some filled bread for the both of them, and some salad leaves for Isha.

"What do you want to do now?" he asked Lim when they'd finished eating.

Lim was feeling a lot better, although he was still feeling weaker than he had when leaving the hospital. Isha was again on his shoulder, and her slight weight and warmth gave him comfort.

"I think I'll go and see Magnon, the healer here. To get my prescriptions refilled, and just to say hi. He wrote to me at the hospital, you know?"

"No, I didn't know," said Vaarem. "But that was nice of him. He only met you once."

"Yeah," agreed Lim. "Which is why I want to see him. Do you want to come with me?"

Vaarem considered this for a few moments, then said, "Sure. If only because I really don't think that Mother would want you wandering the city by yourself."

Lim sighed. "Great," he said. "Not only does Pelleata want to kill me, but now my own mother won't let me live my life. Fucking dragon dung. What a day."

"Yeah," agreed Vaarem. "It sucks. But what can you do?"

"Oh, there's plenty that I can do," Lim assured him. "But I'm sure that most of it would not be very constructive. Come on." He stood up. "Let's go before Mother and Father decide that neither of us can go out."

They walked across the city together, glad to be among elves again. The familiar scent of leaves and earth, and the predominantly green surroundings made Lim feel at home. Isha sat on his shoulder and occasionally chirruped, as if wanting to tell them something. Lim lifted his hand and stroked her head and back.

He walked up the steps to the apothecary, remembering how he'd struggled the last time. He still struggled, but it was easier. He pushed the door open and stepped inside, followed by Vaarem.

Magnon's wife, whose name was Malina, looked up. She smiled as she recognised him.

"Lim, is it?" she asked, getting up off her stool to greet him.

"Yes," he said. "Hello. This is my brother Vaarem." He indicated Vaarem, who extended his hand and said hello.

"I'm glad you came back," said Malina. "Magnon and I have been wondering how you were getting on. You look well."

"Thank you," said Lim, not sure whether she was just being polite. He still didn't feel particularly well, even by his own standards, but he probably was better than he'd been the last time he'd been here.

"Magnon?" called Malina, opening a door that led to the healing practice behind the shop. "That young man Lim is here. Come and say hello."

A few moments later, Magnon came through the door and greeted Lim warmly, then greeted Vaarem when Lim introduced them to each other.

"This is Isha," said Lim, pointing to the critter on his shoulder. "I found her a few days ago in a field."

Magnon smiled at that, then said, "So, you said in your letter that the treatment didn't work?" He looked at Lim over the top of his glasses.

"No." Lim shook his head. "But I do have some new ways to manage, so I guess it wasn't a total loss. Here," he gave Malina the list of his prescriptions, as well as the empty bottles.

"Whoa," said Malina, her eyes widening. "Now, that is quite a list," she scanned it, then said. "I believe that I have everything in store, but it will take me a while to get it all together. You're welcome to wait. Or, you can see Magnon?" she looked at her husband questioningly.

"Sure," said Lim. "I could do with a check-up. I've, I mean, we've." He indicated himself and Vaarem, and Isha on his shoulder, "been travelling with the single most unpleasant young lady that we have ever met. I fear she may have caused me some damage."

Magnon raised his eyebrow. "Indeed?" he asked. "Well, come through. Your brother can stay here."

"I don't mind if he comes in," said Lim.

"Suit yourself," said Magnon, letting both Vaarem and Lim through into his practice.

Lim was indeed interested to see how he was doing. His body often betrayed him, in the sense that he thought that he was well, only to find that some new complication had developed. Right now, he wasn't sure how he felt. He didn't know whether his current lethargy was due to Pelleata's influence and would therefore pass, or whether it was a sign of something more sinister.

Inside the healer's practice, Vaarem took Isha, and sat on a chair in the corner, as he usually did during these times, while Lim lay down on the bed and let the healer examine him.

When it was over, he did his shirt back up and went to sit next to his brother, Isha climbing back onto his shoulder.

"You're an anomaly, Lim," said Magnon mildly. "You really puzzle me."

"I have that effect on many people," said Lim with a cynical smile. "So, what's the verdict?"

Magnon looked at the notes that he'd taken. "You seem better than the last time that you were here," he began, sounding pleased. It was like he genuinely cared. Lim wondered how long that would last. Most of his healers had started out with genuine concern for him, only to eventually give up in frustration when they couldn't do anything. But Magnon was not there yet, and perhaps, because he wasn't Lim's regular healer, would never get to that stage. "You've put on a bit of weight and your lung capacity is greater than the last time you were here."

"That's good." Smiled Lim. It was nice to hear that his condition had improved; for once.

"Yes," answered Magnon. "However, you are still quite significantly underweight, and your lung capacity is still what we refer to as minimal. But I am genuinely pleased to see that you have improved. How long have you been on the new medication routine?"

"About a week," said Lim, trying to remember. It seemed like a lot longer.

"I would be interested to see how you are in a moon or two."

"I can write and tell you," said Lim. "Or, if you really want, I can get my healer in Palinas to write to you too."

"Yes, I would like that," said Magnon with a smile.

They chatted for a few more minutes, with Vaarem offering the occasional comment, then they went back out into the shop.

Malina had prepared Lim's medicines and had put the bottles in a secure bag.

"Here you go, Lim," she said. "Everything is in there. And here," she opened the bag and took out a smaller bag no bigger than a purse, with a shoulder-strap. She opened it up and showed him that it had several compartments, each containing a small bottle. "You can use this to carry your daily medicines with you. I see how those little bottles are falling out of your pockets. This will be more secure."

"Thank you," said Lim, feeling touched.

He put the small bag over the shoulder that Isha wasn't on, and across his body. It felt comfortable, and he was pleased that the bag was black. He wondered whether Malina had guessed at his colour preference, or whether that was the only colour she had.

"How much do I owe you?" he asked, getting out his money.

"Just for the medicines," she said, as she had the last time. "The bags and the consultation are on us. As it is, I feel bad for taking so much money from someone so young, but I have to make a living, and these ingredients don't come cheap."

"It's fine." Lim smiled, again feeling touched that she seemed to genuinely care so much. He handed her several gold coins. He hadn't spent much money on this trip, so he had enough for potions. It was something that he always set a portion of his allowance and earnings aside for. "Thank you so much for all this," he said, looking inside the bags again, counting ninety small bottles, four larger ones, and six jars. Together with his potions from the hospital, he now had enough medicine to last him for six moons, give or take. He smiled in gratitude again.

"Do you want me to carry that?" asked Vaarem, looking at the big bag that Lim was carrying.

"No thanks." Lim shook his head. "I can carry my own stuff."

"Okay," said Vaarem. "Tell me if you change your mind."

"Will do," said Lim. He looked across at his brother's profile and smiled to himself. He really was lucky to have a brother like Vaarem, who looked out for him without being condescending and without using Lim's failings against him.

Chapter 26

The Dinner Party

It was getting dark by the time Lim and Vaarem got back to the inn. Lim gave Vaarem the bag of medicines at the bottom of the stairs. He could have carried it up, but why kill himself when Vaarem was willing to help?

They changed their clothes and tidied their hair, in readiness for going to Ninetta's.

"Take your potion now," said Vaarem before they left.

"Why?" asked Lim. It was still early, and while the evening medication didn't make him drowsy as such, he preferred to take it later in the day, ideally with dinner.

"Because I have a feeling that Pelleata is going to try and do something to you again," said Vaarem. "And with the amount you spent today, you don't want to go wasting it because some dumb bitch knocks it out of your hand."

"Good point," said Lim. "Do we have anything to eat? I don't want to take it on an empty stomach, remember?"

"Oh yeah," said Vaarem. "Hold on." He dug around in his bag, and finally emerged with a couple of stale-looking biscuits.

"Great, Vaarem," said Lim sarcastically. "Really appetising." He laughed. Nevertheless, he took the biscuits and bit into one. "I'm sure it's not supposed to be this chewy," he remarked. But he ate it anyway. He had his evening potion, then he bit into the second biscuit, but couldn't finish it. "Yuck," he said. "That better not give me food poisoning."

"Oh, don't be so dramatic." Laughed Vaarem.

"Fine," said Lim. "But if I puke, I'll make sure to do it on you."

"Whatever," said Vaarem. "You won't and you know it."

"Hopefully," said Lim. In reality, he knew that he would be okay, but it was sometimes fun to joke about problems that he knew he didn't really have. It was a rare occurrence.

They met their parents in the common room. Lim had left Isha sleeping on the bedside table in their room. He didn't want to risk Pelleata hurting her again, and the gargantula seemed to understand, setting down to nibble on some leaves and grass that Vaarem had picked outside.

They'd all dressed up for the occasion, wanting to feel like they were not in constant transit for one evening.

Zareanna had on her lavender dress, and she'd braided her hair and wound it up around her head like a crown. Delicate amethyst earrings decorated her ear lobes, and a matching necklace encircled her slender throat. Garrett had bought the set for her in Sirrock City, Vaarem had told Lim.

Garrett was dressed in a white shirt and purple vest, with purple and black pinstripe trousers tucked into knee-high boots. His golden hair was pulled back in a tight braid, emphasising his lean, well-proportioned face.

"You guys look great," said Vaarem smiling, and Lim agreed. Even more than looking good, their parents actually looked happy together.

Has this trip made them closer? wondered Lim hopefully. He always wanted his parents to be happy, especially his mother, so it was wonderful to see her like this. The positive energy from them both filled him with a sense of strength and vitality that he rarely experienced.

Or is it just the medication kicking in? he wondered at the back of his head, but did his best to dismiss this idea.

"Thank you," said Garrett graciously. "You boys look good too. I like what you're doing with your hair today, Lim," he said, in a rare moment of generosity. Unfortunately, he followed it up with, "Much better than that dwarf style you were sporting before."

"Thank you, I think," grinned Lim. He was in too good a mood to worry about his father's remark.

He'd done up his hair in a bun again, with a few strands framing his face. He was dressed in his black silk shirt with the lace around the collar and cuffs, a black velvet vest that fell to his mid-thigh, and his usual black trousers and boots.

Vaarem had foregone his usual top-knot and had only pulled back the top part of his hair, letting the rest flow loose over his shoulders and down his back. He was dressed in a gold-coloured shirt, with dark-red trousers and vest. Lim thought that he looked kind of garish, but he had the charisma and personality, not to mention the physical beauty, to pull it off.

They took the carriage, as Ninetta and her family lived on the other side of Morliss. When they arrived, Vaarem and Garrett brushed down and settled the horses in the small stable, then the family walked over to the tree that held Ninetta's house. A small staircase led to a short wooden bridge, which led to the front door. The door was framed by leaves and two large, thick branches. A housekeeper in a grey dress and green apron opened the door and let them in.

Ninetta and Lyanna met them in the front hall. They were both dressed in simple satin gowns, Ninetta's a silver-blue colour, her mother's a silver-green. Both had their hair styled in tiny, delicate braids around their temples and pointed ears, and flowing silver-gold down their backs

"Welcome," said Lyanna with a soft smile.

Lim could smell something appetising coming from the kitchen. It seemed that Ninetta's cooking would be as good as she'd promised.

Ninetta hugged Vaarem, then Lim. "I'm so glad that you're okay," she told Lim softly. "I had been afraid that you wouldn't come, that you'd be too sick."

He smiled at her reassuringly. "I'm tougher than I look," he said. "Plus, I had to come and taste this extraordinary food that you promised. I'm starving."

"That's good," she said, taking his hand, then taking Vaarem's hand in her other one, and leading them through the house.

"Where's your pet?" she asked, looking at Lim's shoulder.

"Back at the inn," said Lim. "I didn't think she'd like a dinner party," he said with a chuckle. He didn't mention Pelleata.

Ninetta nodded.

Lyanna's aunt Sereanna came to meet them in the sitting room. She was dressed in a fitted gown of red satin, with flowing chiffon sleeves, and red flowers in her hair, which was stacked up on top of her head in a tall bun.

"Good evening," she said, bidding them all to sit down. "Welcome to our home."

Everyone sat down.

Lim looked around for Pelleata.

Maybe she's not here, he dared to hope. Perhaps she's gone to see Randall, or something.

He sat down on the couch next to Ninetta, with Vaarem on his other side. Garrett, Zareanna, and Lyanna took the other couch, with Sereanna taking the metal-backed chair that stood at the end of the room.

They made pleasant small talk, while the young housekeeper brought them refreshments, such as pieces of fruit, or tiny sweet and savoury biscuits. Lim politely declined them all, but Vaarem ate them enthusiastically.

"Are you not hungry?" asked Ninetta anxiously, as she nibbled on a small biscuit.

"I am," said Lim. "I am saving room for your prepared meal. Surely, you've noticed how quickly I tend to get full."

"Not really," she said gently. "But whatever works for you."

He smiled at her and looked around the room, as the adults talked about the weather and the condition of the roads in Morliss, before moving on to more interesting topics such as their hobbies. It turned out that Sereanna was a teacher too (she taught senior students of Vaarem and Lim's age), and Lyanna was a poet. Ninetta was studying poetry too, which Vaarem thought was very impressive. He kept glancing at her over Lim, and Ninetta kept looking back, making Lim feel like he was in the way, but when he suggested that he and Vaarem swap places, both Vaarem and Ninetta refused. It seemed that they were more concerned for him than for being with each other, which made Lim feel warm and loved, but also a little awkward.

He was glad when it was time to get up and go through to the dining room.

"Where is your cousin?" he asked Ninetta, as they walked to the table.

"I don't know," she replied, looking around nervously. "She said that she was going to take a nap, but she's been napping for an awfully long time. Perhaps she'll sleep through dinner and not bother us." She looked towards her mother, as if for confirmation, but Lyanna was talking to Zareanna and Garrett, and appeared to not have heard her daughter.

But no sooner had they sat down, than Pelleata made an appearance. She looked beautiful in a simple pale-pink gown, with her hair loose, but Lim could immediately feel her malice. He swallowed nervously, glad that he'd sat himself between Vaarem on one side and Sereanna on the other.

"I apologise for being late," said Pelleata, taking a seat on her aunt's other side. Lim moved a little toward Vaarem. "But," Pelleata dropped her voice so that Lim and Vaarem's parents, who were still talking to Ninetta's mother at the other end of the table didn't hear, "I have been feeling most awful all afternoon. I don't know why you three," she indicated Lim, Vaarem, and Ninetta, "go out of your way to make me feel bad. It's not my fault that Lim spilled his medicine and then got magically cold. It's not my fault that he's clumsy and can't control his magic."

"Except that he's *not* clumsy and he *can* control his magic," Ninetta pointed out.

"How do you know?" hissed Pelleata, still speaking quietly. "You don't know him."

"I do," said Vaarem. "And she's right. My brother is not clumsy."

"See what I mean?" Pelleata asked her aunt with a pout. "Precious Limmy can do no wrong. It must be all my fault," she whined.

"Le, stop it," said Sereanna. "You're being rude. Just because Lim dropped something does not make him inherently clumsy. Now, sit down please and behave yourself."

"Of course," said Pelleata sweetly, as she made herself comfortable. "I promise to not upset precious little Limmy." She looked at Lim and smirked. "I wouldn't want you to hurt yourself again, seeing as you're so frail and delicate."

Sereanna frowned at her, but Pelleata simply smiled, before looking up and smirking at Lim again. "I apologise, Limmy," she said.

He sighed and looked down at his plate, as the housekeeper deposited several platters in the middle of the table. His appetite was gone.

The smells coming from the platters were appetising to everyone it appeared, except Lim. Ninetta had cooked different types of vegetables and legumes, with herbs, spices, and sauces. She'd also made a lentil soup, which everyone, except Lim, raved about.

"Wow," said Vaarem, eating a spoonful. "This is seriously orgasmic."

"Vaarem," scolded his mother.

"Not at the table when we are guests," said his father disapprovingly. "Although I must agree, the soup is wonderful."

"You need to give me the recipe," said Vaarem, grinning at Ninetta from the corner of his eye. "Every time I make it, I will think of you."

"Aww," said Ninetta, blushing.

"Eugh," said Pelleata, sticking her tongue out, "You two are so gross. Think of precious Limmy. You're putting him off his food. How rude are you, Nin?"

Lim looked down at his bowl. *Just my luck,* he thought bitterly. *The one time that I could actually enjoy eating, I can't.*

Nevertheless, he dipped the spoon in the soup, then brought it to his mouth, because after Pelleata's little speech everyone, especially Ninetta, was watching him expectantly. So, he forced himself to eat and smiled.

"It is good," he said to Ninetta, "Really." He ate another spoonful, and another, feigning enjoyment, when in actuality, he just wanted to leave.

"So, what did you do today after arriving in Morliss earlier this afternoon?" Sereanna asked him and Vaarem. Lyanna was talking to their parents on the other side of the table.

"I went to visit someone," said Lim, glad of an excuse to stop eating. "His name is Magnon, and his wife Malina."

"Magnon Silverbranch? The healer?" asked Sereanna curiously.

"Yes."

"Why did you visit the healer?" demanded Pelleata. "I thought you said you weren't sick. You better not have infected me with anything," she warned him.

"I'm not sick," he said, as patiently as he could. "He's a friend." He looked over at his parents, but they were still talking to Ninetta's mother, all of them gesturing with their hands. Lim was glad that at least *they* seemed to be enjoying themselves. Pelleata seemed to be deliberately only talking when her aunt was, so that Zareanna wouldn't hear her. A part of him admired her tenacity, but wondered why someone would go to so much effort just to be negative. It didn't make sense to him.

"Fuck you're weird," scoffed Pelleata, echoing his own perception of her. "Imagine being friends with the healer. Don't you have any normal friends?"

"Le!" warned Sereanna. "Watch your language. What's gotten into you? Magnon is perfectly nice. Why would anyone not be his friend?"

Pelleata simply rolled her eyes. "Precious Limmy obviously is," she said under her breath.

"I'm sorry, Lim," said Sereanna. "I don't know what's come over Pelleata. She's very upset about what happened earlier today."

"I bet she is," said Lim pleasantly. "But it's okay. No harm done." He smiled at Pelleata sweetly, mimicking her expression. "Isn't that right, Le? It was all an accident and we're all fine."

Pelleata gritted her teeth and scowled.

Vaarem kept glancing over at his brother. He wanted to make sure that Lim was okay. His parents were talking to Ninetta's mother and not paying any attention to their side of the table. Fortunately, Sereanna was sitting between Lim and Pelleata, so Vaarem was confident that Pelleata wouldn't try anything, but he was still anxious.

After dinner, the housekeeper brought out a cheesecake for dessert.

"Did you make this too?" Vaarem asked Ninetta, as a slice was put in front of him.

"Yes." She nodded proudly. "Mother helped me."

"Well, it looks delicious," he said, taking a spoonful and raising it to his mouth.

"What's the matter, Limmy?" He heard Pelleata say from the end of the table.

Lim was looking at his plate, his expression undecided.

"What's wrong?" asked Vaarem softly.

"Nothing," said Lim, looking up. "What's the matter with you, Le?" he asked Pelleata.

Her aunt, sitting between them was eating her cake, oblivious to her table neighbours.

"Nothing," Pelleata smiled sweetly. "Why are you not eating? Is it not good enough for you?"

Lim took a spoonful of cake and raised it to his mouth.

Pelleata watched him, a look of intense concentration on her face.

Vaarem, all of a sudden, felt very uneasy. He was about to tell Lim not to eat the cake, but before he could say anything, Lim had put the spoon in his mouth.

An expression of extreme panic crossed Lim's face and he gasped for breath. He spat the cake back out onto his plate and put one hand to his chest, the other to his mouth, his eyes wide and frightened.

"Oh, my Fates," said Pelleata, with exaggerated shock. "How rude."

Lim struggled to breathe, as everyone stared at him.

"What did you do?" demanded Vaarem, jumping to his brother's aid. "Lim? Are you okay?" he asked anxiously.

Lim shook his head as he gasped for air, a trickle of blood flowing out of his mouth and down his chin.

"I didn't do anything," said Pelleata with mock innocence.

"Limmy? What's wrong?" Zareanna was also immediately out of her chair and at her son's side.

Lim coughed, then finally managed to draw a breath.

"What happened, darling?" Zareanna had managed to pull Lim's chair away from the table and was crouching down next to him. Garrett and Ninetta had also come over and now stood over him anxiously.

"Something," gasped Lim, "sharp," he managed to say. He put his hand to his mouth and pulled out a shard of something that looked like glass.

Ninetta's eyes widened so much that Vaarem thought that they'd burst out of her head. "I didn't do that," she gasped.

"I know." Vaarem put his arm around her for a moment, before crouching down by his brother.

"I bit into it," said Lim thoughtfully, then paused, as if he couldn't quite describe what had happened. "And it was so cold," he said with a shiver. "And sharp." He paused to draw a breath. "It was like magic."

"Oh, don't be absurd," said Pelleata. "You could have just said no thanks to the cake, without making this kind of scene." She rolled her eyes.

"I didn't," Lim put his hand to his head and slumped sideways. If it hadn't been for Vaarem and Zareanna holding him, he would have fallen.

"What did you do?" Ninetta asked Pelleata accusingly. "It was you."

"What?" Pelleata asked incredulously. "I had nothing to do with it. *You* made the cake."

"Mother, she did something to the cake," said Ninetta to Lyanna. "She wanted to ruin this evening for us."

"Aunty Ly, see how she accuses me?" whined Pelleata.

Lyanna moved to stand next to her daughter, as if unsure what to do.

"If you don't mind," said Lim, looking up at his parents. "I'd like to go home now."

"Your guests are so rude, Nin," said Pelleata to her cousin, somewhere above and behind Lim.

Everyone was still clustered around him. Someone had handed him a napkin, that he was holding to his lip, which was bleeding. He'd managed to catch his breath but his lungs and chest ached with every heartbeat, as he tried to regain his senses. He didn't dare look at Pelleata. He knew she'd done it. He could feel the magical energy in the air, but he could also feel it dissipating. Soon, it would be gone, and there would be no evidence of it having existed.

"I'm so, so sorry, Lim," Ninetta was almost sobbing as she crouched near him.

"It's," he gasped for breath, "okay," he managed to say and touched her shoulder reassuringly, still holding the napkin to his mouth with his other hand. His whole body was shaking. Zareanna and Garrett were standing on either side of him, each one with a hand on his shoulder. Lyanna and Sereanna stood next to them, looking at Lim anxiously.

"I'll get you a cup of warm tea, Lim," said Sereanna, and walked towards the kitchen.

Lim managed to stop shaking. His mother stroked his hair. He looked up at her and tried to smile. "I'm okay," he told her softly. "You can all go and sit back down. Sorry." His mother stroked his hair again, then she and his father, and Ninetta's mother all went back to their seats.

Lim looked at his plate. The shard of magical ice-glass was melting. Soon, it too would be gone.

"Why?" he turned around and met Pelleata's eyes.

"Why what?" she asked innocently.

"You know," he said with a weary shake of his head.

She simply shrugged and turned away.

No one wanted to eat the cake after that, so they left the table and went back into the sitting room. It appeared that Ninetta had appealed to Vaarem and their parents to stay a little longer, so that they didn't leave on a bad note. Lim was beyond caring. It seemed that Pelleata was truly out to get him, and he was now using all of his remaining strength to put a magical barrier around himself. This was High Magic, which meant using a lot of his own energy to manipulate the forces around him, and he knew that he was going to pay for it the next day, but he needed to protect himself, so he concentrated and imagined a barrier of light around his body. Once it was in place, he kept concentrating. A spell like this, like a physical shield, needed to be consciously held.

"I am so sorry about the cake," Lyanna was saying, as the two families sat around on the couches. The housekeeper brought Lim a cup of tea, which he took graciously, but didn't drink. He didn't know what Pelleata might do to it.

"I don't know what happened," Lyanna kept explaining anxiously. "I have never had a shard of ice like that form before. I am really sorry, Lim. I hope your mouth is okay."

"It's fine, thanks," he said. His lip had stopped bleeding and the pain in his chest and lungs from the unnatural cold was beginning to fade. But his shock wasn't. He'd never expected anyone to do what Pelleata had done. He stole surreptitious glances at her, as she sat in one of the armchairs across the room, from where he sat between Ninetta and Vaarem. He was glad that he'd taken his potion before coming, like Vaarem had suggested.

He couldn't believe that neither of Pelleata's aunts, nor his parents for that matter, suspected anything and thought the whole thing a freak accident.

He felt occasional pulses of energy, as if someone was trying to penetrate through his magical shield. He looked up at Pelleata each time, and each time he saw her scowl. She was still trying to get to him and was growing frustrated when she couldn't. Lim had never known anyone to use their magic in this way. He wasn't sure what she was trying to do. Perhaps to freeze the air around him so that he couldn't breathe?

His suspicion was confirmed when Ninetta said, "Is it just me, or was it really cold just before?" She hugged her arms around herself, and Lim saw goosebumps forming on her pale skin.

"It's not just you," he told her.

The adults talked about different topics and Lim

found himself drifting off, as his mother and Sereanna discussed the finer points of teaching theory. Vaarem and Ninetta were talking about school too, and Lim felt awkward sitting between them again, but he didn't dare move. He could feel Pelleata's bad energy from across the room.

Suddenly, Ninetta cried out. "Ouch!" She put her hand to her forehead.

"What happened?" Lim sat up to look at her.

"I don't know," she said. "I feel like something sharp just hit me. Ow," she rubbed the spot on her forehead.

Lim turned to her and touched her face gently. There were no marks on her smooth, flawless skin. "There's nothing there." He shook his head.

They both turned to look at Pelleata, who was staring at them intently.

"It was *you*," said Ninetta accusingly. It seemed that if Pelleata couldn't get to Lim, she was going to try and antagonise someone else.

"What?" asked Pelleata. "Aunty Ly? Aunty Rena? Ninetta and the boys are excluding me again and accusing me."

Sereanna looked at her and sighed. It appeared that she'd had enough of her niece's whingeing for the day. "Pelleata Primrose," she said sternly. "You are not a child. Your cousin and her guests are talking together. No one is excluding you. If you want to talk to them, then please do so politely. If you don't want to, then don't, but please stop whingeing. I am honestly embarrassed at your behaviour today, young lady. Now please stop it."

Pelleata dropped her eyes and nodded.

Lim swallowed. He had no doubt that she was going to take her annoyance out on him or Ninetta.

He was desperate to leave. The constant magic use was making him extremely tired, and he could tell that Pelleata was waiting for the moment he would let his guard down.

Finally, the evening was over.

Everyone stood up and walked to the front hall, where they said their good-byes. Zareanna promised to keep in touch with Sereanna about teaching, and Garrett and Lyanna hugged each other warmly. They'd spent a large part of the evening talking about their lost loved ones and seemed to have bonded over their shared grief. Vaarem and Ninetta stepped away to say a private farewell, where they kissed passionately in the corner. Lim found himself standing next to Pelleata.

"Why?" he asked her again.

"Why what?"

He sighed. "No one's listening. I know you did the cake thing. Why? What have I done to you?"

"It was just a joke," she said. "And if you're so frail that it was a big deal, then perhaps you shouldn't go out at all."

Lim dismissed that with a shrug. "I could feel you jabbing at my aura all evening," he pointed out. "And then, when you couldn't get to me, you hurt Nin. Why? Why do you do these things?"

She frowned. "Why do I need a reason?" she said. "I just wanted to see that expression on your stupid face. And when I couldn't get to you, I did it to Ninetta. She's the one who invited you, so it's her fault really. Before you came, everyone liked me, but as soon as Precious Limmy is on the scene, everyone is falling over themselves to do things for you. It makes me sick. I hate people like you. You're weak and pathetic, and you expect the whole world to bend over backwards and cater to you. If you can't do everyday things, then just stay home and stop making others change their lives around for you. You're an obnoxious, manipulative, spoilt little boy and it makes me sick. Both you and your brother. Spoilt brats the pair of you. I am so glad that I am never going to see you again. I would do something to you now, only I know that everyone would come to your aid and kiss your bony arse. But don't worry, one day soon everyone will get sick of moving their lives around for you. You know you'll never amount to anything. I'm just giving you a taste of what's to come." She smiled coldly.

"Right back at you," said Lim wearily.

There was just no getting through to some people.

He closed his eyes as soon as he got into the carriage and rested his head against the wall. As soon as he released the magic shield, his head started to pound, as he'd known it would. He put his hands to his head and massaged his temples.

"Are you all right?" asked Vaarem, sitting down next to him. Garrett and Zareanna, after making sure that he was okay, had gone to sit out the front on the driver's seat together. Lim was just with-it enough to appreciate how nice this was.

"Yeah," he said, then leaned over so that he was resting on his brother.

Vaarem put his arm around Lim's shoulders. "What really happened in there?" he asked. "I can't believe that she actually did something like that in front of everyone."

"Mmm," said Lim. "She used magic to freeze a part of the cake into a sharp shard. But more than that, it was unreal, the cold. It was beyond freezing. I've never known magic to be used like that before. And she kept telling me that she found magic boring." He chuckled grimly.

"I'm sorry," said Vaarem, rubbing Lim's arm. "That is so fucked. I had a bad feeling and was going to tell you not to eat it, but I was too late."

"I had a bad feeling too," said Lim. "But I thought I was being paranoid. And afterward, she kept poking me magically. I had to shield myself all night. When she couldn't get to me, she poked Nin."

"Yes, I saw that," said Vaarem. "I was wondering what was going on."

"Yeah," said Lim. "Fuck my head hurts. Shielding is hard work." He rubbed his temples again.

"I know," said Vaarem. "I can't even do it for any length of time, so good on you for managing it all evening."

"Mmm," said Lim again. "I really feel like shit now. I may puke after all," he said, remembering their conversation earlier that evening.

"I hope you don't," said Vaarem, rubbing Lim's arm again. "Go to sleep. I'll tell you when we get there."

"Thanks," said Lim, resting his head on Vaarem's shoulder again.

Vaarem continued to hold him. Lim felt extremely lucky. Vaarem always looked out for him. His parents, especially his mother, cared about him a great deal, and he had a good number of genuine friends. Pelleata seemed to think that he manipulated people into caring for him, but he didn't. This was what she hated, the fact that people genuinely liked him. What she didn't seem to realise was that if she dropped her negativity, then people would like her too.

He was pondering all this and must have fallen asleep because the next thing he knew was that he was being carried up the stairs inside the inn by Vaarem. He opened his eyes, but promptly closed them again as a wave of nausea washed over him.

Vaarem lay him down on the bed gently and took off his boots.

"Do you want me to help you into your nightshirt?" asked Vaarem, stroking Lim's hand.

"Yes, please," said Lim softly. With every passing moment, he was feeling weaker and weaker. "And can you pass me my potion?" he asked, pushing himself up onto his elbows.

"Which one?" asked Vaarem.

"The painkiller," replied Lim. "My head is killing me, and my chest hurts too."

"What does it look like?" asked Vaarem, picking up Lim's potion bag and bringing it over.

"The little green bottle with the glass stopper," said Lim.

Isha climbed off the bedside table and hopped down onto Lim's bag, then pointed out the bottle. It seemed that she was already in tune with his needs. He smiled at the thought and stroked her when she walked past his hand.

Vaarem picked the bottle up and handed it to Lim, who opened it and took a large sip. He gave the bottle back to his brother, then lay back down and put his arm up to shield his eyes.

"Thank you," said Lim weakly. He allowed Vaarem to help him undress and then to put on his nightshirt.

When he was ready, he flopped back down onto the bed and allowed Vaarem to tuck him in. Isha rubbed his cheek with her head, then settled to sleep on the bedside table.

Chapter 27

Leaving Morliss

As soon as Vaarem woke up the next morning, he had a feeling that something was wrong. He turned over to wake his brother.

"Lim?" he asked, shaking Lim's shoulder.

Lim didn't respond.

When Vaarem looked over at him, he saw that his brother was unusually pale, and there was a sheen of sweat on his forehead and his upper lip.

Oh shit, thought Vaarem, getting out of bed.

"Lim?" he walked around and crouched down next to the bed, so that he was on his brother's level. On the bedside table, Isha stretched, then blinked all of her eyes, and looked over at Lim. She chirruped questioningly.

Lim stirred and opened his eyes, then promptly closed them again, and put his arm over his face.

Vaarem stood up and shut the curtains.

"You can open your eyes now," he said, walking back over to the bed and sitting down next to Lim.

Isha chirruped again.

"Thanks," said Lim weakly, reaching over to stroke the gargantula's head. "I feel awful."

"I know," said Vaarem. "You look awful. No offence."

Lim smiled thinly at that.

"Can you get up?" asked Vaarem.

"I don't know."

Vaarem leaned down and put his hands beneath Lim's shoulders, helping him to sit up. Lim put his hand to his head and leaned against Vaarem.

"Do you need your potion?" asked Vaarem.

Lim shook his head.

"Why?" asked Vaarem, confused.

"Because I feel like I'm going to throw up," said Lim, putting his head in his hands.

Isha climbed off the table and sat in his lap, her big eyes looking up at him with concern.

"I'm okay," Lim told her softly, stroking her head again.

"Are you up to travelling today?" asked Vaarem anxiously. While he wouldn't have minded another day in Morliss with Ninetta, he was conscious about the time that was passing. He didn't want to miss the Winter Lights festival at the East Borla Inn. He was looking forward to seeing Marla and Jessa again. Even though the two young humans were mostly communicating with Lim, Vaarem still considered them good friends, and didn't want to disappoint them by missing the festival.

Lim shrugged, continuing to stroke Isha. "Sure," he said. "As long as I don't have to do anything."

"Are you hungry?" asked Vaarem. "I assume that you're not up to going into the dining room, but I can bring you something to have here."

Lim shook his head. "No thanks. Like I said, I feel like I'm gonna throw up."

"Okay," said Vaarem empathetically. He put his arm around Lim's shoulders and gave his brother a reassuring hug.

"Have I told you recently that you're the best brother ever?" asked Lim, resting his head on Vaarem's shoulder.

"Not in so many words." Laughed Vaarem. "But I know through your actions and stuff."

Lim rested his head on Vaarem for a while longer, then he lifted it, put Isha on his shoulder, and tried to stand up. Vaarem supported him and held on to Lim's waist tightly, as Lim's legs shook.

"Shit," said Lim, as Vaarem led him over to the chair in front of the dressing table. "I can't walk. My legs shake too much."

"I can carry you down," said Vaarem. "Just as well that you hardly weigh anything."

Lim smiled grimly in response.

Vaarem left Lim at the dressing table, then got dressed himself and went out into the dining room.

His parents had just walked in too and were looking around for a place to sit. The inn was crowded, with the entire clientele consisting of elves. Vaarem raised his hand in greeting and walked over to where his parents were standing.

"Good morning, Vary," said Zareanna, reaching up to hug him and giving him a kiss on the cheek.

"Lim is really sick," said Vaarem.

"What?" Zareanna's eyes widened. "Oh no."

"Yeah," said Vaarem with a sigh. "He claims that he's okay to travel, but I don't know. He looks pretty bad. Apparently, he had to magically shield himself from Pelleata all evening last night."

Garrett sighed. "So, on top of everything else, he's given himself sorcery sickness." He shook his head. "Will that boy never learn?"

"I don't think he had much choice," said Vaarem. "Pelleata kept attacking him. When she couldn't get to Lim, she hurt Ninetta. I'm sure she would have gone for me too if we'd stayed, but clearly, she saw Lim as the weaker target."

"Poor Limmy," said Zareanna, with a shake of her head. "He doesn't seem to get a break. I don't think that we should travel without getting him checked over. There are no elven settlements between here and Palinas, so I think it would be best to get the healer here to look over him before we go."

si"I agree," said Vaarem.

They ate a very quick breakfast, then they all went to see Lim. He'd managed to get dressed, but his strength seemed to have given out, because now he was lying on the bed with his eyes closed and his arms crossed over his chest, Isha sitting on the bedside table, watching over him.

"I wish he wouldn't do that," said Vaarem with a shake of his head. "It looks like he's dead."

Lim opened his eyes when he heard Vaarem speak, proving to everyone that he was very much alive. "Hello," he said, then sat up slowly.

"What's wrong, darling?" asked Zareanna, sitting down next to him and putting her arms around him.

"I just feel bad," he said, resting against her. "But I'm fine to travel. Did you get me any food, Var?" he asked, looking up at Vaarem.

"I thought you said you weren't hungry," said Vaarem, realising that he should have brought something up anyway.

"I'm not," said Lim. "But I need something to take with my potion." He rested his head on Zareanna's shoulder and allowed her to stroke his hair. He hadn't had a chance to do anything with it, so it hung straight and loose over his face and shoulders. "It's okay," he said to Vaarem. "I'll have it later." He closed his eyes and rested against his mother again. "Are we ready to leave?" he asked weakly.

"We're not going anywhere until you get checked over," said Zareanna. "I'm going to ask your brother to get that healer Magnon Silverbranch to come and see you."

"That's really not necessary," said Lim. "I'll be fine."

"I'm sure you will be, darling," Zareanna kissed his forehead. "But I don't want to take any chances. We're going to stay here until mid-morning, then we'll be on our way."

"Okay," said Lim. He really thought it all unnecessary, but he didn't have the strength to argue.

Zareanna asked Vaarem to go and get the healer, and Garrett to tell the innkeeper that they would be extending their stay for a few hours.

When they'd both left the room, she lay Lim down on the bed again and started to pack his things for him.

"I'm sorry about all this," said Lim, opening his eyes, then closing them again. "I don't mean to cause all this trouble."

"It's not your fault," she said gently, sitting down beside him again.

"I really don't think that Magnon is going to do anything," said Lim, turning over onto his side.

"Does it hurt anywhere?" asked Zareanna, lifting her hand and stroking his hair.

"Just my head," said Lim. "And my chest. So, just the usual." He laughed a bit. "I'll be fine. As long as I stay away from Pelleata," he added, with a shudder and a cynical smile.

"Did she really try and hurt you?" asked Zareanna.

Lim opened his eye and looked at her. "No, Mother, I am just trying to get her into trouble and being dramatic," he said. "Yes, really."

"I'm so sorry," she said. "Lyanna said that that girl was troubled, but I had no idea."

"I don't think Lyanna had any idea either," he said, closing his eyes again. "She probably does now. Hopefully. She actually hurt Ninetta. Did you see that?"

"No," said Zareanna. "I didn't. But you're making it sound like she didn't hurt you, and she did."

Lim shrugged. "I guess I was expecting it. Hence, I put up the magical barrier, after the cake. Ninetta had no idea. I hope she's okay."

"I hope so too. She seems like a very nice young lady."

"Yeah," said Lim. "She is. And if it wasn't for me, her cousin wouldn't have hurt her."

"It's not your fault, darling," said Zareanna again, still stroking his hair. "That Pelleata seems like a very troubled young woman, and I think she's just looking for excuses. She hurt you because you were there, and if you hadn't been, she would have done it to somebody else. I really hope that Lyanna and Sereanna get her the help she needs."

"She's blaming me for everything," Lim raised himself up on his elbow and laughed.

"Which just proves how troubled she is. She hardly knows you."

"Thank the Fates," said Lim. "Imagine if she knew me well and used all my weaknesses against me." He smiled bitterly.

"I'm sorry she chose you as her target, darling," said Zareanna, putting her arm around him again.

A short while later, Garrett came back, and both he and Zareanna sat with Lim in silence until Vaarem arrived with Magnon and Malina.

"Who's looking after the shop?" asked Lim anxiously. He didn't want to be responsible for Magnon and Malina losing income because they were shut. They'd given him so much already.

"I have an apprentice," Malina assured him. "The shop is in good hands."

Magnon came over and looked down at Lim with concern.

"Oh, my Fates!" he cried. "What happened, Lim?"

Lim explained about Pelleata, and the magic attacks, and how he'd had to shield himself.

"I see," said Magnon, as he examined Lim. "Well, it seems that you have a serious case of sorcery sickness. This usually passes in a day or two, but with you it's likely to take about a week."

"Okay." Nodded Lim weakly, as he lay back on the bed. He'd had sorcery sickness before. Every magic user got it at some point when they over-exerted themselves. However, Lim was usually careful not to do this. He knew that when *he* got sorcery sickness, it was always bad. It was as if his underlying condition was exacerbated by magic use. It was the main reason why he was still constantly searching for a cure. But it seemed that he wasn't going to get one.

"I've had sorcery sickness before," he said. "I told my parents that that's all it was, but my mother insisted on dragging you here. I'm so sorry."

"No need to apologise, Lim," said Magnon kindly. "Sorcery sickness can be very serious. Especially for someone in your condition. Your mother was right to call me. Now, look after yourself until it passes. Get lots of rest and eat plenty of good food. You will most likely not be hungry, but don't skip any meals if you can avoid it. You need to replenish your strength. And no magic use. That goes without saying. Even simple things like heating or cooling water can set you back. Do you understand?"

"Yes." Nodded Lim. "I understand."

"And make sure you keep taking your daily medication. It will help you to recover."

"Okay," said Lim. "Thank you."

"Now, you folks are leaving Morliss later today? Is that right?" asked Magnon.

"Yes," said Garrett. "Unless you don't think that Lim can travel?"

Magnon looked at Lim. "What do you think, Lim?" he asked. "Are you willing to travel today?"

"Yes," said Lim. "As long as I can sleep in the carriage and not have to do anything, I want to go home."

"There you go," said Magnon. "If Lim is up to it, then there shouldn't be any problems. Just make sure he doesn't exert himself."

"Oh, he won't," said Garrett. "I will make sure of that."

"He should be fine in a week or so," reiterated Magnon. "If he does take a turn for the worse, you can take him to any healer who has experience with sorcery sickness. But, like I said, as long as he doesn't exert himself, he will be fine."

Zareanna rode in the carriage with Lim that day, while Vaarem decided to join his father out the front for a change. When they stopped for a rest, Lim stayed inside the carriage, with Isha on his shoulder. He managed to swallow some food, as well as his potion, after which he went back to sleep.

The next day Zareanna rode with Garrett, and Vaarem rode inside. Lim lay down on the floor of the carriage, as it was more comfortable than trying to lie down on the seat. His legs were too long to stretch out properly no matter what he did, but at least on the floor he could curl up more comfortably. Vaarem sat cross-legged beside him and told him stories when Lim was awake, with Isha chirruping beside him.

As the days passed, Lim started to feel better. On the afternoon of the third day, he managed to eat a proper meal, after which he sat on the seat in the carriage and talked to Vaarem. The day after, he got out of the carriage with the rest of his family when they stopped for a rest.

While on the way there, his father had insisted that Lim help with the carriage and the horses, this time he was the opposite and would not allow Lim to so much as lift a finger, and kept telling him to go and lie down. Lim was starting to feel like a freeloader, but soon realised that he still got extremely tired very quickly.

"When you need to rest, you need to rest," Garrett told him. "We are a family and therefore help each other. We all know that you will help when you're better, so don't exhaust yourself needlessly, and let us help you."

They reached the East Borla Inn in the early evening of the fourth day. They saw the bright lights in the windows from a distance away and as they got closer, they saw that there were decorations in the surrounding trees. The Winter Lights Festival was in full swing.

Lim looked out the window wonderingly. The atmosphere was positive and full of energy, and he immediately found himself able to breathe deeper and easier.

Their carriage had barely pulled up out the front when two young human women ran down the front steps to greet them.

"Lim!" they cried, running up and throwing their arms first around Lim as he stepped out of the carriage, then Vaarem as he followed close behind.

"Vaarem!" cried Marla, after she'd greeted Lim. "It's so good to see you. We've been waiting so long. We were afraid that you weren't coming."

"We wouldn't have missed coming for the world," Vaarem assured them.

Jessa put her arm around Lim's waist and led him towards the steps. Isha had crawled into his pocket as soon as he'd stepped out of the carriage. He would introduce her to his friends later. "Come on up," said Jessa. "I'll get the groom to look after the horses. Hello, Mr Nightingale, Ms Bluebell." She turned to Garrett and Zareanna. "We've been so looking forward to your return. Come on up, and Mam and Dad will get you both checked in. We reserved the best rooms for you. Come, come," she beckoned them.

The family got checked in promptly and a groom came to look after their horses and to park their carriage out the back.

"Are you going to be okay, darling?" asked Zareanna anxiously, as Jessa and Marla led Lim away, into the room that they'd reserved for him and Vaarem.

"Yes, Mother," Lim assured her with a smile. He'd been looking forward to coming here for so long, and now that he was finally here, he felt as if a weight had been lifted and he was better than he'd been in days.

Chapter 28

The Winter Lights Festival

Marla and Jessa helped Vaarem and Lim to set up their room. It was at the far end of the main wing, and it opened out onto the garden, which was hung with little festive lanterns.

"Oh wow," said Lim, taking it all in. "It all looks so great."

"Doesn't it just?" said Jessa proudly. "Marla and I did most of it ourselves. It took us the best part of a week, but it was worth it. It looks gorgeous, if I say so myself."

"I agree," said Varrem, looking around, impressed.

"So," said Jessa, when they'd had a look around and were all sitting down, Lim and Jessa on the bed, and Vaarem and Marla on the lounge in the corner of the room, "the Winter Lights Festival began the day before yesterday. It lasts for four days and there is a dinner and a party every night. The main event is tomorrow night. Please stay for it," she asked, putting her hands together and looking first at Lim, then at Vaarem imploringly.

"We'd love to," said Lim carefully, "but we'll have to ask our parents. I think they only planned to stay the one night. Then again, I've been really sick the past couple of days, so they might agree to an extra day's rest."

"Oh no," said Jessa kindly. "I'm sorry that you're still getting sick."

"Yeah," said Lim with a sigh. "The whole treatment was a bust. But I do have more ways to manage, with extra potions and things. No, I got sick for a different reason this time. I met someone really nasty, who kept attacking me magically, so I ended up getting sorcery sickness." He went on to explain everything that had happened with Pelleata. "So, I'm afraid," he said, "that I won't be doing any magic when I'm here now. But Vaarem can." He looked at his brother and smiled.

"I think we can live with that," said Jessa with a smile. "Now," she stood up, "we'll let you boys relax for a while, then we'll see you both this evening?" she asked.

"Sure," said Lim.

Marla stood up and followed her sister out of the room.

Vaarem and Lim were left alone. Isha crawled out of

Lim's coat pocket and sat on the back of the lounge, looking around the room curiously. Lim gave her a leaf from his other pocket. He'd started carrying around bits of greenery to feed her. When they got home, he would let her out into the garden to build her little web-house.

"Are you up to coming to the party tonight?" asked Vaarem, standing up and going over to his bag.

"I don't think I have much of a choice," said Lim, lying down on the bed on his back.

"You always have a choice," said Vaarem.

"Last time we were here, you told me that I didn't," said Lim with a chuckle. "But to answer your question, I don't know if I'm up to it, but I want to go. Also, I got the girls some diamonds from the Diamond Festival, so I want to give them to them."

"Ooh, you charmer." Laughed Vaarem, walking over to sit down beside his brother.

"I just thought it would be nice," said Lim. "The whole point was to give gifts to friends and loved ones. Marla and Jessa are my friends."

"Sheesh," said Vaarem, rolling his eyes. "Why are you being so defensive? I didn't mean anything."

"I know," said Lim. "Sorry. I'm still kind of feeling weird about Pelleata telling me what an arsehole I am."

"You're not an arsehole," said Vaarem.

"I know," said Lim with a sigh. "At least, I try my best not to be," he shrugged. "She really got to me, made me doubt myself."

"I'm sorry," said Vaarem. "She is wrong and just jealous. You don't have a manipulative bone in your body. You're the nicest person I know, and I'm not just saying that because you're my brother. If you ever acted like an arsehole or off in any way, I'd tell you."

"Thanks," said Lim.

Vaarem then went into the bathroom to wash up. Lim lay on the bed and closed his eyes. He lay there for a while, until Vaarem emerged from the bathroom. He'd pinned up the top of his hair, so that the rest fell down his back, and he was wearing his gold-coloured shirt, with black trousers and a black jacket with gold buttons.

"What do you think?" asked Vaarem, twirling around like a fashion model.

"I think you're going to be the handsomest man at the party," said Lim. "Although you were going to be that anyway. But you look really great."

"Thank you." Smiled Vaarem, then went over to his bag to look for some accessories.

Lim sat up, thinking that perhaps he should get ready too.

Although I don't know why I bother, he thought to himself. *Next to Vaarem's shining star, I am completely invisible. Then again, maybe invisible is better than visibly deficient.*

He went into the bathroom, where he washed and dressed in a black silk shirt, his usual black trousers, and a long black vest. He did his hair up in a braided bun with the strands down the front.

He came out of the bathroom, trying to smile.

It must have worked, because Vaarem smiled back at him and said, "You look great."

"Do I?" asked Lim flatly, sitting down at the dressing table, and looking through the box of jewellery and accessories that Vaarem had gotten out.

"Yes," said Vaarem. "Remember how I told you that if you look or act like an arsehole, I'm going to tell you?"

"You never mentioned my looks," said Lim, "But okay."

Vaarem walked over and sat down next to his twin.

"What's wrong?" he asked.

"Why would anything be wrong?" asked Lim, trying not to sound defensive.

Vaarem rolled his eyes. "Because I know you," he said. "Now, tell me, little brother, what is bothering you?"

Lim grinned. It was impossible to stay down for long when Vaarem was around. But then he sighed and said, "I don't know. I just feel like shit. Emotionally, that is," he added quickly, lest Vaarem think that he was getting sick yet again.

"Oh," said Vaarem, his face falling because he could do nothing to help. "Did Pelleata really get to you this much?"

Lim smiled bitterly. "Yes, she did," he admitted.

"Oh, Lim," said Vaarem, getting off his chair and putting his arms around his brother. "Don't be like this. You look great, and everyone who matters knows that you're a lovely person. And animals know it too. You saw how Isha chose to come with you and kept hissing at Pelleata. That's got to count for something. Now, come on, let's get ready so that Mother and Father don't freak out and think that something's happened to you again."

"Fine," said Lim resignedly. He looked in the jewellery box and found some silver cufflinks in the shape of stars with a black stone inside them. He put these on, then he found a black and silver brooch that he pinned to his vest. Vaarem had put on red and gold cufflinks, as well as a red cravat around his neck. They then put on their dress boots, made sure that Isha was okay with a small pile of leaves on the back of the lounge, and left the room, walking towards the other end of the wing, where their parents' room was situated.

Vaarem knocked on the door and their father opened it. He had on his white shirt and was doing up a lavender tie around his neck. His hair was up in a similar style to Vaarem's, with the top pinned back and the rest hanging loose.

"We're ready for the feast tonight," said Vaarem, walking in, Lim following.

Zareanna was doing up the laces on her lavender-coloured gown. It seemed to be the only one she'd brought with her. Her hair hung loose down her back, with jewels and flowers spread throughout its length. "Oh, you boys are so handsome," she said, clapping her hands as she turned to face them.

"Thank you, Mother," said Vaarem graciously. "See, Lim? What did I tell you?"

Lim gave him a cynical smile. "She's our mother. She has to say that."

"Oh, for Fates' sake," said Vaarem irritably. "What is up with you? Seriously."

"Sorry," said Lim with an impatient sigh. "Still recovering, I guess." He didn't want to talk about this, as there was nothing that anyone could do. He sat down on one of the chairs and put his chin in his hand.

"Which reminds me," Vaarem turned to his parents. "Can we please stay an extra night here? Like, until the day after tomorrow? The main Winter Lights party is tomorrow night and we've been invited. And Lim could probably do with a day of rest."

"So, are you going to be resting or partying, Lim?" asked Garrett sceptically.

"Resting," said Lim. "I'm only going to go to the party for a little bit and then I'm going to go to bed."

"Okay," said Garrett. "Just make sure that you don't overdo it. Don't want to have you passing out all over the place."

"No, Father," said Lim meekly.

"I have to admit," said Garrett, looking in the mirror as he adjusted his tie, "that the humans that run this establishment are most decent. And after that awful Pelleata girl, I don't even mind you two boys hanging out with these human girls. Just make sure that you don't give them any false hope, boys. Because once we leave here, we leave these ladies behind. Is that understood?"

"Why would it be such a problem if one or both of our sons had a human girlfriend?" asked Zareanna. "My father had a human girlfriend and now he has a human wife. It worked out pretty well for him."

Garrett looked at her for a moment, as if choosing his words, then he said, "Yes, but your mother is an exceptional human. She is very resilient, but even so, your father will outlive her. By many, many turns." He paused to let his words sink in. "You also had a human husband," he said meaningfully.

Zareanna looked up at him with hard eyes. "Do *not* even go there again, Garrett," she said warningly.

"No," said Garrett, "I *will* go there. Even after everything that we talked about in Sirrock, it still needs to be said. You had a human husband, and you still mourn him. Every day. I loved him too, and I still miss him, but a marriage connection is different. You forget Vada's birthday, but Malkim's death day is still a day that I know not to approach you."

Zareanna frowned. "So what?" she asked, "So what, Garrett?" What does it matter to you? No matter what may have happened, I am allowed to have a day to myself every now and then."

"That's not my point, Zara," he said softly. "My point is that you still mourn him, and will continue to do so. That it still pains you. And I don't wish that on our sons. I don't wish that on anybody," he hung his head. "I just want to spare them pain."

"Pain is part of life, Garrett," said Zareanna quietly. "For without pain, we do not know joy," she quoted a line from the Book of the Fates, the holy scripture of the Faith. "Yes, I mourn Malkim, but I also remember the good times and I wouldn't change that. I always knew that I would outlive him. He knew that too, so we made the best of the time that we had. I do not mourn his human lifespan. I mourn that I couldn't save him from himself. I mourn that he couldn't stop his darkness from consuming him. But I celebrate his life. All the moments that we had together, the joy he gave me far, far outweighs any sadness that I feel at his passing. The same as I know you do. Nothing is eternal, Garrett, and I would not deny Vaarem and Lim love and happiness with a human because it would be brief. I mean, would you deny Lim his pet because animals have even shorter lifespans?"

Garrett looked at her for a long moment, not saying anything.

Lim felt his breath catch, but he had a sip of his potion to keep himself quiet. He didn't want to interrupt this poignant moment.

Garrett finally dropped his eyes and nodded. "I never thought of it like that," he said quietly. "I'm sorry. I'm sorry for all the pain that I inadvertently caused you, and everyone else."

Zareanna smiled. Her eyes were wet with tears, but Lim could tell that they were tears, not exactly of joy, but of happiness. He reached over and took Vaarem's hand in his. His brother was looking at his parents with wide eyes. For once, he had nothing to say.

Zareanna took a step towards Garrett, then put her arms around him and buried her face in his chest. "I forgive you," she said quietly. "I know you mean well. And I do love you, Garrett."

"I love you too," he replied, putting his arms around her and holding her close.

Lim felt his chest loosen, and he took a normal painless breath, feeling his parents' energy, which was positive for once.

Garrett and Zareanna finished getting ready, and the whole family walked through the inn and into the dining hall, which had been festively decorated with leaves, flowers, and candles, and lit by oil lamps on the tables.

Lim put his arm around his mother's shoulders and allowed her to put her hand on his waist.

The hall was beginning to fill up quickly, so the family found a table near the fireplace and sat down. The food began to be served almost straight away. Marla and Jessa and their parents walked amongst the tables, talking to guests, while several other young men and women served the food, which consisted of many elaborate dishes from around Zemia. Lim saw some fried fish from the southern seas, some roast chicken and wild fowl from the northern deserts, beef and pork steaks, and rabbit pie that was popular in the Sirranna region. There were also several soups, both clear and creamy, roast and boiled vegetables, salads, nuts, and fruit. It was a feast for the senses, looking as appetising as it smelled.

Lim couldn't eat the meat. Up close, the smell made him feel slightly sick, but at Vaarem's urging he tried a piece of fish, which was not bad. However, he preferred the soups and vegetables, so ate mostly these.

Even though he'd been starving when he'd sat down, he found himself getting full quickly. He pushed his plates away, while the rest of his family had barely eaten more than half their meals.

"Lim," said his father warningly. "Eat."

"I am," said Lim weakly.

"Doesn't look like it," said Garrett.

"Well, I'm finished," said Lim.

"Well, no wonder you never put on weight," interjected Vaarem, "if you eat like a child."

"I'm full," protested Lim. "I honestly am."

"Of course, you are, darling," Zareanna patted his hand reassuringly.

Garrett frowned at her, and she shook her head, then turned back to Lim and said, "Why don't you save something for later?" She called one of the waitresses over and to Lim's intense embarrassment, asked her to put some food aside for him.

"You didn't need to say it was for me," he told her accusingly, but she didn't have time to reply because Marla came over to their table.

"How's everything going here?" The human hostess smiled at the family.

"Very good," said Garrett, waving a piece of potato on his fork. "We are all very impressed. Everything is most excellent."

"Thank you," said Marla, with a wide smile.

"We asked one of the waitresses to pack some food for us to takeaway," said Zareanna. "For my son. He hasn't eaten much but will probably want to finish later. I hope that's all right."

Lim looked down at his plate and felt his face colouring.

Why is Mother telling everybody?

Marla put her hand on his shoulder and said kindly, "Of course. Anything for you."

"Thank you," said Lim, looking up at her, his face still burning. "You're all so nice. Thank you."

"Well, you're very welcome," she said. "You're very nice too. You all are." She indicated the four of them. She then went away and came back several minutes later with a basket laden with food.

"Thank you," said Lim again, then put his face in his hands. He hated it when people fussed over him. But what could he do?

After dinner, there was a concert, with a band of human musicians playing in the corner. Lim hadn't taken his evening potion, so he went back to his room to take it. When he came back, he saw that Marla and Jessa had joined them at their table. Marla was deep in conversation with Vaarem, and Jessa was sitting on her own, a little apart.

Lim sat down next to her.

She smiled when she saw him, and she moved aside to make room.

The lights were dim and the music relaxing, and Lim soon found himself getting sleepy. He closed his eyes for a moment and found himself sliding in his seat.

Jessa turned to look at him in the dim light. "Are you okay?" she whispered.

"Yeah." He nodded. "Just tired. But I really don't want to leave."

"That's okay." She smiled and took his hand in hers. "You can lean on me if you want."

"Thanks." He smiled and slouched down so that he could rest his head on her shoulder. She continued to hold his hand as the concert went on.

"What are your plans for tomorrow?" she asked him when the show was over, and the lamps had been lit again.

"I don't know," he said. "I'll have to ask my brother."

"Well, if you have time, Marla and I have the day off work, so we can take you both around the area."

"Okay," said Lim. "Thank you. I would like that."

"Did I see you getting cosy with Jessa?" teased Vaarem, as they were getting ready for bed, Isha chirruping from the bedside table, where Lim had laid out his cloth for her to sleep on.

"No," said Lim, taking his hair down and brushing

it out. "I was just tired, so she let me rest my head on her shoulder." He finished brushing his hair and walked over to the basket of leftover food. He was glad to see that all the foods had been packed separately, each item wrapped in wax cloth. He picked up a small vegetable pie, sat down on the lounge, and began to eat it.

"You can tell me," said Vaarem. "I won't judge."

"I know that I can tell you anything, Var," said Lim. "But there's nothing to tell. There never will be."

"Never say never," said Vaarem, pulling his night-gown over his head.

"Fine," said Lim. "I don't plan on there ever being anything to tell."

"Why?" asked Vaarem, sounding curious and a little confused.

"Why what?" said Lim. "Because I'm going to be a priest."

"But that doesn't mean that you can't have a part-ner. Many priests are married."

"And many aren't," said Lim. "Look, I don't know why you care so much. I'm not preventing you from going out on dates, or from having sex, or whatever else you may want to do. We are allowed to have sep-arate interests. Before this I wanted to be a mage, and they don't normally marry either."

"Even if you don't marry, you can still go on dates and have sex," Vaarem pointed out.

"Yes, but it's not compulsory."

"Why don't you want to date anyone? Is it because

of what Pelleata said? Because you're smart and attractive, and I'm sure that lots of girls, or boys." He raised his eyebrow, but when Lim didn't react, he continued, "Would like to go out with you."

Lim frowned. "Yes, yes," he said impatiently, "I look just like you, therefore if you can get a date, then I can too, otherwise that would make you a loser that can't get laid, right?"

"I didn't mean it like that," said Vaarem, put out by his twin's outburst.

"Look, Var," said Lim with a sigh, "I'm sure that if I wanted to get a date and get laid, I could. But my point is that I *don't want to*. I don't feel the need for it in my life. So, can we please drop this conversation and never have it again?"

"I just don't want you to be lonely," said Vaarem.

"I'm not. Really. Now, can we please go to sleep?" said Lim, finishing the pie and wiping his hands on his legs. "I'm really tired, and the girls want to take us out during the day tomorrow. As friends," he added.

"Okay," said Vaarem. "Just don't sell yourself short, you know. You have a lot to offer."

Lim rolled his eyes. "Thanks, for saying that, and for caring. But, there are other ways to contribute to society. I'm really fine. Now, can we *please* drop this."

"Okay," said Vaarem, as Lim walked to the bathroom to brush his teeth. He still sounded unsure, but he was going to drop it. Lim really hoped that he wouldn't bring it up again.

Lim woke early the next day, as he usually did. He fed Isha, had a snack from the basket and his morning potion, then went back to bed. He was feeling tired, but in a good way; he felt that if he managed to get some more sleep, he might actually feel well. So, he slept until Vaarem woke him.

They went to breakfast together, where they met up with their parents but didn't see either Marla or Jessa anywhere. Lim recalled Jessa telling him that they were having the day off.

After the family had all finished eating, they went back to their rooms. Garrett said that he needed to write some letters for work; the Spring Festival was coming up, and he wanted to make a start on organising the event; while Zareanna wanted to write some lesson plans for the upcoming school term. They arranged to meet back in the dining room for lunch.

"Don't overdo things, Lim," Garrett warned him. "If you want to go to this ball thing this evening, you need to be well rested. I will not have you fainting in the middle of the dancefloor and causing a scene."

"Yes, Father," said Lim. "Don't worry, it won't happen." He wondered why his father was all of a sudden so concerned about him fainting. He hadn't fainted in weeks.

Back in their room, Lim lay down on the bed and picked up the book that he'd gotten from Eliza, and started to read. He was a little over halfway through, and the more he read, the more excited he became.

The type of magic that priests performed, used the energy in the atmosphere, generated by plants, animals, people, and the natural world, rather than the magic user's own, therefore seemed to cater to Lim's innate strengths and talents. He really felt that he could do this, and the idea made him beyond happy. For all of his life, he'd been told that a career in magic was out of the question. He wondered why no one had ever suggested that he become a Priest of the Fates. Then again, when people thought of priests and priestesses, they didn't immediately think of magic, even though blessings and such things were essentially magic, as Lim was finding out.

Vaarem had decided to write to Ninetta, so he sat at the desk and did this.

A little before midday, there was a knock on the door, which Vaarem got up to answer.

Marla and Jessa stood on the other side of the threshold, dressed in casual clothes, without their signature aprons over their dresses.

"We have a day off today," announced Marla, as she and Jessa walked into the room and sat down on the lounge when Vaarem invited them to do so.

"Great," said Vaarem, sitting down next to them. "Lim was saying that you wanted to show us around?"

"Yes," said Jessa, "We do, but we are flexible. What plans do you have for the day? What would you like to do?"

Vaarem grinned at her. "My brother and I have no set plans, other than having lunch with our parents.

What would you suggest that we do? We are open to suggestions, particularly if any activities involve you both being our guides, or otherwise spending some time with us and giving us the pleasure of your company," he said, smiling his most charming smile at Jessa and then at Marla.

Lim smiled too. He'd never known his brother to be so eloquent.

"Well," said Marla, "we could all have lunch together with your parents, as it's nearly lunchtime, then we could go for a walk through the orchard, and then into the forest? There are many pretty spots, and there is a stunning waterfall not too far away. We could pack a picnic. What do you think?"

"Sounds great," said Vaarem, looking at Lim for confirmation.

Lim smiled. "That sounds wonderful," he said. "Let's do it."

Marla's eyes fell on Isha, who was sitting on the bedside table and looking at the girls with all eight of her eyes. "What's that?" asked Marla curiously.

Lim smiled. "It's a gargantula," he said. "I found her in a field a few days ago. This horrible girl we were with hurt her, so I adopted her." He put his hand out and Isha climbed on. "She's friendly. She doesn't bite. Her fangs are for cutting leaves and grasses."

Marla stroked Isha's head tentatively, and Isha chirruped.

"She likes you," said Lim with a smile, then held his hand out to Jessa, who stroked the gargantula too.

"You can bring her on the picnic," said Jessa, smiling at Isha. She seemed to have taken to the critter more than Marla, who was a little apprehensive. "Unless you're afraid that she will get lost?"

"She won't," Lim assured her. "I will bring her. She is naturally an outdoor animal, so doesn't mind being outside."

A few minutes later, the four of them left the room, leaving Isha on the lounge, and went to the dining room to have lunch.

Garrett and Zareanna arrived shortly after them, and the six of them sat together, with Marla and Jessa sitting between Vaarem and Lim.

As he'd been eating all morning, Lim wasn't hungry, but he nevertheless managed to swallow a few bites, and he made a show of pushing his food around on his plate, which he hoped hid how little he really ate. He wasn't worried, as he knew that they would be eating more at the picnic, but he figured that his parents probably wouldn't see it that way.

When lunch was over, Garrett and Zareanna went back into their room, holding hands and looking relaxed and happy. Vaarem and Lim went to theirs.

Isha was asleep on the back of the lounge, so Vaarem and Lim walked around her quietly.

"What are you going to wear on this picnic?" asked Vaarem, taking off his shirt and looking through his bag.

Lim looked at his brother's toned body enviously.

"Clothes," he said with a shrug. What difference would his outfit make?

Vaarem turned to him. "Oh good," he said sarcastically. "I was afraid that you were going to wear a potato sack."

"Nah," said Lim. "It would look better on you."

Vaarem laughed at that. "But then we wouldn't match," he said. "No, seriously," he turned to Lim again. "What should I wear? I fear that I didn't bring enough stuff."

"Well, you can always borrow something of mine," Lim offered, only half joking.

Vaarem laughed at that in a good-natured way. "Yeah," he said, "let's dress as each other. Remember when we used to do that and tried to fool people?"

Lim laughed too. "Yes, I remember. Although I'm not sure it would work now."

"Sure, it would," said Vaarem confidently. He twisted his hair up into a bun and slouched. "All I need is a black shirt now, and people will think I'm you."

"Oh yeah?" countered Lim. "Well, let's see." He put his hair up in a top-knot and stood up as quickly as he could, then did a twirl on the spot. "Look at me, I'm Vaarem," he said. "Come on, everyone, look at me." He did another twirl the other way so that he didn't get too dizzy, then bowed, holding on to the table for support with one hand, his other arm extended above his head.

"Perfect," said Vaarem, clapping his hands. "You could pass for me anytime."

"As long as I don't have to take my shirt off," said Lim glumly, still looking at Vaarem's bare torso.

"Oh, for Fates' sake, not this again," said Vaarem, rolling his eyes and quickly putting his bathrobe on to cover himself. "What's gotten into you? You never used to be like this."

"I never used to be this stupidly skinny," Lim pointed out. "I mean, I've always been thinner than you, but it's never been so noticeable before."

Vaarem sighed. "Yeah, but you've never been so sick for so long before," he said kindly. "You'll get better."

"Actually, I have been this sick for this long before," said Lim. "In fact, I've been much sicker for much longer. By my standards, these past couple of moons are nothing."

"Okay," conceded Vaarem. "You have a point. But you always recovered, and you will now too. Just give it a couple of weeks. And eat. Don't think that I didn't see your little charade in the dining room. You actually have to really eat, not just pretend."

"I know," sighed Lim. "I suppose that's what worries me. I can't."

"Can't what?"

"I can't eat any more than I do," said Lim. "I seem to have one mouthful and I'm full."

"Sure, you can," said Vaarem. "You ate nearly that whole basket of stuff that Marla and Jessa gave you yesterday. I didn't touch it."

"I suppose," said Lim doubtfully.

"You suppose," scoffed Vaarem. "Well, *I* know. So,

just hang in there. You'll be fine. It will just take a couple of weeks. And there are no horrible Pelleatas here to make you feel bad."

"True," agreed Lim.

"Of course, it's true," said Vaarem. "I only speak the truth. Now, seriously, help me decide what to wear. No offence, but I don't want to wear your depressing black clothes. It's a sunny day, so I want to wear something that goes with it."

Lim chuckled. "You're the first person I know who wants to dress to match the weather."

Vaarem rolled his eyes. "You know what I mean."

"Yes, I know," said Lim with a laugh. He walked over to his brother's bag and pulled out a green shirt and vest. "Here," he threw them at Vaarem. "Wear this."

"Green?" Vaarem raised his eyebrow.

"Why did you pack it if you didn't want to wear it? Also, you asked my opinion. Also, also, you want to wear something that goes with the spring weather. So, there you go."

"Okay," said Vaarem. "You have convinced me." He put the clothes on, then tidied his hair.

Lim decided to just wear what he was already wearing. He didn't feel like getting changed and besides, all his clothes looked the same anyway: black and ill-fitting. He sighed and sat down to read his book while he waited for Marla and Jessa to arrive.

A quarter of an hour later, Marla and Jessa came to get them. Both girls were dressed in floral dresses, with bonnets on their heads. For a moment, Lim wished that he'd worn something different, then he remembered that he didn't have anything, so he took one last look at himself, put Isha, who was still sleeping, in his coat pocket, then they left.

Marla held Vaarem's hand as they walked, so Lim held Jessa's. Her fingers felt small and delicate in his hand, which he found surprising, as he knew that she worked hard. Perhaps his own hands were even more worn.

They reached the waterfall that Marla had mentioned within an hour, even as they all slowed down to match Lim's pace. Lim felt happy that Marla and Jessa seemed to do it instinctively. They spread out a blanket and watched the water while they ate the food that Jessa had prepared. Isha stuck her head out of Lim's coat pocket and chirruped, making Marla and Jessa smile. Jessa reached out her hand and Isha rubbed her face against it, then the gargantula crawled out of Lim's pocket and sat on the grass, nibbling on the blades.

"So," asked Marla, eating a strawberry, "you two are twins, right?"

"You mean it isn't obvious?" asked Vaarem.

"Yes, but I try not to assume." She grinned.

"Yes, we are," confirmed Vaarem. "Why?"

"Which one of you is older?"

"That would be me," said Vaarem.

"By how much?"

"One day."

"Really?"

"Yeah," said Lim. "We each get our own birthday, which is kind of cool. We turned twenty-five earlier this turn. What's the age difference between you two?"

"A turn and a half," said Marla. "I'm twenty. Jessa's nearly nineteen."

"Right." Nodded Lim.

"The reason we asked," said Marla, "was that Jessa and I were wondering which one of us would take which one of you to the ball tonight."

"Isn't it the other way around?" asked Vaarem. "Doesn't the boy take the girl?"

"Not when the girl's family owns the party venue," replied Marla smoothly, then laughed good-naturedly. "So, that answers that. Vaarem, will you be my date tonight?"

"I'd be honoured," said Vaarem with a bow.

"Lim?" asked Jessa, her eyes bright.

"I'd love to," said Lim, taking her hand and kissing the back of it. He didn't know whether it was his imagination, but Jessa's expression seemed to say that she'd gotten the better deal.

They returned to the inn in the early evening and had a rest in their room before dinner. Lim took out the little diamonds that he'd saved for Marla and Jessa, ready to give the stones to the girls later that evening.

"Did you see how they both wanted to be your

date?" asked Vaarem, as they were sitting at the dressing table, looking through their box of accessories. Even Lim was starting to get a little excited and really wanted to look good for the ball.

"Really?" he asked. He'd thought that it had just been his imagination, just wishful thinking. Why would anyone ever prefer him over Vaarem?

"Yes," said Vaarem. "That whole speech about who is older." He shook his head.

"You don't mind?" asked Lim tentatively. They'd never been in this type of situation before.

"No." Vaarem shook his head thoughtfully. "I know that they like me too. And let's face it, I've had much better luck with the ladies in the past, so it's high time that you get a turn. Besides, I'm still thinking about Nin. Marla is just a friend."

"I know," said Lim. "Jessa is just a friend too."

"Because you're thinking of, what was that girl's name? Elise?"

Lim frowned, then laughed. "Eliza," he said. "And no, she's just a friend too. Why do you not believe me when I tell you that I'm really not interested in anything more than friendship with anyone?"

"Because it's strange to not want a partner," said Vaarem. "Then again, you've always been strange, so it really shouldn't surprise me." He laughed.

"That's right," said Lim. "And don't you forget it.

They turned back to the box of jewels.

"Would you marry a non-elf?" asked Lim after a moment.

Vaarem looked at him, then shrugged. "I've never thought about it," he said. "But if I ever meet someone whom I really think I want to spend my life with, I don't think her race will matter. It's like Mother said, love is love, and we have to live in the moment, rather than worry about a future that may not even come to pass."

They ate dinner with their parents in comfortable silence, then they all went back to their rooms to get ready for the ball. Zareanna and Garrett seemed happy to be going on a date together again, and Garrett made no snide comments about his sons going with human dates, other than to warn Lim to take it easy.

The girls came to their room a couple of hours after dinner.

Jessa was dressed in a dark-purple gown with a full skirt and narrow sleeves that finished at a point over her hands. Her hair was done up in a braid that wound around her head, and she wore an amethyst necklace and earrings. Marla had on a red gown in a similar style, except that it had no sleeves and was instead held up with thick straps that tied up with ribbons. Her hair was piled up on the top of her head and bound in a flower crown of roses. She wore a single ruby at her neck. Vaarem had decided to wear a red shirt with his black jacket and trousers, while Lim wore a plain black silk shirt, with a black velvet vest and trousers. He pinned the silver brooch to his vest, while Isha sat on the dressing table playing with the contents of the jewellery box. Jessa stroked her head for a long while, while Vaarem and Lim put on their dress boots.

As they prepared to leave the room, Lim presented Marla and Jessa with the tiny diamonds.

"Ooh, wow!" they squealed, looking at the little stones.

"These are from the both of us," said Lim, indicating his brother. "From the Diamond Festival."

"Oh, thank you," said Jessa. "You boys are both so sweet."

"It was Lim's idea," said Vaarem. "I don't want to take credit where it's not due." He grinned.

"Well, thank you both anyway," said Marla, putting the little diamond in a pocket in her dress. She then lifted her arm so that Vaarem could hold her elbow. "Shall we?" she asked as Vaarem took it.

Lim glanced down at Jessa, who was smiling up at him. She too had put her diamond in her pocket. He took her hand in his, and the pair of them followed Vaarem and Marla out of the room, down the corridor, and into the dining hall, which was still decorated for the festival.

The tables had been placed along the walls and there were platters of food on them. A string quartet of human musicians played in the same corner as the previous night. The centre of the room had been cleared and several couples were dancing there already. Lim saw that his parents were among them.

Vaarem led Marla into the middle of the room, and

they began to dance. Because he was such an agile and graceful dancer, everyone in the room stopped and for one song watched them. When the song finished, Vaarem and Marla bowed to each other, then to the room at large. When the next song started, the other dancers went back on to the dancefloor and started to dance again.

Lim held his hand out to Jessa and led her on to the dancefloor. Even though Melissa in Sirrock had told him that he wasn't a bad dancer, compared to Vaarem, he felt completely ordinary.

He told this to Jessa, as he held her close. She must have been wearing very high heels because her head came up to his shoulder, rather than the middle of his chest, which was where she normally rested it when he hugged her. She smiled up at him, reassuring him that he was the best dancing partner she'd ever had.

She stumbled in her shoes a few times, and he held her up.

"You're very graceful." She smiled up at him.

"Thank you." He smiled down at her, daring to think that maybe she was right.

The song finished and they walked over to the tables. Jessa picked up a grape and fed it to him.

"Thank you," he said, then did the same to her.

She ate it and smiled up at him.

"Do you want to sit down?" she asked. "These shoes are killing me."

"Sure."

They walked over to the chairs, which were situated

against the wall further down the room and sat down. They watched the other dancers in companionable silence, holding hands. Lim saw that his parents were staring into each other's eyes, as if they were the only people in the room. He smiled at that. Vaarem and Marla kept dancing, sometimes swapping partners to dance with other people.

After a while, Lim and Jessa stood up and danced again.

They danced to one song, then Marla and Vaarem came over and Lim danced with Marla and Vaarem danced with Jessa. Then, Vaarem danced with his mother, while Garrett reluctantly danced with Marla, then with Jessa. Lim sat and watched, enjoying the atmosphere, then stood up and walked the length of the room looking at the decorations. When she'd finished dancing, Jessa joined him.

Whenever they walked past the food tables, Jessa would pick something up and give it to him, so that by midnight he was feeling very full and very tired.

He danced with Jessa again, then, when the song finished, he walked back over to a chair, his hand to his head. He was starting to feel faint and dizzy.

"Are you all right?" asked Jessa, taking his hand in hers again.

"Yeah." He nodded, "but I think I might have to call it a night. I'm really tired."

"Do you want to go and lie down?" she asked.

"Yes." He nodded.

He stood up again, a little unsteadily, glad of Jessa's arm around him.

They walked back to his room, where Lim lay down on his back on the bed. Jessa sat down beside Lim. Isha was asleep on the bedside table, in her usual spot, so Jessa stroked her head, then turned to Lim and stroked his shoulder. He flinched involuntarily.

"Sorry," she said, taken aback. "Did I hurt you?"

"No." He shook his head. "*I'm* sorry. I'm kind of weird about being touched. I don't like it. I get poked and prodded so much," he tried to explain.

"I'm sorry," she lifted her hand, as if not sure what to do with it. She clearly wanted to comfort him but didn't know how.

"You can stroke my hair," he said. "I don't mind my head being touched. In fact, I like it." He chuckled.

She smiled, then ran her hand through his long hair, which had come loose sometime during the evening. "I'm sorry that your treatment didn't work," she said kindly.

He shrugged. "I am too. I guess it was too much to ask for."

"How do you feel, normally?" she asked. "Are you in pain?"

"No." He shook his head. "Not really. Not anymore, but I still get really tired all the time. And I can't breathe if it gets too cold, or if there's pollen in the air, or negative energy," he explained.

"I'm sorry," she said, still stroking his hair. "That must be hard."

He shrugged. "I'm used to it," he said. "And I do manage most of the time. Especially with these new meds. I really do feel better since I started taking them. But." He smiled sadly. "I still have no stamina. I'm sorry. You can go back to the party if you want. I don't mind."

"It's okay," she said. "My feet are killing me in these shoes." She undid the laces of her shoes, then kicked the shoes across the room. "So, I can't dance any more. Not for a while, anyway. You're so tall, and I wanted to be closer to you." She laughed.

"Well, you look beautiful," he told her. "I really mean that."

"Thank you," she said, lifting her hand and stroking his hair again. "You're so nice. It's not fair that you get so sick."

"Hmmm," he said thoughtfully. "Life's not fair. But in many ways, I'm better off than a lot of people. Like, I have family and friends that genuinely care about me, which means a lot. It's more than a lot of people have. I think that's the reason that that girl that I told you about hates me so much. She's jealous that I have genuine friends. She tried to tell me that I manipulate people into doing things for me and expect everyone to change their lives around to accommodate me, but I really don't. I genuinely try not to be a bother, and to help others when I can. I don't want, nor expect special treatment."

Jessa smiled. "Marla and I meet a lot of people as they come through the inn," she said thoughtfully, "and you and your brother are some of the sweetest people we've ever met. You really care about each other, and others. It's rare to see."

"Thank you," said Lim. "But you and Marla genuinely care about people too. I think that's why we all get on so well." He smiled.

"Yes," she said. She stopped stroking his hair and leaned over to look at him.

"What?" he asked, feeling the sudden tension in the air.

Jessa bit her lip and was about to say something when the door opened and Vaarem and Marla came in. They were twirling around and laughing, both of them a little tipsy. Lim realised that he was probably the only person at the party who hadn't drunk any wine or mead. Not that it made any difference. He rarely drank, and never to the point of intoxication. He sometimes wondered just how sick he would get if he ever got drunk. Not that he wanted to find out.

"Ah, there you guys are," said Marla, flopping down on the lounge.

"What did I tell you?" said Vaarem. He continued to dance around the room. Even though he was clearly intoxicated, he didn't bump into anything, nor trip over.

"Are you okay, Lim?" asked Marla, looking at Lim with concern. At least, that's what he thought she was going for. Her eyes seemed to go cross-eyed every once in a while, and she would have to re-focus.

"Yes," he said, raising himself up on his elbows. "Just tired."

"You and me both," said Marla. "Your brother here seems to have never-ending energy. Just look at him."

"I know," said Lim with a grim laugh. "I live with him. Vaarem, can you please stop. You're making us all dizzy."

Vaarem did a flying pirouette, then landed gracefully on his feet, and bowed. The girls both clapped and Lim did too. Vaarem sat down next to Marla, but after a moment jumped up and started to pace restlessly again. Jessa stood up and started to twirl around with him. She looked tiny and delicate without her shoes, and Vaarem held her carefully.

"Do you want to go back to the hall?" Vaarem asked Jessa. "Just for a little bit. The party is still going."

"Um?" Jessa looked at Lim with a raised eyebrow.

"Go," he told her. "I don't mind. I'll be right here."

"I'll stay with him," offered Marla.

"Okay," said Jessa. She leaned down and kissed Lim on the cheek, then took Vaarem's hand and followed him out the door, only stopping to pick up her shoes.

Marla stood up and walked over to sit on the bed beside Lim.

"Do you want something to eat?" she asked him.

"No thanks." He shook his head. "I've been eating all day."

She raised her eyebrow sceptically.

"It's true," he protested. "You were with me most of the time. You must have seen. And just now at the party, Jessa kept picking things up and feeding them to me," he explained.

"Okay," she said, smiling shyly.

She took his hand in hers and held it, while he asked her about her life.

"It's pretty good most of the time," she said. "I like running the inn with my family. We get to meet lots of people. Although," she mused, "I would sometimes like to travel, to see all the places where our guests come from."

"Well, you're welcome in Palinas anytime," he told her.

"Thank you," she said. "I will surely try to visit when I get a holiday."

"Do you get regular holidays?" he asked.

"Not really," she admitted, shaking her head. "The inn is open through all the seasons, and we always seem to be busy. But we do hire some staff when it gets too busy, like right now, so Jessa and I could potentially have a week or two off. If we planned it well, that is."

"Well, let me know when you do. I would love to, well, Vaarem and I would love to have you both over."

"You and Vaarem are very close, aren't you?" she asked.

"Yes. But we're twins, so it kind of comes with the territory."

"Do you ever think about the future?" she asked him.

"In what way?"

"As in, what are you going to do? How are you going to live? Are you going to have a family? You know, that type of thing."

"Sometimes," admitted Lim. "When I was younger, I never thought about what I'd be when I grew up because I was always told that I wouldn't get to grow up."

Marla nodded, her expression serious. "You were that sick that people didn't expect you to live?"

"Yes." Lim nodded gravely. "But I did. And now that I have grown up, I am starting to think about it. I always wanted to work with magic, but I thought that I couldn't, what with my lack of strength and stamina and all that." He sighed grimly. "But recently, I have found a career option that would suit me, so that's kind of exciting." He told her all about Eliza's book and how being a Priest of the Fates would allow him to use magic, albeit in a different way.

"But other than that, I don't know," he said. "I know that I don't plan on getting married or anything. I don't know about Vaarem. I guess one day he will have a family of his own. I don't know how I would fit into that," he said, sounding a little sad.

"You're not scared of being lonely?" she asked, leaning over and stroking his hair, the way that Jessa had done.

"No," he said. *Why did people keep thinking that?* "You don't need a partner to not be lonely. As I told Jessa just before, I think I'm really lucky because I have genuine friends and family who care about me, I always have. Even being as odd as I am considered amongst elves, there have always been a couple of people who like me, and then I have human friends too." He smiled at her. "There was also a dwarf at the inn where I got the diamonds who was really nice. I'd like to meet some pixies," he added. "And I have Isha." He lifted his hand and stroked the gargantula's head and back. She gave a soft chirrup, which made both him and Marla smile.

"So, you want to travel?" asked Marla, reaching out her hand tentatively to stroke Isha's head.

"I guess I do," he said thoughtfully, still stroking Isha. He found the movement soothing. "I've never considered it like that before, but yes, I do want to travel. This trip has shown me that I can. I was always worried that I'd get sick, but it seems that I can handle it."

"You certainly can," she said. "You held your own on the dancefloor out there, you know. You may not have had as big an audience as Vaarem, but there were quite a few people who watched you dance with envy."

"Really?" He raised his eyebrow. "You sure it wasn't pity?" He laughed.

"Yes, I'm sure." She laughed back. "Don't sell yourself short, Lim," she said. "You are an awesome person."

"Thank you," he said. "But if I am awesome, then it's only because my loved ones and friends make me so. You know what they say about being judged by the company you keep."

Marla considered this. "I guess that's true.

"What about you?" asked Lim. "What do you want to do?"

"I want to travel," she said. "I want to visit all the places that our guests come from. Then I want to settle down somewhere and have a family. Maybe take over this inn when my parents retire, or maybe start up my own. I'd keep in touch with Jessa and my parents regardless."

Lim smiled at that. "Well, like I told Jessa, you are welcome in Palinas anytime."

"Thank you," she said. "Now, it's getting late. I think we should start calling it a night."

"I agree," said Lim, stifling a yawn.

He sat up slowly, then stood up, holding his hand to his head. Marla helped him to stand and smiled up at him.

"Do you need any help with anything?" she asked.

"No thanks." He shook his head. "I'll get Vaarem to help me if I need it. But I think I'm fine. Thank you for a lovely night." He leaned down and hugged her, then kissed her on the cheek. She hugged him back, holding on to him for a few moments before letting him go.

"Thank you," she said, sounding a little breathless. "It's been great seeing you again. I hope that everything goes well for you. I really do."

"Thanks," he said, starting to feel a little embarrassed.

She hugged him again, then turned around and left the room.

Lim watched her go, then walked over to the dressing table and sat down. He ran his fingers through his hair and shook it out, then looked at himself in the mirror. His face looked a little flushed, his cheeks pinker than normal. He smiled and was pleased with the face that smiled back at him. For once he looked normal; not sickly, not freakishly gaunt and pale, just a normal, if very slender, young man home after a night out. He picked up his brush and started to brush his hair, watching it as it shone in the lamp light.

A few minutes later, Vaarem came in. He was followed by Marla and Jessa, who said their good-byes to him, then walked over and said their good-byes to Lim again.

"I'll see you both in the morning," said Marla, with Jessa nodding behind her, then they left, shutting the door behind them.

"Fuck I'm exhausted," said Vaarem, lying down on the bed, extending his arms. He lay there for a while, then sat up and took off his boots. Lim realised that he was still wearing his own boots. He lifted his foot and undid the clasp, then started to pull his boot off, but had to stop because he suddenly felt dizzy. He took a breath and tried again.

"Do you need some help?" asked Vaarem.

"Yeah." Nodded Lim, closing his eyes and putting his foot back down on the floor. He may have been looking normal, but his body wasn't functioning normally.

He wondered why this still surprised him after all this time; surprised and disappointed him.

When will I finally lower my expectations? he berated himself. He undid the clasp of his other boot and allowed Vaarem to pull off his boots and socks for him.

"Do you need help with anything else?" asked Vaarem.

"No thanks." Lim shook his head. "I'll be fine." He could still dress and undress himself.

He stood up and went to the bathroom to wash, then came back into the room and put on his nightshirt. Vaarem did the same and they both got into the bed.

"I can't believe that we are finally going to be home in a couple of days," said Vaarem after turning off the lamp.

"Hmmm," said Lim. He hadn't even thought about the fact that in a couple of days they'd be home and that their adventure would be over.

And for what? he wondered. I am not cured. It's all been a waste.

Only, he couldn't bring himself to think of it quite like that. Because even though he wasn't cured, the trip had been a lot of fun in many ways. They'd met so many people, seen many sights, experienced many things. And their parents had finally connected in a way that Lim had never known them to connect. *Surely the whole thing had been worth it?*

"Are you looking forward to being home?" asked Vaarem.

"I don't know." Shrugged Lim. "Are you?"

"I don't know either," admitted Vaarem. "I think so. But I am going to miss hanging out with you all day, like we have been in the carriage and stuff. And sharing a room with you. It's been like a non-stop party."

"Your whole life is a non-stop party, Var." Laughed Lim.

Chapter 29

Homecoming

The morning sun streamed through the gap in the curtain, indicating that it was later than Lim usually woke up. Vaarem was still asleep beside him. Lim stretched and ran his hand down his body. Was it his imagination, or did his bones not stick out as much as they used to? He was feeling tired, but otherwise well. He closed his eyes again and rolled over, wondering how long it would be until someone came and told him to get up.

I may not be cured, he thought as he recalled all that had happened since they'd set out, *but I survived all the hospital screw-ups, as well as Pelleata's nastiness, not to mention weeks upon weeks of travel in the winter. I am clearly not as weak as I feared.*

Vaarem opened his eyes and rolled over. Lim was

still in the bed beside him, which worried him and made him sit up immediately. Lim usually only slept in if he was really sick.

"Lim?" He shook his brother's shoulder anxiously. He was glad to find that Lim's temperature seemed normal, and that he was breathing easily.

"Yeah?" Lim turned around to look at him.

"Oh, thank the Fates," said Vaarem.

"Huh?" asked Lim.

"I thought that you were sick again," said Vaarem.

"Why?" asked Lim, then shook his head and said, "Sorry. Dumb question. Well, I'm not. In fact, I was just thinking about everything that I have endured and survived on this trip. So, even though I may not be cured, whatever that means, I think, overall, I am better than I used to be. So, maybe, just maybe, I'll keep on enduring and surviving things and getting better slowly, until one day I am well?" The last part of the sentence came out as a question.

"Hopefully," said Vaarem. "I think it makes sense. You should talk to Dr Fantail when you get home. Anyway, let's get up. I hope that we haven't missed breakfast, cause I'm starving, and you've eaten everything in that basket."

"It was mine to eat," said Lim defensively as he sat up, then stood up carefully. On the bedside table, Isha opened her eyes and stretched. She gave a small chirrup, and Lim chirruped back, then stroked her head and back. He was about to go to the bathroom, when there was a knock at the door. He went to open it and found his mother standing outside.

"Lim," she said, putting her arms around him. "Good morning. Where's Vaarem?"

"He's still in bed," Lim pointed to Vaarem, who was still under the blankets.

"Come on, boys. We need to leave soon. Get dressed. They are serving breakfast all morning in the dining room, so go and have something to eat, then pack up."

"Okay," said Lim, letting her in, then going into the bathroom, where he'd originally been headed.

He washed his face and got dressed in his travelling clothes. He looked at himself in the mirror critically. He was still pale and skinny, but not as much as before. He twisted his hair up into a bun, fastening it with a clip, and came out into the room, where Vaarem and Zareanna were packing up their things.

Zareanna looked up at him and her face broke into a smile. "You look lovely, darling," she said. "And so well. How are you feeling?"

"Good," said Lim, then walked over to his bag and had his morning potion. "Come on, Var," he said to his brother. "Let's go down the hall and have some food. I need something soon or that potion is gonna give me a stomach-ache, and fuck it, that's not gonna happen."

"Okay, okay," said Vaarem. He quickly got washed and dressed, then they both left the room, followed by Zareanna.

The dining room was about half-full. The decorations were still up, but it was clear that they would be coming down soon. Nevertheless, there were clean tablecloths on the tables, which gave the room a pleasant atmosphere.

Garrett was sitting at a table near the corner where the band had played the previous two nights, eating a piece of toasted bread. He looked up as his wife and sons entered, and he raised his hand in greeting. Zareanna sat down next to him. There was a plate there, with crumbs on it and a half-drunk cup of tea. She picked it up and sipped it. Vaarem and Lim walked over to the buffet and looked at the offerings. As usual, there were sausages and bacon, eggs, bread, and cheese, as well as fruit and porridge. Lim got himself some fruit and porridge, like he usually did, while Vaarem stood over the food for a long time, trying to decide.

"Oh, for Fates' sake," said Lim irritably after a while. "Just pick something. My hands are getting hot holding this bowl."

"Fine," sighed Vaarem, taking a bowl of porridge for himself.

"I never knew you were so fussy and selective about your food," said Lim, as they sat down at their table.

"I'm not usually," said Vaarem, starting to eat his porridge. "It's just that it is all so good and today is the last day that we're going to be here."

"Well," said Lim, "maybe you could ask for the recipes?"

"I could," said Vaarem, "but we all know that I am not that good at cooking, so there is no guarantee that I could make anything anywhere near as good as it is here."

"You are good at cooking," Lim pointed out, remembering the fish his brother had cooked so long ago now, it seemed. "You're good at everything. But if you're unsure, Mother could help you out, because she is definitely a good cook. Like, Ninetta's food was great, but on par with Mother's."

"True."

They finished their meal, then went back to their room to finish packing. They'd not seen either Marla or Jessa all morning and didn't want to leave without seeing them and saying good-bye.

"I'm going to miss them," said Lim. "I hope that they can come and visit us some time. Or that we come back here."

They walked all through the inn, looking for Marla and Jessa, but couldn't find them. Eventually, they asked one of the on-duty maids, who directed them to the innkeepers' family quarters.

Lim knocked on the door tentatively, as he caught his breath. The search had taken a toll on him, but he was managing.

"Who is it?" asked a sleepy voice.

"It's Lim and Vaarem," said Lim.

"Oh shit," said the voice on the other side of the door, then the door was promptly opened by a dishevelled-looking Marla. Her hair was hanging loose and unbrushed over her shoulders, and she was dressed in a blue silk dressing-gown.

"Oh, my Fates," she said, letting them in. "I'm so sorry. We overslept. After we left you last night, we came back to the party and started to clean up. We didn't get to sleep til it was nearly light." She rubbed her eyes. "Come in, come in." She motioned for the elves to sit down on one of the lounges. "Jessa!" she called quietly, running into the apartment. "Wake up. Make yourselves at home," she turned back to the elves, "but don't be too loud. My mam and dad are still asleep. They were up last night too."

Lim and Vaarem sat down on the lounge awkwardly and waited. A few minutes later, Marla and Jessa emerged, having gotten dressed very quickly.

"I'm so sorry," said Jessa as she leaned down and gave Lim, then Vaarem a hug in greeting. "Come with us."

The elves got up and followed the humans through the inn. Marla and Jessa led them into the kitchen, where they asked the cooks to prepare a food basket, which they gave to Vaarem to hold. When Lim told them that they really must be leaving, the girls led them back into their apartment, saying that they had something for them.

Back inside the apartment, they gave Vaarem a

golden brooch in the shape of a star and Lim a delicate quill and tiny ink pot.

"We wanted to give you both something to remember us by," said Jessa. "We are going to get the diamonds made into necklaces, or maybe bracelets, we haven't decided. But we wanted to give you both something, so please accept these gifts."

"Thank you," said Vaarem, pinning the brooch to his jacket. "Thank you so, so much. You know we'd never forget you, but this is really appreciated. But why us? You must meet a lot of people."

"We do," said Marla. "But you are the first ones to treat us as equals, to see us as more than your servants for the length of your stay here. So, thank you to both of you. It's been lovely having you here. We'll miss you." She reached up and hugged him, then turned to hug Lim.

"Thank you," said Lim, turning the quill over in his hands. "This is lovely."

"To make sure you write to us." Laughed Jessa.

"I will," promised Lim, putting the quill and ink away in his pocket. Isha pocked her head out of his other pocket, and Jessa stroked her head.

The girls then walked them to their carriage.

Garrett and Zareanna were already there, putting their suitcases in the carriage's luggage compartment, and asking the groom to get their horses.

"I still need to get something from our room," said Lim, realising that he didn't have Eliza's book.

"I'll come with you," said Jessa, "I'll take you through the staff corridor. It's quicker."

In the room, Lim picked up the book, which he'd stupidly left on the bedside table. He was planning to read it in the carriage so had not packed it.

"Do you have your medicines?" asked Jessa.

"Yes," said Lim, patting the small shoulder bag that he always carried now. "My other bag is already in the carriage. I just needed to get my book. Fates, I can't believe I nearly left it here."

"I wouldn't have let you forget anything," said Jessa. "And if you had, I would have sent it on to you."

"Thank you," said Lim, taking one last look around the room, to make sure that neither he nor Vaarem had forgotten anything else, then turned to leave.

Jessa put her hand on his arm.

He looked down at her, wondering what she wanted.

"I'm sorry if I made you uncomfortable last night," she said.

"What?" asked Lim. "When? What are you talking about?"

"When we were here," said Jessa, her cheeks colouring. "I wanted to kiss you," she said.

"Oh."

"But then I didn't want to, because I felt that if I kissed you, then I would never be satisfied kissing anyone ever again." She looked up at him.

"Thank you," he said. "That's very flattering. But unwarranted. I am not sure at all that I'd be a good kisser. I've never kissed anyone. Nor been kissed. I wouldn't know what to do."

"Really?" she asked, surprised, as they started to walk back to the carriage through the staff corridor. "You've never been kissed?"

"No." He shook his head. "Like I keep telling everyone, I'm not interested in having a romantic partnership with anyone. I mean, I might change my mind one day, but I really don't plan to. I want to sort my own priorities out first. Also, I plan to be a priest, and while it's not forbidden for priests to marry, it's discouraged. It's something to do with concentration and energy transfer."

"That's very noble of you," said Jessa.

"Huh?"

"Well, you don't want to give yourself to one person so that you can give yourself to everyone. That's very admirable."

"Thank you," he said, leaning down to hug her. She hugged him back, then looked up and gave him a very light kiss on the lips.

"I hope things go well for you, Lim, I really do."

"And I hope that things go well for you too, Jessa," he told her. "We will keep in touch."

They arrived at the carriage and Lim said another good-bye to Jessa and to Marla, who was helping the groom to secure the horses' harnesses, and to the girls' parents, who looked like they'd quickly gotten up to say good-bye to the elves too. It seemed that the family had made a good impression, which pleased

Lim. Inter-race relations were still tense sometimes, despite the alliance that his grandparents had first set up, so he was happy to leave a positive experience here.

He climbed into the carriage, and soon they were off.

He looked back at the receding inn, as the horses pulled the carriage down the road, feeling like he was standing at the threshold of something new. This trip had not worked out the way that he'd planned, but in many ways, he'd gotten more out of it than he'd ever hoped for. He closed his eyes as the carriage rounded the corner and soon enough fell asleep.

They arrived at the last inn, which was also the first inn they'd stayed at, just before dinner. The innkeeper recognised the family of elves immediately and offered them a complimentary dinner, which the family accepted graciously.

"How did you go in Sirrock City?" the innkeeper asked Lim when he went down to the lobby after dinner. "You look well," she remarked.

"Thank you," he said. "I feel quite well."

"I sometimes thought about you," she said. "I was expecting you a couple of weeks ago, and when you didn't come, I was hoping that you'd gone home another way or something, and that nothing bad had happened."

"Thank you," said Lim again, smiling down at her. "That's very kind of you. But as you can see, we're here. It all took longer than expected and ended up not working anyway." He told her about the whole experience, about the three unsuccessful attempts and the injuries he'd sustained, as she gasped and made all the appropriate comforting noises, then he finished with his new medication regime, and he told her about meeting Eliza at the hospital, and finally about finding Isha.

"Ooh, a gargantula?" The innkeeper smiled impressed. "They are quite rare, but great in gardens. They eat all the weeds. They are also very intelligent."

"Yes," said Lim lifting Isha and allowing the innkeeper to stroke her head. "Anyway," he continued, "I always wanted to use magic, and now it looks like I can. If I use it in a non-traditional way, that is." He explained about the book that Eliza had given him, and his decision to become a Priest of the Fates.

"That's lovely," she said. "You know, we perform weddings and other ceremonies here quite often. I have sometimes thought of getting an elf or dwarf priest to officiate some of the ceremonies. It makes it more inclusive and special, you know? I would love to have you once you're ready."

"I would love to do it," replied Lim, once again thinking that even though the hospital treatment had been a bust, the trip as a whole had been wonderful in other ways.

He slept well that night.

Lim picked at the food basket as the carriage

rattled along the road in Palinora and surprised himself by how much he managed to eat. He was feeling as well as he ever remembered feeling. Isha sat on his shoulder and nibbled on a sprig of parsley.

They reached the gates of Palinas in the late afternoon and pulled up to their house in the early evening. It felt strange walking back into their home. Part of him felt like they'd been gone forever, while another part felt like they'd never left.

There was a lot of correspondence waiting for them. Lim sorted through it until he found his own letters. There were three letters from Eliza, one from Terry, and one from the hospital in Sirrock City requesting to know how he was doing and asking him to keep in touch.

There was nothing from Vada, which made him feel disappointed, until he read the last letter. It was from the Temple of the Fates in Palinas, and it said that he'd been accepted into their training programme. It asked him to come down to the premises at his earliest convenience.

"Yes!" he said happily, not caring if anyone heard.

Vaarem came into his room shortly before dinner. Their mother had started to cook, and Vaarem and Lim were expected to come down and help her soon. Their father was tidying up the house. The pictures of Vada and Malkim had been returned to their spots on the wall. Garrett had smiled as he straightened a new one that Lim had never seen before. It showed his parents and Malkim, standing on a clifftop, with a silver dragon flying in the background.

Vaarem flopped down on Lim's bed. "What are you so happy about?" he asked.

"I've been accepted into the Temple of the Fates."

"That's wonderful," said Vaarem, hugging him when Lim sat down next to him. "I got a letter from Nin," he said. "Pelleata is in a lot of trouble. Apparently, she had her aunts wrapped around her little finger, but ever since they saw how she'd hurt you, they have started to see right through her. She is currently grounded, apparently." He laughed.

Lim didn't. "I hope she gets the help she needs. I don't want her to hurt anyone else."

After unpacking, Lim went downstairs to help his brother set the table, while their parents prepared dinner. Lim was tired, but before the trip, he would have been too tired to help. Now he could, which he considered a success. He was not healed, but he was better, which he counted as a win. Isha sat on his shoulder. He would put her in the garden the next day, when it was light.

Their mother had prepared some dried tomato soup, and some roast root vegetables. They hadn't stopped to buy food, so they ate what had survived in the pantry for the past two moons.

As Lim had expected, his father watched him closely as he ate. He forced himself to keep eating. *Communal meals are one of the cornerstones of family life, and social relationships in general,* he told himself. *I can't avoid them forever.* And as he'd told his father back in Sirrock, he did not have the same problems as Eliza or Malkim. He had the ability to participate in mealtimes, so the sooner that he trained himself to be comfortable with it, the sooner his life would get easier. Unlike Malkim and Eliza, he *could* eat, so, therefore he would.

As he'd hoped, his father eventually stopped watching him and turned to his brother.

"Vaarem," said Garrett, "I received a letter from the Council today. Prime Minister Moontail is looking for an office intern next season. I told him about you and he would like to talk to you."

"Why?" Vaarem put his fork down and frowned at his father. "I don't want to work for the Council."

"Why not?" asked Garrett, "It pays well, you meet many influential people, and most importantly, it will allow you to play an important role in helping everyone in the city. You have the brain and the charisma for it. I really think you could take over from the Prime Minister once he retires. There would be an election, of course, but if he vouches for you, you have a good chance. He told me that, I'm not making it up."

Vaarem frowned again, then he shook his head, "No."

"Excuse me?"

"No, thank you?" said Vaarem.

Garrett frowned again. "Why not?"

"Because that type of career does not interest me, Father," said Vaarem calmly.

"Let's discuss this later," said Zareanna, trying to prevent an argument, but Vaarem shook his head.

"There is nothing to discuss," he said, "I do not want an office job. I don't want to work in politics. I want to be a soldier or a peacekeeper, like grandfather Gem and grandma Nellie."

Garrett looked at him for a moment, then he nodded. "Fine," he said, "I will see what I can do about setting up a placement in the peacekeepers or security division."

"Really?" Vaarem raised his eyebrow.

"Yes, really," sighed Garrett, "Fates, Vaaremill, I'm not the monster you make me out to be. I wanted you to carry on in my footsteps. I wanted for you what I missed out on myself, but if you want to pursue a career in a different direction, then I'm not going to stop you. So, if you really don't want the Prime Minister's internship, then I will organise something else."

"Thank you," said Vaarem, his eyes wide. He looked like he was afraid that there was a catch, but as far as Lim could tell, there wasn't. Their father seemed to genuinely respect Vaarem's choice. He was clearly disappointed, but he would get over it, and he would support Vaarem. Lim hoped that his parents would be equally supportive of his own choices.

"You know," said Vaarem to his father, "you can still be Prime Minister yourself. Now that Lim and I are grown-up, you will have the time for it."

Garrett looked at Vaarem for a long moment, then finally nodded. "You're right," he said thoughtfully. "I was so focused on setting this up for you that I forgot that this option is still open to me. Having said that, I do like organising events. But I will think on it. Thank you, Vaarem."

Vaarem smiled in response.

"When I was in Sirrock," said Lim after a moment of silence, "I wrote to the Temple of the Fates in Palinas. Today I received a response. I've been accepted to train as a Priest of the Fates at the start of the next turn."

Zareanna's eyes lit up at that. "Congratulations, darling," she said, "I've seen you reading that book all the way back to Palinas, and I was thinking that it had really captured your interest."

"Congratulations, Lim," said Garrett, "I think that you'll do very well."

"Thank you," said Lim, feeling warmed.

"I think our sons will both be fine." Zareanna smiled at Garrett, who nodded in acknowledgement.

Later that evening, Dr Fantail came over. He examined Lim in Lim's room like he'd done the previous times. Isha sat on Lim's bedside table and watched him with wide eyes. Her calm demeanour made Lim feel less uncomfortable than he'd ever felt during a medical examination.

"Well, I was afraid that I would never say this, Lim," said Dr Fantail, "but I am very pleased to say that you have improved dramatically since I saw you last. These new potions are clearly working very well, so make sure you keep on taking them."

"I will," promised Lim.

When Dr Fantail had left, Vaarem and Lim stayed in Lim's room, sitting on his bed. Lim had decided to try playing his violin again and was currently tuning it. The instrument felt heavy in his arms, but he was confident that with some regular practice, he would build up enough strength to play it again.

"So, you're really going to do this priest thing?" asked Vaarem, as Lim twisted the first peg to adjust the top string.

"Yes," said Lim, smiling at his brother. "I've never been more sure of anything in my life. I really feel like it's my calling. What about you? You really want to be a peacekeeper?" He plucked the next string, then adjusted the peg.

"Yes." Nodded Vaarem. "I'm so happy that Father has finally agreed. I'm going to apply tomorrow. I don't need Father to find me a placement. I can find my own."

"Sounds good," said Lim.

"Yeah," said Vaarem, "I feel like Father was wanting me and you to not end up like him and Malkim, and he's finally let go and trusts us to make our own way."

"Yes." Smiled Lim. "It feels good to know that he's not constantly trying to control us anymore."

Vaarem sighed contentedly in response.

"Speaking of Malkim," said Lim, remembering

Vada's last letter, "Vada wants to re-create his spell. The one that killed him. Apparently, it was something that would rid the world of pain and negative influences, whatever that means. I'm kind of scared for her." He put the violin down and looked at his brother seriously.

Vaarem turned to him and smiled. "Let it go, Lim," he said. "Trust her to find her own way. She's stronger than her father was. She won't make the same mistakes."

"I hope you're right." Nodded Lim, "I need to let her live her life without expecting her to drop everything for me all the time. And you're right, she is strong."

"We need to trust ourselves, and each other," said Vaarem thoughtfully. "None of us will make our parents' mistakes. Now that they've told us, we can avoid the same traps."

"Yes," agreed Lim. "I'm sure we'll make plenty of our own mistakes." He picked the violin up again.

Vaarem frowned.

Lim chuckled. "It's inevitable." He told his brother, "I've been reading about it, and it's the nature of the Fates and the Universe. In order for us to learn, we need to make mistakes to learn from. Pain is a natural, unavoidable part of existence. But it is always balanced out with joy." He looked at the carving above the door, the spiral that represented balance and change. *The Fates may not give you everything you want*, he thought, *but you will always get what you need just when you need it.*

"Well, I'm feeling plenty of joy right now," said Vaarem, "We've had our share of pain for a while, I think."

"Yes," said Lim, "We're due for some joy. Let's make the best of it." He finished tuning the last string and picked up the bow, before running it over the strings.

A sweet joyful melody filled the room.

THE END

Authors Note

for taking the time to read the preceding story. A lot of work and several years of writing have gone into it, and it wouldn't have been possible without the help and support of those around me. I would like to thank my wonderful husband and best friend Stan, who took on all the house and childcare duties (for both the human and the fur kids) so that I could write, Diana for the wonderful cover artwork, and for setting up the website, and to Viktor for preventing me from going crazy by making sure I took some breaks.

I would also like to thank my beta readers, in particular Holly, E.J. Simeon, James Graham, and the New Authors Unite Group.

Finally thank you, dear reader, this is all done for you.

Author Bio

Zofia was born in Poland, lived in Mexico, grew up in New Zealand, and now lives in Sydney with her partner, two children, and four cats. She studied screenwriting, and after graduating wrote and directed a stage play Super Creeps, that played to sold out audiences in the Wellington Fringe Festival. She works at a prominent Australian university providing teaching support to students. When she is not working or writing, she is a breastfeeding counsellor, and sometimes fosters kittens. She has never successfully baked a cake but she encourages others to try.

Easy Chocolate Cake

Ingredients: 200g sugar, 200g butter, 4 eggs, 200g self-raising flour, 1tsp vanilla extract, 2 tbs milk, 2tbs cocoa powder

Method

1: Separate eggs

2: Beat egg whites until stiff

3: Mix all other ingredients together until they form a smooth pale mixture

4: Fold egg whites into mixture

5: Grease a pan, etc, put mixture in it and bake at 180C/356F (pre-heat oven before putting cake in) for 20 minutes or until a skewer comes out clean (which for me is never, but I challenge you all to try)

6: Add icing – or something – I never got to this step...

7: Eat and enjoy.

www.ingramcontent.com/pod-product-compliance
Lightning Source LLC
Chambersburg PA
CBHW061048210726

48294CB00001B/52